Sleeping with the Enemy

LYNN RAYE HARRIS
KATE WALKER
ANNIE WEST

D1471574

MILLS & BOON

All rights reserved including the right of reproduction in whole or in part in any form. This edition is published by arrangement with Harlequin Books S.A.

This is a work of fiction. Names, characters, places, locations and incidents are purely fictional and bear no relationship to any real life individuals, living or dead, or to any actual places, business establishments, locations, events or incidents. Any resemblance is entirely coincidental.

This book is sold subject to the condition that it shall not, by way of trade or otherwise, be lent, resold, hired out or otherwise circulated without the prior consent of the publisher in any form of binding or cover other than that in which it is published and without a similar condition including this condition being imposed on the subsequent purchaser.

® and ™ are trademarks owned and used by the trademark owner and/or its licensee. Trademarks marked with ® are registered with the United Kingdom Patent Office and/or the Office for Harmonisation in the Internal Market and in other countries.

First Published in Great Britain 2019
by Mills & Boon, an imprint of HarperCollins*Publishers*
1 London Bridge Street, London, SE1 9GF

SLEEPING WITH THE ENEMY © 2019 Harlequin Books S. A.

Revelations of the Night Before © 2012 Lynn Raye Harris
Indebted to Moreno © 2016 Kate Walker
An Enticing Debt to Pay © 2013 Annie West

ISBN: 978-0-263-27781-4

0919

MIX
Paper from
responsible sources
FSC™ C007454

This book is produced from independently certified FSC™
paper to ensure responsible forest management.

For more information visit: www.harpercollins.co.uk/green

Printed and bound in Spain
by CPI, Barcelona

REVELATIONS
OF THE
NIGHT BEFORE

LYNN RAYE HARRIS

For Beverly Barton.
You left us too soon, and we all miss you tremendously.
Thank you for your kindness, your encouragement and
your enthusiasm. You were what a true Southern lady
should be. Now that you've arrived, I'm sure Heaven is
breaking out the cloth napkins and good china daily.

DUDLEY LIBRARIES	
000003019581	
Askews & Holts	02-Sep-2019
AF ROM	£7.99
2SE	

USA Today bestselling author **Lynn Raye Harris** burst onto the scene when she won a writing contest held by Mills & Boon. The prize was an editor for a year – but only six months later, Lynn sold her first novel. A former finalist for the Romance Writers of America's Golden Heart Award, Lynn lives in Alabama with her handsome husband and two crazy cats. Her stories have been called "exceptional and emotional," "intense," and "sizzling."

Kate Walker was always making up stories. She can't remember a time when she wasn't scribbling away at something and wrote her first "book" when she was eleven. She went to Aberystwyth University, met her future husband and after three years of being a full-time housewife and mother she turned to her old love of writing. Mills & Boon accepted a novel after two attempts, and Kate has been writing ever since. Visit Kate at her website at: www.kate-walker.com

Annie West has devoted her life to an intensive study of tall, dark, charismatic heroes who cause the best kind of trouble in the lives of their heroines. As a side-line she researches locations for romance, from vibrant cities to desert encampments and fairytale castles. Annie lives in eastern Australia between spectacular sandy beaches and gorgeous wine country. She finds writing the perfect reason to avoid housework. To contact her or join her newsletter, visit www.annie-west.com

000003019581

CHAPTER ONE

SHE could not possibly be pregnant. Valentina D'Angeli's fingers shook as she studied the test stick, the blue line very clearly trying to tell her she was indeed expecting a baby.

It was too crazy to be believed, and yet…

A chill slid down her spine. The night of the masquerade ball had been the wildest she'd ever experienced; the one night where she'd determined to let down her hair and be the person she'd never been able to be. The free spirit who could sleep with a man and leave him in the morning without a shred of remorse.

For one night, she'd planned to be bold and seductive. She *would* experience passion and conquer her shyness once and for all. She *would* be like other women her age—sophisticated, experienced and utterly in control.

Tina set the test stick down and opened another. Surely the first had been damaged somehow. The second would give her the correct answer.

That night had been a good idea in theory, yet even with the anonymity of the mask, she'd been unable to let herself go to the extent her best friend, Lucia, had decided she should.

"You need to get laid, Tina," Lucia had said.

Tina had blushed and stammered and said yes, of

course she needed to—she was tired of being a twenty-four-year-old virgin—but she'd not truly thought it would happen. She'd tried to flirt and dance and be free, but when her partner had pulled her close, his breath smelling faintly of garlic and mint combined, she'd known she couldn't do it. She'd pushed away from him and run from the palazzo, out onto the dock where it had been quieter and cooler, and gulped in the Venetian night air like a balm.

And that's when he'd appeared. Not the man she'd run from, but the man she would give herself to before the night was over. He'd been tall, suave, dressed in black velvet and wearing a silk mask over his eyes.

He'd been utterly mesmerizing, and she'd fallen under his spell with far more ease than she'd ever expected. He'd made love to her so tenderly, so perfectly, that she'd wept with the beauty of it.

And with the loneliness of it.

"No names," he'd whispered in her ear. "No faces."

She'd agreed, because that was what had made it magical—and yet, once it was over, she'd wanted to know him. She'd felt bereft with the idea she never would.

Tina swallowed the fear that rose from the pit of her stomach and grabbed her by the throat. Sometimes, not knowing was the best thing. She wished to God she still didn't know.

But as the light from the full moon had slid between the curtains and illuminated the sleeping form of the man beside her, she'd dared to slide the silk mask from his eyes. Her breath stopped in her chest just remembering that moment.

He hadn't awakened, even when she'd gasped. Even when she'd scrambled from the bed and stood there in the quiet, elegant bedroom of the hotel he'd taken her to. Her heart had turned over, her stomach flipping inside out.

Of all the men in the world.

She'd reacted blindly then. She'd yanked on her clothes as silently as she could—and then she'd fled like the coward she was.

"Right," she said to herself as she waited for the new test stick to negate the first one. The universe was simply playing a huge joke on her, punishing her for that night of wanton behavior with a man she should not have known at all. What kind of woman gave herself to a man she didn't even know?

But you do know him. You've always known him. Always wanted him.

Tina chewed her lip, her heart beating erratically as the seconds ticked by.

And then the answer came, as clear and soul shattering as the first.

Pregnant.

"There is a woman, my lord," the man said apologetically.

Niccolo Gavretti, the marchese di Casari, turned from where he'd been gazing out the window of the exclusive Roman hotel's restaurant and fixed the maître d' with an even look.

There was always a woman. Women were his favorite hobby—when they weren't demanding more than he was willing to give or thinking that because he'd slept with them, he owed them something more.

No, he loved women—but on his terms.

"Where is this woman then," he asked almost wearily.

"She refuses to come inside, my lord." His tone said that he did not approve.

Nico waived a hand dismissively. "Then she is not my problem."

The maître d' bowed. "As you wish, my lord."

Nico turned back to his paper. He'd come here this morning for a business breakfast with an associate, but he'd stayed to drink coffee and read the paper once the meeting was over. He'd not expected a woman to accost him, but then he was hardly surprised, either. A determined woman was often a force to be reckoned with.

Sometimes the results were quite pleasurable and interesting. Other times, not so much.

Only a few moments passed before the maître d' returned, apologetic and red-faced. "My lord, I beg your pardon."

Nico set the paper down. His patience was running thin. He had much on his mind lately, not the least of which was dealing with the vast mess his father had bequeathed to him.

"Yes, Andres?"

"The lady says it is most urgent that she speak to you. But she cannot do so in such a public place. She suggests you come to her room."

Nico resisted rolling his eyes, but only just. Before his father's death, Nico had been one of the top-ranked Grand Prix motorcycle riders in the world. He'd won the world championship a few months ago. He knew all about the kinds of schemes a woman might employ to catch his interest. He had been the object of many such plots in his life. Sometimes he played along because it amused him to do so.

Today would not be one of those times.

"Please tell her she will be waiting for a very long

time," he said smoothly. And then he glanced at his watch. "I have an appointment elsewhere, I'm afraid."

The maître d's face was a study in contrasts. He looked simultaneously uncomfortable and...*gleeful* was the word Nico wanted...all at once. "She said if you refused to give you this, my lord."

He held out an envelope on a small tray. Nico hesitated, furious to be playing this game—and intrigued, damn him, as well. He jerked the envelope from the tray and ripped it open. A business card fell out. It was white, plain, with only a stylized *D* in one corner.

It was the name on the card that pierced him to the bone. He stared at the sweeping font that separated the two words from the paper.

Valentina D'Angeli.

The name sent a slice of old anger ricocheting through him. Not the first name; the last. Valentina's brother, Renzo D'Angeli, had been his greatest rival on the track. His greatest rival in business, even now.

But once, Renzo had been his best friend. Nico and Renzo had worked together building a motorcycle that would take the racing world by storm—until everything had fallen apart amid accusations of betrayal and deceit.

It was a long time ago, and yet it still had the power to make Nico's blood hum with dangerous anger. And sadness.

He focused on the name, tried to remember the girl who'd still been a teenager the last time he'd seen her. Valentina D'Angeli. She would be all grown up now. Twenty-four, he calculated. He'd not seen her since the day he'd walked away from the D'Angelis' house for the last time, knowing he would never be welcomed back again.

Valentina had been a sweet girl, but terribly shy. Her

shyness, he remembered, had bothered her brother. So much so that Renzo had planned to send her away to school once he had the money to do so, in the hopes that an exclusive education could fix her.

Nico had tried to convince Renzo to reconsider. He knew what it was like to be sent away to school, and he'd not been shy in the least. He'd felt isolated, no matter how many friends he'd had or how well he'd done in class. And he'd hated the loneliness, the feeling that his parents were happier without him, and that he was in the way when he was at home.

Nico frowned. It hadn't been far from the truth, but he hadn't found that out until a few years later.

Still, the exclusive education had certainly done its work on him. He had no doubt that it had done its work on Valentina, as well. The raw stone would now be polished to a high shine.

But what was she doing here?

Nico turned the card over. *Room 386* was written on the back. He closed his hand over it. He should walk away. He should get up and walk out the door and forget he'd ever seen this card.

But he wouldn't. He wanted to know what she wanted from him. Renzo must have sent her, but for what purpose? He'd not seen Renzo since that day on the track in Dubai, the first race of the Grand Prix circuit. Renzo had walked away from racing after it was over. He'd married his secretary and was currently making babies in the country, according to everything Nico had heard.

His blood ran cold. Renzo might be done racing, but he wasn't done with motorcycles. They were still rivals in business. And Renzo must want something pretty badly to send his sister to get it.

* * *

She was nervous. Tina stood by the window and watched the cars moving along the street below. She did not know if he would come. What if he didn't? Did she dare to go to his offices and demand to be seen? Or should she try and see him at his country estate instead?

Except he had more than one country estate these days, didn't he? It had been nearly two months since she'd seen him in Venice. In that short time, his father had died and Nico was now the marchese di Casari, a man of far more consequence than he'd been when he used to spend hours working in the garage with Renzo.

Would a man of his stature come to see her? He and Renzo had been enemies for far longer than they'd ever been friends. It was very likely that Nico remembered nothing of her. She'd been a gangly girl, quiet and shy, who had crept into the garage and watched them silently. She hadn't been at all memorable.

But that was a lifetime ago, and now she stood here pregnant with his child. Tina sucked in a tearful breath. My God. How—*how*—had this happened? It had been one night, one erotic and beautiful night in which she'd behaved in a way so very unlike her.

She'd hated being so shy growing up, hated even more that no matter how much education she'd had or how hard she worked at being someone bold and so-phisticated, she was still the same painfully timid girl inside. The one time she'd determined to push past her comfort zone, to *really* be bold, the consequences had been staggering.

If she'd known who her mystery man was, she would have fled sooner. Because she wouldn't have been able to let herself go so thoroughly if she'd known that the man stripping her naked was the same man she'd dreamed about for most of her life.

When she was fourteen, she'd idolized him. He'd been twenty and so achingly handsome that he'd taken her breath away. She'd never learned to relax around him even though he was always nice to her. He'd smiled at her, and she'd turned into a stammering puddle every single time.

And then one day when she'd crept into the garage just to see his handsome face, he hadn't been there. He'd never been there again, and Renzo had refused to talk about it. She'd lain in her room at night for months and prayed he would come back, but he never did.

There was a knock on the door and Tina jumped at the sound like a startled deer. Doubts assailed her. Should she even be here? Should she tell him her secret?

He would be furious. And quite possibly horrified.

But how could she not? He had a right to know he was going to be a father. A right to know his baby. She'd never known her own father and her mother had refused to tell her who he was, other than to say he'd been English. She would not do that to her own child, no matter how difficult this was.

Swiftly, she strode to the door and yanked it open before she could change her mind. The man on the threshold was tall, dark, gorgeous—a more mature version of the young man she'd fallen for so many years ago. Just seeing him again made sparks zing through her body.

He simmered with tension as his stormy gaze met hers. And then he dropped his eyes down her body, studying her so thoroughly that she blushed.

She'd chosen to wear a skirt with sky-high heels and a silk tank beneath her jacket for this meeting. She knew she looked elegant and competent, as she'd intended, but for a moment the hideously shy teenager was back.

"Valentina?" he said, his voice containing a note

of disbelief, and a hint of that sexual magnetism she'd found so irresistible in Venice. How had she forgotten his voice over the years? She could have avoided the situation she was now in if she'd only remembered the silken beauty of his tone, and recognized him sooner.

"Yes. It's lovely to see you again, Signore Gavretti." She stepped back, her heart pushing into her throat. She'd spent a night of bliss in his arms, and he had no idea. Until that very moment, she'd half believed he would recognize her when he saw her. That somehow his soul would know she was the one he'd made love to.

But he did not, and it pierced her to the bone. *Silly.* He was a man, not a magician.

"Won't you come in?"

He crossed the threshold, and for a moment an invisible hand closed around her throat. What had she done? Why had she thought she could handle him? She'd been unable to handle him that night. No, she'd done everything he'd wanted her to do. Willingly, eagerly, thoroughly—as if the shyness she hid from the world had ceased to exist.

Her body heated as the memories rushed through her. Skin against skin, heat against heat, hard against soft. What would he think of her when he knew?

Tina shoved the memories down deep and walked over to a serving cart. "Tea?" she asked, her hand shaking slightly as she reached for the pot. What she really wanted to do was grab a plate and fan herself with it.

"No."

She poured herself a cup—decaf, of course—and turned to find him right behind her. She took an automatic step back. His stormy silver eyes were piercing, his expression hard and curious at once. She wanted to run her hand over his jaw, press her lips there the way she had that night…which seemed a lifetime ago.

"You didn't ask me up here to have tea," he said darkly. "Tell me what your brother wants and be done with it."

Tina blinked, the warm feelings floating through her dissipating in an instant. "Renzo has no idea I'm here." God, no. He'd be furious. Livid. He would probably disown her if he knew.

And he would know, eventually. But that was why she had to tell Nico first. If Renzo found out she were pregnant, he would demand to know the father. There would be hell to pay once he knew who that man was.

Tina set the tea down and pressed a hand to her forehead. It was a mess. A huge, huge mess. Somehow, she had to make it all come out right.

Nico's smile was anything but friendly. "So this is how we are to play it then?" His gaze slid over her again. "You have grown into a lovely woman, Valentina. A great asset for your brother."

Tina wanted to laugh, but she couldn't. She couldn't show that much vulnerability to him. No, Renzo did not consider her an asset. More like a duty. He took care of her, loved her, but refused to consider she might have more to offer than simply being a decorative fixture in his life. She wanted to work for him, but he would not allow it.

"You are a D'Angeli," he said. *"You don't have to work."*

No, she didn't have to work. She *wanted* to work— and if her brother wouldn't hire her, she was going to work for someone else. She'd gone along with Renzo for the past year, but only in the hopes she could convince him that D'Angeli Motors was where she belonged.

Though she'd graduated with honors in accounting and finance, the only thing she could do with her degree right now, aside from dabble in a few investments with the payouts from her trust fund, was balance her own checkbook.

It made her waspish. "You can hardly claim to know what is in Renzo's mind these days, can you?"

He stared at her for a heartbeat, his expression hardening. She'd surprised herself by being so snappish. Apparently, she'd surprised him, too.

"Enough of the games. Tell me why you requested this meeting, or we're through here."

His tone stung. "You did not used to be so abrupt."

"And you did not used to play games."

Tina carried her tea to the couch. She sat gracefully as she'd been taught, and then took a tiny sip, hoping it would calm her suddenly roiling stomach. Perhaps she'd erred in not eating breakfast this morning. But she'd taken one look at the meats, cheeses and eggs arrayed before her on the table and felt she would be violently ill if she ate a bite.

"I'm not playing a game, *signore*. I'm just unsure how to begin this." It was the truth.

"You used to call me Nico," he said. "When you managed to speak to me at all."

She felt herself flushing with embarrassment at the memory of how she used to be so tongue-tied around him. His face was stern and foreboding, his body tense as he loomed over her in his expensive suit and studied her as if she were something he'd stepped in.

If only he knew...

Tina had to suppress a wild giggle. It wasn't amusement so much as hysteria, but nevertheless she could hardly give in to it. Besides, he would know soon enough, wouldn't he? Just as soon as she could manage to say the words.

"That was a long time ago," she said. "Life was simpler then."

She thought a flash of emotion crossed his features, but it was gone as suddenly as it had appeared. "Life is never simple, *cara*. It only seems so in retrospect."

"What happened between you and Renzo?" The words fell from her lips, though she did not intend for them to. Any softening she might have seen on his face was gone again.

"We ceased to be friends. That is enough."

Tina sighed. She'd always wanted to know why he'd stopped coming around, but Renzo remained tight-lipped about the whole thing. She'd been too young to really understand back then, but she'd thought it was probably temporary. A disagreement between friends.

She'd been wrong.

Her stomach clenched again and she splayed her hand over her belly, as if she could stop the churning simply by doing so.

Nico was on one knee in front of her suddenly. His eyes were the color of a leaden sky, she thought wildly. Any minute the storm would break. Any minute.

But for now he looked concerned, and her heart squeezed. "What is the matter, Valentina? You look… green."

She swallowed the bile that threatened and tried to sip the tea again. "I'm pregnant," she said, her heart beating in her ears, her throat.

"Congratulations." It was said sincerely. And it was all she could do to hold in the nervous laughter pressing at the back of her throat.

"Thank you." She felt hot, so hot. She could feel the

sweat beading on her forehead, her upper lip. She set the tea down and peeled the jacket from her shoulders. Nico reached up to help her. He stood and laid the jacket over the back of the couch.

His expression was gentler now, but he was still like a caged lion roaming the quiet space of the suite. Any second, and his fangs would be bared, his claws extended.

Tina closed her eyes and shook her head slightly. *Focus.*

"Can I get you anything?" he asked.

"One of those biscuits would be nice," she said.

He retrieved a vanilla biscuit from the tea table and handed it to her. Tina broke off a piece and chewed slowly.

Nico shoved his hands in his pockets. "If you could state your business, we can solve whatever this is and go our separate ways."

"Yes, I suppose we can." Would he want to be involved? Or would he wash his hands of her the moment she told him? It didn't really matter, she decided. She was strong enough to have this baby on her own. No one was going to stop her from doing so, either.

She finished the biscuit and leaned back on the couch. It seemed the food would stay down this time, but she knew she needed to eat more.

"I had not realized you'd married," Nico said.

Her gaze snapped to his, her pulse thrumming. "I'm not married."

His pause was significant. "Ah."

Tina fumed at the unspoken implications. "I did not plan this, but I won't be ashamed of my baby, either."

"I did not say you should be." And yet she did not believe him. People like him—people who came from families like his—had very stringent views on proper behavior. She'd learned that in boarding school when the other girls had treated her like scum for not having a father. For having a mother who had once been a waitress, and who had never married even though she'd had children.

Those girls had made her life hell at St. Katherine's. They hated her because she hadn't been from old money, because she'd been shy and an easy target for their venom. Rotten snobs, all of them. Except Lucia, of course.

Tina clenched her fingers into the cushion. Nico was one of those people, from old money and lineage. And he was judging her, finding her lacking. It should make her want to hide.

Instead, it made her angry. "No, you did not say anything. But you're thinking it."

He looked cool and gorgeous standing there. Remote. "I'm not thinking anything. Except for what any of this possibly has to do with me."

She stared at him for several heartbeats, as her breath seemed to stop inside her lungs. It was now or never, wasn't it? He'd given her the opportunity. She had to say the words. But forcing them out was like trying to stop snowflakes from melting on her tongue.

"It has everything to do with you," she finally managed, her voice little more than a whisper.

But he heard her. His expression changed, became even icier. He was the aristocrat, and she was the mixed breed dog who didn't even have a father.

"I fail to see how. Until today, I haven't laid eyes on you in nearly ten years. And believe me," he said, his gaze skimming over her again, "I would remember doing so."

His voice was sex itself, and she flushed. But she

looked him dead in the eye and refused to flinch as she said the next words.

"Not necessarily. Not if it was dark and we—we wore masks."

CHAPTER TWO

NICO's stomach felt strangely hollow. He was standing here, looking at this woman who he could hardly believe was the grown-up little sister of his old friend and archrival, and he knew what she was saying even though she did not actually speak the words.

She was telling him she was pregnant. With his child.

But he knew it was a lie. No matter what she said about Venice and the masks, she was not that woman. It was a trick, a ruse cooked up by her brother in order to settle old scores. Oddly, it disappointed him to think she could be as ruthless as Renzo when she'd once been so shy.

He didn't know how they knew, but he would not fall for it.

His gaze raked her body as he tried to recall the woman he'd shared that night with. He'd found her on the docks outside the palazzo, gulping air and shivering. He'd feared something bad had happened to her initially, but that had not been the case at all.

He remembered how sweetly innocent she'd been, and how he'd been drawn to her in spite of his usual preference for more experienced bed partners. He had not thought she would be a virgin, but she'd surprised him on that score, as well.

How could this be the same woman?

It couldn't be. Somehow, Valentina D'Angeli knew the woman he'd been with and she and her brother were using the situation to their advantage. It was too outrageous otherwise.

"You are lying," he said.

Her eyes widened with hurt. "Why would I do that? What could I possibly gain from something like this?"

Fury roared through him in giant waves. She played the innocent so well. "I can imagine a few things," he grated. "I am wealthy. Titled. And my company is a thorn in D'Angeli Motors' side."

Her brows drew down in a dark frown. Unwelcome heat flared inside him as she stood.

It hit him like a blow that she was very beautiful, with strong features and smooth skin and a mouth that needed kissing. Her chestnut hair tumbled over her shoulders in an insane riot of curls. He would have remembered hair like that, hair that twisted and curled and caught the light like it had been dusted with gold. He cast his mind back to that night, saw long dark hair that was thick and shiny…and straight.

Violet eyes flashed fire as she put her hands on her hips and faced him squarely. "Six weeks ago, you did not have a title. And my brother has as much money as you do, if not more. As for the companies, I could give a damn about either of them for all the good it would do me."

Nico tried not to be distracted by the way her waist curved in over the flare of her hips or the way her posture emphasized the full thrust of her breasts against her silk shirt. His body was hyperaware of her, but he could handle that. He simply refused to give in to the attraction.

"Her hair was straight," he said coldly.

She blinked, and triumph surged within him. He had her there. What a pretty liar she was.

Then she laughed at him as she twisted a finger into a curl and pulled it straight. "It's called a blow out, you idiot. Give me twenty minutes with a hair dryer, and I'll show you hair as straight as a file."

He stiffened. "That hardly proves it was you."

She took a step closer to him, and he had the distinct impression she was stalking him. It turned him on more than it ought. For a moment he wanted to close the distance between them, wanted to fit his mouth to hers and see if the sparks he felt in the air also extended to the physical. He had enough self-control not to do so, however.

She tilted her chin up, those eyes still flashing fire at him. She had a temper. He didn't remember that about her, but then she'd only been a teenager when he'd last known her. All he remembered about her then was a girl who hid behind her hair and went mute whenever he spoke to her.

Now she jabbed a manicured finger at him. "Shall I tell you everything about that night, starting with the moment you asked me if I was okay on the dock? Or should I describe your room at the Hotel Daniele? The way you turned off all the lights and told me no names and no faces? The way you peeled off my gown and kissed my skin while I—" here she swallowed "—I gasped?"

She broke off then, her face red, and Nico felt a jolt of need coiling at the base of his spine. He'd bedded a lot of women over the years, but none so fascinating as the one he'd taken that night. It had been a true one-night stand, and in the morning he'd awakened to find her gone. He'd been rather amused with the way it had made him feel, as if she'd used him and discarded him, and yet he'd been wistful, too.

Because, no matter what he'd said to his mystery woman about remaining anonymous, he'd wanted to see her again after that night. There'd been something between them that he'd wanted to explore further. It had only been sex, he knew that, but when he found a woman he enjoyed, he usually spent more than one night with her.

He'd asked the hotel staff if they remembered her or if they had seen which direction she'd gone in when she'd left.

The lone man on duty that night had said she'd left around two in the morning, silk-and-feather mask intact and pale green dress clutched in her fists as she ran through the lobby. He had not noted which direction she'd gone after she'd taken the gondola, and he didn't remember which gondolier had taken her.

A general inquiry of the gondoliers plying that part of the city had turned up nothing.

And that had been the end of that. Nico had been disappointed, but he'd gotten over it soon enough. It was sex, not love—and he could find plenty of sexual partners when the need arose. One sexy, inexperienced woman was not necessary to his life any more than a fine brandy was. They were both enjoyable, but completely dispensable.

"You could have learned those details from someone else. They prove nothing," he told her. And yet his blood hummed at her nearness, almost the way it had that night.

Her head dipped then, her eyes dropping away from his. "This is ridiculous," she breathed. And then she turned and sank onto the couch again, her eyes closing as her skin whitened.

Guilt pricked him. "Do you need another biscuit? More tea?"

"No. I just need to sit a moment." She looked up at him, her mouth turning down in a frown. "You're right, of course. I'm making the whole thing up. Renzo put me up to it so we could embarrass you. Because of course you would be embarrassed, wouldn't you? You, the man who has at least a dozen scantily clad paddock girls clinging to you after your races, the man who appears in the tabloids on a regular basis with some new woman on his arm, the man who famously stood in the middle of a party one evening and kissed every woman who asked to be kissed—yes, that man would be so embarrassed by me and my baby, though we would probably only burnish his bad-boy reputation."

Anger flared inside him. She was making fun of him—and the worst part was that what she said made a perverse sort of sense.

"How do I know what you and Renzo have in mind?" he snapped. "Perhaps you see this as a way to infuse the D'Angeli blood with legitimacy and credibility. This isn't the first time I've had to deal with title hunters, and I'm sure it won't be the last."

He didn't think it was possible she could grow any paler, but she did.

"You are vile," she said. "So full of yourself and your inflated sense of self-importance. I don't know why I wanted to tell you about the baby, but I thought you had a right to know. And I *certainly* don't want anything from you. Now, if you don't mind, I'd like to just sit here quietly. I'd show you out, but I'm certain you can find the door."

Nico stared down at her for several heartbeats. She seemed distressed, and his natural instinct was to stay and help her. But he couldn't forgive what she was trying to do to him.

"You've forgotten one very important detail about that night, *cara.* Perhaps your informant failed to mention it, or perhaps she did and you were hoping I'd forgotten, but we used protection. I may enjoy a variety of bed partners, but I am not stupid or careless."

"I'm well aware of it, but the box does say ninety-nine percent effective, does it not? We seem to be the one percent for whom it was not."

His jaw clenched together so hard he thought his teeth might crack. "Nice try, *bella,* but it's not working. Tell Renzo to think up something else."

And then he walked out the door and shut it firmly behind him.

Tina wanted to throw something, but the effort wouldn't be worth the slim satisfaction she would feel, so she continued to sit on the couch, sip tea and nibble biscuits until her stomach calmed down.

She should feel satisfied that she'd done the right thing and told him, but all she felt was anger and frustration. Whatever had happened between her brother and Nico, it had certainly created a lingering animosity.

She had come to a realization, though. She would not tell Renzo who had fathered her baby. He would demand to know, but it wasn't his right to know. She was twenty-four and capable of making her own decisions. She'd gotten herself into this, and she would deal with the consequences. Perhaps it was for the best that Nico refused to believe her. Now it wasn't necessary that she tell anyone.

Her mother, at least, would support her decision. How could she not, when she'd spent years denying Tina the right to know who her own father was?

Tina frowned. Poor Mama. Her mother had been in and out of love dozens of times that Tina could recall. Even now, she was off to Bora-Bora with her current lover, a man who Tina hoped was finally the right one. If anyone deserved love, it was Mama. She'd worked hard and sacrificed a lot until Renzo had started building his motorcycles and making money at it.

Tina sighed. At least she had a reprieve for a while. Mama was away, and Renzo, Faith and their baby were on their private yacht somewhere in the Caribbean, enjoying their first vacation in months. Not only that, but Renzo was also recuperating from surgery to repair his damaged leg. The last thing she wanted was to disrupt his recovery with her news.

No, as much as she might like to talk to her sister-in-law about being pregnant, Tina knew it was best if she was alone for now. By the time everyone returned, she would be further along and more confident in her ability to deal with them all.

As the afternoon wore on, she started to feel immensely better. She decided to leave Rome early the next morning and head for the family vacation home on Capri. She felt jittery after her meeting with Nico and she wanted to get far away from the city. From him. Not that she expected him to come back, but knowing he was in the same city—sleeping, eating, having sex with other women—was too much just now.

A few days in the lemon-scented breezes of Capri would do her good. But first she would call Lucia and see if her friend wanted to get together for dinner. She hadn't yet told anyone she was pregnant; she would start with Lucia, see how that went. If nothing else, it would be good practice for that moment when she had to tell her family.

Tina had not told Lucia who her mystery lover had been, though she'd admitted to spending the night with a man when Lucia had pressed her about it. Her friend had been so happy to hear it, as if she'd never quite believed that Tina would go through with it.

Tina wasn't sure Lucia would be happy about the consequences, however.

She left a message on Lucia's mobile phone and then decided to go to the Via dei Condotti for some shopping. But first she would walk from the Piazza Navona to the Pantheon in order to clear her head a bit. The walk wasn't long, but it wound through some of the most picturesque of Rome's neighborhoods. She changed into jeans and sandals and added a scarf around her neck.

When she was done, she left the hotel and headed for the Pantheon. She passed gelato shops, antiques shops with paintings and elegant inlaid furniture in the windows, trattorias with chairs and tables lining the pedestrian way, and finally came out on the square where the Pantheon sat, ancient and silent against a bright blue sky.

It was her favorite monument in Rome. She passed inside, beneath the forest of tall columns and into the cavernous chamber with the huge circle cut out in the center of the ceiling high above. Ignoring the tourists with their cameras, she skirted the roped off area in the center and took a seat on one of the benches facing the altar that had been added much later when the structure had been turned into a church.

And then she tilted her head back and watched a wisp of a cloud float over the opening above. For some reason, this building made her feel peaceful. It always had. Once, when she had been home on break from school and didn't want to go back again, she'd snuck out of Renzo's apartment and come here. She'd sat for hours just like this until one of her brother's security team had found her and made her return home and, ultimately, back to the private school that had terrified her until she'd met Lucia and made a friend.

"She had a scar." The voice in her ear was startling. The noise in the Pantheon was always a dull murmur, but this voice pierced her solitude and made her gasp.

Tina whipped around to look at the dark, brooding male now sitting beside her on the bench. Her heart flipped, as it always did, whenever she looked at him. It was very annoying.

"An appendix scar," he continued. "Just here." He made a slashing motion over his abdomen, to the right of his belly button and above his hip bone.

"I had my appendix out four years ago," she said coolly.

His silver eyes looked troubled. "I don't suppose you would show me this scar?"

"I would, in fact. But not at this very moment, if you don't mind. And even if you do," she added irritably. She would not jump to his tune just because he wished it.

The intensity of his gaze did not relent. "Assuming you have this scar, and you are the woman from that night, how did you know it was me?"

She looked up at the perfectly round slice of sky overhead. A bird sailed high over the opening, wings outstretched as it rode the currents. "I slid your mask off. And when I realized who you were, I ran away."

"How do I know that's the truth? That you didn't wait for me that night and set the whole thing up?"

She turned her head to meet his hot gaze, and her belly clenched. It was a different sensation than the one where the baby played havoc with her body. This tightening was a feeling that happened whenever she looked at this man. Only at this man. It was startling and disturbing all at once.

"Don't you suppose that if I'd been waiting for you, I'd have gone about the whole thing differently? I'm pretty sure that hiding on the dock like a frightened, nearly sick child isn't exactly the way to attract a man."

"And yet it worked," he said coldly.

Tina sat up straight, fury vibrating through her. "Look, if you want to believe this is all a ruse, that I'm lying or that I set you up, then fine, believe it. But don't sit here and bother me with your theories, okay? I told you what I thought you should know, and now I'm done. I don't want anything from you, Nico. I don't expect anything. I just thought you might like to know your child."

She started to rise, but he clamped a hand around her wrist and kept her on the bench. His fingers were long and strong, and his touch sent a jolt of energy radiating through her body. She jerked her wrist away and folded her arms over her midsection.

He bent closer to her until only she could hear the hard words coming from his lips. "*If* you are carrying my child, Valentina, I will be involved in his life. I refuse to pay child support and only see him whenever you allow it, or whenever the courts dictate. If you are carrying my child, then *you* are mine, as well."

His eyes were stormy gray pools that slid deep into her soul and tore at her facade of calm. Her instinct was

to recoil, but she didn't. She hadn't lived through boarding school, and the blue-blooded girls—girls from families like his—who'd thought they were far better than
she was, to cave in whenever a man glared at her and
told her how he believed things were going to be done.

When met with icy disdain, she returned icy disdain.

She shouldered her purse and stood. This time he did
not try to stop her. It was a comfort to be able to gaze
down at him, but she realized it was a false comfort.
He was as dangerous as always, as tightly leashed and
volatile as a stick of dynamite.

And she was about to light the fuse.

"You don't own me, Nico. If you want to be involved,
we'll work something out. I want our baby to know
his—or *her*—father. You both deserve that. And I want
you to be in our baby's life. But I won't be part of the
game between you and Renzo. I refuse to be."

The fuse sparked and caught. His smile was cold and
lethal, and she shivered deep inside. He lived for this,
she thought. Lived for mayhem and challenge. It was
why he rode the motorcycles at death-defying speeds,
why he slept his way through the phone book without
remorse, and why he was not about to back down now.

She'd lit the fuse, but the explosion would be a long
time coming. And it frightened her.

"Too late, *cara,*" he said silkily. "You already are."

CHAPTER THREE

THEY sat inside a hotel restaurant facing the Pantheon and Tina stared at the crowds milling in the square. People with cameras, backpacks and books strolled around with their chins in the air, their necks craned to take in the ancient structure. A horse and carriage sat nearby, waiting to take tourists willing to part with their money on a short ride to the next attraction.

They looked happy, she thought wistfully. Happy people seeing the sights while she sat inside the crowded hotel at a table beside the window and waited for someone to bring her a bowl of soup.

Nico sat across from her, his big body sprawled elegantly in the chair, his phone to his ear. She'd tried to walk out on him, but she'd not gotten far before she'd had to stop and lean against a column for a moment.

And he was there, his fingers closing around her arm, holding her up, pulling her into the curve of his body. Then he'd demanded to know what she'd eaten that day. When she'd said only a biscuit or two, he'd hauled her over to this restaurant and plunked her down at the table before ordering soup, bread and *acqua minerale*.

He finished his call and picked up his coffee in a long-fingered hand while she resolutely looked away. She didn't want to study the beauty of those fingers, didn't want to remember them on her body, the way they'd stroked her so softly and sensually, the way they'd awakened sensations inside her that she'd never quite felt before.

Everything about being with Nico had been a revelation. As much as she wished she could forget the whole thing, she could in fact forget nothing. Worse, she wanted to experience it all again.

The soup arrived and she found that she was starving. After a few careful bites, she ate with more gusto than she'd been able to enjoy for days now. She didn't know if the soup would stay down, but eating was preferable to talking to Nico right now.

She could feel him watching her. Finally, she looked up and caught him studying her as if he were really seeing her for the first time. It disconcerted her.

She dropped the spoon and sat back. "Is there a problem?" she snapped. The words shocked her since she didn't usually seek confrontation as she couldn't bear to have anyone angry with her.

And yet she found she did not care when it came to this man. He was already angry with her. What did it matter if she challenged him? It would change nothing about the way he sat there smoldering with fury.

And blistering sex appeal. She couldn't forget the sex appeal.

"Nothing I can't handle," he said smoothly, and she felt angry color rising in her cheeks. He was baiting her and she was falling for it every time. Why couldn't she just keep her mouth shut and let him smolder?

Hard on the heels of anger came fear. It surprised her. But it was a cold fear that wrapped around her throat and squeezed as she considered all the implications of what had happened between them.

Why had she told him about the baby? She should have kept silent. It wouldn't have truly hurt her baby not to know its father just as it hadn't hurt her. And her family would be safe from this man's fury.

Because he was furious, she was certain. Coldly furious. And calculating. She had no idea what he was capable of, but she feared it. He was not the same person he'd been when she'd idolized him as a teen.

"I appreciate the lunch," she said, pushing her chair back, "but I'm afraid I have to go now."

He watched her almost indolently. She wasn't fooled. He was like a great cat lounging in the sun, one minute content, the next springing to life to bring down a gazelle.

"You aren't going anywhere, Valentina." He spoke mildly, but again she was reminded of the cat. He was toying with her.

She thrust her chin out. "You can't stop me."

His eyes gleamed in the light streaming in from the window. "I already have." He motioned to the waiter, and then took out a credit card and handed it to the man when he arrived with the bill.

Tina sucked in a deep breath and tried not to panic. She was not this man's prisoner. She could get up and walk out of this restaurant and there was nothing he could do to stop her. He didn't own her in any way, nor would he.

Tina grabbed her purse and headed for the exit. She didn't run, but she was very aware of what was happening behind her. Nico didn't say a word, his chair didn't scrape the floor, and she breathed a sigh of relief that he wasn't following her. She burst into the open, the sunlight lasering into her eyes as the noise from the square assaulted her.

She turned and walked blindly, not caring where she went so long as Nico did not follow. This time, she would escape him. She would return to the hotel soon enough, but for now she just wanted to get lost in the crowds. He did not own her, no matter what he said. She repeated it over and over to herself as she walked down the cobbled streets, dodging tourists with cameras who weren't paying attention to where they were going, and men who hooted and whistled at her.

These were not the middle ages; women had babies on their own all the time. She did not need a man in her life, and she certainly didn't need that one. He could not compel her to do anything she did not want to do.

Tina walked until she found herself crossing a busy street, and then she was among the pedestrians again, walking alongside booths that had designer knock-off purses, scarves, bottle openers, and miniature Colosseums and Pantheons among their wares. The pedestrian traffic grew heavier the farther she went, and then the sound of rushing water came to her ears. A few steps more and she stood in front of the massive facade of the Trevi Fountain. She clutched her purse tightly to her body as she navigated the crowd and made her way down to the foot of the fountain.

Water gushed from below the feet of Neptune, over the troughs below the horses, and into the vast bowl of the fountain. Tina stood there with her heart aching. People laughed and took pictures of each other. A smiling couple held hands and then threw a coin into the water together. Impulsively, Tina dug a coin from her purse and gripped it hard enough so that the smooth round edge imprinted into her palm. Then she closed her eyes and said her wish to herself before she threw it into the water.

She wished that Nico would leave her alone, and that Renzo would never find out who had fathered her baby. *Too late*, a voice in her head told her. *If you'd wanted that, you never should have told him.*

She stood there a few minutes more before she turned to climb back up the steps as people jostled for position. She came to an abrupt stop when she looked up and realized who stood at the top, waiting for her.

So much for wishes.

He was silhouetted against the purpling sky, his dark form drawing more eyes than just hers. Tina's heart skipped a beat as she gazed up into that beautiful dark face. His hands were in his pockets. He looked, for the barest of moments, *lonely.*

But that could not be right. Niccolo Gavretti was not the kind of man who would ever be lonely. He was wealthy, titled and gorgeous. And, as she knew from experience, a sensual and amazing lover.

He was the last person in the world who should ever be lonely.

He held out a hand to her, beckoning her. She took the last few steps, reluctantly placing her hand in his as she neared the top. He steadied her over the last step and then she was standing beside him, her purse clasped to her chest like a shield.

As if anything could protect her from him.

"I've made an appointment with one of the city's top obstetricians, unless you have a doctor you prefer."

She shook her head, suddenly defeated. If she ran, he would follow, and if she fought, he would fight back. He was a force to be reckoned with, and she did not truly want to fight him. That was not how she wished her relationship with the father of her baby to be. If she had a hope of staving off trouble, she would go with him. For now.

Nico put a hand in her back and guided her through the crowd until they popped out onto a street nearby. A dark Mercedes sat with the engine idling, and when they approached it a man got out and opened the door for them.

Once they were inside, the doors closed and they were soon moving through traffic. The glass was up between the driver and them, and there was nothing but silence in the rich interior of the car.

"Now would be a good time to show me the scar," Nico said at last.

"I'm not sure I want to," she said softly. "I think I liked it better when you thought I was lying."

The leather squeaked as he turned toward her. "I'm not going to hurt you, Valentina."

"Or my family," she added firmly. Because she realized now that it was a very real possibility he would go after Renzo somehow. She had seriously underestimated the depth of his hatred for her brother—and Renzo's for him.

There was silence for a moment. "I can't promise that."

Her heart felt pinched in her chest. She pictured Renzo with Faith and their son, and it killed her to think that she could be responsible for causing them trouble. "I will do as you ask, without complaint, so long as you leave Renzo out of this."

He studied her for a long moment. "I'm still not positive he doesn't have something to do with this situation. Why would I leave him out of it?"

This is your fault.

Yes, it was her fault. Anger began to swell inside her

again, crowding out the despair, glowing and expanding until she thought she would burst with it, until her skin was on fire from trying to contain it all. *Men!*

"I love my brother, but if you think for one moment I would agree to some scheme that involved me getting pregnant just so he could get back at you somehow, then you *are* insane! What woman in her right mind would let her body be used like that for the express purpose of revenge? I have no idea what happened between you, but no one died so I'm pretty certain it wasn't that bad. What you're suggesting is disgusting.

"And not only that," she added when he didn't say anything, "I think the two of you are pigheaded and foolish for allowing this to continue all these years. It's childish to have a *mortal enemy*. No one has mortal enemies these days."

"Rich men do," he said, but for once his voice wasn't harsh or hard or angry.

Tina folded her arms against her body. "I doubt it's that bad. I simply think you make it so."

"What an innocent life you've led," he replied, and a current of old shame flooded her.

Yes, she'd been naive for far too long. She'd grown up sheltered, pampered and scared to say boo. Boarding school, and then university, had done much to erode her shyness—but at heart she was still that girl who hid behind her hair and feared the world.

Except that she refused to show that fear. To anyone. She put a hand over her belly. She had to be strong now, no matter what. No matter that she was scared. No matter that she quaked inside at the thought of what she'd done to her family.

"If by 'innocent' you mean that I fail to see the need to harm others, then fine, call me innocent."

He made a soft noise of disbelief. "In business, my dear, you must always be willing to be ruthless. It's the only way to survive and thrive."

"And yet it's not necessary in one's personal life, is it? Any man who is ruthless in his personal life will soon find himself alone."

"Perhaps it's not so bad to be alone," he said. "Able to choose when you share your life and bed with someone, and able to go home again when you're tired of the work that being with another person takes."

"It sounds like an empty life," she said sadly.

His jaw tightened only slightly, but she knew she'd scored a hit. What she didn't know was why. She'd spent the past few years reading about him in the papers, and he seemed anything but lonely or empty. Yet he reacted to her words as if he had been. It made her wonder what he kept hidden from the world.

"Show me the scar," he commanded her, and her feelings of empathy dissolved like smoke.

Tina clenched her teeth together. She wanted to refuse, but what was the point? She *was* pregnant with his child. She'd started this ball rolling down the hill and she had no choice but to go along for the ride.

Angrily, she ripped her shirt from her jeans and shoved the waistband down just enough for him to see the short scar running diagonally across her lower abdomen. She heard his breath hiss in, and then his fingertips slid along her skin, tracing the edges.

Tina went utterly still while inside her body sizzled and sparked like fireworks on New Year's Eve. Flame followed in the wake of his fingers, and pain, as well. Not from the scar—it was too old to hurt—but from the strength of the need that took up residence in her core and refused to abate.

Nico looked up then, his eyes reflecting the same heat that she knew must be in her own. With a strength of will she would have never guessed she possessed, she pushed his hand away and hastily tucked her shirt back in. Her cheeks were hot, and she refused to look at him.

He didn't speak for a long moment. When he did, his voice was more tender than she'd expected it to be.

"It was you."

Tina realized that tears were pricking her eyes. She looked up at him, uncaring if he saw the emotion written on her face.

"I wish it hadn't been," she told him truthfully. Once, she'd fantasized about him, when she'd been young and naive and didn't know what making love meant. She'd wanted him to fall in love with her, to kiss her and marry her and think she was the most beautiful woman alive—that's all she knew when she'd been a teenager, but it had been her happy fantasy for at least a year. And then, once he'd gone away, she'd continued to dream about him.

Yes, she'd wanted him, but not like this. Not with this kind of animosity and mistrust. What had happened between them in Venice, beautiful though it might have been, was a mistake.

His lips thinned, the corners of his mouth white with suppressed anger. Though they were true, she wished she could take back the words, if only to try and rebuild whatever fragile peace they might have made, but it was too late.

The car stopped while she tried to think of something to say, and the driver came to open the door. Silently, Nico ushered her into the obstetrician's office, his fingers firm and burning in her back. His scent wrapped around her senses and made her throat ache with memories of their night together.

The girl on duty at the front desk didn't even look up as they approached. She handed over a clipboard and told Tina to fill it out without ever once making eye contact.

"We are expected," Nico said tightly, "and I am a busy man."

The girl's head snapped up, her eyes widening as she recognized the man standing before her. "Signore Gavretti—I mean, my lord—forgive me. Please come this way."

From that moment on, things moved quickly. Tina was shown into an ultrasound room and made to disrobe. After the technician took images and dated the pregnancy, she dressed and went into the doctor's office where Nico sat silently sending messages on his phone. A few moments later, the doctor arrived and talked to them about her health, the baby and what needed to happen every few weeks.

There would be regular ultrasounds, and at twenty weeks they would know the sex of the baby if they chose. There were vitamins to take, blood tests to have done and urine samples to give.

There were even classes to be taken, though she wasn't sure that Nico would be coaching her through anything when it came to childbirth. And she wasn't sure she wanted him to do so, either.

By the time they left the doctor's office, Tina's head was reeling. Instinctively, she put her hand over her still flat abdomen as if protecting the tiny life growing there.

A baby. She was truly having a baby, and she'd seen the little tiny lump on the screen for herself. Nico had seen it, too, but in the photo the doctor had handed to him in the office. He'd seemed a bit taken aback at first, as if he still couldn't quite believe it, but there was no denying she was pregnant and no denying that the conception date coincided with the night they were together.

Now he was silent as they rode through the streets of Rome. Outside the car window, traffic screeched and honked, but inside it remained eerily quiet.

Eventually, she realized they were not heading in the direction of her hotel. Her heart began to beat a little harder as she turned to him.

"I'm tired, Nico. I want to go back to my hotel and pack." She'd had a text message from Lucia, but she hadn't yet answered it. Since her friend was unable to get together for dinner, it wasn't crucial that she do so right away.

Nico's expression gave nothing away as he looked over at her. He was like a block of ice, so cold and un-approachable that he made her shiver.

"Your suitcases have already been packed." He glanced down at his watch. "I imagine they've been delivered, as well."

An icy tendril of fear coiled around her heart. "Delivered? Where would they be delivered? I'm off to Capri in the morning, and I will need my things to-night."

"I'm afraid the plan has changed, *cara.*" His storm cloud eyes were piercing as they caught hers and held them. "We are going to Castello di Casari."

Her pulse beat loudly in her ears. "I can't go with you," she said. "People are expecting me."

"No," he said smoothly, tapping the screen of his phone. "They are not. You are on your own right now, Valentina. Renzo and the lovely Faith are in the

Caribbean and your mother is sailing around Bora-Bora."

Tina stiffened. "While that is certainly true, I do have friends. And they are expecting me." Acquaintances, more like, and they were not expecting her so much as expecting a call from her if she wanted to get together.

Which she typically did not. She was happiest on her own. She'd always been a bit of a loner, and she'd never yet outgrown it. It was part of the reason she liked math and numbers so much. When she was in her head, solving problems, she didn't have to deal with the outside world.

"Then you will call and inform them your plans have changed."

"And for how long should I say I am delayed?" she asked tightly, knowing she was not going anywhere tonight that he did not want her to go.

There was ice in his smile. "Indefinitely."

CHAPTER FOUR

CASTELLO di Casari was far more than an ancient family fortress. It was impenetrable. Nico surveyed the castle rising out of the sheer rock in the middle of Lago di Casari and felt the overwhelming sensation of loneliness and despair that he'd always felt when returning here.

The castle had been modernized over the years, so that its medieval character remained but every modern comfort was provided for. Nico had not been here since his father's death just over a month ago. Why he'd thought to return here now, he wasn't quite certain.

Until he glanced over at the woman sitting stiffly beside him in the helicopter. Yes, it was an excellent place to stash an uncooperative female. He could hardly credit that the woman with the riotous hair and lush mouth was little Valentina D'Angeli, but his brain was becoming more accustomed to the fact by the minute.

Just as it was becoming accustomed to the fact she was pregnant with his child.

Until this afternoon, he would have stated it was impossible, but he'd been thinking back to that night and remembering what he'd done differently with her. He had used a condom, it was true, but he remembered it had torn as he had removed it. Now he wondered if it might have torn earlier and he'd only noticed as the tear grew.

Regardless, she was here and she was pregnant. And he wasn't letting her go, because if he did, he had no illusions that her brother would do everything in his power to keep Nico from the child.

And Nico wasn't allowing that to happen. He kept what was his.

The helicopter sank onto the landing pad and the rotors slowed. A man bent over and approached the craft. Then the door opened and Giuseppe's smiling face was there.

"My lord, we are overjoyed that you have come," the majordomo said.

"It's good to see you again, Giuseppe," Nico replied, descending from the helicopter and turning to assist Valentina.

Giuseppe was a short man, not quite five foot five inches tall, and he tilted his head back to look up at Nico. "I am sorry about your father, my lord. We were all saddened by the marchese's death."

Nico clapped the other man on the shoulder. He didn't feel anything inside, hadn't since he'd gotten the news, but he knew he was expected to show emotion over his father's death. It was the correct thing to do regardless that his father had done nearly everything he could in life to alienate his only son.

"Thank you, Giuseppe. He lived life as he wanted to, *sì*? He died as he lived, and I am sure he is at peace."

Giuseppe's old eyes were suspiciously watery. *"Sì, sì."*

A couple of staff members came forward to collect the luggage as Nico threaded his fingers into Valentina's and brought her to his side. She didn't resist, though he could feel her stiffening as her soft body came into contact with his.

"This is Signorina D'Angeli," Nico said. "She will be staying with us for a while."

Giuseppe didn't betray by word or expression that he understood the significance of Valentina's name, but Nico didn't doubt for a moment that the older man did. Giuseppe followed the motorcycle Grand Prix circuit and would certainly know the famous name. He would never ask questions, however.

"Signorina," he said, bowing over her hand in a courtly gesture. "Welcome to Castello di Casari."

"Thank you," Valentina replied without a trace of the stiffness that Nico could feel in her. He had to admire her ability to appear as if she actually wanted to be here. Giuseppe was none the wiser as she smiled at him graciously.

"We will need a meal in an hour or so," Nico said. "Can you do this, Giuseppe?"

The man dragged his attention back to Nico with some reluctance. *"Sì,* my lord. The chef has been busy since we received the news of your impending arrival."

"Excellent. Please have it served on the terrazzo."

"Sì, my lord."

With another smile at Valentina, Giuseppe went off to oversee the staff. Nico still had her hand captured in his, and he led her across the gray helipad and down the stairs to a door, which was a side entrance to the castle.

"I'm sorry about your father," she said as they entered the modern glass-and-chrome room that his father had built as a waiting room for the helicopter. "I should have said that earlier."

"Thank you," Nico said automatically, though it irritated him to do so. Why couldn't he simply tell the truth? That he wasn't sad? That he felt nothing but anger at the man who'd left him the title and the chaos that went along with it? He was right now pillaging Gavretti Manufacturing in order to repair the damage to all the Gavretti holdings.

He would save his legacy, but at what cost? Now more than ever it was important he do so. He had a child on the way, and he intended to hand over an intact empire when the time came. Unlike his father had done.

"I read that he died of a heart attack," Valentina said from behind him.

"He did." Nico stopped and turned toward her. "He also died with a smile on his face, in the bed of his latest mistress. She was twenty."

Valentina's lips dropped open and he had a sudden urge to close them with his own. To plunder their sweetness for one more glimpse of the bliss he'd felt that night in Venice.

"Oh," she said, her cheeks reddening. Nico wanted to laugh, but he didn't. She was still so innocent, no matter that he'd done his best to corrupt her that night. Desire sliced into him then, hot and sharp.

If anything, it angered him to feel this way toward her. Toward a D'Angeli.

"He had money, *cara,* and a title. Women like that sort of thing, whether they are young or old."

"Not all women," she said.

"This has not been my experience."

She looked haughty. "Then maybe you're not meeting the right kind of women."

"If they are women, then they are the right kind."

She made a noise that sounded like disgust. "How did I ever fall for your smooth words that night?"

He reached out and stroked his fingers along her soft

cheek. She gasped as he did so, but did not pull away. Sparks shot through his skin at the touch, made his body hunger sharply for hers.

Her violet eyes were wide. He wondered if she knew they glittered with heat and need. Whatever this was, she felt it, too. Perhaps, for her, it was the lure of the forbidden. Or perhaps it was simply that he was a man and she a woman and they were attracted to each other.

It didn't have to be complicated, and yet it felt as if it was the most complicated thing on earth.

"You fell," he said softly, "because you wanted to."

She had no signal. Tina tossed her phone onto the bed in disgust. She'd tried several times to send a text to Lucia, but there was no signal out here in the middle of this lake.

This place was, she had to admit, magnificent. She pushed open the double doors onto the balcony, which ran the entire width of the house, and stood in the sunshine. The sun's rays were lengthening as it neared dusk, but her view of the surrounding area was not yet diminished. Castello di Casari sat in the lake, but ringing the lake were mountains punctuated by small villages while vacation homes of the rich and famous perched high on the rocks.

The mountains were deep emerald, blooming with plants and flowers; in the distance, the tallest peaks were wreathed in white. Tina sighed. She could see civilization, but she could not reach it. The castle was built on a small island in the lake, its massive towers and walls taking over the entire island.

She went over to the stone balustrade and leaned against it. Below her, the lake rippled in deep blue currents. There was a sailboat a distance out, and a motorboat zipping by closer in. Pots of pink bougainvillea spilled over in regular intervals around the balcony, and there was a grouping of tables and chairs not too far away. She walked over and sat in one of the chairs, content to sit still and be at peace for a while.

She'd been relieved to find that she had her own room, though she hadn't truly expected Nico would try to share a room with her. What for? He clearly didn't want her anymore, no matter that he strummed his fingers over her skin and her body ached for him.

He had simply done it to prove a point. She had fallen because she'd wanted to, he'd said.

And he was right. She had wanted to. Because she'd been overcome by the feelings and sensations ricocheting through her that night, and because she'd wanted more. She'd wanted to see where the feelings led her.

He, however, had seduced her because she was a woman and she was willing.

Tina snorted in disgust. His father had died in bed with a twenty-year-old. Nico would no doubt do the same someday. What a fine father he would make for her baby. She was beginning to understand why her mother had been so secretive—what if her own father had been so terrible?

Renzo knew who his father was, and it had done nothing but cause him pain. He had not told her that, but their mother had. Renzo's pain was the reason her mother gave for not telling Tina what she wanted to know.

Maybe she'd been right after all.

She sat in the sun until it disappeared behind the mountain. It was still light out, but growing darker much faster now. She still wore jeans and sandals, but she'd removed her jacket and scarf. Now she returned to her room and retrieved them.

There was a knock on her door. The man who had greeted them at the landing pad was there, smiling at her pleasantly. "*Signorina,* his lordship asked me to tell you that dinner is prepared. You can reach the terrazzo by going out on the balcony and taking the steps down to the next level."

"Thank you," Tina replied. She wanted to refuse to join Nico, but she was surprisingly hungry. The anti-nausea medication the doctor had given her had worked wonders and she actually had an appetite for once.

She didn't change for dinner, determined that she would not do that at least. She was here under pro-test, not as a willing guest, so to hell with the niceties. Frau Decker would be horrified at her lack of manners, but Frau Decker was in Switzerland. Besides, her old teacher had never addressed a situation in which a lady might be held captive by a gentleman against her will.

Tina frowned wryly. Whatever would the good woman say if she could see this place and the man who waited at the dinner table? Quite probably, like most women, she would giggle and fawn over him.

Tina went onto the balcony and walked the length of it before finding the stairs down to the next level. There, a large table and at least ten chairs had pride of place beside a stunning view of soaring cliffs directly across the lake.

The table was set for two, with crisp white napkins, crystal goblets, silver flatware and pristine white plates. Nico stood with his back to her, looking out at the cliffs and holding a glass of wine from which he occasion-ally took a sip.

She studied his broad back, reluctant to interrupt

his thoughts and turn them toward her once more. He'd changed, she noted with surprise. Instead of the suit, he wore a pair of stonewashed jeans and a black shirt. His hair curled over his collar, and for a moment she longed to go over and slide her fingers into the silkiness of it as she had done that night.

Tina shivered involuntarily, but not from cold. Her body was hot, her blood thick and syrupy in her veins. He did that to her, and it disconcerted her that he still could.

She took the rest of the steps down and Nico turned, his gaze skimming her lightly as he did so. She tilted her chin up, as she'd been taught, and bore his scrutiny as if it were nothing.

"How are you feeling?" he asked.

"I've been better," she replied.

He appeared concerned. "Do you still feel nauseous?"

Guilt pricked her. "I'm not ill anymore, thanks to the medication. No, I was thinking more along the lines of how this is my first abduction."

She didn't expect him to smile, but he did, and it caught at her heart though it should not. "Mine, too."

"How fortunate," she said crisply. "We can enjoy the experience together."

He came over and pulled her chair out, and she realized she'd actually been standing there as if she'd expected it. How silly, and how very like her at the same time. She only hoped he didn't notice how she blushed.

His fingers skimmed over her shoulders after he pushed her chair in, and twined in her hair. She went very still, sparks zipping along her spine and behind her ears. It hurt, and it felt like the most wonderful thing all at once.

She wanted him to keep touching her, to slide his fingers against her scalp and then along her neck, down to her breasts. She wanted it far more than she should.

And then his breath was in her ear, and a deep shiver rolled through her.

"I would not say *enjoy* so much as endure, perhaps," he said before dropping his hand and taking his own seat.

Tina picked up her water and took a sip. She felt raw inside, exposed, as if he'd seen to the deepest heart of her and knew that her body betrayed her every time he was near. "I was being sarcastic."

His eyes glittered darkly. "Yes, I realize this. And I was simply saying what you were thinking."

They were silent while the food arrived. There was an antipasti platter, a delicate angel-hair pasta in sauce, broiled fish, *verdure* and an array of cheeses. The women who'd brought the meal disappeared and Nico proceeded to serve her. She didn't say anything while he filled her plate. Once he finished, he poured more sparkling water into her glass.

She waited while he began to fill his own plate, but he stopped and looked at her. "Eat, Valentina."

"I will," she said softly. "I'm waiting for you."

"Don't wait."

"It's not polite to start eating."

"To hell with polite. Eat."

She picked up an olive and popped it into her mouth. "Everyone calls me Tina," she said. "You might as well, too."

"If you prefer it."

She shrugged. "I don't, but it's what my friends call me."

He arched an eyebrow, and she couldn't help but

think he looked like the devil, all sinful and dark and tempting. "Are we friends then?"

"Hardly. But Valentina makes me think I'm in trouble." She ate another olive and sighed. "Which I suppose I am, really."

"Are you?"

"It certainly seems that way. I started the day in Rome and I'd made plans to go to Capri. This is not Capri."

He inclined his head. "No, it's prettier. And more exclusive."

She took a bite of pasta. It was delicious and she nearly moaned with the pleasure of eating solid food again for the first time in days. A light breeze blew over them then, and she was glad she'd put her jacket on again. It wasn't unpleasant, far from it, but it would be too cool without sleeves. "Did you grow up here?"

"No."

"I imagine your family has a lot of homes."

"Yes."

Tina pushed an olive around her plate. "Which was your favorite?"

His gaze speared into her then, intense and dark and forbidding. His smooth jaw was tight, and she realized that she'd stumbled into something he didn't want to discuss. It made no sense to her. He'd grown up with so much, while she and Mama and Renzo had lived in tiny apartments in back alleys for most of her childhood.

"I have no favorite," he said shortly. "I spent much of my time away at school."

Sympathy flooded her, though she couldn't imagine his experience being bad. He was an aristocrat, wealthy and very beautiful. He would have been the sun around which the other kids orbited.

"I did, too, once I hit fifteen," she said. "It wasn't a good time to go away."

"It never is." He took a sip of wine. "I went to school when I was six. I came home on breaks until I was seventeen." He shrugged. "So I have no particularly favorite house. I spent more time at school than I did here, or in any of the Gavretti estates."

"I didn't know," she said softly. "I'm sorry."

His eyes were as hard as diamonds. "There is nothing to be sorry about. I received a spectacular education and went to a top university."

"And spent summers with Renzo in the garage," she added.

"Yes."

Tina let out a heavy sigh. "Did you at least enjoy the time you spent with us? I had thought you did, but I was young. It's just that you seemed…happy."

She thought she might have said too much, but he only looked toward the cliffs and didn't say anything for a long moment. "I was," he finally said. "I enjoyed building the prototype with Renzo."

"And yet you left. And Renzo refuses to speak of you to this day. What happened?"

His head whipped around again, his eyes spearing into her. "It's not important."

Impulsively, she reached for his hand, grasped it in hers. His skin was warm, and the blood rushed through her veins just from this contact, making her feel lightheaded and confused.

"It *is* important, Nico. I want you and Renzo to be friends again. I want it to be the way it was."

She thought he would jerk away, but he turned her hand in his, traced his fingers in her palm while she shivered deep inside. "It can never be the way it was, *cara.* You are a woman now, not a child. You know life does not move backward."

Hot tears pressed against her eyelids. "I wish it did. For the sake of our baby, I wish I could fix whatever is wrong between you and Renzo."

Because, no matter what happened between them, he was a part of her life now. Through this baby, the Gavrettis and D'Angelis would always be connected. And it made her sad to think it would not be easy for any of them.

He sat back and let her go. The air wafting over her skin made her feel cold suddenly. "You cannot fix it, Tina. No one can."

She sucked in a deep breath. "I refuse to believe that."

"Then you are a fool."

She looked at him for a long moment. "I refuse to believe that, too," she said, her throat aching.

"Believe what you like, but it does not alter reality," he told her coolly. "Now eat, or we will never leave this table."

She did as he commanded, but only for the baby's sake. The food, which was delicious, failed to give her any pleasure. The more she thought of Nico and her brother, of the way they used to be and the way they were now, the less she tasted of the food.

There had to be a way to repair whatever had gone wrong, if only one of them would tell her about it. She thought of Renzo in the Caribbean with his wife and was thankful they were away for now. She shuddered to think what would happen if he were at home.

It would be a true clash of the titans the next time these men met, and she could not bear the idea she would be the catalyst.

Tina dropped the fork. "I want to know what happens next," she demanded, her heart hot with feeling. He'd taken her from Rome, brought her here, but for what purpose? He couldn't really intend for her to stay with him indefinitely.

Nico glanced over at her, seemingly impervious to the turmoil raging within her. "Dessert, I imagine."

"You know that's not what I mean."

The look he gave her was long and heavy with meaning. Her pulse snapped in her veins until she was certain he must see it thrumming in her neck. Dread lay thick inside her the longer he watched her without speaking.

"Tell me," she said when the silence was more than she could bear. "I have a right to know."

"What do you think will happen, Tina?"

She darted her tongue over her lower lip. "I'm not quite sure. I doubt you intend to keep me here for the next few months, no matter what you implied earlier. That would be ridiculous. And unnecessary."

"I disagree," he said, his voice as smooth as fine wine. "It is very necessary."

"Why?" she asked, apprehension twisting her belly into knots. "I want you to be a part of the baby's life. I won't deny you access."

One dark eyebrow arched. "You say that now. But what about when Renzo returns?" He shook his head. "No, that is not acceptable. You aren't going anywhere, Tina. You're staying here with me."

Tina gripped the edges of her seat and willed herself to be calm. "You can't force me to stay," she said, her voice brittle to her own ears.

He leaned back and spread his hands to encompass their surroundings. "Can I not? We are on an island.

The only way on or off is by helicopter or boat—and I control both of those things."

Her stomach plummeted through the stone floor of the terrazzo even as a chill shuddered through her. "You're being purposely contrary. Renzo will come looking for me. You can't prevent that."

Nico took a leisurely sip of wine, studying her through lowered lids. She endured the scrutiny, though he reminded her once more of a cat singling out prey. She sat very still, waiting for him to spring, knowing she was caught even before he did so.

All she could do was wait and see what manner the attack took.

"No," he finally said, "I can't stop Renzo from looking for you. But even he cannot separate a man and his wife."

CHAPTER FIVE

TINA'S breath was a solid ball in her chest. It sat heavy and thick and she couldn't force it in or out for a long moment.

"You look surprised," Nico said mildly.

Surprised? It was too mild a word for what she was feeling right now.

"I can't marry you, Nico," she choked out.

"Why? Because your brother won't approve?" He made a sound of disgust. "He won't approve of you being pregnant, either. If you cared about his approval, you would not have slept with a strange man that night."

It was too close to the truth, but it angered her nevertheless. "I suppose I deserve that, but it doesn't change the fact that you don't love me. I won't marry a man who doesn't love me."

She didn't know quite where that had come from, but the moment she said it, she knew it was what she felt.

His eyes glittered in the candlelight flickering brighter now that dusk was deepening. "Then you should have thought of that before you spread your legs for me."

Tina gasped, stung by his cruel words. "That's not fair. Women are allowed to take lovers without wanting to marry or have babies with the men they choose."

"Yes, but they are typically more prepared than you were that night."

Her cheeks were aflame. "Oh, yes, it's all *my* fault, right? But I'm not the one who used a faulty condom."

"And I'm not the one who chose a random stranger for my first sexual experience. You were lucky you got me, and not someone who might have treated you with less delicacy than the situation required."

"Well, bravo to you then," she snapped. "But I'm still not marrying you. There is no reason for it."

"I can think of a few reasons, not the least of which is that I'm not giving you—or your brother—a chance to change your mind about letting me be a part of the child's life."

She bowed her head demurely, though her heart was racing a million miles a minute. "I understand why you'd think that, but we can have papers drawn up. I'll sign anything reasonable. We'll make sure everything is spelled out."

He threw his head back and laughed, and a feeling of foreboding ricocheted through her. "How perfectly civil of you, *cara*. But this is not a negotiation. I don't trust you or Renzo. There's nothing you can say, nothing you can promise, that I will believe."

"I give you my word," she said.

"Your word means nothing to me." He shook his head, leaned toward her and trapped her hand in his. "No, you *will* marry me, and just as soon as possible."

Tina thrust her chin out defiantly, though her heart hammered and her insides churned. "Even you cannot compel a woman to marry you because you decree it," she said sharply. "I won't do it."

His eyes narrowed. "How selfish you are, *cara*. You would deprive this child of my name? Of my status? You would allow him to grow up without a legal right to my legacy? Do you think he will thank you for it someday?"

Her heartbeat slowed as his words twisted in her brain. God, she hadn't thought of that. She'd grown up with her mother's name, just as Renzo had, and they'd been just fine in the end—though it hadn't always been easy. There'd been no estate to inherit, no vast sums of money to distribute among heirs. There'd been nothing at all, until Renzo made his fortune.

"It's not about money," she said with certainty. "I have money, and our child will want for nothing."

Not only did she have the money from her trust fund, but she'd also been investing a chunk of it over the years. She now had quite a handsome sum that was all from her own hard work. Her brother might not let her work for him, but she did work—managing her money—and she did a damn good job at it, too.

"I went to boarding school, Tina. I know what it was like. Those girls would have made your life hell, and a big part of that would have been your lack of pedigree. Do you want that to happen to your child?"

Fury vibrated through her then. "I won't send my baby away to school, you can be sure of that."

"It's not only school, though, is it? If you want this child to have every advantage, to have doors open for him and to be accepted everywhere, then you will see that marrying me is the only way to achieve that."

She wanted to press her hands to her ears. "You make it sound so medieval, and yet this is the twenty-first century."

"People are not so changed, though, are they? Especially not in my circles." He leaned forward and trapped her hand where it lay on the table. She tried to pull away, but his grip was as solid as the stone cliffs in the distance. "But there is another, even more pressing reason, darling Tina. If you do not agree to this marriage, I will destroy D'Angeli Motors."

A layer of ice coated her heart. Fear pumped into her in waves. "You cannot," she said, proud that her voice did not break. "If you could, you would have already done so."

He let her go and sat back. "You forget, *cara mia*, that I am a much richer man than I was only a few weeks ago. And I will use that wealth—and the power that comes with this title—to destroy your precious brother if you do not agree to marriage."

Horror seeped into her then. She thought of Renzo, of Faith and baby Domenico, and a wave of guilt swept her. Renzo was happier than she'd ever known him to be now that he'd found Faith. He laughed a lot more these days, and he no longer risked his life on the track. His leg was also on the mend now that the surgeons had removed the scar tissue that had built up over time, and he would very likely be walking without a cane once it healed.

He had everything. How could she put his happiness at risk, especially when she'd created this mess by indulging in a single impulsive act solely for her own pleasure? Renzo had done everything to make sure she had a good life, and this was how she repaid his generosity?

"You are really very cruel, aren't you?" Tina asked, her heart throbbing with fury and hurt.

Nico's expression didn't change, though she thought the corners of his mouth tightened. "Life is cruel," he said. "I am merely doing what I must to protect my child."

"*Our* child."

"Yes, our child." He said the words plainly enough,

and yet there was an inflection there, an unspoken threat. *Our child if you do as I say.*

Tina shivered. It did not go unnoticed.

"Are you cold?"

"A little," she said, unwilling to admit that her shiver was born more out of apprehension than the breeze.

"Then let us go inside."

He came and held out a hand to her. She didn't accept it, pushing herself to her feet without his help. He didn't move away, however, and she found herself trying to take a step backward.

The chair stopped her. He was so close. *Too* close. She could feel his heat crawling into her, surrounding her. His scent filled her senses, spice and man mingled with the aromas of leather and wood.

Heat blossomed in her belly, flowed like a river of syrup into her limbs. She felt as if she'd been drinking when she had in fact not had a drop. He did that to her, had done from the first moment she'd met him on the docks outside the palazzo in Venice.

No, he'd always made her feel funny, though when she'd been younger it had only been a hot, hollow feeling right beneath her breastbone. She'd crept into the garage to feel it, to gaze upon him and daydream.

How deluded she'd been about him. How very, very naive. He was not her dream man, not the husband or lover she could have wished for. He was arrogant, cold and very determined to get his way, no matter the consequences to anyone else.

She despised him. And her body wasn't getting the message. Her body was zinging with sparks, melting, aching. Wanting.

Tina sucked in a sharp breath, reminding herself why she couldn't allow that to happen.

She could never allow it to happen again. He'd consumed her the last time, and she'd willingly let it happen. She'd only panicked when she'd known who he was, not because of what had transpired between them. No, she'd been half-ready to do it again, but she'd let her curiosity get the best of her.

If only she'd never removed his mask!

Tina's first instinct was to drop her gaze from the intensity of his, but she forced herself to look him in the eye. Unflinchingly.

His gaze sparked. Heat spread through her body.

"I won't marry a man who threatens my family," she said firmly.

One eyebrow arched. She had the impression he was mocking her. "Oh, yes? Originally, you said you wouldn't marry a man who didn't love you. Which is it, Tina? Love or duty?"

Tina stiffened. "I won't be compelled against my will."

His expression was doubtful. His gaze dipped, lingered on the scoop neck of her tank top before drifting back up to meet her eyes. "I think you shall, *cara*. If you value the things you claim to."

"You are very certain of yourself," she said, her breath hitching in her throat.

"Indeed."

"Renzo is not an easy mark, and you know it." It made her feel confident to say so, but the truth was she had no idea.

Nico's smile was lethally smug. "Do I? And what if I don't care, *bella mia?* What if I am willing to do anything it takes to win?"

"Even immolate yourself in the process?"

He looked thoughtful for a brief moment. "Perhaps. Are you willing to risk it?"

"Are you?"

He laughed at her. "*Allora*, we shall get nowhere if we talk in circles. Come."

He put his hand on her back then and ushered her inside, through hallways and rooms she hadn't seen earlier. The castle had been modernized, but the rooms were still magnificent. Huge vaulted ceilings soared above her head, painted with frescoes that gleamed with bright blues, deep greens, vibrant reds and creamy flesh tones. The floors were inlaid marble mosaic, punctuated with intricate patterns of lapis and gold, porphyry and malachite.

The old wooden panels lining the walls gleamed with oil and care, and lush sheets of silk damask hung over the floor-to-ceiling windows that she knew would look out on the cool blue beauty of the lake when it was daylight.

She didn't realize he was leading her to her room until he stopped in front of her door. Tina dropped her gaze from his, cursing the timid side of her nature for kicking in when she wanted to face him down like a lioness protecting her brood. Her heart kicked up again at his proximity, at the intimacy of standing in front of her bedroom door with the only man she'd ever shared a bed with.

"Defy me if you wish, but you will realize there is only one choice in the end. You will do the right thing for Renzo and his lovely Faith."

"One choice is not a choice," she replied, her jaw aching with the effort it took not to scream at him.

He shrugged, arrogant and unfeeling to the last. "You can choose what is right, or you can choose to let me compel you into it. Either way, you *will* do what I wish in the end."

"How very generous of you," she said, her voice dripping with sarcasm. "I wonder that you even pretend this is a choice."

He laughed, startling her with the rich sound in the dark and quiet hallway. "You amuse me, *cara*—defiant to the last. I can hardly reconcile this with the girl who couldn't speak to me without turning red."

"I was a child then. I've grown up now."

His gaze slipped over her. "You have indeed. Quite delightfully, I might add." Before she knew what he was planning, his long fingers came up and gripped her chin, holding her head up high for his inspection. "There is a connecting door between our suites. Should you desire a repeat of Venice, you have only to open the door and come inside."

Her heart throbbed in her ears, her neck. Surely he could see her pulse beating. Tina swallowed hard. "I don't," she said. "Never again."

She could see his teeth flash white in the dim hallway. His handsome face was so close, the hard angles touchable. Kissable. *No.*

"Never say never, sweetheart," he told her. "You will lose if you do."

"I hardly think so," she said haughtily.

His head dipped swiftly, and she closed her eyes in reaction. She could feel his breath on her lips, and she shivered with anticipation even while her brain struggled to catch up.

"I think you lie to yourself," Nico said, and then he laughed softly as he pulled away.

Tina's eyes snapped open as her brain finally engaged. She took a step backward, thudded into her still closed door. She'd thought he was going to kiss her. And she'd wanted it.

Fire burned her from the inside out—but was it the fire of shame, or of desire? "I don't want you," she said firmly. "I *don't*."

His smile mocked her. "Tell yourself that if it makes you feel better. But we both know it's a lie."

Nico sat in the dark with his laptop and went over the figures again. Then he sprawled back in his chair, raking a hand through his hair in frustration.

Even in death, Alessio Gavretti had the power to irritate him. More than irritate him, apparently.

Nico swore softly. He'd spent years trying to impress the man who wasn't impressed with anything—unless it wore a very short skirt and had very large breasts—but his father had always treated him with a cool indifference that had been the hallmark of his personality.

Nothing Nico ever did made a dent in his father's reserve, though the man *had* come to his races a few times. Nico had been the impetus behind Gavretti Manufacturing in the first place, though it hadn't been his original plan when he'd first gone to his father to ask for support. No, he'd wanted to back Renzo—but his father wouldn't hear of it.

"Why should I invest in this man's business when you are perfectly capable of starting your own business, Niccolo? No, build the motorcycles yourself, but do not ask me for money for another."

Nico frowned. That had been a pivotal moment in his life, though he'd not realized it at the time. He'd built the motorcycles, when he'd realized he had no other choice, and he'd lost the only friend he'd ever truly had. It still hurt in places he didn't like to examine, and for that he blamed the woman in his guest room. Without her, he wouldn't be thinking about this so much tonight.

He'd spent so many years not having a conscience that to be reminded it had not always been the case was more unsettling than he would have liked.

He shoved himself upright and went through the open door onto the balcony. It was quiet outside, dark. He welcomed the solitude. The scents of bougainvillea and lavender filled the air, and far below him the waters of the lake lapped at the rock upon which the castle stood.

It was peaceful. And it made him desperate, as well. He could lose it all if he didn't figure this out.

He'd had no idea, until his father had died and the estate had fallen into his hands, just how much of a tangle it was in. Alessio Gavretti had spent money like he had a printing press in the basement—and so had Nico's mother.

They'd separated years ago, but never divorced. His father spent money on women, and his mother spent it on clothing, jewels and homes. Over the years, they'd managed to rack up an impressive roster of loans and long-term debts. It was as if each one had been trying to outdo the other.

Now Nico had to somehow manage to keep the world from knowing how close the Gavretti fortunes teetered to the brink.

He wanted to laugh at the irony. He'd threatened Tina with ruin for her brother if she did not agree to marry him, and yet he was the one who could be ruined if knowledge of the estate's financial matters became public at the wrong moment. He did not doubt that Renzo D'Angeli would snap up Gavretti Manufacturing and sell it off for scrap.

Nico didn't blame him. In his position, he'd do the same—and without a shred of remorse, either.

Nico leaned on the balustrade and peered at the lights of the village in the distance. He couldn't let it happen, and he damn sure couldn't let Tina refuse to marry him. Without a marriage, he would have no claim to his child, especially if she refused to publicly acknowledge him as the father, no matter what she said about papers and signatures.

And why did that matter so much?

It wasn't as if he knew the first thing about being a father, or even that he had latent fatherly instincts coming to the fore. Nor had he wanted a wife or a child to interfere with the way he ran his life. He was free, unencumbered by entanglements, and uninterested in changing the way he lived.

Yes, if he were to let her walk away, he could work on saving the Gavretti estate and think about finding a proper wife later.

Nico snorted. What was a proper wife? His mother had been a proper wife, hand-selected by his father's family, and look how that had worked out. Two bitter, selfish people who'd produced one child and then used that child in their feud against each other.

Anger ate at him, burning in his gut the way it always did when he thought of his parents and the empty childhood he'd had. Oh, he'd had everything money could buy, but he'd lacked the one thing it couldn't: love.

Maybe that was why he'd been so drawn to the D'Angelis. There had only been the three of them, but they'd had enough love in their home to fill him with its glow simply by association.

He glanced over at the glass doors that led from Tina's room. They were shut, the curtains drawn, but there was a light on inside. The light of the television flickered in the gap where the curtains hadn't quite come together all the way.

A wave of longing filled him, stunning him with its potency. He wanted to walk inside there and take her in his arms again, fill her body with his and shut out the world. It was melancholy and stress getting the best of him, he knew that, but it made the feeling no less powerful.

If he were still in Rome, he'd head out to a club for a few hours, call one of the women on his contact list. He'd engage in a night of wanton sex and wake up refreshed and ready to tackle his problems again.

Love had nothing to do with it.

No matter how much he might have longed for his parents' love, or how much he'd admired the D'Angelis' wealth of it, he knew that love was ephemeral in his world. He'd grown up in a family who loved themselves more than each other, and he expected that was how his life would continue. He was thirty years old and he'd never felt even a glimmering of love for another person.

Until the moment Valentina D'Angeli had walked back into his life and told him she was expecting his child. He didn't kid himself that he'd fallen into instant and overwhelming love with this baby, this collection of cells growing in her body, but something *had* happened.

He'd felt as if she'd punched him in the gut, and the feeling hadn't abated over the past few hours. He didn't know what it was, but he wasn't letting her walk away. He hadn't intended to marry her, but in the end he'd realized it was the only way.

Aside from ensuring him access to his child, marrying Tina would give her brother pause. If Renzo did get wind of Nico's financial troubles, he would think twice about ruining the man his sister had married.

Mercenary, yes. But Nico damn well didn't care. He'd been mercenary for so long now that he couldn't bother growing a conscience for one woman. No matter how she tugged at long forgotten memories of acceptance and hope.

CHAPTER SIX

It was midmorning when Tina awoke, and for a moment she couldn't remember where she was. But then it all came back with brutal clarity and she sat up with a gasp. She was marooned in the middle of a lake, held captive by a dark and dangerous man who insisted that she marry him.

She reached for her phone on the bedside table, searching hopefully for a signal, but there was none. Tina tossed the phone down on the plush comforter and made a noise of displeasure.

But what would she do if there were a signal? She'd text Lucia, of course, but she most definitely would not call her mother or Renzo. A shiver slid along her spine at the thought. That would be a disaster.

She flipped the covers back and went to open the heavy silk drapes. The sun filtered in through the laurels, dappling her face with warmth. The lake was alive with windsurfers in the distance, and here and there motorboats zipped by, some towing skiers and others simply out for a leisurely ride.

It was without doubt a gorgeous view and she stared at the green mountains in the distance before turning her attention to getting dressed. Tina showered—and then, just to prove a point, she blow-dried her hair with a round brush until it was stick straight.

When her hair hung smooth and long halfway down her back, she went into the walk-in closet where a staff member had put away all her clothing. Everything was crisp and ready to be worn, so she chose a pair of shantung silk trousers in bright red and a long silk vest in black that belted at the waist. She added a pair of strappy stilettos, just to add a bit of wow factor, and then put on the bangle bracelet her mother had given her for her graduation. She added the rest of her jewelry for the day—diamond earrings, a gold necklace, three rings—before she was satisfied.

No one seemed to be stirring in the house until she reached the kitchen and found the chef and a trio of helpers at work on something that smelled delicious.

"If you will join the *signore* on the terrazzo, *signorina*, breakfast will soon be served."

Tina thanked the woman and went out to the same table she'd shared with Nico last night. He was on the phone, a laptop in front of him, and she stopped to watch the way the sunlight slanted over his perfect features. He seemed oblivious to her presence.

"It stops now," he grated. "You have an allowance. If you burn through it, you will get nothing more until the next quarter."

A second later he smacked his palm on the table, swearing violently. Tina jumped at the sudden movement and spun to go back inside. Before she could reach the door, he called out to her. She turned slowly. He still had the phone to his ear, but he beckoned her over.

Warily, she approached and took a seat while he continued to argue with whoever was on the other end.

Then he ended the call abruptly and slid the ringer to Silent.

"How is it you get a signal out here and I get nothing?" she asked.

"It's the carrier," he told her. "I use a different service when I am here than I do elsewhere. Though sometimes, when the weather is right and you are in the right part of the castle, other signals will come through."

Well, that explained that. "I don't suppose you'd let me use your phone today."

He shrugged. "Why not? You are an intelligent woman, Tina. You won't call your brother and beg him to rescue you."

Her heart thumped. "How can you be so sure?"

He studied her for a moment, his eyes straying over her hair. Warmth blossomed inside her belly then, spreading through her limbs like hot honey. "So it does straighten out," he said thoughtfully.

"I told you so."

"Women have such tricks at their disposal. I would have never guessed."

She almost laughed. "I wouldn't expect you to be au courant about the things that occur in beauty salons. And I did ask you a question, by the way."

He picked up his espresso, his long fingers dwarfing the small cup. "I am aware of it."

"And what is your answer?"

"I already gave you my answer, Tina. You are intelligent and thoughtful. You also love your brother very much. You do not wish to worry him or cause him to cut his vacation short when he is so happy with his new wife and child."

Her pulse throbbed with every word. It was as if he could see inside her soul. She shook herself. That was silly. Of course he couldn't. But he was a very good guesser.

"Besides," he continued, "you are not in danger. You are in a situation of your own making and you refuse to cry wolf before you've thought it all out."

"Not entirely of my own making," she murmured. "It does seem to take two to make a baby."

"Yes, but I've already thought about it and I know what must be done."

"And what if I disagree? I might think myself justified to call Renzo then. He could at least get his best attorneys onto the situation."

His expression remained unconcerned. "By all means, if you think this is the correct course of action. We can fight about who is more suited to get full custody of the child in the courts."

A chill dripped like acid into her veins. She didn't really think he could take her child away from her—but what if he could?

"I haven't made up my mind yet," she said breezily, turning to smile at the woman who brought her a cup of coffee.

"You will," he said with that arrogant assurance that made her want to grind her teeth in frustration.

His phone buzzed on the table and he pressed the button to send it to voice mail without once looking at the screen. She wondered who was on the other end of the line, then realized with an unpleasant jolt that it must be a woman. He wouldn't treat a business associate that way, she was pretty certain, so it had to be a romantic entanglement.

Something twisted in her gut then, some feeling she didn't want to examine too closely. She'd not thought of what his romantic life must be like right now. They'd spent a single night together nearly two months ago. Though he'd not been linked with any particular woman in the papers lately did not mean there wasn't one—or had not been one that night.

A wave of queasiness swept through her, but it had nothing to do with pregnancy hormones. She pushed the coffee away.

"You can drink it," Nico said. "It's decaf."

For some reason, she was ridiculously touched that he'd known she couldn't have caffeine. But she shouldn't be. It wasn't a romantic gesture; it was a practical one. "Thank you for remembering."

The smile he gave her threatened to melt all her good intentions to remain detached and controlled. How could she even begin to feel that way? He was threatening her—threatening her family. But what he said next cracked the ice she tried to keep around her heart.

"I spent a couple of hours this morning looking up pregnancy. I admit I know nothing."

Tina swallowed. Hard. "I'm afraid I don't, either. I had thought to beg Faith for information."

Nico looked suddenly thoughtful, and the ice cracked a little more. "There is a website with pregnant women on it. They talk about everything. You can even track the stages of your pregnancy. It is quite amazing."

Tina picked up her cup with shaky fingers—mostly because she needed something to do—and took a sip.

She didn't want to see this side of him, not when he'd threatened her with a custody battle and harm to her family if she didn't bow to his will. But when he looked at her like this, when he spoke so earnestly and honestly it made her heart hurt, she remembered the old Nico, the one who used to work in the garage with Renzo and laugh freely.

And remembering made her ache with longing to see them reconciled, though he'd told her yesterday that would never happen. How could it be that bad between them? That unforgivable?

"I'll look into it," she said softly, keeping her eyes downcast while she worked to find her center.

The food arrived then, and once more they were alone and eating together on this gorgeous balcony overlooking the beautiful azure lake. Everything was delicious and plentiful, and she found herself eating more than she'd thought she would be able to.

"I'm glad to see you eat," he said. "You were very pale yesterday when I first saw you."

"The medication helps tremendously. I'm just happy I didn't miss breakfast. I thought I'd slept too late."

His eyes gleamed like purest silver in the shaft of sunlight slanting through the laurels. "You will never miss breakfast so long as you are here, *cara*. The meal will wait until you are ready for it."

A dart of pain pierced her right in the center of her chest and she found herself blinking rapidly to dispel the tears that threatened to fall. Why? *Why?*

It was nothing to cry over. It was ridiculous to think of crying. Niccolo Gavretti was not holding meals for *her*. He was taking care of her because she carried his child, nothing more.

She absolutely would not read more into the gesture than it contained. He was *not* being thoughtful.

But when had anyone ever put her needs and feelings first? When had anyone ever treated her as if she were the center of *their* universe?

Mama and Renzo loved her, she had no doubt, but Renzo had always been the one around whom the family orbited. Because he was male. Because he was older.

Because he was wildly, insanely driven and successful. She'd grown up in his shadow. It hadn't been a bad place to be, but it had also not been a place where she could flourish on her own merits.

"Thank you," she managed to say finally. "That's very kind of you, but there's no need to hold meals for me. Tell me what time you wish to have breakfast, and I will be here for it."

His phone buzzed again, startling her. Again, he sent it to voice mail without looking at the screen. He did it so casually that she almost felt sorry for the person on the other end of the line.

"We will eat when you are ready. A pregnant woman needs plenty of sleep."

Heat suffused her then, made her skin glow. There was something about the way he said *pregnant woman* that made her blush. Absurd.

"I will still endeavor to awaken at a reasonable hour," she said stubbornly. "You shouldn't have to wait for me."

He grinned, and her heart squeezed tight. So, so handsome when he wasn't scowling—and even when he was, damn him. "Truthfully, *cara mia,* I am a night owl. I prefer to sleep in myself. But if you begin to awaken at dawn, then dawn is when breakfast will be."

Tina shuddered. "Never fear, dawn is definitely not my style."

He reached for a roll. "Perhaps this night owl lifestyle will do us well when we have a newborn to take care of. I understand they do not sleep much."

Tina could only gape at him. "Exactly how much reading have you been doing anyway?"

Though, truthfully, that wasn't why she was stunned. No, it was the implication that *we* would be taking care of a newborn. Not her. Both of them, as if he, too, would get up in the middle of the night to feed the baby.

It was a mental picture she did not need.

"I couldn't sleep last night, I'm afraid." He picked up his coffee. "Do you have any idea how much work a baby can be?"

"I have some idea," she said, thinking of Renzo and Faith and the haggard, sleepless looks they'd worn for the past few months.

He looked so serious. "It's rather frightening how much attention such a little person needs."

"Well, they can't do it themselves."

"No," he agreed.

His phone buzzed again. This time he glanced at it before swearing and sending it to voice mail. It was just what she needed to pierce the bubble of dazed delight swirling around her head. He would not lull her with talk of babies.

"Why don't you just answer it?" she asked a bit more sharply than she intended.

There was a sudden chill that blanketed his eyes, and she almost wished she'd kept her irritation to herself.

"Because it will do no good," he told her mildly, though she wasn't fooled he was anything other than angry about the calls. "Some women are incapable of listening to reason, and I refuse to bash my head against the wall repeatedly in an effort to be heard."

Tina's spine stiffened. "I'm rather surprised you would even bother. I thought your usual method was simply to leave once you were finished."

His eyes glittered so hotly she had an urge to apologize. But she wouldn't.

He stood and pocketed the phone, and she couldn't

quite shake the feeling she'd insulted him. Though why she should care, she couldn't say.

"Sadly," he said, "there are some women in a man's life that it is impossible to leave. No matter how much he might wish it."

The island was larger than Tina had first thought when they'd arrived yesterday. On the other side of the castle was a terraced garden, with grapevines twining over a pergola, cobbled walkways, and plots of herbs and flowers. There was also a stone pool with clear turquoise water that looked as if it, too, had been carved out of ancient rock and set here during Roman times.

It had been hours since breakfast. She'd spent some time exploring the castle, and when she'd realized there was actually a garden, she'd changed her shoes into something more reasonable so that she could investigate it further.

She skirted the pool and walked across the grass toward the vine-shaded pergola. From the outside, it looked so private and cool. Peaceful. She could use a little bit of peace in her life right now.

She hadn't seen Nico since this morning, but she hadn't stopped thinking about their exchange on the terrace. *There are some women in a man's life that it is impossible to leave. No matter how much he might wish it.*

Like a woman who was pregnant with his child? She felt like a fool the more she thought of it. Of course he didn't want her in his life, but he was willing to accept her because of the baby. If she married him, would she be the woman on the other end of that phone someday?

She ran her hand along a stand of tall ornamental grass, enjoying the way the fuzzy tops tickled her fingers. No doubt she *would* be the woman on the other end of the phone, whether she married him or not. They were having a baby together and they would always need to be in contact with each other, regardless of whether or not they married.

He would be in her life, and she in his, for as long as they lived. The thought made her shiver—only it wasn't completely out of fear or anger that she did so.

No, more like excitement.

Tina stopped in the middle of the garden as her legs seemed to suddenly be made of jelly. My God, a baby was such a game changer. A *life* changer. A child was forever. It was such a huge obligation that Tina sucked in an abrupt, sharp breath, heavy with responsibility and unshed tears.

My God.

What had she gotten herself into? It was too much. *Too much...*

Her heart beat hard. She thought of Faith and Renzo, of the baby they both loved so much. She could see the pride in their gazes, the love and the utter conviction they would do anything it took to protect their child. And each other.

Tina passed beneath the pergola and found an out-door furniture grouping plush with overstuffed cushions. It was a perfect place to curl up and read—or to think.

She sank onto the couch and lay back against the pillows. Tears pricked her eyes. Such a mess she was in. Nico didn't love her, nor she him, but they'd created this life together. This tiny life that would need so many things from her.

Certainly she could hire a nanny. She could buy her own house and hire around-the-clock care for her child. She could do this alone, she didn't doubt it.

But was it fair to her baby to make him or her shuffle between parents?

Tina put a hand over her belly and concentrated on breathing. Her heart hurt with the chaos of her thoughts. Was agreeing to marry Nico the right thing to do? She pictured Renzo and knew he would be furious if she did.

But if marrying Nico kept him from going after Renzo or D'Angeli Motors, then she had to do it. She would not be responsible for this feud between them growing any worse, nor would she be responsible for bringing harm to her brother and his family.

The sun was warm beneath the pergola, though she was not in direct light. She lay there for a very long time, gazing out at the bright green lawn with red and pink flowerbeds, pencil pines, bay laurels, and even a small grove of olive and lemon trees, until her eyes started to droop.

Tina awoke with a start sometime later, a chill skating over her skin as the sun's warming caress moved on to another part of the garden. Birds chirped in the trees and she could hear the distant sounds of church bells from the nearest village across the lake.

She'd been dreaming about Nico, as he used to be when he came to their house so many years ago. He'd laughed then. Smiled. He'd always had an edge, but it hadn't seemed frightening the way it did now.

Now she was utterly convinced he would do whatever it took to get his way. Ruthlessly.

"You scared Giuseppe out of several years of life when he could not find you," came a cool voice.

Tina gave a little gasp of fright. She turned, found the man she'd been dreaming about sitting in a chair across from her, watching her with an intensity that both warmed and frightened her.

"I'm sorry," she said automatically. "I fell asleep."

"I see that."

She pushed herself upright on the cushions and stretched like a cat coming to life after a long nap. "I don't know what happened. It was warm and cozy, and I couldn't keep my eyes open."

He looked around the sheltered pergola as if seeking the answer somewhere in the leafy green vines. She realized then that they were hidden from the view of anyone in the castle. A person would have to walk across the garden and cross in front of the pergola to see anyone inside it.

No wonder Giuseppe had lost her. She felt a pinprick of guilt as she thought of the little man searching. He'd been nothing but wonderful to her since the moment she'd arrived. He, at least, made her feel like a guest instead of a prisoner.

"It is a lovely spot for a nap," Nico said. "I believe I might have fallen asleep here once when I was six."

Her heart flipped as she thought of him as a little boy. Had he frightened his parents when he'd disappeared that day? Or had they known where he'd gone and left him to sleep in this lovely bower?

He seemed distant, his eyes focusing on some faraway point. Then he swung his gaze back to her. It was cool, hard. Determined. "It is time, Tina."

She swallowed. "Time for what?"

He flicked his fingers against his jeans, as if removing a speck of dirt. "Time to choose."

Her heart skipped. "Who was the woman on the phone?" she asked, fresh anger surging in her veins.

His eyes darkened. She didn't think he would answer. But he surprised her.

"My mother. We were arguing."

Tina ducked her head and studied her clasped hands. So much rage in so few words. She felt as if she'd invaded his privacy somehow, yet she'd had to know the answer. As if it mattered when he compelled her to marry him with threats to her family.

"It's none of my business. I shouldn't have said anything."

She could feel his gaze still on her, intense, steady, penetrating. "You heard me fight with a woman. You saw me ignore her calls. And I've asked you to marry me. You have every right to be curious, under the circumstances."

"Actually," she said, her heart thudding as she lifted her gaze and met those storm-cloud eyes, "you didn't ask me. You told me."

He was so beautiful sitting across from her, his long legs stretched out in front of him, one arm hooked along the back of the big chair as he sprawled casually in it. He wore dark jeans and a white shirt, unbuttoned to show a perfect V of tanned skin that she could remember kissing—innocently at first, reverently later.

He arched an eyebrow as he studied her. She knew her color was high and wondered what he must be thinking. As if it mattered. As if anything but what he demanded of her mattered.

He ran his fingers along the arm of the chair in an absent gesture. "What is the difference? The outcome will be the same."

Her temper flared. "A woman wants to be asked, Nico. It's part of the fantasy."

"Does this mean you've come to your senses?"

Her breath caught, her blood pounding in her temples, her ears. Come to her senses? She felt as though she'd lost them two months ago.

"Promise you won't harm my family or D'Angeli Motors." She said it firmly, her heart racing recklessly fast. It wasn't like her to be so bold, and yet she'd been bolder in the past twenty-four hours with him than she'd ever been in her life. Oh, she was assertive enough usually, having learned to come out of her shell after years of schooling, but not confrontational. She'd been taught to be polite, gracious and ladylike—skills that were somehow lacking when she faced Niccolo Gavretti.

One corner of his mouth turned up. It could not be called a smile. "So long as Renzo leaves me alone, then I will do the same."

Tina closed her eyes, her entire body quivering with fear and anticipation all at once. Was she really going to do this?

Of course she was. What choice did she have? She wouldn't let her family suffer. Nico was titled, wealthy and no doubt in possession of far more power now that he'd inherited his father's estate. Renzo would be no match for him. And she would not let that happen.

"Then you should ask me," she said. "It would be the proper thing to do."

She didn't expect him to do what he did next. He rose from the chair in a graceful movement. And then he was at her side, sinking onto a knee on the gray stone cobbles in front of the couch. His palm came up, cupped her cheek, while his other hand took one of hers and brought it to his heart. It was a grand gesture, even if it was false.

Tina turned her cheek into his palm, though she did not mean to do so. But it was such a tender touch, and she'd ached to feel it for so long. For nearly two months. It stunned her to discover that she'd missed him, missed the aching rightness of his skin against hers.

Oh, she was in so much trouble here.

"Valentina D'Angeli," he said, his fingers suddenly stroking down, along the column of her neck, making her shiver with longing. "Will you be my wife?"

Tina darted her tongue over her lips. She was insane, insane—*insane*—for even considering this. But he was right; she had no choice.

It was the correct thing to do. For her family. For her baby.

"Yes," she whispered, her throat constricting on the word. "Yes."

CHAPTER SEVEN

Tina closed her eyes as his head descended, anticipating his kiss. Longing for it. It had been so long since she'd felt the hot press of his mouth against hers and she was surprised at how much she wanted it. Oh, it was wrong, but she wanted it.

For all her breathless anticipation, however, he did not kiss her. Or, he did kiss her, but not the way she wanted. His lips feathered along her cheek before he tilted her head down and placed a chaste kiss on her forehead.

Disappointment lanced into her as he stood and helped her to her feet.

"There is much to do, *tesoro*," he said. "You will need to pack an overnight bag."

Tina blinked in confusion. "An overnight bag? Why? Are we going somewhere?"

He put his hands on her shoulders, skimmed them down her bare arms. His touch left her glowing and hot, like burning embers on a cool spring night. "We are going to Gibraltar," he told her.

Tina's heart plummeted. "Gibraltar?"

He frowned, but it wasn't unfriendly. "You know why couples go to Gibraltar, Tina. You cannot be that sheltered."

She shook her head as a tide of apprehension began to bubble to life inside her. "I do know why. But why must we? I had thought—"

His pitying look told her he knew exactly what she'd thought. That they would have a normal, though perhaps hurried, wedding. That she would spend the next month or so choosing a gown, flowers, a cake and a venue. That she would somehow persuade Renzo to put aside his dislike and give her away.

She was exactly like other girls in that she'd always imagined she would have a fairy-tale wedding.

But it was not to be. She'd done everything backward, and now this man she barely knew anymore, this man she'd agreed to marry, was taking her to Gibraltar for a quickie wedding. They would be married within twenty-four hours of their arrival on the rock. She would be Signora Gavretti—

But no, she would be the marchesa di Casari.

Tina's knees melted like butter and she nearly sank onto the soft cushions again. Nico steadied her, his strong arms coming around her and pulling her close.

"There is no need to wait," he told her even as he held her against the heat and hardness of his body. "No need to prevaricate."

"But my family…"

His eyes flashed hot. "I am your family now, Tina."

By nightfall, they were on his private jet, winging their way across the Mediterranean toward Gibraltar. Nico sat across from her, his laptop open, his gaze fixed on the screen, while Tina couldn't seem to concentrate on the book she'd been trying to read. Her eReader sat on her lap, forgotten, as she stared at her own sad reflection in the jet's window.

Her life had changed so fast. Two months ago, she'd been looking forward to a masquerade party with Lucia. Everything she'd thought about her life up to that point had been blasted apart in the space of one night, though she had not known how completely it would change her at the time.

Just a little fun, she'd thought. The chance to be someone different, someone more free and spontaneous. Someone brave and bold and in control.

Ha. Some control.

With Niccolo Gavretti, she had no control. She slanted her gaze toward him, her breath catching as it always did when confronted with the evidence of his staggering male beauty. He frowned as he studied the screen, his fingers tapping a key here and there.

She wanted to go to him, wanted to smooth the frown from his face—and she wanted to run away at the same time. She had never been so tormented over one male in her life as she had over this one.

Always this one.

He looked up then and caught her watching him. She didn't jerk her gaze away, didn't try to hide that she'd been looking. What was the point? He closed the laptop and put it away.

"I know this isn't the way you expected this to happen," he said. "But it's for the best."

"The best for whom?" she asked automatically.

His silver gaze didn't waver. "For us. For the baby."

"I don't think waiting a month would have hurt."

He shrugged. "When I decide to do a thing, I do it. I see no point in waiting."

When *he* decided.

"What about your mother? Don't you think she might like to see her son get married?"

His laugh was unexpected. It also sent a shiver over her. "The only thing she cares about right now is the fact I'm forcing her to live on her allowance. I doubt she'd trouble herself to bring me water if I were dying of thirst on her doorstep."

Sadness jolted her at that statement. She knew he was an only child, and of course she knew that his father had recently died, but she'd had no idea his relationship with his mother was that bad. "Perhaps she's still upset over your father's death. Grief does unexpected things to people."

She felt a little foolish for saying such a thing considering how his father had died, but stranger things had happened than a wife still being in love with her philandering husband.

He stared at her disbelievingly. "She is not sad, *tesoro*. Or, if she is sad, it's not because he died, but because I'm now in charge of the money."

"I'm sorry," she said because she didn't know what else to say.

"Not all families enjoy each other's company the way yours does."

Tina dropped her gaze from his. Yes, her family loved one another, there was no doubt about it. But she also thought perhaps they failed to understand one another, as well. They would absolutely not understand, for instance, why she'd agreed to marry Nico.

No, they would be furious. Renzo would pop a gasket when she told him.

Nico's phone rang and he took the call, ending their conversation. A short while later, the plane landed at Gibraltar airport. It was dark when they stepped off the plane. She couldn't see the ocean, but she could smell the tang of the salt air.

They climbed into a waiting car and were whisked to an exclusive hotel high above the city. They checked into the penthouse suite, which the staff assured them came with breathtaking views of the Bay of Gibraltar and the Spanish mainland—as well as the Rif Mountains of Morocco—though it would be morning before they would see the view.

But once they entered the suite, Tina was more concerned about the room. *Room*, as in singular.

"We need another room," she said to Nico when she realized there was only the one.

She wasn't ready to spend the night with him, not like this. Not when everything was spiraling out of control and she felt as if her life was no longer her own. If he'd kissed her earlier beneath the pergola, she might have yielded to him like a flower bending in a storm.

But he had not, and she'd had several hours now to fret about what was happening. From the moment she'd agreed to marry him, he'd shifted into high gear. She should have realized that he would. He was a businessman, and he had every intention of closing the deal before anything could happen to derail his plans.

To him, she was another acquisition. A bit of land, a factory, an exclusive source of some necessary component for his motorcycles.

What did you expect?

Nico crossed the main living area and opened the balcony doors. The bay spread like spilled ink below, and the lights of ships lit up the harbor. Across the bay, the Spanish town of Algeciras glowed in the night.

"There is only this room, *cara*," he said when she came to stand in the open doorway.

Tina crossed her arms over her chest, her heart thrumming along like she'd just had a caffeine injection. "It's happening too fast for me, Nico. I only said yes this afternoon, and now we're here, and we're in the same room together, and my head is spinning."

He turned his head to look at her. She couldn't read him, couldn't tell what was in that enigmatic gaze of his, and her pulse skipped. He was probably annoyed she was giving him trouble.

"There is only one room because it's all they have available, Tina. We'll figure it out, I'm sure."

He sounded cool and guarded, and so very reasonable. Her cheeks felt hot. Sex seemed to be the last thing on his mind, though she couldn't seem to move it from the front of hers. Because she couldn't help but remember the last time they'd been alone in a hotel room overnight.

This one might be sleek and modern, furnished with chrome-and-glass tables, flokati rugs and leather couches, nothing at all like the elegant Hotel Daniele, but her mind didn't know the difference. It kept replaying images of their last night together—cotton sheets so fine they felt like silk, twining bodies, sleek skin and that one perfect moment when she'd discovered how very addictive good sex could be.

"There is a couch," she said, resisting the urge to fan herself.

His expression did not change. "I am aware of it."

She hoped her cheeks weren't as red as they felt. "I'll sleep on it. I'm smaller than you."

He left the railing and stalked toward her. She dropped her arms to her sides, took a step backward. He was so very big, so near, as he stopped only inches away from her. She had to tilt her head back to look up at him, and she wished that she'd put the stilettos back on. At least she wouldn't feel as if he loomed over her if she had.

He reached out and caught a lock of her hair in his hand, twined it gently around his fist. "Is this really what you want?"

She nodded once, quickly.

He lifted her hair to his fine, aristocratic nose. "Do you not think, *cara*, that perhaps the modesty is a bit misplaced?"

The heat threatened to incinerate her from the inside out. "I—I agreed to marry you. So you would not harm my family," she said, her voice little more than a hoarse whisper.

He laughed softly, wrapped her hair once more around his fist until she had to move closer. "Ah, I see. You have given yourself to me as a sacrificial lamb, is that it?"

"No—"

"You think that because you've agreed to the marriage, sex is off the table?" His voice was slightly harder this time.

She swallowed. "I didn't say that. But they are two different things, are they not? We hardly know one another."

"And we knew each other not at all in Venice. I seem to remember this made the entire evening more exciting, not less. Shall I procure a couple of masks to make it easier for you?"

She dropped her chin, hiding her eyes from his. Not because she was embarrassed or ashamed, but because if she did not he would see the flare of excitement that even now dripped into her bloodstream, drugging her with need.

"That was different. And there were consequences neither of us expected."

His playful tone disappeared. "I fail to see how these consequences affect the topic at hand. Or how sex on one night is different than sex on another. Unless, of course, it's the man you object to and not the sex."

That wasn't it at all, and yet she couldn't tell him that. She'd already lost so much of herself to him—if they spent the night together, how much more would she lose?

"I—I'm not ready," she said, still keeping her eyes downcast. "It's not you. It's me."

She felt him go completely still. "How...amusing," he murmured, before he dropped her hair and stepped around her, into the room and away from the currents swirling between them.

Tina's throat was thick with words that would not come, with feelings and emotions she did not fully understand. She'd blundered, and yet she'd only been trying to preserve her sense of self for a little while longer.

He prowled across the carpet, his shoulders tight as he opened the liquor cabinet and poured a finger of Scotch into a glass before turning back to her, the drink cradled in his hand.

"No matter what you might think, *cara*, I am in full control of my libido. You waste your time imagining that I intend to take you to my bed and have my wicked way with you. We have one bed because one bed is all that was available. You may sleep in it unmolested, I assure you."

He downed the Scotch and grabbed his briefcase. "I have work to do, and no inclination to coerce you into doing something which is obviously distasteful to you."

* * *

Tina awoke the next morning in the bed, though she'd started the evening on the couch. She sat up groggily and swung her head toward the direction of the bathroom. The sound of the running shower came through the closed door. A few minutes later it stopped, and then Nico strode into the room wearing nothing but a towel slung low over his hips.

Tina bit off a gasp as she grabbed the sheet and pulled it up to her chin. Nico stopped in his tracks, his expression wry.

"You're wearing the same thing you wore when you went to sleep on the couch, Tina."

She glanced beneath the sheet. So she was, though her attire hadn't quite been the foremost thing on her mind. She let the fabric fall again as hot embarrassment crept through her. He had to be laughing at her on the inside for acting like a startled virgin—though that was not why she'd gasped.

No, she'd gasped because seeing him nearly naked like that was an assault on her senses.

And she wanted more.

"I was fine on the couch," she said, pushing those thoughts away. "You didn't have to bring me in here."

"You didn't look fine. You looked cramped. And cold." He reached into the closet and took out a pair of khaki trousers. Tina jerked her gaze away automatically when he dropped the towel—and then swung it back with a sense of glee. He stood with his back to her so that she could look to her heart's content without him being the wiser. And what a view it was: muscled shoulders, narrow waist, tight buttocks and long, strong legs.

Something flared to life in her belly, something hot and dark and hungry. She gripped the sheet in her fists. Oh, my...

She didn't remember him carrying her into the bedroom last night—and yet she did remember one detail. She remembered shivering and curling up tight under the blanket, and then something warm and solid had cradled her until she forgot she'd been cold.

But had it only been him carrying her, or had he lain down in the bed and held her tight? She didn't know, and she didn't want to ask.

He slid into a pair of briefs before pulling on the khakis and flipping through the closet for a shirt. When he turned back to her, the dark shirt hung open to the waist, affording her a view of sculpted chest and abs that made her mouth water. Tina bit her lip to stifle a whimper.

Nico's gaze was sharp as he looked over and caught her staring at him. "Never fear, *cara*, you slept unmolested. I prefer that my bed partners participate in the activities. It is much more fun that way."

Tina let her gaze drop. "I did not doubt it," she said, because she knew that if he *had* tried to make love to her, she wouldn't have slept through it. "Thank you for making sure I was warm again."

He shrugged as he began to button the shirt. "You are the mother of my child, Tina. Regardless of how this began between us, I will take care of you. Nothing is more important than this baby."

Her stomach hollowed. Of course the baby was the most important thing—and yet it hurt to hear him say it. To him, she was a possession, a vessel carrying a precious cargo. The thought made her ache inside. What would it be like to marry a man who loved her? To have him be excited about the baby instead of resigned?

"I have business to take care of," he told her when he finished dressing. "The wedding will be this evening, so try to amuse yourself for a few hours."

Tina sat in the middle of the big bed once he was gone, feeling dejected. Amuse herself. So typical. He went off to run his company and expected her to entertain herself until he returned.

He was exactly like her brother in that respect—except that Faith had kept working for Renzo until she'd hired her own replacement. There was no way Renzo would dare to tell Faith she couldn't do what she wanted to do.

Even now, Faith oversaw his calendar of appointments and basically ran his entire life while taking care of a newborn. Faith was loved and valued and, though Tina would have never thought it possible with her macho brother, she was very much his equal. His other half.

It was his attitude toward his wife that had given Tina the hope he would eventually cave to her desire to work in the D'Angeli accounting department. She knew he'd been worried she couldn't handle the pressure, the people, or that her innate shyness would somehow stop her from fitting in. He was wrong, though she didn't suppose she would get the chance to show him that now.

Tina showered and breakfasted, then decided to go for a swim in the hotel pool. The exercise would do her good and it would make the time pass until evening. But first she checked her phone for messages.

There was an email from her mother, who was having the time of her life in Bora-Bora, and a quick text from Faith with a picture of baby Domenico and Renzo.

Tina's throat hurt as she swallowed tears. Renzo and Faith were so happy, while she and Nico were merely going through the motions. What would it be like to be so overwhelmingly happy? So in love?

She pushed those thoughts down deep and went

down to the pool. She swam laps for a while, and then sat in the shade of an umbrella and stared at the harbor below. Her thoughts kept going around and around. She almost called Lucia, just to have someone to talk to, but she didn't know what to say. How could you tell anyone that you were pregnant and about to marry the baby's father even though he did not love you?

It was too pitiful, and so she sat and stared at the blue water until she finally gave up and returned to the penthouse suite.

The last thing she expected to find as she opened the door was a seamstress and a selection of wedding dresses. Shock rooted her to the spot as she stood in the entry with the key card in her hand and the door wide-open.

There were racks of gowns—gorgeous, expensive gowns with lace and silk and pearls—that must each have cost a small fortune.

He'd ordered them without her knowledge. Without her input. He'd made the choice for her, just as he'd made so many other choices since barging back into her life in the Pantheon.

It hurt in ways she hadn't imagined possible. She was already feeling sorry for herself, feeling like a burden and a possession rather than a cherished companion and equal after seeing Faith's text earlier, and her hurt feelings bubbled over until she had to act or burst with the effort not to.

She spun on her heel and marched into the office, uncaring that she was still in her bikini and flimsy cover-up.

Nico was not alone. Three men looked up in surprise when she entered the room. Nico's expression could have stopped a bear in its tracks—but she refused to be intimidated. The two men with him excused themselves, slipping out of the office and leaving them alone.

She stood with her hands on her hips, glaring at him. It was only when his gaze dropped down her body that she realized the pose thrust her breasts forward. It was all she could do not to hug herself, but she refused to shrink beneath his simmering gaze.

He met her eyes again, a flicker of interest kindling in his. "What is this about, Tina?"

She took a step toward him, her heart thundering in her chest. "Wedding dresses? You picked out *wedding dresses* for me?" She was so angry that she could barely get the words out without them tripping over each other.

His brows drew down. "No, I did not," he said evenly. "You may pick what you want. I only asked for several for you to choose from."

She dropped her hands to her sides, clenching her fists together rhythmically. Violent emotion swept through her. He was no different from her brother in the way he viewed her. No, he *was* different. Renzo might view her as an accessory, but he loved her. This man did not.

At least Renzo didn't think so little of her that he would pick out her clothes for her.

No, but he picked your schools. And when you wanted to major in finance, you had to convince him he should approve.

She was so damn tired of men making decisions for her. It was going to stop. Now.

"I don't want any of them," she said tightly. Angry tears threatened to spill over as she worked to control her temper. She knew he thought she was being unreasonable, but she didn't expect him to understand. How could he?

He waved his hand as if it were nothing. As if she were a bothersome mosquito flitting around his head. "Then send them away. It's nothing to get upset about."

"You have no idea, do you?" she flung at him. "Women are taught from the time they're little girls to look forward to their wedding day. There are entire magazines dedicated to weddings—to gowns! You don't pick a woman's dress, or pick a selection of dresses, and tell her to choose one. It's arrogant, unfeeling—what are you doing?"

He'd stepped around the desk and started moving toward her, stalking her, until she backed into the closed door with a gasp.

He looked angry—and so very handsome he stole the breath from her lungs. When he reached out and hooked an arm around her, she could only squeak in surprise. Then he hauled her against his hard body until she was pressed to him, breast to belly to hip.

"How is this for unfeeling?" he growled before his mouth came down on hers.

CHAPTER EIGHT

FOR a moment, Tina was stunned into immobility. But only for a moment.

Though her brain told her to resist his kiss, she wound her fists into his shirt instead and arched her body into his. He threaded one hand in her hair and tilted her head back, his other hand sliding down to cup her bottom.

Excitement shot through her in a chain reaction of sparks and sizzle and longing so sharp it made her moan.

She thought that she'd remembered what kissing him was like, but she hadn't remembered even a tenth of it. He consumed her, his tongue sliding against hers, his mouth demanding everything she could give.

Had it been like this in Venice? Yes—and no. Yes, he'd kissed her with this kind of passion—but he hadn't kissed her without restraint. Now there was no restraint. He was a sexual animal, pushed to the edge of control, and she welcomed his fierceness.

His kiss turned her inside out, and she only wanted more.

His hand slid beneath her cover-up—beneath her bikini—and she gasped. He cupped her bare bottom, squeezed, pulling her harder against him until she could feel his erection straining against her abdomen.

Liquid need melted into her core. She wanted him, wanted to feel his body inside hers again. She wanted that perfect storm of passion and heat, the tactile pleasure of touching him everywhere.

She'd never felt more beautiful, more alive and wonderful, than she had when they'd made love the last time. She desperately wanted that feeling again even if it was bad for her. Even if she'd wake up afterward, feeling hungover and hating herself for giving in.

She. Did. Not. Care.

Tina yanked his shirt from his trousers, desperate to feel his bare skin beneath her palms, but a sudden noise outside the door startled her and brought her crashing back to reality.

There were people out there. And dresses. Dresses that had made her so angry she'd come in here to confront him about his lack of respect for what she might want.

But before she could summon the energy to push him away, he stepped back abruptly. He looked wild, his eyes gleaming, his hair mussed where she'd threaded her fingers into it. Not only that, but his body was still aroused, still ready for her. She could see the outline of an impressive erection straining against the fabric of his khakis.

A part of her wanted to close the distance between them, unzip him and wrap her hand around that steely velvet part of him.

But she wouldn't. She wasn't that bold. And besides, she'd come in here for a different reason altogether. A reason she'd forgotten the instant he'd touched her.

"*That* is why we are marrying," he said, his voice

lashing into her with its coolness as he tucked in his shirt again. "Not because this is a fantasy, or a love affair, or any other reason that suits your romantic sensibilities. We are marrying because we have passion, *cara*. And because, as you so helpfully pointed out to me last night, there were consequences to that passion."

He turned and walked back to his desk, raking a hand through his hair as he went. "Now go and choose a dress. Or send them all away. But don't come in here crying to me because you believe you've been cheated out of your little girl fantasy."

Tina sucked in a fortifying breath. She felt like a fool, and it wasn't a feeling she enjoyed. "It's not my fantasy," she told him angrily. It wasn't entirely true, since she and Lucia had often dreamed of their wedding day when they were teenagers, but she was quickly adjusting her expectations of what her adult life was going to bring her.

He looked thunderous. "*Maledizione*! Then why did you barge into my meeting as if someone had stolen your puppy?"

Chastened, Tina felt her anger crumple under the weight of embarrassment. She'd wanted to be taken seriously, and yet she couldn't manage not to storm into a business meeting because she'd been focused on her own hurt feelings. No wonder her brother didn't think she could handle the pressure of working for him.

"You didn't ask me what I wanted. You simply assumed," she told him. She took a halting step toward him, clasped her fist over her heart, which beat hard. She *wanted* him to understand. Needed him to understand.

"I'm a person, Nico. An individual with wants and needs of my own. I don't need to be told what to do. I want to be *asked* what I want."

He picked up a pen and tossed it down again. Then he sat at the desk and pushed both hands through his hair, resting his head in his palms. The move stunned her. "What do you want, Tina? What will make you happy?"

Her throat ached at that single gesture of defeat. Now she felt petty. How did he do that? How did he move her from blazing anger to embarrassment and then guilt in the space of a few seconds?

She realized that he must have gone to a lot of trouble to bring the gowns here. After all, they'd left Italy quickly and arrived in Gibraltar with no preparation.

He'd done something miraculous, something he'd not had to do but that he'd probably thought she might want. Tina's throat ached. Outside this room, a seamstress waited with several top designer gowns. All she had to do was choose one, and the woman would fit it to her body in the space of a few hours.

It was all too real, too fast. She swallowed hard. She didn't know what she was doing. She wasn't ready for any of this—and neither was he. They were like two people turned loose in a vast forest without a compass or a map. They were stumbling, fumbling and getting more and more lost.

And hurting each other in the process.

She knew what she wanted, what she wished she could do. It was impossible, but she said it anyway.

"I'd like to go back to that night in Venice and make a different choice," she whispered. For both their sakes.

He looked up, his eyes sharp, hard. "Clearly, that isn't going to happen. I suggest you find a way to be happy now."

If only she could.

* * *

Tina chose a gown. In the end, she'd been unable to send the seamstress or the dresses away. The one she picked was a gorgeous creation, a strapless gown that hugged her torso and then fell in a lush fall of voluminous fabric from her hips. The dress was unadorned, which was part of the reason it had appealed to her. The beauty of it was its simplicity.

She chose to wear her hair up, though she left it curly, and tucked in a few sprigs of tiny white daisies. The wedding was to take place in the hotel, so there was no need to worry about piling herself and the fabric into a car.

No, all she had to do was go downstairs at the appointed time and arrive at the small chapel the hotel had set up for the purpose. She'd chosen to walk down the aisle by herself, since Renzo was not here to give her away. She refused to allow one of Nico's security detail to do it though he had suggested it. When she'd declined, he'd shrugged.

Now she gathered the small bouquet of flowers the hotel had provided her while the woman who'd helped her dress sniffled.

"You look so lovely, miss," she said. "He will be so proud when he sees you."

Tina managed a smile. She didn't think Nico would be anything other than relieved to get this over with, but she didn't say so. "Thank you, Lisbeth."

Lisbeth dabbed her eyes with a tissue. "It's so romantic, isn't it? Your man flying all those gowns in to surprise you. I could have melted on the spot."

Tina's fingers shook as she twisted a curl that had fallen over her brow. Her stomach dived into the floor. He'd flown the gowns in special, and she'd reacted so furiously over it. She felt childish and hollow inside as she remembered him with his head in his hands.

It made her remember the younger him, oddly enough. He'd been different then. More human. She could picture him at their kitchen table, laughing with Renzo and her mother while she sat very quietly and tried not to blush or stammer or let her adoration of him show whenever she looked at him.

He was a harder man now. He wasn't vulnerable in the least, and yet he'd shown that single moment of emotional vulnerability. As if the weight of the things pressing down on him had, for a moment, been too much to bear.

She'd wanted to go to him and put her arms around him. She'd wanted to ask him to share his burdens with her, but she had known he would not. Now she was ashamed of herself. She'd been so focused on her own feelings that she'd failed to consider his.

He'd insisted they marry for the baby, but it couldn't be what he'd planned to do with his life. A family was such a life-changing decision; to have it forced upon you was not what *anyone* would wish for. It wasn't just about her feelings. It was about his, as well.

Tina left the suite and took the elevator down to the main level, Lisbeth making the trip with her in order to guide her to the right place. Nico was waiting for her outside the chapel. Tina nearly stumbled to a halt, but managed to keep walking anyway. It was just a superstition that it was bad luck for him to see her before the wedding—though how could it get any worse than a wedding neither of them truly wanted?

He was dark and forbidding in his tuxedo as he stood near the entrance. He looked so serious that her heart notched up. His gaze raked her, those stormy eyes smoldering with heat when he met hers again.

"Is something wrong?" she asked.

"There is one last thing we must do before we wed," he told her. He led her into a small adjoining room with a desk and chairs. The two men she'd seen with him this morning were there. With a jolt, she recognized them for what they were.

Lawyers.

If the serious expressions on their faces didn't give it away, then the briefcases and neat pile of papers would have. Nico handed her a pen as one of the lawyers pushed the papers toward her, which were conveniently flipped back for her signature.

And she'd actually felt a glimmering of sympathy for him earlier? Tina turned to look at him, anger kindling in her belly.

"Certain things must be spelled out before we marry, Tina," he said before she could speak.

"I am aware of that," she said tightly as she settled into a chair and jerked the papers from beneath the lawyer's fingers. A prenuptial agreement wasn't unusual or even unexpected. But there was something about the cold-blooded efficiency with which he'd orchestrated this entire marriage thus far that had her on edge.

Yes, he'd gone to a lot of trouble to get the gowns. And she'd actually felt badly that she'd been mad over what she'd considered to be his high-handedness—but now she was angry again. Angry because he'd waited until the last moment, when she was dressed and ready for the ceremony, to spring this on her.

No doubt because he expected her to sign without question. Because he thought she was empty-headed and in need of someone to tell her what to do. Maybe he expected her to simply do as she was told, which made him no better than Renzo in that respect.

She glanced up at him, the agreement in her hands, and hoped she looked coolly controlled. "You may want to sit down," she said. "This might take a while."

His lips twitched. She wasn't certain if it was annoyance or humor that caused it. Regardless, it only made her more determined.

"It is a fair agreement," he said. "You get quite a generous settlement should we divorce, and maintenance for life."

Tina flipped to the pages where the financial portion was spelled out. "Very generous," she said after she'd scanned the numbers. "And yet you've made a mistake." She tapped the pen against the page.

One of the lawyers cleared his throat, and Tina sliced her gaze in his direction. The look she gave him must have been quelling because he subsided without speaking.

"I believe that Pietro wanted to say there is no mistake," Nico said. She thought he sounded vaguely amused, but she was too irritated to be sure.

"Well, there is. You are forgetting that this sum—" she tapped the pen on the page again "—must be adjusted for inflation. A divorce in a year is quite a different animal than a divorce in twenty."

"So it is," Nico replied.

"You've also failed to take into account any money I may bring into the marriage."

"I don't want Renzo's money." His voice was harder this time.

Tina fixed him with an even stare. "I'm not talking about Renzo's money. I'm talking about mine."

One eyebrow lifted. "I wasn't aware you had any."

"I do, in fact," she told him evenly. "I've made investments of my own."

"I'm not interested in your petty investments," he snapped, and anger seared into her. Petty investments, indeed. She wasn't about to tell him what she'd accumulated, unless it became a point in the contract. Her wealth came nowhere close to his, or Renzo's, but she'd earned it herself through the strength of her skills—and she wasn't going to give him control over it.

"Great. Then you won't mind adding a clause that states that fact." How typically arrogant of him to assume that she brought nothing to the marriage other than what Renzo had given her.

Nico's eyes burned hot as he took the pen from her and bent over the papers. He crossed out the figure that was written there and substantially increased it. And then he flipped to the end and added a clause about any money she brought into the marriage.

The first lawyer took the page and read it, then handed it back with a nod.

"Satisfied?" Nico asked as he shoved the document toward her again.

"I'll let you know once I've read the whole thing."

It took over twenty minutes, but she finished reading and attached her signature in bold strokes. She'd worked hard on that signature, ever since Frau Decker had told her she wrote like a mouse that expected to be eaten by the cat at any minute.

"Grazie, cara," Nico said, taking her hand in his and helping her from the chair. A frisson of excitement rolled through her at his slight touch. How very annoying in light of what had just happened.

He lifted her hand to his mouth, as if he knew how she reacted to him, and pressed his lips lightly to her skin. A tingle shot down her spine. "Now, let us get married."

Tina forced a smile. "Yes, let's."

She might be a mouse, and Nico might be the big cat waiting to pounce on her—but she fully intended to choke him on the way down.

They returned to Italy as soon as the ceremony was over. Nico thought about staying in Gibraltar for the night, but he had urgent business to attend to and no time for dallying.

He could hardly credit that he was a married man now. It wasn't something he'd expected to do anytime soon, if ever. Not even to preserve the title within his direct line. It would have gone to a cousin, so it would not have been lost to the family, and that would have been good enough for him.

But now he was married, and to the most unlikely woman of all. Tina sat across from him as the jet winged its way back to Italy. She was still in her gown because he'd insisted on leaving immediately. He'd expected her to change on the plane, but she had not made a move to do so. She simply sat and read her eReader, as if flying in a wedding gown was the most ordinary thing imaginable.

She looked, he had to admit, incredible. Her riot of hair was contained in an elegant loose twist, though several strands had come free to frame her face, with its pert nose and long lashes that made her eyes look as if they were closed when they were merely downcast and concentrating on her book.

Her shoulders were bare, and her breasts rose into lush, golden mounds that threatened to spill over the stiff bodice. He remembered kissing her this afternoon, when she'd burst into the office in that ridiculously small bikini, and his body grew hard.

It had taken everything he'd had not to untie her bikini bottoms and thrust into her right there up against the door. He'd been about to do just that when the noise had reminded him they were not truly alone.

Nico shifted in his seat, unable to concentrate on the spreadsheets before him. He closed the computer with a snap, and Tina glanced up. Need jolted through him as their eyes clashed and held. He could feel the tension in the air, the electric snap of sexual promise that flowed between them like water gushing over a fall.

It would be so good when he stripped her naked again. So, so good.

"Why did you not change into something more comfortable?" he asked her.

She shrugged a pretty shoulder. "You can be forgiven for not knowing it, I suppose, but wedding gowns require a bit of help to get into and out of."

He didn't think his body could get any harder. Apparently, he was wrong.

"I'll help," he said. Growled, really.

Her violet eyes were wide. And blazing, he realized. As if she, too, were doing everything she could to not think about sex and failing miserably.

"I'm not sure you wouldn't tear the fabric," she murmured.

"I might," he said, his blood beating hot and fierce in his veins. Urging him to take her.

"I'd rather you didn't. If we have a daughter, I might like to give this dress to her someday."

A fierce wave of possession swept him then. Why did the prospect of a child cause his gut to clench and his heart to throb?

"And if I promised to be careful?"

Her tongue darted over her pink lower lip; in response, the pain in his groin shifted to an excruciating level.

"I might have to accept your offer, since there is no other way to get out of the dress."

Dear God, he wanted her right now. He wanted to take her hand and lead her to the plane's bedroom and have his wicked way with her.

But they'd been airborne for an hour already and he knew they weren't far from landing. Besides, he wanted far more than a quick tumble from her. He wanted to explore her thoroughly. He wanted to strip her slowly and build her excitement until she begged him to possess her. And that would take time. Time he did not have right now.

There was no choice but to control this need raging inside him like a hurricane.

"I will take you up on that, Tina, but not until we are safely home again."

She dipped her head, but not before he thought she looked somewhat disappointed. The knowledge she wanted him, too, sent a slice of raw lust burrowing deep into his gut. When he'd taken her to bed in Venice, he'd thought she would be like other women. And she had been, until the moment when he'd realized he couldn't quite forget the sexy virgin siren he'd bedded that night.

What was it about her? He'd been asking himself that since the morning after their encounter in Venice.

If he'd known who she was, he wouldn't have touched her, regardless that doing so would anger Renzo. He might be bad, but he wasn't that bad. Or, he was that bad, but he wouldn't have been able to do it when he remembered her as a shy teenager, hiding behind her hair and gazing at him with puppy dog eyes when she thought he wasn't looking.

She'd been sweet, shy and so very innocent. Her adoration had amused him at the time, though he'd been careful not to let her know that he knew how she felt.

She didn't gaze at him that way any longer, and he found he missed it in a perverse sort of way. She'd worshipped him once, and now she did not. Now she looked cool and almost indifferent at times. He was certain, however, that she was not.

"What are you reading so intensely?" he asked, determined to change the subject in an effort to get himself under control.

She looked down at the eReader as if she'd forgotten it existed. What she said next was not even close to what he'd expected her to say. "Oh, just a journal article on rational option pricing and derivative investment instruments."

Nico blinked as he dredged up memories of university. "You're reading about financial engineering?"

He should have realized there was more inside that lovely head than he'd assumed, considering the way she'd gone after the financial arrangements in the prenup. She'd been a tiger. He'd thought she was just very savvy, but now he realized it was something entirely different.

It turned him on in ways he hadn't imagined. And it made him wonder about those investments she'd mentioned. Not because he thought she'd made a fortune, but because he was suddenly curious.

She looked fierce. "And why is that so hard to believe? Not that you've ever asked, but I have a degree in finance. With honors, I might add."

No, he hadn't asked. Why hadn't he asked? Because

he'd thought her expertise was in shopping and look-ing pretty, that's why. It was the sort of thing he was accustomed to from the women in his life. Not that he didn't have seriously smart women working for him, but he'd never actually dated any of them.

"That's impressive," he told her sincerely. "I'm sur-prised you aren't working for your brother with that kind of résumé."

She looked angry. "Yes, well, Renzo has certain opinions about what I should be doing. And working for him was not it."

"Then he is a fool."

Her eyes were suddenly sharp. "Really? Does that mean you'd consider allowing your wife to work in the finance department of Gavretti Manufacturing?"

He flicked an imaginary speck of lint from his tux-edo. "Perhaps. One day." He had no intention of letting her anywhere near his financial department. She was a D'Angeli, and he didn't kid himself that her loyalties had suddenly switched when she'd said her vows.

Still, if he'd been Renzo, he would have used her ex-pertise. He could say that honestly. He always used the best tool for the job.

"I suppose I can't ask for a better answer," she said. Then she laughed, the sound so light and beautiful that it pierced him in unexpected ways. "I bet you thought I'd tell you I was reading a romance novel, or perhaps a tome that everyone claims to have read but really haven't."

He couldn't help but smile in return. She was infec-tious when she laughed. "Such as?"

"Oh, *Ulysses* maybe. Or *Moby-Dick*. Something giant and meaty and excruciating in the extreme."

Nico put a hand over his heart in mock horror. "I happen to like *Ulysses*."

The corners of her mouth trembled as she worked to keep a straight face. "Then I am sorry for disparaging it. I'm sure it's a fine piece of literature."

"You aren't sorry," he said, enjoying the way her face lit up with mischief.

She gave up the pretense and laughed again. "No, not really."

"Don't worry," he told her. "I've never actually read *Ulysses*. I was just teasing you."

She shook her head. "That's very bad of you."

He took her hand in his, his thumb ghosting over her palm. He could feel the tremor that ran through her body. An answering thrill cascaded within him. Soon, he would take her. He had to.

"I like being bad," he murmured as he nibbled her pretty fingers. "I excel at it, in fact."

Her only answer was another shiver.

CHAPTER NINE

TINA was on edge in a way she hadn't been since the night she'd met Nico in Venice. That night, when she'd gotten into the gondola with the enigmatic stranger, she'd known they would end up in bed together even if she hadn't fully admitted it to herself.

Tonight, she was admitting it. And she wanted it so desperately her skin tingled with anticipation. It didn't matter that she'd been furious and hurt earlier. Nothing mattered except that she'd stood in that tiny chapel and promised to love, honor and cherish until death do us part, while her heart thrummed and her palms sweated and the man standing beside her gazed at her with piercing silver eyes.

They were in this together now, officially, and tonight was their wedding night. She couldn't quite wrap her head around it. She was a married woman, the marchesa di Casari, and her family had no idea. Guilt slid deep into her bones. Renzo would hit the roof when he found out. Thank God that wouldn't be for another couple of weeks at least—more if she was lucky. Still, she had time to figure out how to tell everyone what she'd done.

And time to get to the root of the problem between Renzo and Nico. If she could just understand that, she could help to fix this thing between them. She didn't expect they would be best friends ever again, but if they could at least be in the same room together without wanting to kill each other, that would be a start.

The plane had landed half an hour ago now. She'd thought they were returning to Castello di Casari, but instead they were in Rome. She expected that Nico had a huge villa somewhere in the city, but rather it was an exclusive apartment overlooking the ancient rooftops and splendid ruins.

There was no staff waiting to greet them, no Giuseppe with his kind smile and brisk efficiency. There was only Nico, and the lights of Rome spread out like a carpet of fireflies.

She felt suddenly awkward as she stood in the darkened living room and watched Nico prowling toward her, his dark good looks emphasized by the formality of the tuxedo. He'd undone his tie a while ago, and unbuttoned the top couple of buttons of his shirt to give a tantalizing glimpse of bronzed skin.

She focused on that slice of skin until he stopped in front of her and her eyes drifted up to meet his. It jolted her again just how very handsome he was, with those piercing eyes and perfect cheekbones.

He took her hand in his without breaking eye contact, placed it on his shoulder.

Then he did the same with the other one, placing it on his opposite shoulder as her heart thrummed and her body warmed to dangerous temperatures.

"Alone at last," he told her with a wicked smile that made hunger slide into her veins.

"So it would seem."

"I want you, Tina," he said, dipping his head to place a soft kiss on her cheek. She closed her eyes and tilted her head back as his mouth traced a path along her jaw and down the column of her throat. "Too much," he murmured against her skin, and the vibration of his voice dripped into her bloodstream like pure adrenaline. "I've thought of nothing but this for hours now."

A thrill rocketed through her. "I should tell you no," she said on a little half gasp as his lips found the sweet spot behind her ear.

"It's inevitable, *bella*. You want me as I want you."

"I might," she admitted. "But I'm not exactly thrilled with how you've treated me."

He lifted his head to look at her. "The prenup was necessary. You know that."

She shrugged, but she didn't remove her hands from his shoulders. "I do know. But you could have picked a better time."

He sighed, his palms sliding along her hips. "It wasn't ready before then. It takes time to put together a document of that size."

"I realize that, Nico. I'm not stupid. But you could have told me earlier that we'd be dealing with it at some point."

He dipped his head and ran his mouth along the column of her throat while she tried not to moan or fall apart in his arms. "I'm sorry," he said. "I should have mentioned it."

She sighed. She had an apology of her own to make. "Thank you for getting the dresses. It was nice of you."

His hands slipped around to cup her bottom. "I thought you were angry over that."

Tina swallowed as heat swirled inside her belly. "I was. But I realize you were trying to be nice. You just went about it in a typical male fashion."

He pulled back to look down at her. "A typical male fashion?"

She nodded as she gazed up at him. "Yes. You assumed I would be happy so you proceeded without consulting me."

"And you would prefer I consult you in the future about decisions of this nature?"

"About decisions that involve me. Yes."

He dipped his head and ran his tongue along the top of her bodice. "And what about this, Tina? Do you wish to continue? Or shall we say good-night here?"

"Nico," she breathed.

"You have the power to say no," he told her. "I want only a willing wife in my bed."

Tina shuddered as he pulled her against him, the evidence of his need for her pressing into her abdomen. He was hard, ready, and liquid heat slid through her in response.

"I think I'm ready," she said, a shiver running through her because he'd asked. *He'd asked.*

"Think? Or know? Because I don't want any ambiguity, *cara.* Choose me now, or go to bed alone."

He was truly asking what she wanted—and she was a goner.

"I know. I *know.*" Tina wrapped her arms around his neck at the same moment his mouth sought hers, capturing it in a kiss so scorching she nearly melted from the heat. She moaned when he slid his tongue against hers, and her knees suddenly felt as if they were made of water.

She was hot and ready, like a pot that had been on the burner all day—and Nico seemed to know it.

Her pulse thrummed in her ears, her throat, her breastbone, pounding out a beat that made her dizzy while his tongue licked into her with such devastating skill that all she could do was cling to him.

He made her feel so much. So many conflicting emotions crashing through her along with a healthy, hungry appetite for what they were about to do. How could she want him so acutely? And how could he be so very bad for her at the same time?

Nico pulled her hips against his again, until she could once more feel the evidence of an impressive erection.

Tina whimpered. Just like that, it was suddenly too much to wait even a minute more. She'd decided to do this thing, and there was no going back.

She ripped at the studs holding his shirt closed until he laughed deep in his throat and shrugged out of his jacket, letting it fall where he stood. Then his hands came over hers, helped her tear the shirt open as studs popped and flew.

Her hands were suddenly on his hot flesh, her palms sliding along his skin, learning the texture of him once more. He was so hot, so hard and muscular, and she wanted him naked before another minute passed. She couldn't think about anything but him. He drove her crazy with need.

She tugged the shirt from his trousers and then went after his belt and zipper while Nico fumbled with the buttons at her back. She could feel his frustration mounting with the tiny buttons.

He broke the kiss and turned her in his arms. "Don't rip them," she gasped.

"I won't." His voice was clipped, rough, and it made her tremble. Soon the bodice began to loosen, but he lost patience and turned her again, pulling the front of the gown down just enough so that her breasts spilled freely into his hands. Her nipples were hard little points that he flicked with his thumbs while a deep shiver rolled through her.

"*Dio*, you are so beautiful."

A skein of pleasure uncoiled in her belly, along with the bone-deep need that made her sex ache. Niccolo Gavretti had said she was beautiful. Nico, the notorious playboy, the man she'd mooned after as a love-struck teenager, had just said she was beautiful. It was a dream come true in some ways.

She wanted to tell him that he was beautiful, too, but his mouth captured hers again, driving all thoughts from her head except one: *need you now.*

His mouth was questing, demanding, and she responded in kind, her heart hammering, her skin on fire as she tried to get closer to him. He gathered fistfuls of her skirts, shoved them up her hips so he could hook his fingers into her panties and push them down until gravity took over and they fell to her feet.

Tina was never so glad she'd not worn garters as she was at that moment. "Now, Nico," she said against his lips. "Now."

He guided her backward until she bumped into something. Before she could tell what it was, he lifted her and sat her down on a table. She was so focused on him that she had no idea where they were—dining room, kitchen, living room—and she didn't care. All she cared about was this man and this moment.

Tina wrapped her legs around him as he pushed her thighs open and stepped between them. His hands were on her hips, holding her in place as their mouths fused again and again, their kisses drunken and hot and utterly addictive. She fumbled with his zipper, jerked it down with shaky fingers. And then her hands were in his trousers, freeing him.

He groaned as she wrapped her hand around him, slid her palm along his hot, velvety shaft. He shoved her skirts higher and pulled her hands away from his body. She made a sound of disappointment, but a moment later she felt the blunt head of his penis pressing into her and every last thought flew out of her mind.

He cupped her bottom, tilting her backward slightly before he thrust deeply inside her—it wasn't a sudden movement, but it was overpowering in its intensity. One moment she was craving him, the next he'd filled her. Tina cried out in surprise and pleasure, and his entire body stilled.

"Have I hurt you?" His voice was rough.

Yes, she wanted to say. *Yes.*

But the pain wasn't physical. "No. Please don't stop."

His laugh was ragged. "Stop? Not possible, *tesoro.* Not possible." He leaned forward and kissed her again, and she could feel his body pulsing inside hers. Had it been this exciting the first time? Had she wanted him so desperately that she'd been willing to do anything to have him?

Possibly, but it didn't matter. *This* was what mattered. Now, when he was inside her, his entire being focused on her. He was the kind of man who knew how to make a woman's body sing, and she knew this night would be even better than the first because she wasn't as naive as before. Because she knew what to expect— and she craved it.

Craved him.

Tina didn't want to let him go, as if she would wake up and find it had all been a dream if she did. She wrapped her arms around his neck, her body bending into him as he began to move. Their tongues tangled as he stroked into her with such skill she wanted to weep.

She knew he tried to be gentle, but it wasn't really possible.

For either of them. They were joined together with no barriers between them this time—and they'd waited for two long months to be in this place again, though they did not know it was what they'd been waiting for.

Nico pushed her back until she was supporting herself on her hands, her back arching, her breasts thrusting into the air for his pleasure. His lips closed over an aroused nipple, spiking the pleasure within her until she wasn't certain she could hold out another second.

"Nico," she gasped, her senses filled with him.

Deep within her, the explosion began to build. His lovemaking was raw, powerful, almost desperate, as if he'd held back for far too long and even now perched on the edge of his control. His fingers dug into her hips as he held her hard and drove into her.

Tina dragged her eyes open to look at him, to look at the picture they made. He bent over her body, the ruins of his shirt clinging to his broad shoulders. His skin glistened with moisture and she lifted a hand to rake it through his hair. He dragged his mouth across her breasts then, his lips closing around her other nipple. Tina clasped his head to her with a soft moan, loving the sharp, sweet spike of pleasure that tugged at her. Her breasts were so much more sensitive than they'd been only a few weeks ago, and she cried out as his tongue swirled and teased and tormented.

He drove her relentlessly, almost savagely, until she shattered with a sharp cry, her entire body clenching with the force of her orgasm. Her legs tightened around him, as if she was afraid he might try to leave her.

But he didn't leave. And he didn't stop, gripping her

buttocks in his hands and lifting her to him until the new angle made her breath catch once more.

"Again," he said, the muscles in his neck and chest and abdomen corded tight as he held her up and drove into her.

Tina lay back on the table, her arms over her head in helpless surrender, her eyes closed as she pushed her hips up to meet him. She was a creature of pleasure now, a being who existed for this alone. He came down on top of her, the fabric of her dress rustling, no doubt wrinkling hopelessly.

She didn't care.

He dominated her with the strength of his body, and she wrapped her legs high around his back, tears squeezing from her closed eyes to leak down her temples and into her hair.

It was too beautiful, too perfect to be with him like this. He destroyed her. And she was far happier than she should be.

"Tina," he groaned. "*Dio*, don't cry."

He threaded his fingers through hers, his mouth seeking hers once more. He kissed her far more sweetly than she'd thought he was capable of at that moment. Fear swirled in her belly then. Everything about being with him felt right—but did he feel it, too, or was this simply the consummate ladies' man doing what he did best?

Tina squeezed her eyes tighter. She couldn't think like that. She simply couldn't. They were married now and they had a child on the way. He was hers.

And, oh, God, that's just what she'd wanted, wasn't it? She wanted him to belong to her—had from the first moment he'd walked into their tiny kitchen with Renzo and smiled at her. He'd been so strong and handsome and perfect—and she'd been shy, awkward and unworthy of ever getting such a man, even in her wildest dreams.

He raised his head, as if he sensed the turmoil in her heart. "You're thinking too much," he said gruffly. "Stop thinking."

And then he made it impossible for her to think as he thrust into her again and again, harder and harder, until she caught fire, until her body shattered in a million bright shards of color and her breath tore from her in a long, broken cry.

She was still gasping and reeling when he followed her into oblivion, holding her tightly to him, his hips grinding into her one last time as a deep shudder racked him.

Her heart throbbed in the silence, filling her ears with the sound of her blood rushing through her sensitized body. Tina put her hand in his hair, held him to her as he buried his face against her neck. His hair was damp, hot, and his breath ghosted over her heated skin, cooling her.

She gazed up at the ceiling, dazed by what had just happened between them. She was still in her wedding gown—her very crumpled wedding gown—and lying on a long table. A console table, she realized. They hadn't even made it out of the living room.

She'd married someone her family hated and now she was having wild sex with him on a table. She ought to be ashamed—and yet she wasn't. She was thrilled at the illicitness of their encounter.

He wasn't a bad man, she told herself. He wanted what was best for the baby, the same as she did, and he'd flown wedding dresses in for her so she wouldn't have to get married in something that she'd worn to lunch or shopping with Mama and Lucia. He'd tried to make sure she had something special. That didn't make him good by a long shot, but it made him human at least.

She was still breathing hard when he pushed off her and turned to tuck himself away. A frisson of alarm crept through her then. They'd had sex and he was done. He would leave her while he went to work on his laptop, or maybe he'd leave the apartment and go into the city and not come back until she'd fallen asleep waiting for him to return.

He caught her gaze then and quirked an eyebrow. "I'm not leaving, Tina."

She hated that he knew what she was thinking simply from looking at her—and yet she was relieved, too.

"I hope not," she told him, pushing herself up on her elbows. "I was quite enjoying that."

Nico's gaze was sharp and hot as he smoothed her gown down before he helped her to stand. Her legs were wobbly and she swayed into him. He caught her close, his fingers burning into the exposed skin of her back.

His smile scorched her. "We definitely aren't finished yet," he told her, tucking a lock of hair behind her ear. "That was merely a prelude."

Tina's heart was still racing. "Some prelude."

He kissed her. In spite of everything that had just happened, in spite of the fact she was spent, excitement blossomed in her belly, kindling like a flash fire.

"You haven't seen anything yet," he promised.

Nico lay in the dark and listened to the breathing of the woman beside him. She'd fallen into an exhausted sleep hours ago, but his mind wouldn't quiet enough to let him do the same. His body was replete, drunk on sex and high on the endorphins a good release could bring—and yet, if she turned to him now and ran a soft hand over his thigh, he'd harden in an instant.

And that was what he didn't quite understand. What was this nearly insatiable need for her?

Oh, he loved sex and women, and he'd been known to spend long nights making love to whichever woman had caught his fancy. That was not unusual in the least. Nor was the fact she was beside him in the bed. He didn't mistake sex and sleeping for love, and he made sure the women he was with knew that.

He knew that some men left in the middle of the night, or made the woman leave, but what was the sense in that? If he woke up aroused, he wanted a soft female body in which to spend himself.

No, he didn't leave in the middle of the night like a vampire, and he didn't kick a woman out of bed until he tired of her. How quickly that happened depended entirely upon her.

The instant the games began—the jealousy, the pouting, the efforts to make him say that he was beginning to feel something more—she was gone.

But now he had a wife, and that wife intrigued him more than he could remember being intrigued in quite a while. His life, while full of beautiful women and all the finer things money could buy, had left him empty of late. More lonely than content, more restless than happy.

Tina, however, excited him again. He'd been so hot for her that he'd taken her on a table in the living room with the lights of Rome stretched out below. He should have made it more special for her, but he'd been unable to wait. She'd asked him not to ruin her dress—he hadn't, but he'd damn sure creased it. After that first frantic coupling, he'd carried her to the bedroom and taken the time he should have taken initially. He'd explored her, aroused her, and satisfied her over and over.

He loved the sounds she made when she came, the way she said his name, her soft voice breaking at the end as if he were the one thing she needed in this world to survive. It was a plea, each and every time—and yet it wasn't. He sensed there was something about her he could not touch, and it drove him crazy wondering what that was.

Did she purposely hold a part of herself back? Or was he imagining things?

He turned in the bed and slid a hand along her hip before pulling her into the curve of his body. She felt good there, and he lay beside her and just listened to her breathing.

Valentina D'Angeli. *Valentina Gavretti*, he corrected fiercely.

How was it that he lay here with Renzo's little sister and the only thing he felt was protective? He should feel triumphant, as if he'd finally found the way to get beneath Renzo's skin—but he didn't.

She turned in his arms then, her hand coming to rest on his cheek. It made him feel fierce inside. If Renzo tried to take her away…

"Nico," she sighed.

"Yes, *cara*?"

He could see her smile in the dark. "Nothing."

His body was already reacting though he tried to think of something other than sex. But his penis was throbbing to life regardless. Sometimes it definitely had a will of its own. He did not doubt that women were right when they accused men of thinking with their genitalia.

He pushed a lock of curly hair out of her face. "Tell me something, Tina."

"What's that," she asked sleepily, burrowing into him even more.

"I don't understand how you were still a virgin." He'd been thinking about it since she'd blasted back into his life. She was so passionate, so honest and open in her sexuality, that it didn't make sense. She burned him up with her heat, and he craved more of the same—had since the first night he'd been with her.

She shrugged. "I never found anyone I wanted to be with."

He'd never claimed to understand women's minds, so he didn't argue the point. To her, it made perfect sense. "Then why did you choose me?"

"Actually, I chose someone else," she said, and he couldn't stop the slice of jealousy that slammed through him. "But he smelled like garlic. You didn't."

Nico blinked. "You mean it came down to garlic?"

She nodded. "Yep. Garlic. One really shouldn't eat garlic if one expects to seduce a woman."

He couldn't help but laugh at that. "Then I suppose I should be grateful I skipped the garlic."

She tilted her head back on the pillow to look at him. He could feel the intensity of her gaze, even if he couldn't actually see what was in her eyes in the dark. "Do you really mean that?"

Everything inside him grew still. He didn't know what he meant, but he wanted to tell her not to read too much into it, though he knew that she already had. She was young and naive, at least as far as relationships went, and he couldn't tell her the truth right now. He couldn't tell her that he didn't believe in love between a man and a woman. He only believed in sexual chemistry—which they had an abundance of—and that usually fizzled after a while.

Except nothing was fizzling at the moment.

"I don't regret being your first lover, Tina." That was most definitely true. He shifted his pelvis so she could feel the evidence of his continuing need for her.

"Oh," she said, her voice husky. And yet he sensed she was somehow disappointed in his answer. Was it because of the baby? Or because she hoped there could be something more between them than simple lust?

He didn't know, and he didn't want to ask. He didn't want to talk about expectations, or about what he thought might happen when they tired of each other. It was too soon, and he was still growing accustomed to the idea of a wife.

He wouldn't allow this to disintegrate to the point it harmed their child, but he knew they would have to address it one day. What happened when they were ready to go their separate ways?

"Go to sleep, Tina," he told her somewhat gruffly. He was aroused, but he'd get over it. "You need your rest."

She made a disapproving sound. "And if I don't want to sleep?"

He didn't think he could grow any harder than he was in that moment. "What do you want, *tesoro*?"

"I think you know."

He gathered her closer, nuzzled the hair at her temple. "Can I possibly be so lucky?"

She slid a hand over his hip. "Enjoy it while you can. I imagine things will change once this baby really starts to grow."

She pressed her mouth to his chest, her tongue swirling against his skin as she wrapped her fingers around him and squeezed.

"Tell me what you want," he said—groaned, really. He didn't expect her to push him onto his back and straddle him, but he was damned happy she did. He groaned again as she sank down on top of him. Her movements were slow at first, inexpert, but they increased in tempo until he didn't care about anything but what she did to him. He gripped her hips and thrust up into her while she gasped and moaned. When she stiffened and choked out his name, he came in a hot rush that left him gasping and spent.

"That was lovely," she said huskily. Then she leaned down and kissed him slowly, clearly pleased with herself. His heart tapped an insane rhythm in his chest as he lay beneath her and concentrated on breathing evenly. "Really lovely.

"And, Nico," she added when he was still trying to catch his breath and couldn't manage to say a word. "I'm glad you were my first, too."

A stab of unexpected emotion pierced him as he keyed in on one word. *First.*

First implied there would be a second. It twisted his gut into knots.

Chemistry, he told himself, as he closed his eyes and hugged her to him. It was only chemistry that made him want to punch something at the thought of her with another man.

CHAPTER TEN

THEY spent the next few days in Rome while Nico attended to business. During the day, he went to meetings, worked on his computer at home or had long conference calls in his home office.

But at night, he was hers. Tina shivered to think about what happened at night. And sometimes during the day, when he came home early or ended a call and came back inside to find her on her computer or reading.

She'd thought that sex couldn't get any more exciting or amazing than it already was.

She'd been wrong. When he turned to her in the night and slid a palm along her hip, she shuddered, her body coming alive with sensation. And then she melted into him, fusing herself to him, taking him deep inside her and losing herself in the rightness of it.

He owned her body, and he knew it. Whether she straddled him and rode him frantically or whether he made love to her with his mouth before filling her with that part of him she craved, it didn't matter. He owned her as surely as if he'd taken a brand and seared his name into her skin.

It was…shocking. And frightening. How could she need him so much in such a short space of time?

"Hello, earth to Tina. Yoo-hoo."

Tina focused on Lucia, who sat across from her in the restaurant and waved her hand back and forth in front of Tina's face.

"I'm sorry," Tina said, smiling at her friend as she picked up her water glass and took a sip. "Just thinking."

Lucia made a face. "I can guess what about. That man is simply gorgeous, and you are one lucky girl."

"There's more to a marriage than having a gorgeous man," Tina said wryly. She'd told Lucia everything, even the part about their hasty marriage in Gibraltar. Rather than being horrified, Lucia was giddy, as if they were still sixteen and sneaking cigarettes in the janitor's closet. Tina shook her head. She'd hated cigarettes, and hated the sick feeling she got whenever she sneaked around.

She had that feeling today, in the pit of her stomach, as she thought about Renzo and Mama. Soon, she would have to tell them what she'd done.

"Oh, I'm sure." Lucia lifted her glass. "But it doesn't hurt a bit, I'll bet." She took a sip before putting the glass down again and leaning forward. "So tell me if his nickname is well earned. Is he Naughty Niccolo in the bedroom as well as on the track?"

Tina colored. "Lucia, I don't think—"

Lucia sat back again and blinked. "Don't tell me you've fallen in love with him. Tina, he's not the sort of man you love."

"No, of course not." She would be crazy to love him. She knew that.

And she *didn't*. How could she? They'd been together a week, and sex was not enough to base such a strong emotion on. Of course she'd thought she'd loved him once long ago, but she'd been a kid. She knew better now. Desperately wanting someone because they seemed out of reach, because they were gorgeous and kind to you and took your breath away with a smile was not love. It was infatuation.

She'd definitely been infatuated with him.

Tina waved a hand as if it were the silliest thing ever. "I'm pregnant, not stupid."

Lucia stabbed her salad. "I still don't know why you married him. You don't have to marry a man just because you get pregnant anymore. You also don't have to have the baby," she added.

Tina told herself not to get angry. Lucia was only speaking the truth, and she was the best friend Tina had ever had. She was not saying that Tina should get rid of her baby, just that it had been an option *if she'd wanted it.* Which she did not.

"I know that. But I want this baby. And Nico was rather insistent once I told him."

"I suppose he would be with the title and all." She dropped her fork, her eyes widening. "My God, I've just realized this means you are a marchesa now. Wouldn't the girls back at St. Katherine's be surprised!"

Tina laughed. "Disbelieving is more like it."

"Thank God those days are over." Lucia sighed.

"Definitely," Tina agreed, and put a hand over her belly beneath the table. Her stomach was still relatively flat, but it wouldn't be for much longer. "And you can rest assured I won't be sending this little one away to that awful place. Or any boarding school."

Lucia grinned again. "I just can't believe you're going to be a mother! I'm happy for you—but, Tina, what an amazing thing. The odds of that happening on your first time must be one in a zillion."

"Or more."

"Are you scared?" Lucia looked very serious then, and Tina reached over and clasped her hand, squeezing.

"No, actually. I'm learning a lot about being pregnant." The morning after she and Nico had arrived in Rome, she'd awakened to find him on his laptop in bed. When she'd stirred, he'd turned the computer to where she could see it.

"Look, *cara*, this is the site I was telling you about. You can join and track your pregnancy. There are articles, discussion groups and a bulletin board." He'd tapped a key, his eyes rapt on the screen. "So much to learn."

It still caused a pinch in her heart when she thought of the look on his face. How could she think he didn't care about her when he did things like that? It was true they never talked about feelings—but he *must* feel something. Mustn't he?

"When are you going to tell your mother and Renzo? They have a right to know, Tina."

Tina leaned back in her chair and sighed. "I know." It was the thorn in her happiness, the idea that she'd betrayed her family by marrying Nico. If they hadn't been half a world away, what would have happened?

She expected the news to hit the tabloids any day now, but she hoped that Renzo and Faith were so busy in the Caribbean that they weren't paying attention to gossip. She *would* tell them, but when she was ready.

After lunch, she and Lucia did a bit of shopping, and then Tina said goodbye and climbed into the chauffeured car that Nico insisted take her everywhere. She even had bodyguards, which she found slightly ridiculous, but two men in dark suits and headsets shadowed her every move now, though they traveled separately and never intruded.

Except for that one time when the crowds and hawkers around the Spanish Steps had been a bit boisterous. The man who'd shoved a rose in her face and wouldn't leave, even when she said no, had been jerked away and thrust in another direction.

Lucia hadn't even noticed, and their afternoon had continued pleasantly enough. But now Tina was tired and happy to return to the apartment. She almost wished they were back at Castello di Casari, with the sun and the water and the lovely garden, where she could lie underneath the pergola and dream.

And check her stock portfolio. She loved the thrill she got whenever she made a successful trade, when she watched the balance on her portfolio climb yet again because she'd taken a risk no one else had seen and it paid off.

Dammit, she was good at numbers and calculations. Very good. And Renzo didn't know it. Wouldn't have acknowledged it if he had, she thought sourly. It was a matter of pride for him that the women in his family didn't work after a lifetime of struggling to make ends meet—though Faith had certainly challenged that assumption quite successfully.

What would Nico think? He'd said he would consider letting her work for him, but she didn't imagine he would do so anytime soon. More likely, he'd said it to appease her because he'd made no mention of it since the plane ride back from Gibraltar.

When she let herself into the apartment, she could hear Nico's voice coming from the open door to his home office. He did not sound happy and she stopped, unsure whether to turn around and leave again until he was finished or to let him know she was home.

But the cold tone of his voice with its underlying hint

of despair had her moving forward until she stopped in the living area, her heart pounding in her throat. Her progress ceased when she heard a woman's voice.

The woman sounded haughty. She had the cultured tones of an aristocrat, and she seemed very angry. It took Tina a moment to realize that her voice was coming from the speakerphone.

"You are an ungrateful son, Niccolo," she snapped. "I sacrificed everything I had for you."

"What did you sacrifice, mother? As I recall, it was very little."

She sniffed. "You're just like your father. You don't care about me at all. You took his side against me. You always did."

"I did not," Nico growled. "I was a child. I had no idea who was right or who was wrong. But I knew one thing, and that was that neither of you seemed to want me around."

"It was difficult," his mother said after a long silence. "We pretended for your sake until you went to school. There was little point in it afterward."

"Yes, and when I begged to be allowed to come home, you were always unavailable for some reason or other. Traveling abroad or checking into a spa. How difficult life was for you, Mother."

Tina's heart ached to hear him sound so bitter. And she ached for the little boy he must have been, so lonely and unwanted. How cruel this woman was! And how Tina wanted to wrap her hands around his mother's neck and squeeze. What kind of mother did that to her child?

"It is difficult now," she said. "I put up with your father's philandering for years. The humiliation. But I always knew I would be taken care of in my old age.

And now you have inherited and I'm begging for alms at your feet."

"You are not a beggar," Nico said, his voice a harsh growl full of emotion that stunned her with its intensity. "You have a very generous allowance, and you will live within your means from now on. I will not allow the Gavretti holdings to be siphoned off and sold piecemeal in order to gratify your urges."

"That is ridiculous," she said. "There is no danger of that. You are simply a cruel and ungrateful son who would see his mother suffer rather than take care of her needs."

"It's time this conversation was over," Nico said.

"But I'm not finished—"

"I am."

His mother didn't speak again, and Tina knew he must have hung up on her. She walked to the entrance of the office, a lump in her throat. How awful it must have been to grow up with a woman like that, a woman who'd had no warmth for her child. Tina may not have known her father, but her mother was the most effusive and lovely person on the planet.

Mama had done everything possible to keep her and Renzo fed and clothed and happy. The only harsh words in their home came when someone was upset or angry over something—but they were gone quickly, and everyone was happy again. Tina had never felt like a burden to her mother, even when she probably had been at times.

Nico sat with his head in his hands and her heart squeezed hard at the sight of him like that. He looked defeated, the weight of his worries pressing down hard on those strong shoulders.

Something twisted inside her then, something

that stole her breath and made her stomach sink into her toes. She stood there as a maelstrom of emotion whipped her in its currents. Everything she had within her wanted to go to him and put her arms around him. To hold him tight and tell him that someone loved him even if his mother did not.

Tina pressed her hand to her mouth. She'd just told herself all the reasons why she did not love him. And yet none of them made sense any longer. Not in light of the feeling swelling in her heart.

But it couldn't be love. *Sympathy.* Yes, it had to be sympathy. She couldn't bear to see him hurting like this, and it made her want to hold him close and soothe him.

She must have made a sound, a sniffle as she tried to keep from letting any of the tears welling in her eyes fall, because he looked up, his dark gaze clashing with hers.

"I didn't know you were home," she said lamely, her body trembling with the force of the feelings whipping through her. She felt as though she'd tumbled over the edge of a cliff and there was no going back. She couldn't seem to find her equilibrium.

He pushed to his feet and shoved his hands in his pockets. He looked uncomfortable, restless. "I finished my meetings early."

She wanted to reach out to him, take him in her arms. But she didn't think he would welcome it. She tried to smile as if everything were normal. As if her heart weren't breaking for him.

"I went to lunch with my friend Lucia. It was nice to get out for a while."

The look on his face told her that she probably shouldn't have added that last bit. It was an innocuous enough statement, and yet it sounded as if she'd been feeling trapped.

"Do I make too many demands on your time?" His tone was dangerously cool. She knew he was only lashing out because he was still angry over the conversation with his mother.

"That's not what I meant. You've had so many meetings lately and it was nice to see my friend. That's all."

He shoved a hand through his hair and turned away. "I have work to do, Tina."

She walked over and stood behind him. She started to put a hand on his arm, but thought better of it. "Do you want to talk, Nico?"

He spun on her. "About what?" He jabbed a finger in the direction of the phone. "About my mother? There is nothing you can say, *cara*, that will change the situation."

Tina took a deep breath. "No, I didn't think I could. But you're obviously upset about it. Sometimes it helps to talk."

His laugh was harsh and bitter. "You know nothing of my life, Tina. Nothing. You can't just come in here and ask me to talk and think it will make everything better."

"I didn't say it would make it better. I said that sometimes it helps."

"You are a child," he spat at her. "A naive woman who knows nothing of relationships. You grew up sheltered by your family and loved no matter what. What would you know about a life like mine? My only value to my parents was that I was a boy and an heir."

His words stung her to the core, and yet she refused to walk away. She didn't know what it was like to be shuffled between parents, but she did understand what it was like to feel lonely. Though how could she compare her loneliness to his? She couldn't and she knew it.

"If it makes you feel better to heap scorn on me, then fine. Do it."

He stared at her for a long minute, his eyes flashing with pain. And then he swore as he took a step backward. "Just go, Tina. Leave me alone. I'll get over it soon enough."

Tina was sitting on the terrace with a cup of tea and her phone, texting Faith and pretending that everything was well. Faith sent pictures of Renzo and baby Domenico that caught at Tina's heart and made her ache with longing for what they had.

She didn't know if she and Nico would ever have that, but she could hope. Though it seemed a somewhat futile hope at the moment, she had to admit.

She felt guilty sending texts back and forth with no mention of her pregnancy and marriage, but it was clear that her brother didn't yet know. Thankfully. She couldn't imagine how angry he would be when he did, but she was certain it was going to be bad.

Faith had asked her to fly out and join them, but Tina refused, saying she and Lucia had plans to go to Tenerife. She felt bad telling a lie, but sending a text with the truth wasn't quite how she envisioned breaking the news to her family.

Finally, the texts ended and she sat and looked at the dome of St. Peter's in the distance. The bells sounded the hour while below the apartment she could hear the traffic whizzing by and the occasional shouts of people greeting or cursing each other in the street.

Rome was always bustling with activity. She loved the city, but right now she felt as if she would like to be somewhere quieter, more placid. Castello di Casari. She could still picture the beauty of that pergola—and the look in Nico's eyes when he'd got down on one knee to propose. It hadn't been real in the sense that they'd been in love, but he sure had made her believe for a second there.

"Tina."

She turned toward his voice. He stood in the terrace doors, watching her. His hands were in his pockets, his shoulder leaning against the door frame. He looked delicious, as always, and a tiny thrill flared to life in her belly. He was wearing a white shirt, unbuttoned to show a slice of skin, and a pair of faded jeans with loafers.

He walked over to her and stood beside her chair, not looking at her, but gazing out at the city lights. She wanted to twine her hand in his and press it to her cheek. *Love*, a voice whispered. *You love him.*

No, not love. Sympathy.

"Finish your work?" she asked brightly. She would not let him see how much he'd hurt her by shutting her out earlier.

He pulled a chair out and sat across from her. *"Sì."* He didn't say anything for a long minute. And then he pulled a small box from his pocket and set it on the table between them. When she didn't say anything, he pushed it toward her.

Her heart began to thrum. "What's this?" She took the velvet box, but she didn't open it.

"An apology," he said. "And something I neglected to do."

She popped the top open and stared. The diamond inside caught the light and refracted it, sparkling in the Roman dusk. It was at least six carats, she decided.

And it was surrounded by yet more diamonds. A very expensive and elegant ring.

"It's beautiful." It was true, and it made her heart ache. Perversely, she wanted it to mean something to him. But it didn't. He'd bought her a ring and now he was giving it to her along with an apology. As if the way to make up for not trusting her enough to talk to her was to buy her things.

Silly, silly Tina. But what had she expected?

He took the box from her and removed the ring. Then he slipped it onto her hand and she pulled it closer, turning her hand this way and that to catch the light.

"If you don't like it, you can pick something else."

She shook her head. The ring was gorgeous, and definitely something she would have chosen for herself. It wasn't modest or understated, but it wasn't gaudy, either. It was elegant, the kind of jewelry worn by a marchesa.

"Thank you," she said, keeping her eyes downcast so he wouldn't see the hint of sadness in them. He'd given her a wedding ring, but it didn't feel as if it meant anything to him. It was just one more thing to check off his list of things to do. And a way to soothe any hurt she might be feeling over the way he'd treated her earlier.

"I'm sorry I snapped at you," he said, as if on cue.

"You were upset."

"Nevertheless, it was not your fault."

"I shouldn't have said anything." She shrugged and played with her phone where it sat on the table. "Who am I to give advice? I'm pregnant and married and I still haven't told my family. Until I solve my problems, I probably shouldn't attempt to give advice on yours."

"Your family loves you, Tina. Renzo loves you. He's going to be angry, not because of what you've done, but because of who you've done it with. But he won't stop loving you."

It was her turn to be taken aback. "I'm sorry, but I don't see how you can possibly know that. He hates you, and I've betrayed him." She shook her head. "No, I don't think he'll stop loving me. But he won't want to see me."

He blew out a breath. "Why did you tell me about the baby? You didn't have to. If you hadn't, you wouldn't have to worry about what happens next."

The lump in her throat hurt, but she swallowed it down. "I can't believe you're asking me this when you wouldn't talk to me earlier." She spread her hands on the table, shaking her head. "But I'll tell you. I'll prove that you *can* talk about the things that bother you and the world won't end if you do. I told you about the baby because I grew up without a father. I always wanted to know who he was, but my mother wouldn't tell me. And I was determined that wouldn't happen to this child. I didn't expect you'd insist on getting married, however."

His eyes flashed. "No, you thought we'd live separate lives and I'd come visit the baby from time to time. When it was convenient, of course. And only so long as your brother didn't decide to prevent it."

She wanted to deny it, but the truth was that's exactly what she'd thought. She'd thought it would be so easy, that she would tell him she was pregnant, tell him she wanted nothing from him, and they'd arrange civilized visitation as the baby grew. She'd known Renzo wouldn't approve, but she'd intended to put her foot down.

She dropped her gaze from Nico's. "I won't deny it," she said. "I truthfully didn't think you'd be interested in being a father. I had hoped you would want to be a part of the baby's life, but I didn't expect it."

"I'd ask what gave you that idea, but I'm sure I can guess."

They both knew he'd been quite a fixture in the tabloids over the years. "You haven't exactly had any long-term relationships."

"In my experience, they don't work out."

A pinprick of pain throbbed in her heart. "Is that from personal experience or from observation? Because I'd say the two are not interchangeable."

He looked resigned for a moment. Uncertain. But then his expression hardened again. "My parents have rather warped my view of what a marriage is supposed to be."

"They are only two people," she said. "They don't represent everyone." She didn't even want to think about how his views impacted *their* marriage.

He shook his head. "Nevertheless, they are what I grew up with. They should have divorced years ago, but they stayed together instead and made each other miserable."

"And you," she added softly.

She expected he'd grow angry but he only ran his palms over his face before spearing her with a glare. "And me. Yes, they made me miserable. They still do."

"Why did you marry me, Nico?" She had to ask, in light of what he'd said about his parents' marriage.

He looked away, as if he couldn't quite face her at that moment. "You know why."

"Yes, I suppose I do. But what happens after the baby is born?"

He shrugged. "We take it a day at a time, Tina. I can promise you I won't ever let this child feel the way I felt.

And I'm confident you won't, either. We'll figure something out, and we'll be far better parents than I had."

Her heart thumped. He was actually talking to her, though she didn't know for how long. "I appreciate that. And I think I understand now."

"Understand what?"

She shrugged self-consciously. "You looked uncomfortable when Giuseppe expressed his sympathies for your father's death, and later, when I did, as if you didn't want them but felt you had to accept them anyway."

He didn't say anything for a long minute. He just stared at her, his nostrils flaring as if he were holding in a great deal of emotion. "The truth is that I despised him. But not always. I worshipped him for years, craved his affection—yes, even beyond my mother's. She's right about that. I did side with him when I grew older. She was so...bitchy and petty, while he seemed regal, controlled. But I soon realized he only cared about himself."

Tears sheened her eyes. She didn't care if he saw them. She reached for his hand, squeezed it tight. "I'm sorry, Nico."

He didn't jerk his hand from hers. Instead, he squeezed their palms together. "I wanted what you had," he said, the words almost choked from him. "I came to your place so often because I wanted to be a part of what your family had together. Your mother is kind, accepting. I loved sitting at the kitchen table with all of you and eating dinner. It felt far more real than anything else in my life at that time."

"I loved having you there," she admitted. "I think we all did. Renzo looked upon you like a brother."

He pulled his hand away then, and she regretted the

impulse to say such a thing. But it had been the truth. He and Renzo had been so close, and now they weren't.

And now he was closing up again. Closing in on himself like an exquisite flower that only bloomed for a few hours and then shut the world out once more.

"It was a long time ago," he said stiffly.

She swallowed the lump in her throat. "It could be that way again. If only you and Renzo would talk—"

"Maledizione," he swore, rocketing to his feet, his entire body vibrating with anger. She could only stare up at him in shocked fascination. "Don't you understand? I am a Gavretti. I ruin everything I touch."

He turned and stalked inside while she sat helplessly and stared at the suddenly shimmering dome of St. Peter's in the distance.

Not *everything*, she hoped.

CHAPTER ELEVEN

WHY had he told her those things? Nico paced inside the darkened study, angry with himself for letting her see that far into him. He hated being vulnerable. He'd sworn to himself, when he'd been eight years old and crying because his mother wouldn't let him come home on a school break, that he would never let anyone see how much he hurt ever again.

It was about survival. About appearing strong and self-sufficient. The world couldn't exploit what it didn't know. If he appeared strong, then he was strong.

Nico swore softly. He could see her through the window, sitting there on the terrace and not moving. The ring he'd given her sparkled in the lights, drawing his attention.

She sat so still. He wondered what she was thinking. He had an insane urge to go to her, to pull her into his arms and tell her—once more—that he was sorry. What was wrong with him? Why was he feeling soft when it came to her?

Dio, he'd already revealed things to her that he should not. He'd opened up a window into his soul when he'd told her how he felt about his parents.

And then, to compound his mistake, he'd admitted to her what her family had meant to him. How he'd been desperate to sit in their warm glow and just soak it up as if he belonged.

He'd been pitiful, like a starving dog staring into the back door of a restaurant, hoping for a few scraps to come his way. He, a Gavretti, the heir to an ancient title and estates around the world, had envied the humble home of the D'Angelis. He'd wanted to be one of them much more than he'd wanted to be Niccolo Gavretti.

But of course he hadn't belonged. It had taken almost two years, but he'd found that out the hard way. He'd told her he ruined everything he touched—and it was true. He and Renzo had been friends, working together on a project that meant everything to Renzo's future, and Nico had screwed it up.

He'd taken that feeling of belonging and thrown it back in their faces as if it had meant nothing. That's not at all what he'd intended when he'd gone to his father, but it's what had happened nevertheless. And he'd been powerless to stop it. Worse, he'd been complicit when he'd eventually done what his father had demanded of him.

She would hate him if she knew what he'd done. If she knew that he was directly responsible for Renzo's setback in the first year, that he had as good as reneged on his word, she would despise him. Even a baby wouldn't change that.

For the first time, he couldn't bear the thought of her knowing. Of her hating him. He'd forced her into this marriage with threats to her family because he'd believed marrying her was a shrewd move, as well as the right thing for the child, and he'd done it all without a care for how she felt about him.

Now he couldn't bear the idea she would hate him. God, what was wrong with him?

Nico stood with his fists clenched at his side and watched her through the window. Was she angry? Was she crying? He was on edge watching her. A sliver of desperation curled around his heart. He wanted to go outside and gather her in his arms, and then he wanted to take her to bed and pretend this had never happened. That he'd never spoken to her of his love-starved childhood and that he'd never let her know what her family had meant to him.

Because when she learned the truth, when she hated him and wanted out of this marriage, she would know how much he'd once cared about the D'Angelis. And she would pity him for it.

Dio, he was screwing this up in so many ways. He refused to have a marriage like his parents had had—a cold, bitter, soul-destroying relationship that had warped not only their lives but his as well—and yet he'd set himself up for it when he'd insisted on marrying the sister of the man he'd betrayed.

He wanted to go to her. He wanted to take her to bed and see her eyes darken with passion, wanted to hear her soft cries as he took them both over the edge of control, and then he wanted to lie beside her and go to sleep with her body tucked into the curve of his.

She fit there so perfectly. He loved resting his hand on her belly. It was far too early in the pregnancy to feel anything, but he liked knowing that his child nestled beneath his hand. He felt a connection there, something he'd never felt with another person, and he liked the way it made him feel inside.

Tina stood up then. Her beautiful body was outlined against the light, so lush and curvy that it made him ache just to look at her. Then she turned and came back inside. He held his breath for a long moment, hoping she would come into the office and challenge him, that she would put her arms around him and tell him she wanted him.

But she kept walking, down the hall and into the bedroom. He did not go after her.

"We're returning to Castello di Casari," Nico said, and Tina looked up from where she sat with her computer open on the couch. She'd been engaging in some light trading this morning, moving funds around and diversifying into a few tech stocks that she thought were poised for growth.

The financial papers were at her side, but she'd not read them yet. She usually liked to read them over breakfast, but she'd been too preoccupied. Even now, thoughts of last night warmed her cheeks and made her squirm in her seat.

Nico had come to bed late last night, slipping in beside her and lying on his back with an arm behind his head.

She'd pretended to be asleep, though she'd hoped he might reach for her anyway. He did not, so she'd turned toward him and put a hand on his chest. He still didn't reach for her, so she sidled closer and ran her palm down his flat abdomen.

He'd shuddered beneath her touch. And then he'd turned to her as if she'd flipped a switch inside him and tugged her into his arms.

"Tina," he'd groaned into her neck. "Tina."

She'd spread her hands on the hot, silky skin of his back. "Make love to me, Nico. Please. I want you so much."

What followed had been the most intense lovemaking between them yet. He'd worshipped her body reverently, as if he'd had forever to do so. As if they were suspended in time and the only thing that mattered was the two of them. He'd kissed his way down her torso, and then slid his tongue between her folds, swirling and sucking her clitoris until she came apart with a cry.

He did it again and again, until she'd begged him to join his body with hers and end the torture. He'd slid inside her, his body hard and strong, filling her so exquisitely. She'd thought she'd felt it all with him, but she'd realized in that moment she hadn't.

Because it felt different when you realized you really were in love with the man whose body knew yours so perfectly. But perhaps *different* was the wrong word. It felt like something...*more*.

More intense, more thrilling. More heartbreaking. Especially when the man you loved did not love you.

Tina gave herself a mental shake as she looked up at him now, her heart aching for him. How had she let it happen? How had she fallen in love with him between one breath and the next?

She'd thought she'd been on her guard, thought she'd been in control. She hadn't.

"I'd like that," she said in answer to his announcement. "I didn't get to explore it quite enough the last time."

Besides, there were shadows under his eyes and she worried that he'd been working too hard. It would be good to go somewhere more remote and peaceful. Somewhere that she wouldn't be worried about her brother showing up unannounced and having a meltdown.

"I've finished what I needed to do in Rome. We'll leave after lunch."

Tina was busy for the rest of the morning, packing

and getting ready to leave the city. She texted Lucia, who wished her a *buon viaggio* and told her to call every day, and then they were on their way.

This time when the helicopter swooped over the mountains and headed down to the imposing castle sitting in the lake, Tina paid attention to everything she had not before. The water was crystalline blue, turquoise in places, from the melt waters that came down out of the mountains and fed the lake.

Today, the sky was clear. Sailboats and motorboats dotted the lake. People sunned themselves on yachts, looking up with hands shading their eyes as the helicopter passed overhead.

"What a beautiful place," she said. "How they must envy you coming into the manor in the lake."

He laughed. "Perhaps they do. I've often thought we should open to tourists, but that was before I married you. Now I think we will keep the castle as our own private refuge from the world."

She liked the sound of that, though she felt slightly sorry for the tourists who would never get to visit. On the other hand, there were plenty of other tourist attractions nearby.

But even better, she liked that he'd said it would be *their* private refuge.

She turned her head to look out the window as the craft began its descent onto the helipad. The emotions whirling inside her were almost too much, and she was afraid that if he looked at her she would cry.

She desperately wanted to grab his hand, hold it to her cheek and tell him she loved him.

Instead, she swallowed the impulse and waved as she saw Giuseppe. He stood at the edge of the landing pad, his hair whipping in the breeze from the rotors even though he had very little of it. Behind him, several staff members waited, no doubt to help with the luggage.

Giuseppe waved back, and she smiled to herself, suddenly sure that it wasn't the most dignified thing in the world for him to do but that he'd done it for her.

"My lady," he said, bowing over her hand when they'd alighted from the helicopter and moved away from the rotors. "Congratulations on your marriage, and welcome once again to Castello di Casari. This time, you are her mistress and she is happy to have you."

"Thank you, Giuseppe," she said, smiling happily. Her world wasn't perfect, that was certain, but it had been a pretty good day thus far.

Nico put his arm around her and pulled her into the curve of his body. She wanted to turn into him, tuck her cheek against his chest and breathe him in.

Giuseppe grinned broadly as his gaze moved between them, and she knew that he'd seen what she couldn't hide.

"So happy to see a couple so deeply in love," he effused. "Maybe soon we can hope for the bambino, yes?"

She wasn't certain how Nico would react to that, but he only smiled and clapped Giuseppe on the shoulder. "Perhaps we can, Giuseppe. I'll see what I can do."

The other man laughed, and then they were going down the steps and into the castle the same way they'd gone before. This time, however, Nico took her up the stairs and into his room instead of the adjoining one she'd had the last time.

Once the door closed, he pulled her into his arms and kissed her at the same time he slipped the straps of her dress off her shoulders.

"What are you doing, Nico? They'll be bringing the

luggage up soon," she said, laughing as he dipped his lips to her shoulder.

"That's what locks are for, *cara*. Besides, I did promise Giuseppe I'd get started on the baby making."

"I think it's safe to say that task is done," she replied. His fingers went to her zipper and started sliding it down slowly.

"Just to be certain, I think we should get naked anyway." He reached behind him and flipped the lock on the door, then picked her up and carried her to the bed. He quickly divested her of her clothes, though he still wore all of his as he hovered over her on his palms. It was rather erotic to feel the scrape of his jeans against her sensitized skin.

"Wait," she cried as a thought occurred to her.

He looked up, his beautiful stormy-gray eyes hot and intense. "What, *cara*? Do you have a request?"

Now, there was a thought. "No," she said quickly. "But your father—it, um, it wasn't this bed, right?"

Nico laughed. "Definitely not. He was in Florence at the time. Besides, I have ordered new mattresses for all the residences."

"I'm relieved to hear it."

He bent and licked her nipple, and a shot of liquid desire melted in her core. "Now, about that request," he murmured. "Tell me what you desire from me, Tina... anything you desire."

The next few days were glorious. Tina had never been happier. She felt so free, as if she really could be whomever she wanted. As if she truly were bold and brave, and not a cowering mouse deep inside. Nico made her feel that way—as if she could conquer the world and not regret a single moment of it.

Each day, they started with breakfast on the terrace where they laughed and talked and teased each other with hot looks and silly innuendo.

They sometimes went for walks around the garden, or took a swim in the warm pool. Once, they went out in a yacht and floated along the lake's shore, stopping at one of the towns for lunch and some shopping.

Every night, they stayed up late, making love, watching television, or sitting side by side in the bed and working on their computers. It was domestic and blissful and she looked forward to the days stretching before her so long as they began and ended with Nico.

Today, they'd been swimming when he'd suddenly given her one of those heated looks that she knew preceded an afternoon of hot lovemaking. She hadn't even pretended not to notice. Instead, she'd climbed out of the pool and toweled off while he'd watched her.

And then she'd told him she'd race him to the bed. She could hear him lifting out of the water behind her as she'd started to run, laughing, but he'd never managed to catch her. She'd made it to the bedroom first, and when he arrived, he'd still had water dripping down his hard, tanned muscles.

He hadn't even dried off before stripping her bikini and coming down on top of her.

After they made love, she fell into a sound sleep, waking sometime late in the afternoon, her body replete, her skin still glowing and sensitive. She turned toward Nico, but he wasn't in bed. She frowned as she sat up, yawning and stretching.

She had to stop sleeping in the middle of the day. And she had to tell him to stop letting her do so.

Except that she knew he wouldn't listen. He'd nod and say of course—but if she slept, he would let her sleep. Apparently, according to him, the pregnancy website said excessive tiredness was common in the first trimester. Nico was turning into quite the authority on pregnancy, she thought wryly.

Her phone buzzed with a text. Occasionally, she got enough of a signal to get a message or two, usually when the sky was clear. Tina reached for her phone, pleased that someone was getting through. There were three bars today, which were a good sign, and a text from Faith.

What's going on there? Is everything okay?

Tina swallowed a sliver of dread and texted back. Of course. Everything is fine.

A second later, her phone buzzed again. Renzo is worried about you.

I'm fine.

There was something in the paper about you being seen with Niccolo Gavretti in Rome a few days ago.

Tina's heart sank. She'd been expecting something to happen, knowing the way the tabloids usually covered Nico, but she'd allowed herself to be lulled into a false sense of security when nothing had happened. At least they didn't have the story of her hasty marriage yet.

Nico and I move in the same circles sometimes. It wouldn't be unusual to see him at an event. Oh, the irony of lying about seeing Nico while sitting in his bed.

The pause before the next text was long. Finally, her phone buzzed. He's dangerous, Tina. He wouldn't think twice about using you in order to get to Renzo. Be careful.

Tina's heart twisted. She wanted to call Faith up and tell her how wrong she was, but it would do no good. Faith had her information from Renzo, and of course she would take her husband's side.

Tina sighed. What a mess she'd gotten herself into. She loved the man her brother hated, and she still had no idea what had happened between them. Clearly, her reprieve was nearly up and she had to tell Renzo the truth before the papers said anything more. But she wasn't going to do it through a text to his wife.

I will.

Faith texted a few more things, a picture of baby Domenico sleeping in his crib, and they said their good-byes. Tina got up and dressed, and then took the newspapers she'd not read this morning and went out onto the terrace. The afternoon sun was less intense, and the shade of the laurels kept her cool while she flipped through the papers.

They were financial papers, not tabloids, but she still scanned them for any news about Nico that might appear.

When she found it, her chest felt tight.

Gavretti Manufacturing Cash Flow Shortage, Order Cancellations.

She read the article twice to be sure she understood everything the reporter speculated. Then she got up and went to find Nico. They'd been here for days, and he'd said nothing. It bothered her and worried her at the same time.

She found him where she expected, in his home office with its gorgeous paneled walls, floor-to-ceiling bookcases and overstuffed leather furniture. He sat at the desk and tapped on his computer. Three phones lay on the desk in front of him.

Nico looked up as she walked in, the frown he'd worn easing when their gazes locked.

She ignored the jolt of electricity buzzing through her system and held up the paper. "Is this true?"

The warmth in his eyes faded to something akin to resignation. "Not all of it."

"Which part is true then?"

She thought he wouldn't tell her, but he sighed and leaned back in the chair. "My father left me a mess. I'm trying to fix it."

"By raiding your company?"

"By shifting assets temporarily."

She came over and sat down in front of his desk. "I want to help."

He shook his head. "I have it under control. I have advisers and a crack financial team. We're handling it."

Worry spiked in her belly. "You're vulnerable right now."

His eyes flashed. They both knew what she did not say. "Somewhat, yes. But trying to take me over would strain D'Angeli Motors. It would not be the wisest of courses that Renzo could take."

"And yet whatever this thing is between you doesn't seem to care about logic." Tina shook her head and swore. "So stubborn, the both of you!"

She hadn't brought up the subject in days, and he'd not, either. Now, he looked irritated.

"It's complicated, Tina."

She smacked her hand on the desk, startling him if the way he flinched was any indication. "It's not complicated at all. You talk, you solve what needs to be solved, and you walk away with a clear conscience.

No one says you have to be best friends again, but for God's sake, there is a child on the way and he or she will need a whole family, not half of one."

"The baby will have the two of us," he grated. "That is enough."

She shook her head furiously. "There is also an aunt and uncle and cousin, as well as a grandmother, who would all spoil this child rotten if given the chance."

His jaw flexed stubbornly. "I won't stop you from seeing them, Tina."

She could feel angry tears welling behind her eyelids. "No, but you won't join me, either. You'll force me to choose between spending time with you and spending time with them, provided Renzo will see me at all after he finds out I've married you." A bubble of hysterical laughter escaped her throat. "My God, it's like you and my brother got a divorce and I'm being torn between you."

"Don't be melodramatic," he snapped. "You aren't a child."

"No, I'm not," she said fiercely. "But I still lo—care about you both."

She couldn't say *love*, though she wanted to. She couldn't bear for him to look at her with pity when he knew how she felt. By now, she knew enough about him to know that love was not something that would ever come easy for him. He would always be suspicious, always mistrusting. He'd been hurt too badly by the lack of love in his life to believe it could be so freely given or genuine.

Tina leaned forward, palms on the desk, determination vibrating in every bone of her body. "Let me help, Nico. I know what I'm doing, and I can help you get the company back in the black. Renzo won't be able to touch it. I'll make sure of it."

He looked stunned. And then angry. "By doing what? Begging him not to?"

"I wasn't going to beg him, no." Though she had intended to have Faith put pressure on Renzo in the interim, she also intended to inject enough cash into the coffers to make the prospect unappealing to him.

Nico shot to his feet and swore. "Do you honestly believe I'd trust you, Tina? We've been married for less than a month. We have a child on the way, and we have great sex—but you've been a D'Angeli your entire life. Your loyalty is to your family, not to me."

She felt as if he'd slapped her. But what had she expected? Of course he was suspicious, and why not? She would be, too, if she were him. She stood and folded her arms beneath her breasts, feeling angry and drained and frustrated all at once.

Her loyalty *was* to her family—but he was her family, too. That was the part he hadn't managed to get through his thick skull yet. She loved him, and Renzo didn't *need* Gavretti Manufacturing. Oh, she didn't doubt he would do everything in his power to obtain it if he could, but the fact was that D'Angeli Motors was thriving and growing, and her brother was in no danger of losing a thing.

Nico, on the other hand, was dancing on the edge of a precipice and too infuriatingly stubborn to see that he needed her.

"I know why you think that, Nico. It hurts to hear you say it, but I understand why you would." She crumpled the newspaper and tossed it on the desk. "And don't think I don't realize, in light of this news, that at least part of why you married me was to buy leverage against Renzo."

He didn't deny it, and though her heart throbbed, she told herself it didn't matter. She knew enough about him now to understand that he didn't trust anyone. He might have been from a privileged background, but he'd been so lonely that he'd learned to do whatever it took to protect himself.

"It wasn't my only reason," he said stiffly.

She shook her head. "No, I realize that. Now what you need to realize is that I may be what you need to get out of this mess, though not in the way you imagined." She reached for a pen and wrote some figures down on the notepad sitting beside his computer. "This is what I've done with my money. Tell me you could have done better and I won't say another word."

CHAPTER TWELVE

"WHAT's your plan?"

Tina looked up to find him standing in the entrance to the pergola, watching her. She'd been reading—or trying to read, since she was in fact fuming and unable to concentrate. She'd fled his office and then fled the house, angry and sad and in need of some distance. Since there wasn't really anywhere to go, she'd opted for the shaded pergola.

Now, she set the eReader on the table in front of her and searched his eyes. He looked serious, though unhappy. He didn't want to ask her this, she knew. And yet the numbers on the paper didn't lie. She *did* have a good head for finance.

"You need cash," she said, deciding not to dance around the obvious. "I have cash. We'll cover the loan payments to buy time to restructure the debt. And then, if you'll let me see the complete picture, I'll have a better idea what else can be done."

He didn't even blink when she mentioned loan payments. But she'd done her research and she had a far better idea of what he was trying to do now. The state of his father's finances at the time of his death was a matter of record. Anyone determined to do so could find out the information.

In trying to save the ancient estate from ruin, Nico was putting his company at risk.

"And what makes you think my financial advisors haven't already suggested this course of action?"

"Oh, I'm sure they did. But the cash is clearly coming out of Gavretti Manufacturing. You may not be damaging the company, but you're putting your entire personal stake at risk. Someone could buy your loans and take the company out from under you. You're right that it wouldn't be easy just yet—but that day is probably coming, and sooner than you wish."

He looked at her for a long minute. And then he shook his head. "Your brother is indeed a fool not to use you."

She shrugged self-consciously. "I'm not a genius. I'm just good with figuring these kinds of things out."

He pulled the paper she'd written the numbers on from his pocket. "I don't know. I'd say this is impressive. No wonder you were so insistent about your money in Gibraltar."

She laced her fingers together in her lap. "It's what I enjoy doing. I have fun with numbers—and with taking chances on them."

"You're good at it, apparently."

"I think I am," she said.

He set the paper on the table. "Nevertheless, I don't need your money, Tina. Your analysis is interesting— and even, I admit, tempting—but I already have a plan."

Disappointment ate at her. Stubborn man. He didn't want her money because of who she was. "You still don't trust me."

He blew out a breath. "I shouldn't have said that."

"But it's what you feel."

His eyes gleamed hot. "Haven't you figured it out by now? I don't trust anyone."

Her heart hurt for him because she knew there was so much more underlying that statement than he would admit to. He didn't trust anyone because he'd never been able to depend on anyone. He was used to doing everything alone, to taking care of himself and asking nothing of those from whom he should be able to ask the world.

In that moment, she despised his parents more than she'd ever despised anyone in her life. Her fingers clenched. If she could get her hands around his mother's neck right now...

Not helpful.

Tina swallowed, her throat aching with the weight of unshed tears. "You need to learn how, Nico. Not everyone is your enemy."

He looked remote and cool and untouchable, and it hurt to see him withdraw from her after all they'd shared. "I learned a long time ago that it was easier to live life as if they were. It keeps me from being disappointed."

"I'm not everyone," she said. "I care."

"Yes, but for how long?" He took a step closer, his hands thrust in his pockets, his eyes glittering bright as diamonds. "Everyone has a limit, Tina. Even you. You haven't asked me in days now what happened between Renzo and me. Why not? Are you afraid the truth might change your mind?"

He watched her struggle and knew he'd said something that pierced to the very heart of her. Yes, she said she cared—but if she knew the truth, what then? Would she believe him guilty, or would she still try to see the best in him?

He very much feared it would be the first option. And that's what bothered him—the fact he actually *cared* what she thought. Why?

He'd initially decided to marry her for the child—and for leverage, yes—and to hell with the consequences. He didn't care what she thought of him, so long as she was a good mother to their baby.

But somewhere along the way, that had changed. He craved her like a drug. He didn't like it. Or he did like it when he was deep inside her and making her scream his name, but he didn't like the way it made him feel out of control to want her so much.

It was almost as if he *needed* her somehow. And that was not true, because he didn't need anyone. He'd made sure of it.

"I'm not afraid," she said. "I stopped asking because it makes you angry."

What made her different from other women? She was smart and beautiful, but so what? She challenged him in unexpected ways, which should irritate him and yet somehow managed to thrill him. He didn't quite know what it was, but it was something.

He'd sat in his office after she'd left and stared at the figures on the paper as though they were written in Sanskrit. And, *Dio*, he'd been tempted. Tempted to accept her money and let her forge this path by his side. It would certainly make what he was trying to do easier.

But then he'd wondered just what in the hell he was thinking. She was still a D'Angeli, regardless of their marriage, and she would inevitably side with her brother against him. It didn't matter that she craved him in bed, or that she was pregnant with his child. Blood was thicker than water.

Hell, in his world, even blood wasn't enough to ensure unwavering loyalty. How could he expect it from her?

No, he wouldn't take her money, no matter how tempting.

"Are you planning to tell me now," she asked, one delicate eyebrow arching imperiously. "Or was that simply a cryptic teaser designed to put me off?"

"It's simple enough," he said, his heart pounding much more quickly than it should now that he'd determined to tell her everything. Once he told her, she would despise him—and then he could go back to living the way he always did, the way he understood. He would still have her in his bed and in his life, but neither of them would mistake what they had for anything other than sexual chemistry and a shared future for the sake of their child.

"Renzo and I worked on the design for the prototype for months. I promised to get the financial backing for us to make a test version of the motorcycle."

She nodded. "I remember how excited he was. It was all either of you talked about."

He remembered those days as if they'd happened only yesterday. The memory of them still had the power to slice into him with pain and regret. He should have been stronger.

"Yes, well, I failed. And not only that, I betrayed him in the process. Gavretti Manufacturing was up and running a full year before D'Angeli Motors."

She sat there with her jaw slightly open and her eyes wide. So she had not known that fact.

"That's right," he said, pressing in for the kill, though

it destroyed him inside to watch the expression on her face. "I stole the prototype. I made the motorcycle without Renzo. That's why he hates me. And that's why you shouldn't want to give me your money."

"I don't believe it," she said after a long minute in which he could hear everything around him as if it were magnified a thousandfold. The chirping of birds, the beat of a butterfly's wings, the sticky slide of a spider in its web.

He refused to allow that tiny leap of his heart to give him hope. "Why not, *cara*? You already know I don't trust anyone. Why wouldn't I take the plans and start my own company?"

Her hands clenched into fists. "You might be bad, Nico—or you've made everyone think you're bad—but that's not who you are. You wouldn't steal the prototype when you'd spent months working on it together. When you knew what it meant to Renzo."

"How can you be so sure?"

"Because it's not who you are," she repeated.

"You don't know that. It might be exactly who I am."

She shot to her feet with a growl and glared at him. "It's *not*, so stop trying to make me think it is."

Something broke inside him then, something he hadn't even known was there. The force of it was too much, whipping him in a maelstrom of emotion while he stood there and focused on her beautiful, angry face, unable to say even a word.

How could she look at him like that and believe, to her core, that he had not done what everyone else thought he'd done? No one had ever believed in him that strongly. No one had ever stood toe to toe with him and insisted he wasn't what he said he was. When he'd felt petty and mean and unloved, no one had ever told him differently.

When he'd been ruthless and hard and colder than New Year's Day at the North Pole to survive, no one had ever told him they didn't believe that's who he was.

But she was standing here now, this woman he adored, and telling him he was so much better than he thought.

This woman he adored.

Dio!

Panic followed hard on the heels of that revelation. How could he adore her when she would leave him in the end?

Nico took a step backward. He didn't adore her. He *wanted* her. He was confusing the two in his head, that's all.

She looked miserable. A tear spilled free and slid down her cheek and his heart turned inside out. He wanted to gather her to him and hold her tight, tell her everything. But he couldn't. He couldn't be that weak ever again.

Nico turned and walked away.

Tina despised crying. But she'd been doing a lot of it over the past few hours. First, she'd watched in stunned silence as Nico had left her in the garden. She'd been torn between chasing after him and making him talk to her, or staying where she was until she got herself under control again. She'd been so angry and so hurt at the same time.

And, yes, even confused. He'd told her that he'd stolen the plans from Renzo—but she didn't believe him. She simply didn't, and yet she was furious with him for not telling her the rest of the story. For turning and walking away like a coward.

As if he *wanted* her to believe the worst.

She didn't know how much time passed—a half an hour at most maybe—when she'd heard the helicopter coming in for a landing. Fear had slid through her like oil then. She'd shot to her feet and started running toward the castle.

But she was too late. By the time she bounded up the stairs to the helipad, the craft had lifted off and started banking toward the mountains. She knew without being told that Nico was on it. She'd stood there with her hands twisting together in front of her and felt empty inside.

He'd left her. He'd climbed onto that damn helicopter and left her.

She went to her bedroom—their bedroom—and raged for a good hour. Then she'd cried for another. And then she'd picked up her phone and tried to text Lucia. But the signal was intermittent and she couldn't get it to go.

Giuseppe brought her dinner on a tray. He looked confused, and apologetic. "It was business, madam," he said, as if that explained everything. "His lordship will return in a day or two. I'm sure it must have been important for him to leave you on your honeymoon."

"Thank you, Giuseppe," Tina said numbly. Yes, business. Important business. Perhaps he was even now prowling the nightclubs of Rome and finding a woman to spend the night with.

The thought made her heart hurt so badly she thought she might throw up. *No*, she told herself fiercely. *He would not do that.*

Just as he wouldn't have stolen the prototype. How

could the man who spent hours on pregnancy websites, who flew dresses in for their wedding, and who sat with his head in his hands and fought the specter of his unfeeling mother *not* have a heart? He'd told her how much he'd loved her family, and knowing what she did about his past, she didn't believe he'd lied about that.

He *did* have a heart. He was a man who felt things deeply, no matter that he tried to hide that fact from everyone, including himself. He was afraid of feeling. Afraid of loving.

And so was she, apparently. Tina frowned. Why hadn't she told him that she loved him? That she believed in him because she knew it in her bones that he was worthy of that belief?

Coward. She was no better than he was. He'd run from her, but she'd been running from the moment he'd walked into her hotel room in Rome. How could they possibly have a future together if they both kept running?

Tina lifted her chin as sudden determination rushed through her. She was finished running. No, from now on she was facing life head-on and demanding only the best it had to give. No more half measures for her. And no more hiding.

Determined, she flipped open her computer and started writing the emails that would change everything.

She gave him three days. When Nico still hadn't returned after that time, Tina dredged up every shred of haughty at her disposal and told Giuseppe she wanted the helicopter. She'd thought he might argue with her, or that Nico had given him orders to keep her on the island, but he merely nodded his head vigorously and said, "Yes, madam. Of course, madam."

She felt bad for being so brusque after that, but she'd been afraid he would refuse her. When she stood inside the glassed-in waiting room and watched for the helicopter on the horizon, she turned to him and smiled.

"I'm sorry if I was rude earlier, Giuseppe."

He dipped his head. "Not at all, madam. You miss his lordship. It is quite understandable."

The helicopter soon arrived to whisk Tina back to the airport and then to Rome. She didn't know for certain that's where he was, but she suspected it since there was so much going on with Gavretti Manufacturing. Once she landed, she took a car to the apartment. Nico wasn't there, but the doorman recognized her and let her in when she claimed she'd forgotten her key.

That was another item on her list of things to do: get keys to all Gavretti residences. Nico wasn't hiding from her ever again.

She went down the hall to the bedroom, discovered that he was indeed staying there, and then turned and went back to the living area where she made a couple of phone calls before settling down to wait.

She didn't even have to wait an hour. The door burst open and he was there, looking so delicious in his navy blue custom suit with the pin-striped shirt open at the neck.

He also looked furious. Obviously, the concierge had done as she asked and called Nico to let him know she had arrived.

"What are you doing here, Tina? And why didn't you let me know you were coming? You should have had security."

She stood and faced him squarely across the couch.

Her heart swelled with love for him. He looked so angry, but she only wanted to touch him. She wanted to put her palms on his face and tell him how much she loved him.

But she was too scared. She would do it, but not quite yet.

"You didn't steal the prototype, Nico," she said, ignoring his questions. "I want you to tell me the truth."

He swore violently. She expected him to fight her, but he went over and poured a Scotch from the liquor cabinet before turning back to her.

"I might as well have. It was my fault."

"How?"

He sank onto a chair across from her and rubbed his forehead. And then his gaze snapped up, glaring at her.

"I took a copy of the plan to my father, to ask him for the money. He refused. He told me he would only back us if I built the motorcycles and made it a family enterprise." He took a sip of the Scotch. "I told him no. But he had friends who followed the sport, and he took the design to them, looking for investors. The next thing I knew, the financing was in place for Gavretti Manufacturing. Renzo didn't believe me. We said terrible things to each other—and I went to work for my father."

"I thought it was your company?"

"I bought it from him a few years later, but no, it was not at first."

Tina blinked. "But he didn't care about motorcycles, did he? Why would he try to start a factory that built them?"

Nico took another swallow of the Scotch. "Greed. He saw something in the plan and wanted to capitalize on it. He was right, as the success of the company proves."

Tina clenched her fingers in her lap. "You have to tell Renzo this."

His eyes flashed, his jaw hardening. "I did tell him, Tina. He didn't believe me." He laughed harshly. "Can you blame him? In his eyes, I betrayed him because I believed I was better than he was. Because I was a rich and privileged Gavretti."

She couldn't stop the feelings swelling in her another minute. He was a good man, and he tortured himself so much. Not only that, but he expected people to believe the worst of him.

She went to his side, knelt on the floor before him, and grasped his free hand in hers.

"No," he told her, setting the Scotch down and trying to make her get up. "Don't get on the floor."

"Nico," she said, tears rushing into her throat and eyes. "I believe you. *I* believe you."

He pulled her up and into his lap, and she clung to him, buried her face against his neck and breathed him in. He was everything to her, everything. Him, the baby. She couldn't imagine her life without them now. And she was more than prepared to do battle with her brother over it.

"You're too trusting, Tina," he said, stroking her hair. "I *did* go to work for my father. A better man would have refused."

"And let him steal all the hard work you and Renzo did? I don't think so."

"I asked Renzo to come work for me. I thought we could still do what we wanted—but he refused. And he was right to do so, as the success of D'Angeli Motors proves."

She pressed her palm against his chest, felt how fast

his heart was beating. "You were both so stubborn. And wrong to let this fester between you."

"It can't be fixed, Tina," he told her. "There's too much bad blood between us now. We've spent too many years feeling bitter and angry. I know I've said things, done things, that can't be forgiven."

She squeezed him tight. "We'll see about that."

The door buzzed then, and she took a deep breath to fortify herself for what came next. It wasn't going to be an easy afternoon.

She just hoped the two men she loved most didn't hate her by the end of it.

CHAPTER THIRTEEN

HER brother was so furious he vibrated with it. Beside him, Faith had a hand on his arm. She squeezed it at regular intervals, as if to remind him he couldn't do what he so obviously wanted to do, which was to punch Nico.

Faith shot Tina a worried look, and Tina clenched her jaw. She'd done this, and now she had to see it through. Worse, she'd dragged Faith into it when she'd asked her to help set up the meeting. Renzo would not be happy about that, either. Right now, he was too focused on her and Nico to be angry at Faith.

"This is a low blow even for you, Nico," Renzo snarled. "You couldn't touch me, so you went after my sister?"

"Renzo," Tina snapped, and he slanted his icy gaze at her. "Didn't you read the email I sent you? We met at a masquerade. We didn't know each other's identity."

"That's what he wants you to think."

Tina rolled her eyes. My God, he sounded like Nico had in the hotel room when he'd accused her of setting him up. "The two of you are exactly alike. It's no wonder you won't talk."

Nico was standing over by the liquor cabinet again. He hadn't refilled his glass, but he stood there with his hands in his pockets, his gaze flashing furiously at her and Renzo both. He looked like a cornered animal. And a dangerous one.

"There's nothing to talk about, Tina," Nico growled. "You see how he thinks."

Tina resisted the urge to pinch the bridge of her nose. Instead, she went over to her brother and touched his arm, even though he was so very angry with her.

"Renzo, for God's sake, there's a baby on the way. Nico is my husband now. You *both* made mistakes, you know. And I want you to talk to each other about them."

Renzo's expression was thunderous. "You can't be serious, Tina. He cares nothing for you. This is all a game to him."

"I *am* serious." So serious that her chest hurt with the chaotic emotions buffeting her. It was an effort not to cry. Her eyes stung, her throat ached and her heart tattooed the inside of her chest at light speed. She loved them both, and they were idiots. "It's not a game."

Renzo swore. "You're a fool, you know that?"

She lifted her chin and stared at him with all the imperiousness she could manage. It hurt to hear him say that but, strangely, she wasn't feeling cowed. She'd always wanted her brother's approval—but now, for what must be the first time in her life, she realized she didn't need it.

"I'm twenty-four years old, Renzo. Old enough to make my own decisions. I don't need you deciding what's best for me anymore. I'm married to Nico and pregnant with his child—and that's not going to change."

He looked fierce. And so worried for her that it broke her heart.

"Tina, for God's sake, he betrayed me. Betrayed *us*. I almost didn't get the financing for the company after that. If I had not, you'd probably be waiting tables in some restaurant and trying to make ends meet. Our lives would *not* be what they are today. He tried to take that from us, *cara mia*."

She leaned toward him then, feeling fiercer than she'd ever felt in her life. "If you believe that, *you're* the fool."

"Renzo," Faith said in that syrupy Southern drawl of hers. "Why don't the two of you talk, for Tina's sake? You can at least be civil for her, can't you?"

Tina had the feeling that if anyone else had said that, including her, he'd have snapped their head off. Instead, he closed his eyes and squeezed his wife's hand, as if seeking patience and strength.

"Fine, yes. We will talk."

Tina went over to Nico, her heart in her throat. He was every bit as murderously angry as her brother, and she wasn't sure he would agree. She took his hand, and when he didn't stop her, she felt hopeful.

"I want you to do this for me, Nico. For our baby. Please."

His eyes flashed. And then he squeezed her hand and she drew in a shaky breath. "For you," he said. Then he lifted his head and glared at Renzo. "We can talk on the terrazzo."

"No," Tina said. "Faith and I will go outside. You two stay in here."

His brows drew together in concern. "It's hot out there, *tesoro*."

"We'll sit beneath the umbrella. Besides, I'm fairly positive neither of us will try to throw the other one off the roof. I'm not so sure about the two of you."

* * *

When the door to the terrazzo closed, Nico turned to look at the man glaring at him so murderously. They'd been best friends once, almost like brothers, but they'd been enemies for so many years now that he remembered that time as if it had happened to someone else.

"Drink?" he said.

Renzo shook his head. Nico refilled his own and leaned against the bar. He waited for it to happen, waited for the storm brewing inside Renzo to break. The man might have promised his sister to talk, but that hadn't changed his view in the least.

"I can't believe you went after Tina," Renzo said, his voice low and hard. "She had nothing to do with what happened between us."

"No," Nico drawled, "she didn't."

"Yet it didn't stop you."

Suddenly, Nico was tired of this charade. He turned to glance out the window at Tina, who sat beneath the umbrella with her sister-in-law and cast worried glances toward the door. She was beautiful, fierce and lovely. Special.

She believed in him, and nothing he said or did had shaken that belief. He'd been expecting her to leave, to hate him, but she didn't. No, she followed him and confronted him and demanded he face his past head-on in order to free his future.

And he wanted to do it. For her, he would do anything.

Anything to see her smile, to have her in his bed beside him, soft and warm and sexy. He wanted her there, on her computer, making her stock trades and giving him hell. And he wanted to watch her grow big with their baby, knowing she loved this child so fiercely that she'd come to him in the first place so that her baby would have a father.

Their baby.

The feeling that had gripped him in the garden the other day seized him again. Only this time it wouldn't let go until he acknowledged it for what it was.

Love. He loved her, and it stunned him. He'd never loved anyone—or hadn't since he'd been a child and learned that loving your parents didn't mean they had to love you back.

He wanted to go to her, wanted to sweep her into his arms and tell her how he felt. She'd fought for him so hard, fought against him, too, when he'd tried to keep her at arm's length. She'd crawled beneath his defenses and curled up in his heart.

Nico turned back to face Renzo, his chest swelling with emotion. He didn't really care what this man thought of him—but he did care what Tina thought. And Tina loved her brother. He hoped like hell she loved him, too. Because he wasn't ever letting her go.

"I love her, Renzo." The words felt so foreign coming out of his mouth. So new. "I don't care if you believe that or not, but it's the truth. And I will do anything to make her happy. If that means talking to you, then I'll do it for as long as she wants me to."

Renzo looked taken aback. But then his eyes narrowed. "Why should I believe a word of what you say?"

Nico took a deep breath. "I don't care if you believe it. Whether or not you do doesn't change the truth of how I feel."

Renzo snorted. "My God, you're unbelievable. Somehow, you've got her believing the lies you spout. And don't think I don't know you're doing this to protect your company. I've heard whispers of your trouble.

You think the only reason I won't destroy you is because of my sister. Don't bet on it, Nico."

"You once said to me that the motorcycles weren't my passion as they were yours. You were right." He shrugged. "I enjoy what I do, but it's not my life. If you want to take it away from me to prove a point, then do it."

"You're bluffing."

Nico shook his head. "No. Not only that, but I'll also tell you exactly how to truly destroy me, if that's what you wish." He turned to look at Tina again, felt his heart swelling with feeling. "Take her away from me, Renzo. That's how to do it."

Renzo didn't say anything for a long moment. "If you're lying to me about this—" He broke off, swore.

"I don't want to fight with you anymore. I should have never gone to work for my father. I should have found another way. I should have blown up the plant before allowing the first motorcycle to come off the line, but I didn't. I've made mistakes. I regret them. But I won't let them harm the woman I love any longer."

Renzo looked fierce. "If you hurt her, I'll make you wish you were never born."

"If anything ever happens to Tina, you won't have to."

They didn't seem to talk for as long as she'd hoped, but they had at least spent twenty minutes together without either of them throwing a punch. Faith gave Tina a hug and said she'd call soon, and Renzo stood in the door looking more thoughtful than he had when he'd walked in earlier.

"*Ciao*, Tina," he said softly. And then he opened his arms and she went into them, relieved and shaken and so very grateful that he wasn't going to shut her out. He kissed her on the head. "If he makes you happy, then I am content."

"I'm sorry for causing you pain, Renzo. But I love you. And I love Nico, too."

Renzo squeezed her before setting her away from him. "We will see you soon, I hope? Domenico has grown. You will be very surprised when you see him."

Tina wiped her eyes as she laughed. "I look forward to it."

Renzo and Faith left then, and Tina turned around to look at Nico. But he wasn't standing by the terrace door any longer. He was outside, standing in the middle of the terrace, lost in thought.

She went out to him, her heart thrumming. She didn't doubt he was angry with her, but she hoped that, like Renzo, he would forgive her. She didn't think he and Renzo had solved their problems, but she hoped they might have at least managed a truce. One day, maybe, forgiveness would come for them both. But for now, she'd settle for them being together and not looking like two wolves circling for the kill.

The sun had dropped lower in the sky, and the shadows lengthened across the terrazzo. Across the way, she could see an old woman hanging washing on her balcony.

Nico turned, as if he could feel her approach. What she saw in his eyes made her heart skip a beat.

"I'm sorry, Tina," he said before she could say a word.

"For what? I'm the one who forced you to spend time with my brother."

He took a deep breath. "For leaving you. For doubting that you could believe in me. For everything."

"Hopefully not everything," she said lightly, trying to keep from throwing herself into his arms and begging him to love her the way she loved him.

Love would come in time, she was certain. She could be patient. She *would* be patient.

She took a deep breath. "I'd be grieved, for instance, if you said you were sorry for the way you can't keep your hands off me. Or if you said you were sorry you'd married me."

He shook his head. "I'm not sorry for that."

Then he reached out and tugged her into his arms, and relief melted through her.

"I'm not sorry for it, either." She sighed and pressed her cheek to his chest. "I'm going to prove to you that this can work between us."

He lifted a hand and pushed her hair from her face. "I already believe it."

She tilted her head back to look up at him, her entire body tensing with hope. "You do?"

His smile lit her world. "I love you, Tina. And I believe there's nothing you can't do when you set your mind to it."

Tina felt her jaw drop. "You love me? Really?"

"I do."

"Oh, Nico, I love you, too," she said, tears filling her eyes. Good heavens, these hormones were making her weepy.

"I know you do."

"But I've never said it. How did you know?"

He laughed, the sound breaking as if he, too, were feeling overwhelmed with emotion. "You stood up to your brother and told him you believed me. I think you even called him a fool." He kissed the tip of her nose. "I truly enjoyed that, by the way. But you've also defended me fiercely and never once backed down, not even when I tried to make you do so."

"Of course I did. I love you."

"Yes, that's what I thought. You'd either have to love me or be insane. I chose the option I most wanted."

She curled her fists into his shirt. "I used to want this when I was a girl, you know. You, me, marriage. But I didn't really know what any of that meant. I just knew that you were perfect and I wanted you to love me."

He shook his head. "I've never been perfect. But I'm going to try every day of my life to be the best man I can be. For you and our children."

Tina laughed, though a tear escaped and rolled down her cheek. "You already are the best man you can be, Nico. You always have been. And your best is pretty damn good."

He dipped his head and kissed her fiercely. "I want to shout it to the rooftops how much I love you. In fact...*I love Valentina D'Angeli Gavretti!*"

Across the way, the woman hanging laundry stopped. *"Brava, amore,"* she shouted back.

Others took up the cry until Tina was laughing and crying and trying to hide behind Nico. He took her hand and dragged her inside.

"I love you," he told her, his mouth against her skin, his fingers divesting her of her clothing. "I love you..."

Tina never doubted him for a moment.

EPILOGUE

TINA looked up from the computer screen when Nico walked in, holding their son in his arms. The baby's little head lolled against his father's chest as he fought sleep, and Tina's heart squeezed hard with love for her men.

"What are you working on?" he asked.

"The latest projections. I believe you're going to turn a profit, *caro*."

Nico dipped and kissed her on the forehead. "Thanks to you, my beautiful financial guru."

In the last year, they'd managed to infuse Gavretti Manufacturing with the cash it needed, sell off some of the Gavretti assets, and put the bulk of the estate back in the black. True to his word, Nico had put her to work right away in his accounting department—and he'd given her access to his entire fortune and all his business ventures. As a busy wife and mother, she often worked from home—and she loved what she did. Every day, she had her fingers in billions of euros worth of assets. And it felt damn good. She was proud of what she'd accomplished, and excited about what the future held.

"Faith called," she said as Nico bounced the baby. "They want us to come for dinner tomorrow."

"Then we shall go."

Tina smiled. It hadn't been an easy year for her brother and Nico, but they were learning to tolerate each other. Perhaps even to like each other again, though it was too soon to really know that for certain.

"I love you, Nico," she said, standing and hugging him and the baby both.

"You should," he teased. "Name another husband who would get up in the middle of the night to feed the baby while his wife slept."

She could think of a few—her brother most certainly, according to Faith—but she didn't say so.

"I think he's asleep," she murmured.

Nico looked down. "So he is."

They took him to his room and then lay him in the crib. Nico's fingers twined with hers as they stood there together and watched their son breathe.

"He is the most perfect thing I've ever done."

Tina slid her arms around him and kissed his jaw. "I'm sure I can think of one or two other things you do perfectly."

He turned until their bodies were melded breast to belly to hip, until she could feel the burgeoning evidence of his desire for her, until his lips slid along her throat and she gasped softly.

"Tell me what these things are," he whispered in her ear, "and I'll do them for you."

Tina shivered. "You might want to prepare yourself then," she said. "Because it's going to be a very long night."

He chuckled softly. "I'm counting on it, *amore mio.*"

* * * * *

INDEBTED
TO MORENO

KATE WALKER

For Alison and Malcolm, aka Malison—a fine poet
and my favourite Tech Support guy. With many
happy memories of Writers' Holidays and other events.

PROLOGUE

THE ALMOST FULL moon was burning cold and high in the darkness of the sky as Rose slipped out of the door, shutting it cautiously behind her. She winced inwardly as the battered wood creaked on rusted hinges, the sound seeming appallingly loud in the stillness of the night, and froze in a panic, waiting for someone to stir upstairs, to come after her as her stepfather had done on that day almost three months ago. But the house remained silent and still, apparently empty, though she knew that there were half a dozen or so figures hidden behind the filthy, cracked windows on the upper floors.

She had to be grateful for the moonlight that illuminated her way down the weed-clogged path towards the street. It helped make sure that she didn't stumble over the beer cans or plastic bags of rubbish that littered her way. But for the few minutes it took her to reach the road and scurry out of sight, panic screamed a need to run along her nerves fighting a vicious battle with the need to move carefully and avoid making a sound. At any moment she expected to hear movement behind her, the sound of a shout waking and alerting everyone in the squat.

And one dangerous person in particular.

Rose's heart clenched as she tried to pull her thoughts away from the man she was leaving behind. A man she had once seen as her rescuer, coming to her aid when she needed help most. The man she now had to leave behind or lose herself once and for all.

It was a bitter irony that she had once seen this squat in the abandoned shell of a once elegant town house as a sanctuary as she'd fled the unwanted attentions of her hated stepfather, only to find that she had well and truly jumped from the frying pan into the fire.

'Oh, Jett…'

The name slipped past her lips, and, despite everything she did to push them away, images slid into her mind. The picture of his long, powerful body lying on the dusty floor of the bedroom they had claimed as their own, his head with the overlong jet-black mess of hair pillowed on the olive-skinned arms in which he hid his face. He had always slept like that, even after they had made burning, passionate love, tumbling deep into sleep as if at the press of a button. But she knew that the appearance of deep slumber was a false impression. One awkward move, the faintest sound and he would jolt awake in a moment, coming upright and alert in the space of a heartbeat, every wary sense on high alert.

He'd stirred in his sleep as she'd left his side and only by murmuring something about needing to use the toilet had she persuaded him to let his head drop back onto his arms.

'Don't be long' had been the curt, brief command and although she'd known he couldn't see her she had shaken her head, letting the long fall of her bright red hair conceal her face.

'I won't be a minute,' she'd managed, knowing that he wouldn't take that the way she meant it. She was not going to be absent from his side for just a minute but for ever. This would be her one and only chance to get out of here before all hell broke out and she was going to snatch at that chance and run with it.

Yet even as she ran down the road there was a terrible tearing sensation inside her, in the region of her heart. A sense of loss and yearning for what she had thought she had, for what she'd dreamed of, that now, with a bitter realisation, she knew to have been a fake all the time.

If only... But there was no room, no time for 'if only'. There was no future for her with this man, the man she had been foolish enough to fall head over heels for, to give herself body and soul to until she had realised the truth about the sort of person he was.

She should have known he was no knight on a white charger when he'd, literally, picked her up off the street. But then she'd been so lost and alone that she'd been grateful for any help, caught up in the dark spell he had woven around her from the start. Now she could no longer ignore the evidence that told her that Jett was involved in the abominable trade of dealing illegal drugs. A trade that had resulted in the horror of the death of one of the other squatters. She shuddered fearfully just thinking of it.

Which was why she had to get out of here right now. She had to go as far and as fast as she could and never once look back.

The sound of cars coming down the road caught her ears. She knew why they were there. The police had acted on her information, and their approach meant that time really had run out for her.

Speeding up, she dashed away from the house that had been the only thing she could call home for the last few months, breath catching in her lungs as, skidding slightly, she whirled around the corner. Behind her, the convoy of police cars came into the street and pulled up sharply outside the door to the squat.

It was over. But the real truth was that it had never truly begun and her naïve foolishness had blinded her to the reality until it was almost too late.

CHAPTER ONE

NAIRO ROJA MORENO stepped out of the door of his private jet and frowned savagely as the icy blast of air and rain crashed into his face, making him blink hard against the cold.

'*Perdición!*' he swore, pulling up the collar of his jacket, the wind whipping the word from his lips and whirling it up into the steel-grey sky. 'It's raining!'

Of course it was raining. This was England, and it seemed that the weather had conspired to remind him just how much he loathed the place.

London, where he'd once thought his life might start afresh only to find that what was left of his heart had been taken and carelessly discarded without a second thought.

'*No.*'

He made his way down the steps, tossing back his hair in defiance at the weather. The memories that swirled in his thoughts had nothing to do with the temperatures, except for the fact that it had always been cold in that damn house. Cold and miserable except for the times that he had been able to persuade Red to join him in the tatty, inadequate sleeping bag.

Be honest. It wasn't the weather or the house that had got to him. It was the coldness of betrayal. The coldness of a heart he had once thought was warm and giving. Until she had left him with nothing when she had vanished out of his life and into the night.

Well, good riddance to her, he told himself, shaking off his memories in the same moment as he slid into the car that was waiting for him. He had had no inclination to go after her, and there had been no time to even consider it. He had been so occupied turning his life around and making his way back to his family—a reconciliation that she had almost destroyed by her actions—that she had been the last thing on his mind. He'd managed a second chance and he wasn't going to stuff it up. This trip to London would be the final part of the task he had set himself.

'Dacre Street,' he told the driver in response to the man's request for a destination. He could only hope the driver knew where the damn place was; it was in no part of the London he usually frequented.

Nairo settled back on the seat, frowning darkly as he raked his wet hair back from his face. He had to get into the city, do the job he'd come to do, keep his promise to Esmeralda. He had so much to make up to his sister and this one last thing to make her happy was what mattered. After this, his duty was done.

If there ever was a day when it was the worst possible moment for Louise to need to go home sick, then it had to be today, Rose told herself, sighing as she pushed back a floating strand of bright auburn hair that had escaped from the neat braid for the nth time. Obviously her normally efficient and organised assistant had been feeling worse than she had let on the previous day, if the state of the reception area was anything to go by. Everything needed tidying, and the diary that detailed today's appointments had been splashed with coffee, blurring the details.

Not that Rose needed any reminders. The appointment

had been made a week ago, the first contact being with a heavily accented voice on the other end of the phone. Nairo Roja Moreno's PA as she declared herself to be.

'Nairo Roja Moreno…' Rose murmured to herself as she considered the blurred words in the diary. The eldest son of an aristocratic Spanish family, his PA had informed her. And he wanted to talk to her about a wedding dress?

She'd meant to look up this Spaniard on the Internet last night, but her mother had been so unwell that it had taken all of her time and attention to get them both through the evening.

When she'd got the confirmation email she'd been overjoyed. It had seemed like a rescue mission arriving just in time. Caring for her mother through her illness had drained her resources, taken all her energy, mental and physical. She'd had no new commissions in an age. The mess of her marriage that had never been and the scandal that had followed it had seen to that. She was behind with the rent on the boutique, had barely been able to meet the costs of her flat. But if this Nairo Moreno really did want her to design his sister's wedding dress together with the bridesmaids' outfits, the flower girls and pageboys of which there seemed to be dozens, well, it might just save her from going under. Save her reputation publicly, save her life financially and perhaps even save her mother's life in reality.

Joy had endured a long and difficult battle with the cancer that had assailed her. She was weak and drained by chemotherapy, the operation, and was only just starting to recover. Any new shock, any extra stress might be dangerous, and, after all the time it had taken to rebuild their relationship from a perilously rocky point ten years before, Rose hated to think that everything could be destroyed now.

Her aristocratic visitor would be here any moment. Tapping her pen in a restless tattoo on the appointment book, Rose frowned as she looked out at the lashing rain that was splattering the plate-glass window of her design rooms. Not the best day to imagine a summer wedding.

Jett had hated the rain, particularly in the unheated squat. As a result, so many rainy days had been spent cuddled up together...

A rush of dark memories swamped her mind, loosening her grip so that the pen dropped from her hand, falling to the floor and rolling away under a display cabinet.

'Darn it!'

Getting down on her hands and knees, she groped in the darkness, fumbling for the pen just out of reach. It was then that she heard the door open behind her, the rush of cold damp air telling her that someone had come into the building from the street.

'Sorry! Just a moment.'

'De nada.'

It was the sexiest voice, deep and dark and so beautifully accented.

Of course! The Spanish aristocrat—what was his name? Nairo something. Suddenly becoming aware of the way she must look, bottom in the air, narrow skirt stretched tight, she made one final lurch, banging her head on the shelf before grabbing the pen, then turning to push herself upwards.

It *was* no problem to wait, Nairo reflected. He was perfectly happy to stay here and enjoy the spectacle of a deliciously rounded bottom stuck up in the air as its owner groped for something under the shelving. Folding his arms across his chest, he leaned back against the door feeling his pulse kick up and thud hard and heavy in his veins as he enjoyed the view before him.

If there was one thing he hadn't anticipated on this unwanted trip to England, then it was the possibility of indulging in a little sensual pleasure. There was so much to
be planned and organised back in Spain, with the demands
of his sister's soon-to-be in-laws to take into consideration,
that he had allowed himself only the freedom of a couple
of days away from the chaos and uproar that The Wedding
of the Century had created.

Now, with this tantalising display of female charms
on display before him, he allowed himself to reconsider.

It had been a long time—too long—since he had had
the pleasures of a woman in his bed. His father's final illness, the need for ferocious commitment to work on the
family estates, restoring the Moreno fallen fortunes, and
now, of course, Esmeralda's engagement and upcoming
wedding had ensured that he had had little time to breathe.

Suddenly the prospect of a few days' relaxation, even in
the grey, rainy city of London, had infinitely more appeal.

'Got it!'

The triumph in the woman's voice made him smile,
but it was a smile that leached from his lips as he saw her
lift her head.

Red hair. His personal curse. A bronze, auburn red it
was true, not the bright red that had been one of the glories
that he had so loved in the woman who had once filled his
days, haunted his dreams.

Red...

The echo of his own voice sounded inside his head as
memories threatened to surface. He had fought against
those memories, pushing them behind him as he set about
restoring his life to some degree of order and rebuilding
it from the mess it had become. The last thing he wanted
was the resurfacing of anything that connected him to the

time when he had lived in London in such very different circumstances.

Scarlett. It was the name of this shop—the designer that Esmeralda had sent him to find—that had put these thoughts in his mind.

'I'm sorry— I— Ouch!' The sharp cry of pain broke into his thoughts.

She had lifted her head rather too quickly in her triumph at having found whatever it was she was looking for and so had caught her face on the side of the shelf. Immediately he moved forward, holding out his hand to her.

'Allow me...'

That voice was designed to turn any woman to mush, Rose told herself. And the firm, warm grip of his hand was like touching a live wire, sizzling reaction sparking all along her arm.

'Th-thank you.'

The sharp bang on her forehead had brought tears to her eyes so that she was blinking hard to clear them as he swung her to her feet, the strength of the movement bringing her up and close to him. So close that she almost fell against him as she rocked on her toes before she managed to snatch back her balance and settle her feet on the floor.

She was assailed by a rush of heat from the closeness of a powerful male body, her senses tantalised by the heady combination of the musky scent of clean male skin, a sensual tang of some citrusy aftershave, all topped off with the fresh, wild trace of rain and wind that he had brought in from the street outside.

Suddenly, shockingly, all she could think of was one word, one man, one memory.

Jett... The word slammed into her mind without thought, without control.

No!

Why was she thinking of him? It was almost ten years since the night she had fled from the squat. A decade in which she had picked herself up, dusted herself off and built her life back up again. To the stage where this Spanish aristocrat was here today to discuss a commission to design a wedding dress for his sister.

A commission that she desperately needed. It would be the first time ever she had been asked to design a dress outside the small spread of the local area, unless you counted the dress that her friend Marina Marriot had worn just last month at her wedding to an up-and-coming actor.

'I'm fine now...'

She wished she didn't sound quite so breathless. Wished she had let go of his hand before this so that it didn't look quite so embarrassing as she had to ease her fingers from his.

'De nada.'

Again the sound of that sexy accent coiled around her, bringing memories of another man who had spoken with just that hint of an exotic pronunciation.

But there was no way that Jett would wear a suit like this one that made this man look so sleek and powerful and magnificent. That had to have been custom-made to flatter the powerful straight shoulders, the width of his chest and the lean length of his legs down to where his feet in polished handmade shoes were firmly planted on the tiled floor. Jett had never owned a suit. Like her, he had barely had a change of clothes. The tee shirt and jeans she wore as she fled from the house where the unwanted attentions of her stepfather had made sure it had never felt like a home being the only items that she'd had to drape over the door to what was laughingly called their bedroom.

Her eyes had cleared now and she was looking up into the carved, hard features of the most stunning man she had ever seen. Amber eyes framed with impossibly lush, black lashes burned down into hers. Hard bones shaped the lean cheeks, touched with a darkness of stubble even this early in the day. That mouth was an invitation to sin, warm, sensual, full lips slightly parted over sharp white teeth.

And she knew how that mouth felt, how it tasted…

She felt the world tilt on its axis, the room swinging round her.

'Jett…'

There was no holding it back this time. She didn't even try. It escaped on a breath that was all she could manage as she realised just who this man was.

A man who had once filled her days and haunted her nights. Even when she had run from him she had still taken him with her in her thoughts, her nights filled with memories that jolted her awake, left her drenched in sweat, her heart pounding. A man she had had to hand over to the police when she had learned the source of the money he had suddenly come into, then left to face the repercussions of his actions.

'Jett?' She heard him echo her response sharply, a frown snapping the black, straight brows together, cold eyes looking down into her upturned face.

Those amazing eyes narrowed, the beautiful mouth tightening as his head came up and he took a step back, away from her.

'Red… I didn't know *you* worked here.'

Worked here. Perhaps that was a score one to the fact that he really was here by accident. That he hadn't sought her out—because why would he do that after all this time? The thought didn't help with the thumping of her heart, the feeling like the beating of a thousand butterfly wings in the pit of her stomach. He hadn't come looking for her and it was all just a terrible misstep of fate.

But that dark emphasis on the word *you* twisted something in her guts, bringing home an awareness of the fact that she was all alone, not even Louise in the office, within call. Tension stiffened her back, tightened her shoulders.

'And I didn't know *you* worked for Nairo Moreno.'

That brought an unexpected twist to his mouth, the sensual lips twitching into something that could have been described as a smile but was totally without any warmth in it. His eyes seemed to impale her where she stood.

'Not worked…I *am* Nairo Moreno. I came here to see Ms Cavalliero. Oh—what, my darling Red…?'

The smile grew wider, darker.

'Did you think I was here to see you? That I would have hunted you down after all this time, determined to find you?'

She had actually considered that fact, Nairo told himself. It was written all over her beautiful face. The young girl he had once known as 'Red' had always held the promise of being a looker, but he had never anticipated her growing into the sleek, sexy vision who stood before him.

That pert bottom that had caught his attention from the start was only a small part of a slim, shapely figure displayed to full advantage in the cream lace blouse and navy blue, clinging skirt. The hair that had once been the vivid, vibrant colour that gave her her nickname was now a more subtle auburn shade, still with the glint of red blending in with the glossy darker tones. Those almond-shaped, slightly slanting hazel eyes were even more feline than before when accentuated with the subtle use of cosmetics that she would never have been able to afford back then.

A swift, sharp inward shake of his head broke the train of his thoughts, dragging them back from the path down which they had wandered.

She was the last thing he wanted in his world right now.

Hadn't she come close to ruining his life all those years before? Ten years younger, and a lifetime more naïve, he had risked losing everything for the sake of a few short nights of heedless passion. He had even, foolishly, blindly, come close to giving her a piece of his heart. Only to discover that he had been nothing to her when the promise of a reward for information had more appeal instead.

'It's taken me rather a long time—don't you think? Ten years. So why should I suddenly turn round and want to see you again? You can relax about that, *Red*—I am not looking for you but for your boss.'

'My boss?'

'*Sì*. Ms Rose Cavalliero. The owner of this business, and the designer of...'

An autocratic wave of his hand indicated the two beautiful dresses displayed on mannequins in the corner of the room. Of course, Rose realised, he was here to discuss the design of his sister's wedding dress. But the realisation that he still thought she was only the receptionist, that he hadn't put two and two together to recognise that the 'Scarlett' in her business name was in fact her, was in no way eased by the thought of that commission he'd come to discuss.

Oh, no, no! She couldn't work for him. She wouldn't do it. OK, so it might mean a real coup for her business. A boost to her reputation that would be of immeasurable value. But would it be worth it?

All the money in the world couldn't compensate for spending time with Jett—with this Nairo Moreno as he now called himself. Even if he hadn't come looking for revenge, it was obvious that he could barely bring himself to be polite to her.

But how could she get out of it?

'So where is she?'

The question came coldly, curtly, and seeing the hard set of his face Rose was swamped by a rush of cold unease.

To see the smoulder of dark anger in his eyes made her feet feel unsafe on the floor, her mouth drying sharply. If only she had known who this Nairo Moreno really was, then she would never have agreed to meet him today.

But of course he didn't realise exactly who she was. He still believed that she was only the receptionist. For a second the desire to put him in his place by pointing out that she owned the whole establishment and was the designer he had said he so wanted to meet warred with a sense of self-preservation. What she really wanted was to get rid of him before he brought his malign influence back into her present as he had done to her past.

'She couldn't be here. Her mother isn't well.'

Well, that was true enough. And the closer she could get to the truth with this man, the less likely she was to give herself away.

'She didn't think to send a message to let me know?' The anger was there now, in a frigid form. 'That's hardly good business practice.'

'It—it was an emergency. She got called away unexpectedly.'

'I see.'

His tone said the exact opposite as he pushed back the immaculate white cuff of his shirt and checked the time. On the sort of platinum watch that the man she had once known could never have afforded.

Unless of course… The coldness at her spine turned into a slow, icy creeping sensation that made her remember just why she had had to run out on him, the darkness of the world that she had discovered she had fallen into.

'I'm sure she'll be in touch…'

When she had some excuse ready. Some reason why

she couldn't take on his commission. She'd think of something when she wasn't faced with telling it to him in person. Right now, all she wanted was for him to get out of her life and stay out. For good this time.

'I'll be waiting for her message.'

The dark thread of anger that laced the statement turned it into an unspoken threat, making her heart clench painfully so that she had to struggle to draw her next breath.

'I'll tell her.' Embarrassingly it was a revealing squeak.

Unable to meet those coldly assessing eyes, Rose hurried to the door, deliberately moving so as not to risk touching him, or come within reach of one of those long-fingered hands that now rested lightly on the smooth leather belt that encircled his narrow waist. She didn't want to remember anything about the touch of those hands, and the thought of them coming anywhere near her again set the butterflies fluttering wildly in her stomach all over again.

'You do that.'

This was not at all how he had expected the day to go, Nairo reflected as he watched this new Red march to the door and yank it open, standing there stiff and taut, rejection in every inch of her slender body. The meeting with some society designer he had anticipated had not happened and instead he had found himself confronted by memories from his past stirring the silt in which he'd believed they were buried.

Forcing him to remember how this one slip of a girl had turned his life upside down, blackening his name just when he was fighting to win back his father's respect, and then walked out on him.

To remember how soft her skin had felt, the warmth of her body as she had curled up to him on the rough and ready 'bed' that had been all the furniture their room had possessed. He could still catch her unique, individual scent even if now it was hidden under some crisp fresh perfume and it awoke a hunger he had thought he'd forgotten. A hunger that he had spent the last ten years trying to obliterate. He'd indulged his masculine needs indiscriminately but never, it seemed, managed to wipe it out. Not if it could be woken again so fast and so easily.

'As soon as I see her,' Red came back at him with what was clearly a pointed reminder that she wanted him to leave. And it was because she so obviously wanted him gone that, perversely, he found himself lingering.

She felt it too, this disturbing hot flood of memories and awareness. It was there in her face, in the wide darkness of her eyes, the pupils distended until they almost obliterated the mossy softness of her irises. Her breathing was tight and unnatural and he could see the faint blue tinge under the pale skin at the base of her neck where a pulse beat, rapid and uneven. A kick of reaction hit him in the gut, keeping him where he was instead of leaving as she clearly intended he should.

'Is she always this unprofessional?' he asked icily, watching as her mouth quivered, then tightened again.

How was it possible that after all this time he could remember how that soft mouth had tasted, the warm yielding of those pink lips against his own?

'She…has so many demands on her time. More than she can cope with sometimes.'

'She's so busy she can risk losing an important commission?'

Rose flinched inside at the sharp stab of the challenge. Just moments ago she had thought of the Moreno commission as the chance of a lifetime, a rescue package that had landed on her desk wrapped in beautiful paper and tied with golden ribbon. But now it was as if she had opened that magical parcel only to find it filled with black, stinking ashes, with a deadly poisonous snake lurking at the bottom just waiting to strike.

She had to get out of this contract somehow, but for now she would settle for having Jett—or Nairo as it seemed she must call him—out of the shop, out of her space, to give her time to think about the way she could possibly deal with this without ruining her professional reputation once and for all.

'I can't tell you about that.' The fact that it was actually the most honest thing she had said gave a new strength to her voice. 'So, if you don't mind…I'd like you to leave now.'

His smile was dark, devilish enough to send shivers down her spine.

'But we've only just found each other again.' The mockery that lifted his tone had the sting of poison.

'Well, you obviously haven't missed me in the past ten years.'

No, that sounded too much as if she regretted it. The last thing she wanted was for him to think that *she* had missed *him*, even if it was true. But all her courage had seeped away, leaving her feeling weak and empty, genuinely afraid of what she might spark off if she challenged him too strongly.

'I wish I could say it's been a pleasure to see you again, but I'm afraid that just wouldn't be true. And I really must ask you to leave now. We have this event—a bridal fashion show—tonight. I have to get ready for that.'

That she wanted him to go wriggled under his skin and stayed there, irritating him furiously. She'd got under his skin in a very different way in the past. He had let her do things to his heart that he had never allowed any other woman—any other human being except perhaps Esmeralda—to do to him before or since. But now that they had met up again, all that she wanted was to be rid of him as soon as possible.

The temptation to dig his heels in and refuse to move at all almost overwhelmed him. But a moment's thought left him realising that he didn't have to tackle this right now. Not yet. He knew where Red was; she wasn't going anywhere. He could afford the time to wait and discover rather more about her, and then he would act in the way that would give him the best satisfaction possible.

Shaking her life right to the roots just as she had done to his when she'd walked out on him, leaving behind a mess it had taken years to sort out.

A curt nod was his only response to her pointed remark. It amused him to see the way her shoulders dropped slightly in relief, the easing of the tension about her mouth as she believed that she had got rid of him.

'You'll tell Ms Cavalliero that *I* kept our appointment? And I expect to meet up with her at her earliest convenience.'

Left to himself he'd dispense with the designer and her frills and fancies and go straight to the result he most wanted—the settling of the score he had with the woman he'd only ever known as Red. But he'd promised Esmeralda and he wasn't prepared to take any risks with his sister's health that not keeping that promise might result in.

So he'd see to this damn dress—the dress of his sister's dreams—first. And then he'd deal with Red. He'd waited nearly ten long years already. He reckoned he could wait a little while longer.

The burn of his memories suddenly flamed up again, hot and hard, as he saw the way that she stood at the door, stiff-shouldered, taut-backed, her chin lifted in a sign of defiance. There was a flare of awareness in those mossy-golden eyes that pushed him just too close to the edge of the restraint he was holding so tight.

His feet came to a sudden halt, not letting him move forward. He caught her swiftly indrawn breath, noted the extra tension in every muscle that held her slim frame tight, drew in her stomach and lifted the swell of her pert breasts above the embroidered belt that circled her waist.

'Red…'

If only he knew how much she hated that once affectionate nickname! That focussed stare held her transfixed, unable to look away in spite of the fact that she felt as if his gaze were searing through her skin, burning her eyes to dust. Slowly he lifted a hand, touched her face, the blunt tips of his long fingers resting so lightly on the cheekbone under her right eye.

'I never thought I'd see you again,' he said flatly. 'It's been…interesting…meeting up like this.'

'*Interesting*—that isn't the word I'd use to describe it.' *Devastating*, *earth-shaking*, came closer. So many times in the past she'd dreamed of just this meeting happening— and dreaded it in the same moment.

'But I need to tell you. I am not the man that I was.'

'I can see that. That is, if Moreno is really your name,' she challenged.

'Jett was only ever a nickname. Moreno is my family name, though I didn't use it then—before.'

Abruptly his mood changed, his eyes becoming darker.

'They let me go, you know,' he said. 'There was no evidence against me.'

The conversational tone of his voice was at odds with what she read in the taut muscles of his face. Just how had Jett become this Nairo Moreno?

The man who stood before her was light years away from the wild, rough-haired youth she had once known.

The one who had stolen her heart only to break it just a few weeks later, crushing it brutally under his booted foot. Was he the member of a Spanish aristocratic family he claimed to be or—that nasty slimy feeling slithered down her spine again, making her shiver—had his obvious wealth and position been bought with the proceeds of other activities in the years since they had known each other? There might have been no evidence of the crime she'd suspected him of, but he had clearly come a long way in ten years and that spoke of a ruthlessness and focus that few men possessed.

Something she didn't want to dig into too deeply. And a very good reason to get out of the contract to design a dress for anyone in his family if she possibly could.

'You will not tell anyone about the time we knew each other.'

It was a cold-blooded command, laced through with a powerful seam of threat, a warning as to what would happen if she was fool enough to reveal anything he wanted kept hidden.

'Not even Ms Cavalliero.'

'I doubt if she'd need to know.' Not when she already knew every dark detail about Nairo Roja Moreno. And wished she didn't. 'I certainly won't be telling.'

'Make sure you don't.'

The finger that rested on her cheek traced a slow, gentle path down the line of her jaw, to rest against the corner of her mouth, hooded eyes watching every flicker of expression across her face.

It was all that Rose could do not to turn her head sharply, pull away from that small, lingering touch. She wanted to move, desperately longed to back away, and yet at the same time that simple touch was so familiar, bringing back memories of the feel of his hands on her skin, the taste of his mouth…

She couldn't go there. She *mustn't* go there!

'Take your hand off my face.' She hissed the words out as much against the feelings that were stinging her as at him. 'I didn't give you permission to touch me and I…'

She couldn't continue in the face of his unexpected soft laugh and the way that he deliberately twisted his hand so that the backs of his fingers were now against her skin. Deliberately he stroked his fingers down her cheek again.

'I said don't do that!' This time she couldn't hold back and jerked her head away in angry rejection.

His laughter scoured her spine, but he lifted his hand slowly, bronze eyes gleaming with wicked mockery.

'My, you do have a tendency to overreact, *querida*. It didn't use to be that way. I can recall a time when you would beg for my touch.'

'Then you must have an amazing memory. It was a very long time ago.'

'Not long enough,' Nairo drawled, the smile evaporating fast. 'Some things you just don't forget.'

'Really? Well, I'm afraid my recollection isn't as good as yours—and it's certainly not something I want to revive.'

Making the movement look as if she were only wanting to ease his departure, she slipped away from him, holding open the door again.

'I'll pass on your messages.'

The words showed every trace of the effort she was making to get them out, fighting against giving in to the burning response even that most gentle of touches was sparking off all over her skin. One flick of a glance up at him was more than she could cope with. She could see herself reflected in those burnished eyes, small and diminished in a way that made her legs feel weak as cotton wool.

'I'll tell her—everything you said.'

'Except that you knew me before.'

How did he manage to inject such deadly poison into six simple words? The stepfather she had run from in a flight that had ended up with her living in the squat might have ranted and roared, bellowing threats, but he had never managed to make her quail inside in the way that this quietly spoken command could do.

'Except for that,' she managed jerkily.

For another dangerous moment his fingers still lingered too close to her face, but then, just as she thought that she couldn't keep control any longer, he lifted his hand away and let it drop to his side. The smile that he flashed on and off was like burning ice, no emotion at all in it.

'See you around, Red.'

'Not if I see you first.'

The words were muttered to an empty space. He'd gone, striding out into the darkness and the rain without a single glance back. It was as if defiance of his presence was all that had been holding her upright as she sagged back against the wall and let the door slam back into place.

He was gone. And she was free, safe—for now.

But it was only a temporary reprieve. There was no way she could hold off having Jett—in the form of Nairo Moreno—back in her life while he still wanted to see Rose Cavalliero. Right now he had no idea that *she was* the Rose he'd come to talk to, but she couldn't hope to let that last for very much longer. He would put two and two together, and when he did, then he would be back.

She had to get rid of him; she couldn't cope with him intruding into her life. Not just because of the past but because of the shocking effect he still had on her today.

Slowly her hand crept up to her face, covering the spot where Nairo's fingertip had touched her. She almost expected it to have etched a brand into her skin, marking her as his. He had done that long ago, hadn't he? He had touched her life and encircled her with bands of emotional and sexual steel so that she had never been able to break free. Even now, all these years later, he could still invade her life and if she wasn't careful he would leave it in ruins all over again.

CHAPTER TWO

HE SHOULD NEVER have let himself touch her.

Nairo slid his car into the nearest empty parking space, stamped on the brakes with uncharacteristic lack of care and switched off the engine. His concentration had been shot all afternoon, in a way so untypical of him that it felt as if he was teetering on the edge of a form of madness. The tips of his fingers still seemed to burn with the imprint of that touch, the connection of skin on skin, even though it was hours since he had walked out of the shop and left Red behind. He was sure that if he brought his hand close to his face he would still inhale the perfume of her skin, the fresh, unique combination that was this woman mixed with the light floral scent she had worn.

Or perhaps that was because the cloud of her personal body perfume seemed to enclose him ever since he had re-alised just who she was. It had been like that after they had first become lovers. In the squat she had always washed every day, even in the freezing water that was all they had available, and the scent of her skin had been the only thing that was fresh or clean in the grubby little room that they had called 'home'.

Waking up each morning to find her curled against him, the soft hair, longer and redder than she wore it now, falling over her face, had made him feel as if life was worth living at a time when he had had serious doubts on that matter.

She'd had her own problems too. Running from an aggressive and abusive stepfather, a mother who had been too weak to protect her, she had still given him a reason to wake up—if only because waking up usually meant another opportunity to take her in his arms, and give in to the heated passion that burned into his soul every time he touched her.

He had even thought about changing his life for her.

'Change—for her—hah!'

The words punched into the air as he pushed open the door to the hall where the wedding fayre was being held, the violence of the movement expressing the way the memories burned like acid.

He had thought about change—had even taken the first steps towards it—and she…she had just walked out on him, never looking back. She'd also added an extra little sting to her departure that had come close to ruining every chance he had had of rebuilding what was left of his relationship with his family.

The burn of that memory almost had him turning and marching right back out again. He wanted nothing to do with Red—and yet he couldn't get her out of his mind. Her betrayal, her desertion, demanded some sort of retribution and yet he had no wish to tangle himself up with her all over again. He had just about found peace after ten years' hard work. Did he really want to stick his head right back in the lion's mouth and risk it all over again?

But the promise he had made to Esmeralda held him prisoner. He had sworn he would bring her this designer she had set her heart on, and he was not going back on his word. Only with that contract secured and his sister happy would he consider just how he would deal with Red.

The sound of the buzz of many voices from the end of the corridor told him just where the event was being held and had him heading towards the glass-paned door.

The noise of conversation hit him along with a strong wave of perfume—a heady mixture of so many different fragrances. The room was full of women of all ages, shapes and sizes. There were flowers everywhere too, and a small runway set up in the centre of the hall with a white floor, leading to a fall of heavy velvet curtains in rich red. The colours of the flowers, the curtains, the women's dresses and suits whirled and blurred into a kaleidoscopic haze.

'And now, ladies, we have a special treat for you...'

The voice was immediately familiar and Nairo cursed under his breath. Because there she was again. The woman he had known as Red.

If he had felt that she had grown into a beautiful woman when he had first seen her in the boutique, then this was even worse. Now she was groomed, and sleek, elegant in a silky peacock-blue shift dress, simple and sleeveless, that clung lovingly all the way from the softly scooped neck, over the curves of breasts and hips to end just above her knees and reveal a heart-jolting slender length of leg. The ridiculously high-heeled shoes were exactly the same colour as the dress, except for a perky little white bow at the toe. The whole effect had him clenching his hands into tight fists and pushing them deep into the pockets of his trousers as he fought with his immediate and primitive response.

He'd thought he'd put her out of his mind. He'd tried his damnedest to do just that, but it had taken only one look, one touch, and it had become obvious just why he'd been hooked in that way. She'd had the power to entrance him as a skinny girl and now she'd grown up, matured, he was swamped by a hunger he hadn't felt before or since. Then he'd been naïve enough to label it with a softer emotion because then he'd been fool enough to believe that emotion existed. He'd soon learned his lesson.

Now was not the time he wanted to remember how he had once been able to hold one slender foot in his hand, lift it to his mouth and kiss it from the long, delicate toes all the way up to where her legs disappeared under her skirt…

…and beyond.

Infierno! He could feel an unwanted heat flooding his body, hardening him and making his heart pulse in a hungry response to the erotic memory that had him in its grip. Violently he shook his head to drive it away and only succeeded in drawing the attention of the women closest to him. Their expressions of surprise and the widening of their eyes a sure giveaway of how unexpected his presence was, here in this ultra-feminine environment.

Nairo ruthlessly determined to ignore them—he had no interest in any woman here except for Red—and the important designer, wherever she was. He pointedly directed his gaze towards the runway, and the woman on it, her auburn hair gleaming glossily under the spotlight.

He watched Red lift the microphone again and announce, 'As I said—a real treat—for the first time ever an exclusive preview of my brand-new designs for spring.'

My.

The word exploded inside Nairo's head, battering at his thoughts. *My brand-new designs…*

Of course—he'd been a complete fool. How could he have not realised? It had all been there in front of him, but he had been so set on his mission for Esmeralda—and so stunned to find himself face-to-face with Red after all these years—that his intelligence had failed him and he hadn't made the connections that he should have done.

Red. *Scarlett.* The name written above the window of

the small boutique. And the designer's name was Rose Cavalliero.

Rose red. *Scarlett*.

The velvet curtains had opened and a model had emerged from behind them, walking up the runway, her progress marked by gasps of delight and admiration. She was a willow-slim beauty, and the dress she was wearing was a masterpiece of lace and silk, a fairy-tale wedding gown.

But he spared it only one brief glance. There was no space in his mind to focus on anything but the woman who stood on the side of the runway, microphone in hand, talking about trains, beading, boned bodices…

All he could think was that *she*—Red—was also Rose Cavalliero—

Scarlett's talented designer—the one his sister dreamed of having to create a dress for her upcoming wedding.

The woman he had once known as Red was the woman he had come to London to meet—and to persuade her to come back to Spain with him.

Suddenly the room that had already felt so alien to him in its total focus on femininity, the overwhelming reek of clashing perfumes, seemed to constrict around him, the lights dimming. It couldn't be any further from the rooms in his father's home where he had lived as a boy. The old-fashioned high-walled castle so wrongly named Castillo Corazón—the castle of the heart! But the feeling of being trapped was just the same.

As an adolescent, he had felt this sensation of being cornered when his new stepmother had insisted that he meet all her female friends—the wives or daughters of acquaintances, some of whom had once been or still were his father's mistresses. They had almost mobbed him, circling round him like brightly painted predators. He had learned fast and young to recognise when someone was genuine and when they were fake.

Or he'd thought he had.

He hadn't recognised the secrets behind Red's green eyes. And he had known the slash of betrayal when he had found out the truth.

'And perhaps for an older bride, this elegant look…'

The clear, confident voice carried perfectly, no real need for the microphone, but it was not the woman on the runway whom Nairo was seeing. Instead it was the woman he had met in the boutique that morning.

Hell, she'd still deceived him even then. She had known who he was, known that he had come to see *her*, and yet she had let him linger in his belief that she was just the receptionist and that Rose Cavalliero was someone else entirely.

She had had the opportunity to tell him the truth then, but she hadn't taken it. Instead she had dodged the issue, kept it to herself, and then she'd dismissed him once again in a brief and curt email.

Scowling, Nairo remembered the message that had reached him in his suite just an hour and a half ago. Rose Cavalliero was sorry, but she was afraid that she couldn't manage to fit in a meeting with him after all. She apologised for the inconvenience, but the truth was that she wasn't taking on any more commissions at the moment. She was sorry that he had been inconvenienced in coming to London for nothing, but she needed to take time to care for her mother…

Coldly polite but dismissive. All of which could only mean that she had something to hide.

'And this is the highlight of the Spring Collection. I've named it the Princess Bride.'

Perhaps it was the name, perhaps it was the sound of the

murmurs of appreciation that flowed around the room, but something made Nairo look up to see yet another model emerging from behind the scarlet curtains.

In that instant he knew just why Esmeralda had been so insistent that this particular designer should create her dress. If she could make these women—every one of them—look so stunning, then what would she do for his sister? She would turn his shy, uncertain sibling into a glorious beauty—the princess she was meant to be—and surely that would give Esmeralda the confidence to face up to Duke Oscar's critical and demanding family without making herself ill again. And that was what he owed to his sister.

A memory stirred in his mind. The image of Esmeralda when he had come back from Argentina, where his father had sent him as penance for his adolescent rebellion. His sister had always been slim, but then she had been frail and delicate as a tiny bird. He'd even been afraid to hug her in case she might break. It had torn at his conscience to realise that the truth was that she was suffering from anorexia. It had taken him months to encourage her to let go her hold on her appetite and eat.

There and then he'd vowed that he would never let her down again. That he would do whatever it took to make her happy—keep her healthy and strong. To do that he now had to bring Rose Cavalliero back with him. Even if she had turned out to be the woman he had known all those years ago.

And when he had Red—or Rose or whatever her name was—in the castle in Andalusia, then he could tie up all the loose ends that were left hanging from when they had been together before. He would get rid of this unwelcome desire that still made him burn for her and he would teach her how it had felt to be the one cast aside when something better presented itself.

Leaning back against the wall, he folded his arms and prepared to wait and watch until it was time to talk to her.

Rose had been so focussed on the fashion show and making sure that everything ran smoothly that she had had no time at any point to actually look up and take notice of the crowd. But now, with the last dress displayed and the final parade of models down the runway, she could relax and look up, take a breath, glance out across the room…

And that was when she saw him.

Apart from the fact that Nairo Moreno was the only male in the room, it was impossible to miss him. He was leaning against the wall, arms folded, dressed all in black, with his shirt open loose at the neck. Like a big dark bird of prey amongst a flock of gaudy, chattering parrots. The burn of his golden-eyed stare was like a laser beam coming across the room.

He must have read the email she'd sent trying to get out of the commission he wanted. She'd asked for a receipt, so she knew he'd opened it. But he had determined to ignore it. She'd tried to avoid telling him who she was—who the designer Rose Cavalliero really was—but it seemed she'd failed miserably. Because now he was here—waiting, watching like some dark sentinel at the door.

'Rose!'

'Ms Cavalliero!'

Belatedly becoming aware of the way that she had been standing, silent and stunned, while her audience grew restless, Rose blinked hard, clearing her eyes of the haze of panic that had blurred her vision and forced herself to focus. At the front of the audience were the special guests, the reporters who had been invited specially in the hope of giving the new collection a great opening. That even more hopefully would lead to the sort of sales that would save her business, pay the rent for another twelve months. Give her mother a place to live and rest as she recovered from the draining bouts of chemotherapy. They'd only just found each other again properly; she couldn't bear it if their time together was so short.

Dragging her gaze away from the dark figure at the door, she switched on what she hoped was a convincing smile as she turned her attention to the first reporter to get to her feet—a well-known fashion writer for a luxury magazine.

'Do you have a question?' she managed. 'I'm happy to answer...'

'I'm glad to hear that.'

It wasn't the fashion reporter who spoke but another woman, a blonde she hadn't spotted before. Rose's heart sank. She knew this woman and so what was coming.

'Don't you think it's something of an irony, the fact that you are publicising your new collection now—with images of love and happy-ever-afters—when your own story is so very different?'

The bite in her voice was unmistakeable, sharp as acid. Rose recognised her as Geraldine Somerset, a person she had seen at one of Andrew's parties. The woman everyone had expected to be his fiancée before he'd met Rose.

'I don't know what you mean.'

'Oh, I'm sure you do.'

Geraldine lifted a newspaper that had been lying on her chair. Rose had no need to see it to know that it was a notorious scandal rag. She also knew just what headline the woman wanted everyone to see. Geraldine unfolded the sheet to its full length, waved it above her head, turning so that everyone could read the banner headline: *'Dream-maker or dream-breaker?'*

Rose even knew what pictures went with that story. How could she not when a copy of just that paper had been pushed through her letter box less than a week ago? On one side of the text was a picture of Andrew, head down, frowning and glum. The other was a picture of Rose herself, striding into her boutique—the name Scarlett perfectly clear and in focus. It had been taken shortly after the news of the broken engagement, the cancelled wedding, had hit the fan.

'Would you want to buy your wedding dress from a woman who only cancelled her own marriage just three days before the ceremony?' Geraldine was demanding now. 'Would you entrust the most important day of your life—or your daughter's—to someone who had so little care about her fiancé that she left him broken-hearted practically at the altar?'

'That isn't the way it was...' Rose protested, only to have the newspaper waved even more violently in rejection of her words.

'"Dream-maker or dream-breaker?"' Geraldine declared, clearly very proud of the headline it was obvious she had created.

It was equally apparent that she was having the effect she wanted. The whole mood of the evening had changed. The murmurs of appreciation and approval that had marked the end of the fashion show had now changed to darker, more critical comments. Already people were pushing back their chairs, getting to their feet.

'This has nothing to do with my work!' Rose tried, but it was like Canute asking the sea to go back. Everything had changed and Geraldine, with her emotive headline, the carefully slanted photographs, had turned the tide of opinion.

Rose had forgotten that Nairo Moreno was here. That he was watching all this.

The moment the thought had crossed her mind she lost her concentration as she flicked a hasty, nervous glance to where Nairo leaned against the wall by the door. Or rather, where Nairo had been leaning. Even as she watched she saw his eyes narrow sharply, the beautiful, sensual mouth tighten until it was just a thin, hard line. The frown that snapped his black brows frankly terrified her.

Not meeting her eyes, his gaze fixed on the scene before him, he levered himself up from his position and stood tall and dark and powerful as he surveyed the room.

'The woman's bad luck—she taints everything she touches.' Geraldine was getting into full flow again, her voice rising to almost a screech, the newspaper flapping wildly as she waved it high. 'I mean—who would want *her* to design a dress...?'

'I would.'

Cold and clear, the response cut through the buzz of outrage and comment that had filled the room. The silence that fell was as if a huge blanket had been dropped over everyone, stifling any sound. The audience stilled too, as Nairo moved forward, his movements the dangerous prowl of a predatory wild cat. A path opened up to let him through and even Geraldine froze to the spot, her words deserting her as he came closer.

Rose couldn't blame her. Seen like this, Nairo Moreno was the sort of man who could suck all the air out of a room simply by existing. She found herself struggling to breathe, waiting and watching...

'I said *I would*.'

Nairo had reached Geraldine's side now and he snatched the newspaper away from her, sparing it only the briefest, iciest glance before he crushed it brutally in one hand

and tossed it aside, contempt in every inch of his powerful body.

'I would have Miss Cavalliero design a dress for someone I loved. Anyone with eyes to see would do the same—
wouldn't you?' he challenged, his fierce gaze raking over
the rest of the audience. 'Anyone but a fool could see that
as a designer Miss Cavalliero is hugely skilled. As a man,
I'm no expert in fashion…'

Rose watched in amazement as he actually shrugged
his shoulders in a gesture of assumed self-deprecation.

It had to be assumed, didn't it? Even as the Jett she'd
known he wouldn't willingly admit to any sort of weakness in his own make-up. But the gesture had worked.
The women surrounding him had actually smiled. Some
of them were nodding.

'But even I can see that these dresses are works of art.'

He had the room in the palm of his hand, Rose realised.
He was turning the tide of disapproval that Geraldine had
threatened to direct against her.

'Miss Cavalliero…'

Nairo had moved closer, was holding out a hand to her.
For the space of a dazed heartbeat she stared at it, only
realising after a moment that he meant to help her down
from the runway, onto the floor of the main ballroom.

She needed that help. Needed the support of his strength
and the warm power of that hand. But even as his grip
closed over her fingers, she knew a sudden stunning
change, felt the sting of burning electricity fizz through
her so that the hold she took on him was more than to get
down the steps to the floor. It was like being taken back in
years, to the days when she had been just a stupid, crazy,
hormone-ridden teenager and she had first met Jett. Back
to the days when she had given him her heart, her soul,

her virginity. And he had only to touch her to send her up in flames.

From being cold with shock, she was now burning with response and could feel the colour heating her cheeks.

'Now can we talk about the dress you will create for my sister?'

Rose knew that everyone was watching, that she was the focus of all eyes, and she knew there was only one answer she could give. He had saved her reputation, her business, and the slam of the door told its own story: that Geraldine had conceded defeat and was on her way out of the room, out of the building—please heaven, out of her life.

She had caught that firm and deliberate emphasis on the word *now* even if no one else had. He knew she had tried so hard to get out of the commission he had proposed. The commission that would mean she would have to work with him, for him, all the time she was planning the dress for his sister. At least it was not for his *bride*.

But she'd been here once before, when Nairo had seemed to be her saviour and turned out to be a threat of danger she had barely escaped. So now had she been rescued or entrapped? Was he offering her freedom and a new security or had he actually caught her tight in some carefully planned and deliberately achieved spider's web? Did he really just want her to design a dress for his sister or was there more to his intervention than that?

Right now it seemed that he was her saviour—at least that was what everyone else would think. And because of everyone else, all those eyes on her, she knew she had no option but to give him the response he wanted.

'Miss Cavalliero?'

The prompt sounded easy, almost gentle, but she had regained enough composure to look into his eyes and easy and gentle were not what she saw there.

What she saw was ice, resolve and the sort of ruthless determination that warned her that if she didn't do as he wanted, then he was more than capable of turning this apparent rescue mission into one of total, devastating destruction.

She had been offered a lifeline as long as she went along with what Nairo Moreno wanted. Her life had been full of problems before, but now it seemed that by escaping one set of difficulties she had landed herself with a whole new adversary. One who she suspected was much more formidable than anyone she'd come up against before.

Out of the frying pan and into the fire. But what else could she do?

'Of course, Señor Moreno...' She forced her stiff lips into what must have looked like the most wooden and unbelievable of smiles. 'I'd be happy to discuss your commission with you.'

CHAPTER THREE

NAIRO MIGHT HAVE said that he wanted to discuss the design for his sister's wedding dress, but he showed no inclination to deal with that business right then and there. Instead he waited, smiling, courteous—apparently patient—while Rose spoke to the women who wanted to talk to her about designing their dresses, or their daughters'. The endorsement that Nairo Moreno had given her was apparently enough to convince them that Scarlett was the designer that everyone wanted now.

Which was not surprising really, Rose admitted to herself. After all, as she had discovered earlier in a quick, mind-blowing search on the Internet, the wedding that he was organising for his sister was to be the society event of the year. Esmeralda Roja Moreno was to marry into powerful Austrian aristocracy, it seemed. Duke Oscar Schlieburg was the eldest son of Prince Leopold of Magstein and his wedding was to be almost a state occasion. Her head was spinning simply at the thought of the boost of publicity and the prestige that would come to her business as a result of her involvement with such an event.

A boost that had already started, it seemed, as she collected up the lists of names and addresses of all the potential new customers she'd gained.

'That seemed to be a success,' Nairo's cool voice drawled as the last customer went out the door.

'Success is an understatement.'

Her response came faintly. She had been so absorbed in the matter in hand that she hadn't really been aware of the fact that he had been there all the time, a silent observer, sitting on the edge of the runway, his long black-clad frame standing out so starkly from the white and silver décor. She'd been fooling herself, of course, if she'd let herself think that he had gone. He had set this response in progress with his intervention for his own personal reasons, and now he was going to claim what he felt he was owed.

A chill breeze seemed to blow across Rose's skin as he dropped down from his place on the runway and started towards her and she wished everyone hadn't left her quite so alone.

'Th-thank you for your help. I really appreciate it.'

His dark head nodded, bronze eyes hooded to hide any emotion he might feel.

'There is a price for my assistance.'

Of course there was. This was Nairo Moreno she was dealing with now. A man who had somehow built himself up from the shabby, broken beginnings of their lives when they had first met and who now was this powerful, wealthy man. There had to be a price on anything he did. He was no longer Jett, the youth she had run out on so long ago.

'A price?'

'Oh, don't look so panicked,' he mocked as she turned uncertain eyes on him. 'I'm not going to demand your body in return for my favours in some odd modern version of *droit du seigneur.*'

He paused just long enough for her skin to smart under the bite of his mockery.

'There wouldn't be much point, would there? After all, *we've* already been there, haven't we, *querida*?'

The pointed reminder that they had once been lovers, that he had been the one to take her virginity all those years before, drained the strength from her muscles, making her grab at a nearby chair for support. An innocence that then she had relinquished happily and unhesitatingly, she had been so much under the sway of the heated hunger she had known for this man, blinded to anything but her need for him.

'Been there, done that—didn't bother to stay around to get the tee shirt,' she flashed at him, then immediately regretted her too-aggressive tone.

He might have stepped in to save her business earlier this evening, but what he had decided so surprisingly to give her, he could take away in the blink of an eye. Just as so many new customers had followed his lead to want to use her services, they could easily follow him *away* from her again if he chose to reject her after all.

She must not forget that she was no longer dealing with the Jett of ten years before. This man was a very different sort of male. Tall and powerful, his broad frame had filled out and strengthened where Jett had had a whipcord leanness that had been defined even further by the fact that there was never quite enough to eat in the squat.

Added to that he was someone else entirely—a man of status, with power and money no object. He had a sister who was marrying into the aristocracy and an estate which, if the Internet reports were to be believed, was more than the equal of his prospective in-laws. How he had come by that she had no idea; she didn't want to think about it too closely. She had bitter memories of the appalling ways he had planned on acquiring more money ten years before. But it all added up to someone who was light years away from the scrawny, long-haired Jett she had once believed herself in love with.

Thank heaven she was well over that particular nasty infection! But the scars the past had left on her soul reminded her that she would do best to play this particular game very carefully. Every instinct warned her that Nairo Moreno played to win and that he would prove a spectacular opponent if she was foolish enough to challenge him too far.

'*Querida...*' she echoed cynically. 'How come you're suddenly living in Spain and tossing about Spanish endearments?'

'Not suddenly,' Nairo corrected flatly. 'I always did live in Spain—or, rather, my family home was in Andalusia. And so, naturally, I grew up speaking Spanish.'

'You never used Spanish when we— In the squat.'

'No.' There was even less emotion in the response this time if it was possible. 'I didn't. But then I didn't want anyone there to know who I was.'

Shockingly the fact that he included her in the 'anyone' he hadn't wanted to know the truth about his background, combined with the fact that he had only ever used his native language to her in the brutally sarcastic way he had said *querida* just now, stung at her deep inside.

'And obviously neither did you. So tell me, when did "Red Brown" become the much more exotically named Rose Cavalliero?'

The room suddenly felt chill, as if the heating had been turned off, as from a shadowy corner of her mind came the echo of her mother's voice on the day she had been called to the hospital to find Joy recovering from a brutal beating that Fred Brown had given her.

'My own fault, darling,' Joy had admitted. 'I was a

sucker for a handsome face, a sexy body, a promise of support…and I thought he'd change.'

Wasn't that how it had been with her daughter when Rose had met Nairo?

'Rose was always my given name,' she responded stiffly. 'It's just that Brown was the name I'd been going by—my stepfather's name. You know why I was more than happy to change that when I found I could. It was only when I reunited with my mother and we started talking—really talking—that she told me my father had been an Italian artist she met on holiday—his name was Enzo Cavalliero.'

Another of the good-looking men her mother had fallen for, only to find herself abandoned when things got tougher. Joy had tried to contact him when she'd found herself pregnant, but he'd never responded.

'I've used it ever since. But I don't think that you should throw stones, Señor Moreno. You weren't exactly forthcoming about your true background either.'

A slight inclination of his head was all the acknowledgement of the hit she'd made he was prepared to give.

'Jett was a nickname the gang in the house gave me. It was easier to stick with that.'

But Rose didn't want to linger on the past. The present had enough complications of its own to be dealt with.

'So what exactly is your help going to cost me?' she asked now, determined not to let him see that anything he'd said had had any effect on her.

She was sure that he had expected she would want to know why he had never told anyone the truth about his background and that by deliberately not asking any such thing she had frustrated and irritated him in equal measure.

'More than designing a dress for your sister, I mean.'

A lot more, the hard twist to his mouth warned. But his answer was not what she'd expected.

'I expect you to come and live with me for a month— Oh, not in that way…'

That twist became more pronounced, mocking the startled reaction he had deliberately provoked and that she had been fool enough to give him.

'I doubt that either of us would care to go back to the way things used to be. No—you will come to Spain with me, meet Esmeralda, get to know her properly. You'll work with her on the details of the wedding—the bridesmaids' dresses, the pages' outfits… Everything.'

'I can't manage that,' Rose put in hastily, thankful that there was at least a real excuse for her not to fit in with his plans. She had no wish to spend any more time with him than she absolutely had to. If she had to design his sister's dress, then she would—she had too much to lose if she didn't. But the swirl of personal memories threatened to put her completely off balance and she desperately wanted to get this back onto a purely business level.

'I was telling the truth when I said that my mother is unwell.'

The way his dark brows snapped together warned her of what was coming and she knew the question was one she would have wanted answering for herself. Nairo had been the only other person she'd confided in about her stepfather's abuse and, worse, he also knew that Joy had sided with her husband in the face of Rose's accusations. That was why she had run away, a desperate move that had ended by throwing her into the arms of the man who had called himself Jett.

At that time Nairo had understood unquestioningly. That was one of the reasons she'd fallen head over heels for him, wildly, crazily, until she'd learned her lesson. She was secretly stunned that he even remembered, never mind felt some of the anger he had showed then.

'And you'd put your life on hold, ruin your business for her?'

When she had done nothing of the sort for her daughter. The implication was there and Rose knew she couldn't deny it. It was the way she had felt herself and it had taken long years of distance and slow, painful reconciliation before she had managed to reach the place she was in now.

'She's my mother.'

He was obviously not convinced.

'And did she act like a mother when she took your stepfather's side against you?' There was something new and shockingly savage in his tone so that Rose had to hurry to reassure him.

'She regretted that deeply. She was scared—terrified. She'd been a single mother once and found it so hard. No money, no support.'

So Joy had thought her salvation lay in the support of a man, any man. And she was, as she had admitted, a sucker for a handsome face. Fred Brown had been a very good-looking man. A handsome face that hid a personality as black as pitch. But admitting that took Rose down paths she didn't want to follow as they reminded her that at one point—more than one—she had found herself to be very much her mother's daughter.

'But when I found her again she was in a real mess. Brown had been treating her as a punchbag because he was so angry I'd got away from him.'

'Is that what's wrong with her now?'

'No—she had breast cancer. She had the operation and now she's recovering from treatment. She's getting better every day, but I wouldn't feel right about leaving her even...'

'Then I'll make sure that she has the very best care.' Nairo dismissed her objection with a wave of his hand. 'A live-in nurse—anything and everything she needs.'

Just the thought of Joy having professional care, the attention that Rose hadn't been able to devote to her and run the wedding boutique as well, brought such a rush of relief that she almost grabbed the offer right out of his hands. She'd felt so guilty at the way she'd had to neglect her mother recently, leaving her in the tiny flat for far too many hours on her own. The demands of just scraping a living, finding the money to keep a roof over their heads, had forced her to focus on her work far more than she'd liked and it had given her an insight into why her mother had been prepared to grasp at anything—anyone—who seemed to offer an alternative. But the uneasy, apprehensive feeling that came with wondering why he was offering—and demanding—so much forced her to hesitate.

'I don't usually work this way!'

Everything was happening too fast. Only yesterday she had been barely aware that Nairo Moreno even existed, let alone that he was actually the boy she had once given her naïve foolish heart to, all grown up and turned into this unstoppable masculine force.

'It's this way or no way,' Nairo retorted.

'And if I don't agree?'

'I reckon Geraldine would be able to point me in the direction of another designer.'

It was said so lightly, even carelessly, that she couldn't believe he meant it. But meeting his stony eyes told a very different story. He meant every word and if he did go elsewhere, with Geraldine's recommendation, then her business was dead in the water. Her reputation would be shredded for ever if it got out that Nairo Moreno had withdrawn his commission from her.

'But why can't your sister come here and talk things over with me? That's how I usually work—how it would be with any other client.'

'Esmeralda is not just any other client. This wedding has to be perfect, and my sister has to have everything she wants.'

She sounded like a spoiled little princess and already Rose was regretting having anything to do with this wedding. Yet how could she regret taking on the commission that might turn her life around? If the response to Nairo's announcement that she was to design Esmeralda's dress was anything to go by, once this commission was completed, then surely everyone would forget the cancelled wedding, the 'broken-hearted' groom left almost at the altar? She would put her heart and soul into creating the most beautiful gown for Nairo's sister so that the wedding would be the perfect showcase for what she could design in the future.

How long would it take? A month, he'd said. Maybe less? She could cope with that, couldn't she? After all, she probably wouldn't have to see Nairo himself for any real amount of that time. He was a man, and from her experience the males involved in weddings, even the most doting grooms, stayed well back for as much of the time as they could.

'You'd really make sure that my mother has a nurse?'

'If that is what it takes. A live-in carer in attendance twenty-four hours a day. I know of an agency...'

Nairo named an exclusive and highly rated agency, the sort of establishment with fees that Rose couldn't even dream of being able to afford.

'You can choose her yourself—I'll set up the interviews for tomorrow if that will suit you.'

It would more than suit. It was far more than she could

ever have anticipated. If only it hadn't been Nairo who was behind it all. Surely he couldn't want her that much.

But of course. She almost laughed aloud. *He* didn't want *her*. He was here at the bidding of his sister. That demanding little princess.

'I understand how you feel about leaving your mother,' Nairo put in unexpectedly. 'My sister has been ill too. That is why she is not here with me.'

'Oh. I'm sorry to hear that.'

A kick of guilt left Rose feeling uncomfortable. She should be grateful to Esmeralda; because of his sister Nairo was offering her a lifeline that she had never anticipated.

'I'll look forward to working with her on the designs for her wedding—to make her dream dress, for a perfect day.'

'I'd appreciate that, thank you,' he said, his voice unexpectedly rough at the edges, and something had changed in Nairo's face. A relaxation of the muscles in his jaw, an unexpected light in his eyes, turning Rose's feelings upside down. She didn't care if the concern was all for his sister, only knew that the sudden rush of release from the tensions of the past year or more had gone to her head like the prosecco she had served earlier that evening.

'No, thank *you*!'

Her head spun with such relief it pushed into an unguarded response and before she had quite realised what she was doing she had come up close and pressed her lips against his cheek.

A kiss of thanks. That was all it was meant to be. Just a peck on the cheek. There and gone again in a minute. But as soon as her lips touched his skin, felt its warmth and the hardness of bone beneath her mouth, the moment the taste of him touched her lips she knew that it wouldn't stay that way. It couldn't end there.

It was like putting a match to a drift of dried tinder deep

inside her, setting everything burning, making her control crack dangerously. She remembered what that taste had been like before, what a simple kiss had led to. Something so wild, so passionate that it had been impossible to control. It was reaching out to grab hold of her already, turning her blood white-hot, melting her bones so that she swayed on her feet. She would have fallen if Nairo hadn't reached out and grabbed both her arms, holding her upright. Holding her close.

'Red...' Nairo said roughly, and the rawness in his voice told its own story. One she wanted and yet feared to hear.

It was still there. The sparks that flashed like lightning when they looked at each other, the flames that flared if they touched. She'd felt it in that moment when he had touched her cheek in the shop doorway and it was bubbling up inside her now like lava in a volcano, threatening to spill out and swamp her in a scalding flood.

'Rose...'

The fact that he had corrected her name only seemed to make matters worse. His tone was tight, constricted as if he was having trouble getting words out of his throat. But then he gave up on even trying. The proud dark head bent swiftly, his mouth coming down on hers in a hard, bruising kiss. It crushed her lips back against her teeth, opening them to allow the stroke of his tongue, tasting her, tantalising her. She could barely snatch in a breath under the pressure of his kiss as she let her head fall back, opening to him so that he could plunder her mouth. Time evaporated, sweeping all memories before it, and in her thoughts she was once more back in the scruffy darkness of the squat, alone with this man who had come to her rescue when she had most needed him, and who had stolen her naïve heart as a result.

The ten years in between had vanished. She was once

more the girl she had been then, young, innocent, lost in a world of sensation that she had never known existed.

Something she hadn't experienced since in all the time between.

It was like opening a door and letting in the sunshine. Nairo's strength was a powerful support, one she still needed as she swayed against him again. Her arms came up, reaching for him once more…

'*No!*' he said harshly, wrenching his mouth away, shocking her out of her dream world.

It had been a dream then too. Like the sort of fairy tale her mother had been looking for. She had thought him her rescuer, but she hadn't known the truth.

The long body so close to hers had frozen, stiff and taut. She could feel him staring down at her even though she couldn't see it, and she had to force her eyes open to meet his.

The darkness of desire had changed his eyes, distending his pupils so that there was only the faintest gold at their rim, and yet, in spite of that one betraying reaction, he couldn't have been further from her if he had been on the opposite side of the world.

His hands clamped hard and tight around her shoulders, pushing her away, the ferocity of rejection in his movements.

'*No!*' He didn't need the extra emphasis. His feelings were perfectly clear. 'This isn't going to happen. It isn't what I want.'

Liar! The word sounded in Rose's head and she wanted to throw it at him, to challenge him with it. The way her body was stinging in response to that kiss screamed at her to defy his hard-voiced declaration. How could he say that when she had felt his reaction in the tightness of his body, could still see it shadowing his eyes?

But even as her mouth opened to speak she caught the word back, swallowed it down, knowing that it was safer that way. But she wasn't going to let him get away unchallenged.

'My, you do have a tendency to overreact, don't you?' she tossed at him. 'It was just a little kiss.'

'Some *little* kiss.'

Nairo couldn't stop his mouth from quirking up into a smile at her response as he recognised her repetition of the comment he had turned on her in the boutique earlier. She had spirit, he'd give her that. But 'a little kiss' went no way towards describing what they'd just shared. A little kiss wasn't possible between them.

The taste of her was still on his tongue, his lips. His senses burned and every nerve still throbbed from the response that had blazed its way through him. The heat and hardness below his belt made it impossible to think straight. But when he looked into her eyes he knew he *had* to think straight. Hell, someone had to or he would give in to the primitive demands of his body that screamed for appeasement, throwing her down on the thickly carpeted floor, crushing her under his weight.

She would let him, he knew that without a doubt. She might scratch and hiss like an angry kitten, but she could not deny the enticement, the welcome that had been there in her eyes, in her touch—in that far from *little* kiss.

'However little it was, it's not what I want from you.'

'I should hope not, because that's not what I want from you either.'

She might try to disguise the flinch away from his words, bring her head up a little bit higher to declare defiance and rejection, but she was still fighting a disappointment that was every bit as strong as the one that was biting at him. The wide, blurred pupils gave away the fact that she was as turned on as he was. Even after ten years he still remembered how she looked when she was aroused and hungry for the pleasure he could give her.

'I might sign up to design your sister's dress—but that's all. It's a business deal, nothing more.'

'A business deal suits me fine,' Nairo echoed with a curt nod, holding out his hand to her.

She took it, even clasped it firmly and shook it in a very businesslike manner, but not before he'd noted the hesitation, the tiny jerk of her fingers as his palm touched hers. He knew just what that meant. Hell, wasn't he feeling it too? How could he miss the way her tongue slipped out, slicked across dry lips, the forced way she swallowed against an obviously tight throat?

He could have her right now if he wanted, and—*querido Dios*—he *wanted*. The need was like a searing brand on his body. He wanted her and he could have her if he just pressed a little more…kissed her again…caressed her…

He could have her, but what good would this be if, after all this time, after ten years' waiting, it was fast and furious, totally uncontrolled?

The demanding pulse that had taken prisoner of his senses insisted that it would be worth it—*right now*. But the little part of his brain that was still rational told another story. One that offered a fuller, deeper satisfaction.

Waiting would be worth it. Waiting would build the hunger, the sense of need, in her as well as himself. If he kept her waiting, then he would keep her hungry. The hungrier she became, the more complete his triumph would be when he finally made her his. This time she wouldn't be able to walk away from him.

This time he would be the one doing the walking.

'Can I give you a lift home?' It wasn't easy to make it sound careless, relaxed.

Her head came up, eyes wary at even that simple question.

'No, thank you. I still have some tidying up to do here. And I have a taxi coming…'

'Then I'll see you tomorrow—for the interviews. I'll call the agency and set them up.'

'That would be perfect.'

Her smile was a fake flash on and off, not meeting her eyes, not warming her face in the slightest. She might think that she was showing nothing, but he knew Rose Cavalliero, as he must now call her, of old. The harder she worked to project the fact that she was feeling nothing, the more she had to conceal.

It wouldn't be a problem keeping her wanting. He'd seen the disappointment in her eyes when he'd pulled back. It had almost been worth the difficulty he'd had to wrench his lips away from the warm, soft invitation of hers just to see the way those mossy-green eyes clouded with disbelief and frustration. The fire that had flamed between them all those years ago was still there, totally undimmed by ten years' absence. If anything, it was stronger now. The desire of a grown man for a woman rather than the adolescent rush of hormones he had known before. He had thought that he had wanted her then, but it was nothing compared to what he felt now.

'Tomorrow, then.'

Not a man to let grass grow under his feet, this Nairo Moreno, Rose reflected as she made herself take the business card he passed her. He had come prepared for this and would allow for no other possible outcome.

If anything should tell her just what his trip to England was really all about, it was that. All her earlier fears, the secret thrill of dread that he might actually have come looking for her after all this time, evaporated in a hiss that almost sounded like laughter at her own stupidity.

She couldn't have been more deluded.

He didn't want her. He couldn't have made that any plainer if he'd tried. The flat, emphatic statement left no room for doubt. He didn't want her and that should have made things so much easier. She should feel relieved, because she was going to have to travel to Spain with him, to stay there for a month while she worked on his sister's dress, and it would be so much easier knowing that she meant nothing to him, that he didn't want her in any way.

So why, instead of the relief she should feel, the soar of elation and freedom, was the emotion that filled her built on the sort of disappointment that shrivelled her heart?

CHAPTER FOUR

'You need to tell me about the wedding.'

'What?'

Rose lifted her head from the sketches she was concentrating on to see Nairo standing in the doorway of the workroom that had been set apart for her in the Castillo Corazón. This was the first time that he had approached her since they had arrived at his magnificent family home, and she'd been grateful for his absence as she tried to get her head round what had happened to her.

It seemed that in the time since Nairo Moreno had appeared in her life her world had been turned upside down. Was it really possible that it was less than a week since that moment and yet she seemed to have lost control of her life as surely as if someone—Nairo obviously—had wrenched the reins from her hands and was directing things the way that *he* wanted.

Nairo didn't wait for anything, it seemed. He wanted a carer for Rose's mother—one had been selected, appointed, moved into the tiny flat that she and her daughter shared, while Rose was whisked off to the airport in a chauffeured car, escorted onto a sleek private jet and transported here to Andalusia, where the luxurious golden-walled *castillo* was to be her base for the next four weeks or so. It felt as if she had been transported into a different world instead of just to another part of Europe. Her work-room alone, opening out onto a Moorish-style patio, would have swallowed up more than half of the shabby little flat that she had struggled to pay rent on and the suite she had been installed in with its tiled floors and decorated ceiling was almost twice the size of her London boutique.

When she had first seen her room, it had been like going back in time, with the huge canopied bed and the rather old-fashioned furnishings giving the place a formal, rather stiff, dark look. The most wonderful aspect of the room was the wide balcony overlooking the gardens and the river below. But she didn't have time to explore, to enjoy the beauty of her surroundings or even have a swim in the large outdoor pool. She was here to do a job and it was so much easier if she focussed on that and nothing else. It would also mean that she could get out of here as soon as possible.

'I didn't think that you'd be interested. But here...'

'Not that.'

Nairo waved away the pages covered with designs and colour swatches she held out to him.

'Not Esmeralda's wedding—I understand that that is going fine. No, I meant the wedding that never was—the one you were supposed to have with Lord what's-his-name...'

'Andrew,' Rose supplied flatly.

'Yes, Lord Andrew Holden. The man you supposedly left at the altar on the day of the wedding.'

'Three days before the wedding, actually.'

Rose knew she sounded snappy when really she was fighting with the rush of tension that stretched each muscle tight as she answered him. The thought of the day she had realised she couldn't go through with her wedding was particularly uncomfortable with Nairo before her, reminding her of the memories that had driven her to make that decision.

'Why do you want to know?'

'Because Oscar and his parents are getting concerned.'

Rose had seen Nairo's prospective in-laws, the Prince and Grand Duchess, only once, but that was enough to make her understand exactly why he was so insistent that things would be perfect for them. Their emphasis on propriety and social esteem meant that they would expect nothing less. And it was obvious that Nairo's sister was very much in awe of them.

From the moment that she had met Esmeralda Moreno she'd understood even more. Nairo's sister was almost nine years younger than him and, while she shared his black-haired, golden-eyed colouring, she had nothing of his powerful build and strength. Instead she was tiny, delicate, finely built. Too thin and nervy, speaking too quickly, worrying about too much. Rose suspected that she showed signs of suffering from some sort of eating disorder in the past, which made it clear why Nairo was so concerned and protective.

Esmeralda was definitely not the spoiled princess she had anticipated but a vulnerable woman who desperately wanted people to like her. And Rose did like her, very much.

'Oh, come on, I'm only the dress designer!' she protested. 'When the big day arrives, I'll be out of here and gone.'

She sincerely hoped that would be the case. Living here like this with Nairo likely to appear at any moment was stretching her nerves so tight she felt they might actually snap. It should have been an easy matter to avoid him in the huge *castillo*, but somehow she always seemed to bump into him when she least expected it. She was beginning to feel like a hunted animal, on high alert at every moment, while Nairo was perfectly polite but totally indifferent and businesslike.

This isn't going to happen, he had said and it seemed that he was determined to keep to that.

Still she found herself tensing up whenever Nairo walked into a room, focussing so hard on what she was doing that it was almost a discomfort. She was so aware of him, of the lean length of his tall dark figure, the glint of the sun on the rich darkness of his hair, the beautifully accented sound of his voice, the scent of his skin blended with a tempting citrus cologne. It was only then that she realised how deep she had dug a gaping hole at her feet and foolishly allowed herself to fall into it. She had fallen back into the bonds of his physical spell as badly as she had done all those years before, when she had been just an adolescent, and every day she spent at the Castillo Corazón pulled those bonds tighter and harder around her, stopping her from thinking straight and from sleeping at night.

She couldn't even use her mother as an excuse. The nurse that Nairo had provided for Joy had proved to be perfection in a human form. 'My guardian angel' her mother called her and under the woman's gentle care Rose's mother had not only been more comfortable than she had ever been when Rose had struggled with her care as well as running the boutique, she had actually thrived. The two women had become great friends so that as well as providing her medical care, Margaret also gave Joy the sort of female companionship she had been longing for. The sort of friendship that, try as she might, Rose had never been able to really have with her parent. There were too many shadows between them. Margaret and Joy shared knitting patterns, read books, enjoyed cooking together and Rose knew that she would be going a long way towards risking the steady progress of her convalescence if she was to take Margaret away.

There was more to it too. The last time she'd spoken to her mother there had been a new, very different note in Joy's voice. One she hadn't heard in so long—if ever at all. Pushed to describe it, she'd have had to say that there was a lack of the guilt that had always been just under the surface ever since they had reunited when Rose had gone to visit her in the hospital after Fred's last attack on her.

They'd determined to put the past behind them, made a home together, but Rose knew that her mother's conscience always troubled her when she looked back, particularly when she'd seen how hard her daughter worked to keep the roof over their heads. So now the relief and delight at what she saw as Rose's newfound success lightened every word, every phrase. After all the time it had taken them to rebuild their relationship, could she really risk going back on that?

'It's not as simple as that,' Nairo said now. 'There has already been a lot of interest in the fact that you're here— and involved in Esmeralda's wedding. I need to know how to handle it if the paparazzi come hanging round the gates, trying to take photographs. There's a risk that they're becoming more interested in *you* than the bride and groom and they're starting to demand to know whether you're a curse on any wedding you're involved with.'

'Oh, that's just stupid and you know it.'

Rose used the need to put the papers back into order and down onto the table as a defence against the rush of colour she knew had heated her cheeks.

'I saw the effect just the mention of the story had on the audience at your fashion show,' Nairo stated coolly. 'It could have turned pretty nasty.'

'Because Geraldine stirred it up. She won't be here at Esmeralda's wedding.'

'But you will be, and if you come trailing the shadows of your past life behind you and bring the paparazzi to our door, then it will turn this whole thing into an ordeal for my sister instead of the happiest day of her life.'

'Well, you should have thought of that when you asked me to design the dress for her and made sure that I would do it.'

You have a nerve to talk about past scandals, Rose wanted to fling in his face, but the memories of how she too was connected to that past dried the words on her tongue. Combining those memories with the thought of her mother's happiness and health now made sure that she didn't dare risk opening another can of worms. She couldn't forget the unspoken threat that had been in his warning that she was not to talk to anyone about the time when they had met before.

Echoes of that time had surfaced on the first day when they had reached the *castillo*. As she had got out of the car, Rose had stared up at the huge, beautiful golden building, with the darkening rays of the setting sun vividly reflected in the glass of every wide-paned window.

'Is all this yours?' she'd gasped, unable to believe it. Unable to connect this glorious, elegant building with the man she had first known to be living in a squat, no job, no money of his own.

'It is now,' Nairo had responded flatly. 'I inherited from my father. What?'

He'd looked down at her sharply.

'You don't think all this is bought with the profits from my dirty dealing?'

It was the first time he had breached the wall of silence they had built around the past. The wall she had had to build around it in order to be able to go on with this 'business arrangement'.

'I never...' she'd begun, but at that moment the great wooden door of the *castillo* had opened and a tiny whirlwind in the shape of his sister, Esmeralda, had rushed out to meet them, flinging herself into Nairo's arms and hugging him tightly so that there had been no chance of continuing the conversation.

It still hung there between them now, unspoken, not dealt with, and Rose knew that one day it would have to be faced or it would blight the rest of her life.

'You saw enough to realise that I have a "past",' she flung at him. 'That was the time to get out of things if you'd wanted to keep this squeaky clean so as not to offend your in-laws. Instead you made sure that I got this commission and that everyone there knew it. Why?'

It was a question he'd asked himself so many times, Nairo acknowledged. If he'd had any sense, he should have turned and left her to the ruin of her fledgling business. He'd have found another designer to please Esmeralda. He'd have appeased his sister somehow and not jumped, feet first, into the murky puddle of complications and memories that this woman brought with her. But, Esmeralda or not, he had known from the start that he couldn't just turn and walk away from her. Not until he'd got her well and truly out of his system.

'You were the designer Esmeralda wanted. And I hate bullies. Geraldine was a born bully, anyone could see that. She wanted the attention to herself and she was determined to do anything to win it. I enjoyed making sure she didn't succeed.'

It was true he hated bullies, and he had no trouble recognising an emotional tormenter when he saw one. Hadn't he seen enough with the way his young stepmother had treated Esmeralda, whom she'd considered a rival for her husband's affections? Though he'd never reckoned that she would start on him as well. That was why he had moved forward to act when Geraldine had been trying to stir up trouble. But there was more to it than that. In spite of everything, the memory of the way Rose had walked away from him, in spite of the fact that the tall, elegant woman who stood on the runway in that clinging peacock-blue dress was light years from the girl he'd befriended and protected in the squat, he had still seen some faint and unexpected traces of the Red he had known back then. He'd seen the stress lines round her eyes, the way she was biting her lower lip. The memory had disturbed his responses so sharply that he had moved forward, acted, spoken, before he had even realised what he was doing.

'She was supposed to be marrying Andrew before he met me. She wanted her revenge.'

'I would have thought she'd have been happier to have him back on the market.'

'Mmm.' Rose looked uncomfortable about that. 'The problem was that he didn't want her back. He'd been looking for an excuse to break off with her and—well, I provided it.'

'Are you saying he didn't love you?'

'No.' Bright auburn hair caught the blaze of the sun as she shook her head, sending it flying in the air. It also sent the aroma of her perfume, light and delicate, wafting towards him, threatening to scramble his thoughts so that he had to drag them back into focus. 'The opposite. He was crazy about me.'

The emphasis on the word *crazy* warned him there was more to this story than she was happy to acknowledge.

'So what happened? Why did you call the wedding off? He was too "crazy"?'

And Nairo was too aware, Rose reflected secretly. He'd caught on some betraying note in her voice, a look in her eyes, and seen part of what she would have liked to have kept hidden from him.

'He was...rather obsessed,' she managed, finding it embarrassing to say any such thing to this man. Why would he believe that Andrew had been so over the top in his avowals of devotion and adoration when Nairo himself had found her so totally forgettable? 'I—I realised that I didn't feel the way that he did. He took it badly.'

'Three days before the wedding,' Nairo murmured darkly.

'I know! I know! You can't make me feel any worse than I do already.' She'd lived with the guilt ever since.

Her voice sounded too uneven, too raw, and she had to move away, riffling through the papers in her hand as if looking for something special amongst them. There was no way she was going to admit that she had tried so hard to care for Andrew as he'd wanted. She knew there was no great passion between them; they hadn't even made love. But she had thought that would all come in time. Until the day when, sorting out her belongings, ready for the move to the elegant apartment that was to be her new home, she'd come across a dusty, faded box at the back of a cupboard.

In that box had been the one and only photograph of herself with Nairo she had ever owned. Creased and battered, it was one of a set they had taken in a cheap photo booth on an afternoon when they had actually had a few pounds to spare. A joyful, laughter-filled day that she had wanted to record for ever and so had dragged Nairo into the booth with her in spite of his protests.

The sketches in front of her blurred now just as that photograph had done then and she blinked hard. How could she have married Andrew—married anyone—when she knew she didn't feel anything like the overwhelming power of emotion that had swept over her when she had been with the man she had known as Jett? She couldn't have given herself to anyone else unless she had felt something that had at least come close to what she had felt then. The man she still felt that way about, she realised with a feeling that left her fighting for breath.

Even worse, she knew she had proved herself to be her mother's daughter when she'd rushed in without thought, just as Joy had plunged into marriage to Fred Brown. She'd believed she'd found someone who would care for her, someone who would take the burdens from the shoulders that had supported them since she'd promised to help her mother escape from her stepfather's brutal influence. In a weak moment she'd seen hope and so she'd said yes, only to realise that she'd done so for the worst possible reasons.

'I should never have said yes to his proposal. Our engagement was a terrible mistake.'

'Why such a mistake?' Nairo questioned. 'Looking at it from the outside, I would have thought that Andrew Holden was the perfect choice.'

'Oh, really? And why was that?'

He'd caught her on the raw there, he could hear it in her voice as she tossed the question over her shoulder at him, the muscles in her face stiff and tight with rejection.

'Good-looking, tall, successful, with a great position in society. Wealthy...'

That brought her spinning round to face him. Her eyes were unusually bright as she turned them on his face.

'And you think that his money was the answer to everything? The reason why I wanted to marry him in the first place?'

Nairo shrugged indifferently, brushing off her challenge to him.

'Isn't that what women want in a marriage?'

It was what his mother and stepmother had wanted from his father. The old man had always been a sucker for a pretty face, a sexy body. He had been so convinced that he was 'in love' that the thought of a prenup had never entered his head. Between them, his two wives had drained almost everything the old man had to offer and then headed for pastures new when there was nothing left. The first Señora Moreno had been happy to leave her children behind, not wanting her pleasurable lifestyle with her new partner to be restricted by a son and daughter, then just nine and one year old. The second, Carmen, had even tried to take Raoul's son from him in the end.

He'd vowed that he would never leave himself as vulnerable to any woman as his father had done, and for most of his life he had kept to that vow. The only reason he had ever come close to breaking it was standing before him now. He'd had a lucky escape there. One that had taught him a much-needed lesson on the risks of weakening. At least he had had the sense to keep the truth about his family from her, though he'd come close to telling her that Christmas when he'd tried for a reconciliation with his father. She'd still found a way to make money out of their relationship when she'd gone to the police.

'Not me!'

The fury of her indignation clashed with his own challenging stare so that he could almost see the spark where they met in the air between them.

'But your business was in difficulties—you're oceans deep in debt.'

That made her head go back, green eyes widening in shock.

'How do you know that?'

The smile he couldn't hold back wouldn't have looked

friendly. It wasn't meant to. It was just an on-off twitch of muscles, an uncontrolled response to the realisation that even now she still didn't recognise the difference between the raw youth he'd been and the man he was now.

'I make it my business to know everything about any-one I'm dealing with. If I want the information, it's easy enough to get it. So wouldn't marriage to him have solved all your money problems?'

'Maybe—yes. But shouldn't the fact that I *didn't* marry him show you that that wasn't what I was looking for from him?'

He had to concede that, Nairo acknowledged. But if that was not the reason she'd been prepared to marry this Andrew, then why had she backed out so late? For an uncomfortable moment he was back at the fashion show, watching the woman called Geraldine brandishing the newspaper with the scandalous headline right in Rose's face. He'd stepped forward to stop the obvious attack right then and there, but he'd never actually really challenged himself on *why* he'd done that. He'd claimed that he hated bullies—and he did—and the sight of her pale, strained face had taken him back ten years to the moment when he'd first set eyes on her looking lost and alone on a London street.

But there was more to it than that.

'Wouldn't I be much more comfortable, more settled, as Lady Holden?'

'As I recall, you always dreamed of marriage and a happy-ever-after...'

He let the rest of the sentence fade off into a dark growl, not liking the memories that came pushing to the surface as he spoke.

I don't do love. I don't do commitment... Through the years his own voice came back to haunt him. He'd been so sure, looking at the ruins of his father's two marriages, the destruction they'd left behind—particularly for Esmeralda. *I certainly don't do marriage. If you want those, then you'd better find yourself someone who does.*

But the irony was that in the moment that Geraldine's announcement had made him realise Rose had done exactly that—found someone else, agreed to marry him—then his world had rocked off balance and he'd found himself moving forward, taking action without really thinking things through.

It hadn't even been the fact that he wanted to please Esmeralda. This went deeper, was more personal than that. He didn't want Rose being with anyone else. He wanted this woman back in his life, in his bed.

He hadn't had enough of her ten years ago and he didn't intend letting her be with anyone else until he'd got her out of his system.

'Perhaps I did,' Rose acknowledged. 'But there would have been no happy-ever-after. I was very fond of him, but I could never give him what he needed from me. My timing was really really bad, but it would have been far worse if I'd married him and then realised my mistake.'

It all sounded so perfectly rational, so believeable. At least, it would have been if it hadn't been for the way that her eyes wouldn't quite meet his. She was holding something back, hiding something from him. But before he could try to drag out of her just what it was, the door opened and his sister hurried into the room.

'So have you finished your sketches, Rose?' she asked, her voice bubbling with excitement. 'Have you got something to show me?'

'Yes, I have them here...'

Rose reached for the sketches from the table once again and it was only now that he saw how much her grip on them had been crumpling the paper so that she had to smooth them out to show Esmeralda her designs.

'If we've finished...'

Her hazel eyes went to Nairo's face, her eyebrows lifting in question. He knew what she was asking, what put that faint frown of concern between her fine dark brows. Was he going to leave things there, with whatever she'd kept hidden still unsaid?

It seemed he was going to have to because her question, the look she turned on him, alerted his sister to his presence in the room.

'I didn't see you there, big brother! Don't tell me you've suddenly developed an interest in bridesmaids' dresses—because that's all we're going to let you have a peek at! No one but Rose and I will see *the* dress before the big day. It's our secret.'

'And that's how you must keep it.'

Rose could only blink in astonishment as she heard the change in Nairo's tone as he addressed his sister. The cold stiffness had melted away, leaving a warmth that flowed over her like liquid honey. But only for Esmeralda. When he turned back to her his eyes were opaque and hooded, hiding any emotion.

'Would I dare to get in Esmeralda's way?' he drawled. 'We're finished here—for now. We can carry on this converation at another time.'

So was that a promise or a threat? Rose had no way of knowing because as he finished speaking Nairo moved to drop a quick, affectionate kiss on his sister's head, then strolled out the door. The gentle gesture wrenched at her heart, reminding her of how she had once believed that he had cared for her too.

No—bitter realism made her add it as the door began to swing to behind Nairo's tall figure. Gentleness and warmth were not what there had ever been between the two of them. Their relationship had been based on a searing sexual passion that had caught them up in a conflagration too wild, too ferocious to be resisted. She might have thought there was concern at first, when he had come up to her when she had been sitting on the stone steps in Trafalgar Square, cold and miserable, too tired to go any further. One of her shoes had split, letting in the wet, and her hair had hung in damp rat's tails around her face and shoulders. Perhaps then he'd felt a touch of concern for her. He couldn't have felt anything else.

Quite frankly, then she'd been a mess.

'So—Rose—do you have the designs—the dress...?' Esmeralda's excited voice broke into her thoughts as she tugged the sheets of paper from her hand. 'Let me see.'

Rose could only be thankful that the younger girl's enthusiasm and excitement meant that she didn't notice her own distraction, the way that her mind was far from focussing on anything like the plans for the wedding dress but instead had followed Nairo out the door and back into the past they had once shared.

'Oh, but these are *gorgeous*! *Maravilloso!* Perhaps we should have let my brother stay and see these. Then he'd understand why I insisted that it had to be you designing my dress and he should fetch you for me.'

She sounded so determined, so resolute that for a moment Rose remembered once again the way she had dismissed Nairo's sister as a spoiled, demanding little princess. But she'd seen with her own eyes since she had come to stay at the *castillo* that Esmeralda was a charmer, a delight. She could easily wind anyone round her delicate fingers, but she only used that appeal on her obviously besotted brother. No one could have missed the way he watched his little sister so closely, a faint frown deepening the lines around his stunning eyes. There was more than just brotherly affection behind that watchfulness. Some memory that it seemed only the two of them shared.

'Surely they would impress even him,' Esmeralda was chattering on, unaware of the way that Rose's thoughts had drifted away. 'They might even convince him that romance really does exist.'

'Your brother is not a romantic?'

By imposing enough control over her voice she managed to make it sound relaxed, even light.

'Surely someone living here amongst all this beauty…' The wave of her hand took in the high decorated ceiling, the tiled floor that led out onto the patio, the sun streaming through the wooden blinds from the garden, where the sound of the river below in the valley was a gentle background song to the formal beauty of the *castillo*. There was so much to the place that she still hadn't seen.

'Oh, *no*…' Esmeralda shook her dark head sharply. 'He has no time for looking at his surroundings, not even to bring this place up to date really. He's had to work too hard to make sure that the estate was saved and that we could still live here.'

'The estate was in danger?'

Seeing the elegant luxury that surrounded her when contrasted with her own small flat, Rose found it hard to believe any such thing.

'We almost lost everything,' Esmeralda assured her. '*Papá* was ill and he let things slide. That was when he brought Nairo back from Argentina after seeing the great job he did there.'

'Argentina?' It was a strangled sound of surprise.

So Nairo had lived abroad for some—how much?—of the time since they had been together in the squat. No wonder he'd seemed to have disappeared off the face of the earth and she had never seen or heard anything of him since that fateful night.

Esmeralda nodded. 'We have an *estancia*. That was almost derelict too. But my brother, he knows how to work—and work.' Her endearing, bright smile quirked her mouth up at the corners. 'Even if *Papá* didn't approve of so much he did out there.'

'No time for romance?' The uncomfortable fluttering of her heart made it a struggle to speak.

'No time—and no *heart* for romance. I'm not quite sure what happened, but I know that when he was in England he met someone.'

Esmeralda shook her head as if in disbelief.

'Some cold, cruel little witch who stamped on his heart and then betrayed him without a care. She got off unscathed, but my brother... Pah! If I could get my hands on her...'

Rose's head was spinning. *When he was in England...* Could Esmeralda mean *her* as the 'cold, cruel little witch'? But that was not how it had been. Nairo had been the one who deserved those accusations. He must have told the story differently.

Nairo had once told her why he was in London, living in the squat. A huge row with his father, so he had just walked out, taking no money with him. 'A woman' had been behind it was all he would say. So did Esmeralda have it wrong and the woman who had hurt her brother was actually someone he'd left behind in Spain?

Or perhaps Rose was too sensitive to this account of things? Perhaps there had been some other woman in England... Unfortunately that version of things didn't bring any sense of relief, only a tangled mess of complicated feelings that twisted and burned at the thought of Nairo being so involved with someone else that the other woman had left him feeling that she had 'stamped on his heart'.

Stamped on his heart! That made it obvious that *Rose* couldn't be the woman Esmeralda had meant. The Nairo she had known had had no heart to be stamped on.

From the depths of her thoughts a flash of dark memory came back to haunt her. Nairo holding Julie, the girlfriend of Jason, an older man who also shared the squat, the blonde woman's head on his shoulder. The burn of jealousy she had felt had been like nothing she'd ever known.

A faint noise out in the hallway made Rose glance up. Reflected in the mirror on one wall, she could see the tall dark figure of Nairo just beyond the doorway almost blending into the shadows of the wooden-panelled corridor beyond. He hadn't walked away at all but must have heard every word of the last conversation. As her head came up, she saw the heavy lids that hooded his eyes lift so that he was staring straight at her.

Just for a moment their eyes locked in the reflection in the glass, the intensity of his stare making her blood run cold in her veins. Then he turned on his heel and strode away.

CHAPTER FIVE

ROSE WAS OUT on the patio, at work on her designs, the sun gilding her arms exposed by the sleeveless white cotton top. She had pulled her chair right to the edge of the swimming pool and let her bare feet fall into it so that the water lapped against her lightly tanned toes as her head was bent over the sketch pad on her knees. Her pencil moved swiftly and confidently over the paper, adding a flurry of lace here, a waterfall of a train there. Her auburn hair tumbled forward over her face as she concentrated, the copper strands in it caught and illuminated by the setting sun until they glowed a fiery red, much closer to the colour they had been when Nairo had first seen her.

He had been away from the *castillo* for only four days and yet coming back to her now was like seeing her anew.

It had been the red of her hair that he had first seen, spotting her slumped wearily against a wall, the brilliant glow shining out in the dull grey of a wintry afternoon in spite of the fact that it had been raining heavily and her corkscrew curls were limp around her head. Long, thin legs in faded black leggings had been splayed out on the steps she was sitting on as if she didn't have the energy to place them any other way, and her head was down-bent then as it was now, but then it had been a sign of depression and withdrawal, not the current focus on creativity.

He had easily picked her up from the pavement where she sat and carried her when she had swayed against him in obvious weakness. She hadn't eaten for two days, she'd told him later. She'd left home in a frantic rush, running from her abusive stepfather, no time to collect more than her handbag. But her purse had had so little cash in it, and that stepfather had put a stop on the bank card he had once let her have.

A card he had later expected her to pay for with sexual favours.

A red haze burned before his eyes and he cleared his throat to ease some constriction that had unexpectedly closed it off.

'Buenas noches,' he said hastily as Rose started at his approach, scrambling to her feet, her eyes wide as she turned towards him.

'How long have you been there?' Her tone was stiff with tension, warning him to stay away. A warning he had every intention of ignoring.

'Not long. But you seemed so absorbed, I didn't want to disturb you. '

He gestured with his hand towards the sketches that lay open on the table, a dress in a swirl of pink lace, the one she had been working on, uppermost.

'Aren't you supposed to hide those from me? Some ancient superstition about no one seeing The Dress until the big day.'

A wash of colour swept up into her cheeks at his teasing tone, and she moved the sketches around, fanning them out and then back again before answering him.

'Oh, no—that's just the bride's dress—Esmeralda's gown. And I'm past the point of drawing sketches for that. We've already had a couple of fittings and it's almost ready. These are some other designs—suggestions for the weddings of other clients. Women who were at the fashion show that night…'

She let the sentence trail away, but there was no mistaking which night she meant. Deliberately he waited and watched the struggle that went on behind her eyes before she opened her mouth again.

'I really am very grateful to you for what you did to help me.'

Grateful was fine. Even if she made it sound like something that was the exact opposite. He could use 'grateful'. He would have preferred something much more passionate, but at least it was better than the frozen mask that she slapped on her face whenever she was forced to be alone with him. She managed that as fast as she could, but he had still been able to catch the glint of awareness in her eyes, the way her white teeth had dug into the rosy softness of her bottom lip when she had thought he hadn't noticed her. But of course he'd noticed her. How could he do anything else?

His resolve to wait was coming back to bite him and bite him hard. Being with her and not being able to touch her in a sensual way was a torment, all the more so because it was self-inflicted.

He could sense where she was in the *castillo* even in the silence of the night, imagining her up in her suite, asleep on the high canopied bed or lingering in the deep roll-top bath, the water scented with some floral oil. Every instinct seemed to home in on her even when he tried to focus on something else. He could tell if she had been in a room and had left it just before he'd entered by the whisper of her soft slippers in a corridor, the trace of her perfume that drifted on the air. And to sit in a room with her, hear her voice, the bubble of laughter that seemed to well up so often when she was sharing something with Esmeralda, made his skin feel too tightly stretched across his body, pulling painfully taut across his scalp.

Just to watch her move across a room, see the sway of her breasts and hips, the smooth curve of her behind, the length of her legs, made his blood pound, his groin ache. This was why he had never been able to forget her. It was the reason for the burningly erotic dreams that had plagued his nights, forcing him to wake in a knot of sheets, with sweat sheening his skin. He had thought he'd suppressed those dreams after all this time, but from the moment she had come back into his life he'd been tormented all over again.

Being with her and not having her made him curse his blind stupidity in ever starting out on this idea. And now, when she had no trace of make-up on her porcelain skin, lush black lashes framing those mossy-green eyes, it was all he could do not to lean forward and crush the soft pink lips under his demanding mouth. Her long, fine hands were slightly stained with a wash of colour from the water-colours she was using on the designs, making a memory twist in his guts. Those fingers had once been smudged heavily with coal dust as she had tried to light a fire in the grate in their room in the squat, using a few battered, damp pieces of coal that had fallen from a passing delivery lorry in the week before Christmas.

'Perhaps I should save this for the big day itself,' she'd said, holding her grimy fingers out towards the weak, spluttering flame. 'Then we'd have something special to celebrate. But I can't wait...'

He hadn't encouraged her to wait either. Because it had been in that moment that he had resolved to make a move to change his life for her and with her. He'd known his father would demand a high price before he'd allow the prodigal son to return home, but it would be a price he was prepared to pay if it meant that he could offer Rose a better future. But he hadn't reckoned on her desertion, the betrayal that meant his Christmas Eve had begun with a visit from the police and had continued to go downhill from there.

It had almost lost him his honour, his family. And the damage it had done to Esmeralda was something he could hardly bear to remember even now.

'I've just been talking to my mother,' Rose said. 'I ring her every night and Maggie—the carer who is looking after her—has been a godsend. She and Mum are getting on so well, it's like having her best friend come to stay.'

He knew how that felt. When his father had been in his final illness, just four years before, the trained care of the professional nurses brought in to help him had been invaluable. He couldn't imagine having to cope with the round-the-clock care the old man had needed, and the business of dragging the estate into the twenty-first century without knowing that they were dealing with everything that was needed in his sickroom. They had also been able to keep an eye on Esmeralda too when he couldn't be there. But Rose had had to manage on her own. And her mother...

Her smile, the light in her face caught on a raw nerve. With the memory of that miserable winter day in the squat so clear in his mind, it was impossible not to contrast the way she looked now talking about her mother, and the bleakness that had dulled her hazel eyes when she had thought about not being able to be home at Christmas. *Infierno*, hadn't that given him the final push to hold out an olive branch to his father?

'I'm pleased for you.'

'For me?' She had obviously caught the distance in his voice and it made her frown. 'But you've been really kind to my mother and I'm glad to see her happy.'

'You can forgive her that easily?'

'Forgive—but she's my mother.'

'You ran away from her.' The memory made his voice hard.

'No!' Rose shook her head, sending her hair flying, the softness of it and scent of floral shampoo tormenting his senses. 'Not from her—from her husband.'

'She married him—her choice,' he dismissed. 'And she didn't protect you from him.'

'No,' Rose admitted with obvious reluctance. 'But she was scared.'

'And you weren't?'

'Nairo—I saw what he did to her. Her face—the bruises all over her body. Broken ribs.'

Her earnest tone, the expression on her face made it plain that it was important to her that he understood. And now, perhaps he did as he couldn't have done back then.

Her mother had been little or no help to her, he recalled, remembering the anger that had tightened his muscles, burned in his veins at the thought that in her own way Joy Brown had been as much of a waste of space as his own vindictive stepmother. That was why he'd been astounded to find that mother and daughter were now living together, with Rose doing everything she could to support her ailing mother. With a generosity he hadn't expected, she had obviously forgiven the older woman's neglect even before Joy had been taken ill. But then hadn't he been able to reconcile with his father once the old man, recognising how ill he was, had asked for his help after finally acknowledging the foolishness of believing Carmen's selfish lies?

I only wanted to give you and Meralda a new mamá... Raoul's voice, rough with the after-effects of too much wine, too many cigarettes, came down through the years to haunt him. That would have been so much easier to believe if that 'new *mamá*' hadn't been an ex-showgirl who'd worked in the casino where Raoul regularly lost more than he could afford—and no more than six years older than his adolescent son.

'Is it any wonder that I detest bullies?' he murmured, seeing some of the tension leave her body as he spoke. 'In that case, I'm glad that I could help. So how is your mother?'

'Making great progress. She's feeling stronger every day and she sounds so relaxed. There's a new lightness in her. It was like hearing her coming back to life. Really I don't know how to thank you!'

'Ah, well, I can think of a way. I came to ask you something. Esmeralda has gone to spend the evening with her fiancé and his parents, so I came to see if you wanted to have dinner with me.'

'Oh—there's no need.' Rose placed her hands flat on the top of the table in order to control the way that they had started to shake nervously. 'I was looking forward to a quiet night on my own. Perhaps a bowl of soup.'

'We can do better than that.' His smile burned through the defences she had struggled to build around herself. 'I know that you've come here to work, but I'm no slave driver. Surely you can give me a chance to say thank you.'

'Th-thank you?' Her tongue stuttered over the words in the face of the unexpected warmth of that smile. 'No, really, I am the one who should be thanking you.'

Nerves twisted into knots in her stomach, forcing her to face the fact that she had no alternative but to agree to his invitation. It would look so ungracious to refuse it now.

Besides, when he smiled like that, he made her forget all about the man he had once been, the cold manipulator who had been hidden behind the sexy, whipcord-lean youth with unkempt black hair and gleaming eyes. But where had that youth gone—if in fact he had gone anywhere? Wasn't he just hidden under the sophisticated veneer that Nairo Moreno presented to the world? She had been deceived by him once and it had shattered her heart. Was she going to risk letting that happen to her all over again?

But it was only dinner, and here in this house. It wasn't even a *date*.

'It's only dinner,' Nairo said, echoing her thoughts with unnerving accuracy. 'Nothing to be scared of.'

'I'm not scared. Of anything.'

But it was too fierce, too emphatic to be fully convincing. As she watched that smile deepen in his eyes she suddenly knew that she was in big trouble. There was no way she could back out without making it obvious just what she had been dreading and so risking even further humiliation if she had this all wrong.

'Dinner, then.' She started packing away the sketches carefully in her portfolio. 'I hope you'll forgive me if I don't change my outfit. It's been a long day and...'

She let the sentence drift when he actually laughed at her concern.

'I'm only offering a casual meal, Rose. I'm not like my soon-to-be in-laws insisting on everyone dressing for dinner. I thought this would be an opportunity to escape all the formalities and relax.'

'Oh, that sounds great!'

Her relief was genuine. The past weeks had been something of a strain when she had found that she was expected to change for dinner every night. The formal meals around the highly polished table in the huge ornate dining room had been something of an endurance test and she'd already worn the few smarter dresses she'd brought with her at least twice. Her blue linen trousers and white sleeveless shirt were cool in the heat but hardly the sort of dressing up she had had to become used to.

'To be honest, I'm just in the mood for something simple like an omelette or cheese on toast.'

'Or fish and chips?' Nairo inserted lightly, taking the breath from her lungs with an instant vivid memory of just what had provoked that comment.

They had both managed to get temporary jobs in the run up to Christmas and to celebrate their first income in weeks had indulged in fish and chips, fresh from the paper, with fingers prickling from the icy cold. That cold now seemed to reach out from the past and encircle her heart. In spite of having so few comforts, and nowhere secure to live, she had thought that she was happier then than she'd ever been in her life before. Head over heels in love with the man she called Jett, she had adored and trusted him so much that she had given him her body, her virginity without fear or hesitation.

It had been less than twenty-four hours later when the bitter truth began to dawn on her as Nairo had started to talk about a way of making sure they had more money, a plan to secure their future.

'I don't eat chips any more,' she managed. 'Too much fat.' She regretted that comment as she saw the way it drew his burning gaze to her body, drifting slowly and deliberately over her shape, lingering blatantly at her waist and hips.

'You know you have no need to worry about that, Red,' he drawled, golden eyes challenging her to find an insult in his obvious admiration. 'And you don't have to fish for compliments.'

'I'm not fishing! And my name is Rose. No one ever calls me Red any more.'

'You'll always be Red to me.'

It was impossible to interpret just how he meant that comment and he didn't give her time to think about it as he turned to go back indoors.

'I can't offer you fish and chips, but I reckon I could rise to an omelette if that's really your choice.'

'*You* could...' Rose gave up on trying to hide her confusion as she was forced to trot in his wake.

That confusion grew even worse as she followed him, not towards the elegant dining room, where she had had all her meals so far, but across the tiled floor of the spacious hall and...out the main door?

'No—hang on a minute.' She hoped he'd believe her breathlessness was caused by her efforts to keep up with him. 'Where are we? I thought...'

'I invited you to dinner. You accepted.'

'Yes—but...' Unnerved, she looked back into the house, then turned again in time to see the amusement grow in his eyes.

'I thought you wanted a rest from the formality.'

'I did—but...'

'This way.'

He caught hold of her hand, leading her out into the still, soft warmth of the evening. Unable to break free without an awkward struggle, Rose let him take her with him along the gravel path towards another door set into the wall of the *castillo*.

'What is this?' she asked as he paused to slide a key into the lock.

'My home—my apartment.'

He flung the door open and stood back to let her past him.

'*Mi casa es su casa.*'

Rose stepped onto polished wooden floors, stared up at the high white-painted ceilings that soared above the hallway and the wide, curving staircase. Through the doorway she could see a living room, with more wooden floors, huge multicoloured rugs and large squashy sofas in a rich deep red. The walls were lined with bookshelves and, even at this point in the evening, the whole room was flooded with light. As soon as she stepped into it, the room spoke to her of comfort and relaxation more than any of the huge, formal rooms in the main *castillo*. It had the same elegant proportions of course as anywhere in the rest of the main building, but it was so much more of a home than those rooms with their old-fashioned, stiff furnishings.

This explained something that had puzzled her before. She had assumed that Nairo had been out and about when he didn't eat with his sister and her. That he had work to do or he might have been wining and dining—and more— one of the beautiful women he was so often seen with according to the gossip magazines. She had never thought that he might have this separate section of the *castillo* to himself. Something about the room tugged on a memory but one she couldn't bring to mind as it hovered on the edge of her thoughts.

Nairo watched Rose stand in the centre of the room, staring round at her surroundings, her confusion evident on her face. He'd aimed for that and obviously he'd more than succeeded. It gave him a grim sense of satisfaction to see that this separate section of the *castillo*, his private home, had surprised her as much as this.

It would surprise Esmeralda too if she had known that he had brought Rose here tonight. He never brought anyone to this apartment, least of all any woman he was seeing. Those sorts of relationships were conducted away from the *castillo*, in the woman's home, or the privacy of a suite in a luxury hotel. The apartment was his, and only his. It had been his refuge from the time he had come back from

Argentina, a place where he had the privacy and isolation that had never been his while his stepmother, or one of his father's more recent conquests, had been in residence in the main building.

His personal apartment had been a place of retreat when he returned to try to drag the value of the estate back from the brink of bankruptcy. A place that was his alone. Much as he loved his sister, and, towards the end, he'd rediscovered a connection with his father, he'd needed privacy for his own thoughts and a space to relax in.

Though relaxed was exactly the opposite of the way he felt right now. He didn't know what had possessed him to invite Rose here, to bring her into his private sanctum. He hadn't thought beyond the fact that he was tired of waiting, that he couldn't hold back any longer.

Seeing her in the main rooms of the *castillo*, with Esmeralda or perhaps Oscar and his family around, was becoming totally intolerable. He wanted Rose on her own. Just the two of them. The feelings she inspired in him were not for public times, for the company of anyone else. They were hot thoughts, burning desires that were just for the privacy of his own apartment. And ultimately for his bedroom.

But for now, he would play things casually; they had the whole night ahead of them.

'Pour yourself a glass of wine and come and talk to me while I cook.'

'You cook? You really meant it?'

'Of course—simple meals at least. An omelette, wasn't it?'

If he had offered anything else, she might have tensed up, decided this was a very bad idea, but this was so relaxed, so simple that it felt like coming home.

No! She couldn't let herself—wouldn't allow herself

to think like that. There was no way this apartment was anything like home to her even if the warm colours of the furnishings and the polished wooden floors were so very different from the formality of the main part of the main house, which had made her feel as if she were living in a museum most of the time.

'Pour one for me too.'

Nairo had headed through a door at the far side of the room, into the kitchen, Rose assumed. Spotting the bottle of rich red wine on the table, opened and left to breathe, she felt her heart hiccup once again.

Had he been so sure that she would join him? For a moment her steps turned towards the door, then she caught herself up, refusing to give in to the twist of nerves in her stomach.

She had told Nairo she wasn't afraid and she wasn't going to let him prove her wrong. Not when she had the chance of facing up to the mess their past had been and dealing with it once and for all. Determinedly she turned back, reached for the bottle of wine. She was lucky that she had already launched her steps towards the kitchen when the realisation of just why this apartment had seemed strangely familiar hit home with a head-spinning rush.

One night when the wind had rattled the window panes in the squat and they'd huddled together against the cold, she had spilled out some of her secrets, her fears, her unhappiness. Not just in her stepfather's home but before that, when her mother had struggled to find them anywhere to live, when one room had often been all they'd had to share together. Fred Brown's comfortable semi had seemed like heaven in contrast to that. At first. When they hadn't known the fear and distress that had hidden behind that safe suburban door.

In order to distract her, Nairo had set her to imagining what a real home would be like, creating the rooms in her imagination. Then he'd done the same. The place she was in now, she realised, was one of the rooms he had described to her then.

In the kitchen Nairo was already at work; he had pulled onions and peppers from the huge fridge and was busy slicing into them with a brutally sharp knife, his movements quick and efficient.

'Wine…'

It was all she could manage as she placed the glass beside him on the huge central island and then leaned back against the nearest worktop, sipping at her own wine as she did so. She couldn't take her eyes off his hands, lean and strong, and the speed and neatness with which he sliced and chopped. He had rolled the sleeves of his crisp white shirt back from his wrists to just above his elbows, exposing a long stretch of tanned olive skin liberally shadowed with crisp black hair. The way that the hard muscles bunched and moved under the satin skin transfixed her and she took another hasty swallow of the delicious wine.

Her whole body tingled under the memory of how it had felt to have those powerful, long-fingered hands stroke over her, making her quiver in uncontrolled delight.

'What is it, Rose?' Nairo had noticed her abstraction, and he paused in his preparations, dark head coming up, deep bronze eyes fixing on her face. He followed the track of her stare, glancing down at his arms, then flashing back up again to clash with her green ones. 'Not seeing what you wanted to see?'

There was danger in his question and in the darkness of the eyes that watched her intently.

'I—'

Straightening up, he stretched his arms out, flexing those elegant muscles all over again, as he waved his hands in her face. The burn from the acid onion juice on his skin made her eyes sting as she blinked in shock.

'No needle tracks, no scars, no trace of drug abuse. Not the arms of a junkie—hmm, *querida*?'

The hiss with which it was tossed in her direction made frightening nonsense of the term of affection so that her shocked and startled eyes lifted sharply, locked with his, unable to look away.

'Or do you think it all went up my nose?'

'No! Oh, no, no!'

She didn't even have time to rationalise her response, it was instinctive, escaping without a thought. Not this Nairo, the hard-working businessman, respected by so many, devoted to his sister...

But this Nairo was the same man as the Jett she'd known all those years ago. She'd been so *sure*.

No. It hit hard as a blow. She'd been so *scared*.

She'd thought she should fear him then, but the cold rage in his eyes told her that she had more reason to be afraid right now. And yet scared was not what she felt—not in the same way. Because she knew that right now that icy rage was justified.

'I never thought...I mean, I spent all those weeks with you. We lived together—I saw you night and day. Saw you dressed and...and...' her voice shuddered on the word '...undressed. I knew there was nothing like that. I knew that you were not an *addict*!'

She didn't know how she expected him to react. She only knew that it wasn't with the cynical laughter that made him throw back his head in a dark travesty of amusement. Disturbingly all she could think of was the way it had felt to lie in the sleeping bag with him, her head on his shoulder, nose pressed close against the bronzed skin of that strong neck, feeling the muscles move underneath it, breathing in the scent of his body. Even after ten years the memory still had an intensity that slashed at her heart.

'But you thought that I was prepared to feed others' addictions—for profit.'

If he'd raised his voice, shouted at her, then she knew she would have backed away, heading for the door. But his tone was flat and low, almost gentle, as if this were a casual conversation and not an exhumation of the darkness of the past that still lingered between them. Yet, for all that soft, steady tone, there was no hiding the ruthless control that went into keeping it that way. That had always been the difference between him and her heartless stepfather. But now she had to face the fear that that ruthlessness had blinded her to differences that went so much deeper.

She'd known this had to come sometime. At some point the silt that had gathered around their time together would have to be brought to the surface, exposed to the cold light of day. It was inevitable. But life had been so peaceful, so easy for the weeks she had been here that she had actually allowed herself to think that perhaps it didn't matter. That maybe she could complete her commission and get away again, unscathed...

Oh, who was she kidding? She hadn't been unscathed from the moment he had walked into her boutique and back into her life. The truth was that the past had left its scars, heart deep, and his return had shown that those wounds were still only barely healed. One word, one touch, one kiss like the one at the fashion show, and the delicate covering behind which she'd hidden them was ripped away, leaving her emotions raw and exposed.

The only surprising thing was that he'd waited so long. Why had he held back until now?

But then he said, 'And yet you were prepared to put up

with vile—my criminal past—in order to get this wedding dress commission?' And it all became so obvious.

It was for Esmeralda, of course. He'd wanted to make sure his sister got the dress of her dreams. Nothing was to come between that and the wedding. But now it seemed he was satisfied with how that had turned out and he'd decided to challenge her.

'You thought so little of me.'

She'd thought the world of him once and that was why disillusionment had hit so hard.

'I saw you.'

Nairo tossed the knife down onto the chopping board, clearly dismissing all idea of preparing any sort of meal for them.

'You saw what?'

'You—and Julie…'

'Julie?'

He could barely remember the name, but slowly the image came back to his mind. The bosomy blonde who had been the latest to warm Jason's sleeping bag, but who had made it more than plain she had an interest in him. Whenever Jason had been out of the squat she had tried to flirt with him, stroking his face, pressing unwanted kisses on his lips. But she'd usually waited until Rose was out too. Had Rose seen her…?

'Julie meant nothing to me.'

'Nothing?' Her wide eyes challenged that statement, but the sheen of tears that glistened in them told a different story. 'I saw you kissing her.'

'*Infierno*, you saw no such thing.'

Nairo reached for the knife again, pulling a pepper towards him and starting to slice into it, his movements hard and vicious. It was either that or reach for her—and he didn't know just *how* he would do that. Right now to touch her for any reason would blow this whole thing apart.

'You saw nothing. You saw *her* kissing *me*.'

'Oh, and you were fighting to get away from her, were you?'

Scorn and disbelief rang in Rose's voice and in that moment he knew just what kiss she had seen. The time when he had tried to convince Julie to get out of the squat—get away from Jason and his dirty deals. She had said that she would go if he went with her, her eyes even filling with tears when he had said no. He had tried to let her down gently, telling her that he was already committed. That had been the one and only time that he had admitted to anyone the way he had felt about Rose. He hadn't even told Red herself—something for which he was to be so very grateful later.

'No, I was not. But at least she didn't betray me.'

'Do you really think I could stand by and…?'

'And what, Red? And *what*?'

The knife slashed through the firm red skin of the pepper, hacking into the wood of the chopping board and leaving a cut so deep that he almost had to wrench it free.

'Fine—I kissed her—if that's the worst that you can accuse me of, then…'

Had she really just walked out on him because she had seen him comforting Julie? Had what they had meant so little to her that she could just turn her back and walk away? The slices of pepper dropped into rough, shapeless pieces, any attempt to dissect them carefully abandoned completely.

'So you didn't give her heroin?'

'What?'

Once more the point of the knife hit the chopping board and stuck, his fingers clenching so tight around the handle that his knuckles showed white. He couldn't make himself look at her, knowing that he would lose what little was left of his control if he did. Had she really thought him capable of that?

'You gave her drugs.'

His mind was back in the darkness of the squat, after that one lingering kiss. Lingering on Julie's part, never on his. He had tried one last time to make her stop, change the path she was on. A path that would lead all the way down to hell if she didn't get off it.

'Get out of here,' he'd told her. 'Get away and start again. That's what I'm going to do. I can't stay here any longer.'

He'd unpeeled her fingers from around the tiny wrap of drugs she'd clutched in her hand and held it up.

'No more, Julie,' he'd said. 'No more… If you leave it, you can come with me if you like.'

Was it possible? Could it be that Rose had actually seen that as him encouraging Julie in her habit, but, cold and controlling, he had told her she could have no more that day?

He knew—hell, he'd always known—that Rose had had good reason to go to the police. That the poisonous atmosphere in the squat had to be exposed and dealt with. Hadn't that been the reason he had wanted to get her out of there? The one thing that he had never ever been able to come to terms with was that she actually believed *he* was capable of being behind it all. So convinced that she hadn't even stopped to ask, to give him a chance to put his side of things. She had just turned and walked, leaving him behind without a backward glance.

Now it seemed that she had added other imaginary crimes to the list. But the ultimate betrayal was that, like his father, she had gone with what she had thought she'd seen, believing in the way things had looked rather than actually asking him for the truth.

'I gave her nothing.' The knife moved again, the sharp blade chopping faster and faster, dicing the pepper into tiny pieces. 'Not drugs. Not a thing.'

Absolutely nothing. Not a thing. How could he when at that time the only part of his heart that he had allowed to open was given to someone else entirely? To the woman who was standing at the other side of the island accusing him of...

His head came up, eyes blurred as he tried to focus on her face. The face that had once meant so much to him. Still so beautiful, but no longer the Red he had thought she was. The Red he had never ever really truly known. For such a short time she had made everything make sense— given him a path to follow, when all the while she had believed that he was lower than the grubby floorboards of the squat beneath her feet.

'Did you really think that *I* was the dealer in that place? That *I* was the one selling heroin?'

CHAPTER SIX

'TELL ME THE TRUTH. Is that what you thought?'

The expression on her face gave him his answer. But it was obvious that she couldn't hold back any longer.

'You had it in your hand that day and you suddenly had money. You said— You told me…'

I have a plan—a way of getting us out of here. The words hung between them in the stillness of the night, dark and determined and—as he now saw—so easily interpreted in a totally different way. By her at least. *But I need to get more cash together. Just give me a few more days.*

'I said I would get us out of there. I was working on it—but you didn't wait. You walked—you *ran*… You told the police that I…'

'I had to, Jett…'

Impossibly, she had reverted to the old familiar name, the one she had once used with warmth, he had believed, with love, he had deluded himself.

'I couldn't just sit back and let that happen.'

'Let what happen?' His voice sounded raw and cracked. 'Let *what* happen, Ms Cavalliero?'

'Jett—Toby *died* from an overdose, from a bad batch of that stuff. I couldn't let that happen again.'

'You couldn't— You— Oh, *infierno!*'

The curse broke from him as an unwary, unthinking

movement had lifted the knife again, bringing it down onto one of his fingers, slicing in deeply.

'Hell…'

For a moment it was all he could say as the pain shook him out of the daze of anger and denial that had held him.

'Oh, Nairo…'

Suddenly she was beside him, hands coming out, reaching for him. She took his fingers in hers, letting the knife drop back onto the work surface with a clatter as she turned towards the sink, taking him with her.

She turned on the taps, splashing water onto the cut finger, letting it wash away the blood that had sprung to the surface as she reached for a paper towel, folded it into a pad and clamped it down onto the wicked-looking cut, pressing it hard to stop the bleeding.

'Hold that—tight!' she said, her voice trying for authority but threaded through with a quiver of concern. 'I'll find something—do you have a first-aid box?'

'That cupboard over there.' He indicated with a nod of his head. 'Second drawer.'

Rose found the sterile dressings easily, even though her hands were shaking as she grabbed at them. Ripping off the protective plastic, she was back at his side in a moment, seizing his injured hand with a roughness that betrayed the way she was feeling. The sight of the ugly cut under the stained paper pad made her stomach roil and she almost slapped the dressing down onto it, needing to hide it. Stretching the fabric, she fastened it tight, then added another one on top of it, making sure it was secure.

'*Gracias.*' It was raw, husky, and it made her keep her head bent, her eyes fixed on his fingers.

The job was done; it was time to let go. And yet somehow she couldn't pull her hand away. Her fingers curled around Nairo's, twisting, smoothing. She was stunned by how passively he let his own hand lie in her grasp.

'Thank you,' he said again, his voice deep and rough-edged in a new way that brought her gaze to his face. 'Rose...'

She felt she could drown in the fathomless pools that were his eyes. Her own face was reflected there, eyes wide, skin pale. Her hands still held, his but now it was for a very different reason. She felt the burn of his skin against hers like the sizzle of wild electricity, singeing her nerves.

'Rose, listen to me, damn you...'

His words seemed to scrape along her senses, making her breath catch and snag in her throat. She had to listen. She couldn't let go, couldn't move away.

'I did *not* sell any drugs to Julie or to anyone. You can believe me or not, but that is the truth. I was not dealing. I would rather die.'

He'd offered no proof, but the shock was that she didn't need any. The fact that he hadn't even tried to produce anything to convince her but had simply stated the facts hit her like a slap in the face, making her thoughts reel. How had she got it so wrong? How had she let herself be deceived so easily?

The full realisation came like a dagger out of the darkness, slashing at her in a way that wounded more brutally than the chopping knife had sliced into Nairo's finger. It had been there in the moment just now when she had realised how scared she had been when she'd been in the squat. Not just scared of Jett—but everyone. Anyone.

Her mother, her stepfather—they'd all let her down in their own way. Deep inside, wasn't the truth that she'd believed everyone would act that way? Particularly the men.

Even Nairo.

She'd thought she'd loved him, but had she truly trusted

him? Could you really say you loved someone without the deepest, most absolute trust?

The thought of the cruel wound she had just bandaged still made her shiver deep inside and now this new thought made the shudders colder, crueller. Had she let herself lose someone she had once cared for so deeply in the biggest mistake of her life?

Even as she asked herself the question there came a low, icy little thought at the back of her mind. Someone *she* had once cared for so deeply—but who had never actually said that he cared about her. She thought she'd loved him, but she hadn't trusted him to love her back.

'But the police…'

His grip on her hand tightened until she winced under the pressure.

'Oh, yeah, the police came—they had to, after you called them, didn't they?'

Molten bronze eyes burned down into hers, but Rose was back in the past, in the dark and the cold of that Christmas Eve. She had been unable to leave, to run as far and as fast as she should have done, and she had crept back to hide in the shadows across the street. She had seen the police raid the house, bringing out everyone inside. And she had seen Nairo bundled into a waiting car, speeding off towards the police station. Arrested, she had believed.

'No.' Nairo had seen the look on her face, watched the thought processes that changed her expression flit through her eyes. 'No, they didn't arrest me. Nothing to arrest me for. They searched the place, took everyone in for questioning—you should have stayed around longer. You might have learned a truth or two.'

That caught her on the raw, had her biting her lip hard, teeth digging deep into the softness of her flesh. There had been one moment when he had looked out from the back of the car, staring into the darkness. She had flinched back into the shadows, but...

'You saw...'

'I saw.' The confirmation was dark, brutally cold.

He'd seen her. He'd known she was the one who had reported him to the police. Who had had them raid the squat and arrest everyone they found there.

'I had to—surely you could see that? I couldn't have such a thing on my conscience...'

'And you thought that I had offended that delicate conscience? What was it, Rose—was it that, after your vile stepfather, you were seeing villains everywhere? So you thought I was one too? Or was it really something else?'

'What else could it be?' The way he'd come so close to her own disturbed thoughts earlier, the fear of what might be coming, made her voice tremble, her hands tighten on his.

'They found nothing on me, Red.'

Somehow he managed to imbue the once affectionate name with the burn of acid so that it seared over her skin, taking a much-needed protective layer along with it.

'Not a trace of powder, not a single syringe. There was nothing on *my* conscience, then or any other night. But there was plenty to find on Jason. It was Jason who was the dealer in that squat. So you see, you didn't earn your money—not really.'

'My money?' This was new, and unexpected. 'What money?'

She watched his beautiful mouth twist into a cynical sneer and in a sudden panic tried to pull her hands from his only to feel his fingers tighten around hers, holding her prisoner. She couldn't have moved away anyway. Her legs were numb, unfeeling as the shock of what he was saying punched into her chest, taking her breath from her.

'The reward that Toby's parents offered to anyone who could help them find who sold him the drugs that killed him. Wasn't that what stirred your *conscience* so that you just had to act?'

'No—no way!'

Once more she tried to wrench her hands from his, only to have those strong fingers curl around hers again, twisting so that he could pull her closer to him, her breasts crushed up against the hardness of his chest, his breath warm on her skin as he bent his head to stare straight into her eyes, searching deep as if to find the truth he wanted there.

'It wasn't— I couldn't...'

'Do you know, *querida*?' Nairo's drawl was slow and lazy, totally belying the intensity of his stare. 'If I wanted to, I could almost believe you.'

If I wanted to.

'But you don't—do you?' Rose snapped, fighting against the sharpness of the stab of that careless response. 'You want to believe that I only betrayed you to the police because it would profit me.'

His shrug was a masterpiece of indifference, brushing aside her protests effortlessly.

'It was a long time ago, a third of a lifetime—I've put it all behind me. And betrayed?' It came with a deadly softness. 'You might think that, my dear Red, but let me tell you that before I could feel betrayed, I'd have had to care.'

The poisonous bite of his words tore at her inside, though she was determined not to let it show. It was a fight to find more defiance against him, but she dragged it up from deep inside, tilted her chin higher, tightened her mouth.

'So you think that the only reason I could leave you was for money?' she flung at him. 'That otherwise you were so irresistible I wouldn't have been able to tear myself away? Did you ever consider that perhaps I'd realised that I wanted—*needed*—more?'

That memory slashed at her now, the one that had tormented her when she'd first come into this apartment and recognised it as the home that Nairo had described to her. He'd wanted her to respond with her own dream home, but she hadn't been able to do that. She'd had no idea what a real home looked like. Only that it was safe. With people she trusted.

'That I wanted what *Rose* wanted, what I have now—not to exist, as Red did, in a place like that, with a man like you?'

'If you did, then you were lying to yourself,' Nairo returned harshly, squashing her protest. 'And you've been lying for the past ten years with your Lord Andrew and your non-marriage.'

His dark head bent, came so close that his mouth was just inches away from hers. If she was to lift her head, then their lips would meet—and she shivered inside at the thought of the conflagration that would sweep through her if that happened. She feared it and yet she wanted it so much.

'You couldn't put anything in place of what we had—the passion that burned so hot and hard from the moment we met. That made me pick you up from the street where I found you. That made you give yourself—your virginity—to me without a second thought. You couldn't find anything to match it.'

There were no words to deny his accusation. She had wanted it then and, no matter how hard she tried to deny it now, she still felt exactly the same way.

No, not exactly. In the past she had fallen into his arms in the throes of her first, her only, blaze of naïve passion.

Nairo had come to her rescue when she had been lost and alone, homeless and helpless on the streets of London. She had thought that he was her knight in shining armour, her saviour. But he'd had nothing more than that passion to give her, and, needing so much more, she had let her fears grow until she'd convinced herself that she had no alternative but to run. But she'd been running from the lack of love, never from a man who dealt in drugs.

But the hellish thing was that even knowing that didn't change anything.

From the moment that she had seen the knife slice into his finger and had felt the shock of horror at the thought of his beautiful hand being damaged in that way, she had known she was in deeper than she dared to admit. Once long ago, in the squat, she had caught her hand on an exposed nail, just a graze, far less damaging than the knife cut, and instinctively he had reached for her, bringing her hand to his mouth, to kiss away the soreness of the shallow graze, looking straight into her eyes as he did so. She had loved the slow smile that had curved his lips, felt herself drawn irresistibly into the darkness of his eyes, and he had pulled her to him and crushed her mouth with his. They had ended up in bed—if the battered sleeping bag could be called a bed—that night, coming together again and again, only having to reluctantly put a check on the passion that burned between them when they had run out of the small supply of condoms that had been all Nairo could afford to buy.

She had been prepared to make love one more time without, she recalled, heat rushing over her body at the thought of how naïve she had been. She had never been able to impose any control on herself where he was concerned, as irresponsible as her mother, who'd been only the same age when she'd fallen pregnant. Nairo had always been the one to insist on a degree of sanity—out of consideration for her, she had always thought. She'd believed it was because he didn't want her to have to deal with unwanted consequences of their relationship so young. She had seen it as evidence of how much he cared, but later she had been forced to consider the possibility that it was really to protect himself. To ensure that he wouldn't be burdened with any responsibilities that might tie him to her for a future he had no desire to face.

Now she knew where he disappeared to at night, to this private apartment, she was again confronted with all the thoughts that had filled her mind when he hadn't joined them for meals, of Nairo being out on the town with a succession of beautiful women. In her imagination he had escorted them home, taken them to bed...

But perhaps if he had been here all the time... If he had spent the evenings in his apartment—alone?

Was she a fool to imagine that that was possible? To allow herself to think that Nairo had no one special in his life right now—no one, full stop?

The passion that burned so hot and hard from the moment we met. You couldn't find anything to match it.

Was it possible that that passion was the way he felt—had felt—still felt—too?

'You still can't, can you?'

'No?' She tried to make it into a challenge, bringing her chin up defiantly, but that only brought her lips even closer to his, the warmth of his breath on her skin, the taste of him so close that she could almost sense it on her tongue. 'You think not?'

She was teetering on the edge of a dangerous cliff, balanced so precariously that the tiniest puff of a breeze would send her flying, tumbling head over heels into the pit of molten need that was already threatening to enclose her.

She didn't want to say no, didn't want to put a stop to this. The need to acknowledge the reality of what he said was a burn in her veins, the tiny connection between their hands like putting her fingers into a live electric socket. She knew it was safer to let go—but at the same time she knew that it was the last thing she could do. She wanted this touch, needed more of it, as common sense fought a nasty little war with the hungry sexuality that was making her pulse thunder hard against her temples.

She wished he would make the first move, but deep down she knew that was just cowardice. She *wanted* this, she should own it, acknowledge it. If she chickened out now, she would only regret it so hard tomorrow.

But if she acted, would she regret it even more?

'I know not,' Nairo declared. 'If you'd found someone else to give you what we shared, then you would be with him now. But no, no one—definitely not your Lord Andrew. So can you face the truth—or can you actually claim that what I say is a lie?'

The danger was that he was talking to himself, Nairo knew. He wasn't just challenging Rose to admit how it had been, how it still was, for her, but forcing himself to look the truth in the face and review his own life in the ten years that had passed since they had been together. There had been no one else who had affected *him* so strongly, no other woman who had trapped him in her searing appeal, since the day Rose had walked out on him on that dark December night. Oh, there had been other women—too many—who had warmed his bed and eased the appetites of his body. But none of them had made him yearn as she had done. None of them had truly satisfied him.

They had been enough to stave off the hunger of his most basic needs, but he had left every bed with a feeling of emptiness and discontent so that in the end he had simply given up. He had nothing to give these women and they did nothing to fill the emptiness inside him. He had focussed instead on the work of the estate, the business deals that kept his mind from straying onto other, more sensual paths. In the beginning he had told himself that he was doing this only to rebuild his relationship with his father, to regain Raoul's respect, but the truth was that he was still trapped by the memory of how it had been with Red.

That was why he had had to keep her with him now. Why he couldn't let her go until he had gorged himself on her warm and willing body, to wipe away all the hunger she had left him with and know that at last he was done with the blind, foolish obsession he still had with her, sated and fulfilled so that he was at last ready to move on.

'No,' Rose said softly.

The single syllable was so unexpected that he felt it like a start inside his head, his gaze going to her face in shock, searching her eyes.

'Is that no, you don't want…?'

'No, I can't claim that what you say is a lie.'

If her voice had had the slightest shake in it, any sort of hesitancy, then he would have let her go, stepped away from her, forcing his attention back onto the preparation of the simple meal he'd been planning, though it would kill him to do so. He wanted her. *Infierno*, but he ached to possess her, to taste her mouth, feel the warmth of her skin under his touch, the softness of her body yielding to him.

But it was that *yielding* that he wanted. He wanted her willing and he wanted her as eager for his touch, his kiss, as she had been all those years before. Nothing else would give him the satisfaction he craved. He had been through every form of hell keeping his hands off Rose since she had come to live at the *castillo*, and now his blood was thundering in his veins so that he was hard and hot as hell, aching with need, unable to believe what she was saying.

'I'd like to be able to say that I don't feel that way about you, but I'd be lying...'

Nairo's only reaction was a long, slow blink, but she knew she'd stunned him.

'So?' Nairo questioned very softly. 'Rose, what are you saying?'

Could he bring his face, his mouth, any closer, without touching her? Did he know how much it tormented her to be this close and not to reach out to him? To be surrounded by the warmth of his body, the scent of his skin, feel his breath on her cheek? Her mouth had dried painfully and she had to slick her tongue over her parched lips in order to be able to speak. The way that his darkened eyes dropped to follow the betraying movement, the brush of the rich dark arcs of his lashes over the bronzed high cheekbones almost destroyed her.

'I—I...' she tried, failing to find any words to express the denial that self-preservation demanded she turned on him. The denial that would be every sort of a lie. 'I... Oh, Nairo...'

It could not be held back any longer.

'Kiss me! Kiss me now!'

CHAPTER SEVEN

WHO MOVED FIRST she had no idea. Had she lifted her face so that the tiny gap between their waiting lips was obliterated, bringing their mouths together in a clash of wild and searing passion? Or had he brought his lips down on hers in response to her wild-voiced demand? Or perhaps to silence any attempt she might make to deny what she'd said, to retract the command she had been unable to hold back?

He needn't have worried. There was no way that she could even consider denying the hunger that had been eating at her from the moment that he had walked into her boutique, back into her life. It was as if she had been asleep for the past ten years and like Sleeping Beauty had only been waiting for that one kiss from a very special prince.

A prince? Oh, who was she kidding? Certainly not herself. Nairo was no fairy-tale prince now just as he had never been that knight in shining armour she had dreamed of when she had first met him. He had promised her nothing, no happy-ever-after, but the truth was that now she didn't care.

All she wanted was Nairo the man, right here, right now. His brutally devastating kiss forcing her mouth open under his to taste the innermost essence of him, to let her tongue dance against his in intimate passion. The caress of his hard fingers on her skin, pushing under her blouse at the waist of her jeans, skating over her nerves so that she shivered in urgent response, pressing herself against the heat of his long body. Her breasts were crushed against the powerful wall of his ribcage, against her hips the hotly swollen arousal that told her he was feeling every bit of the hunger that seared its way through her.

In a burning haze of need, she felt her feet leave the floor as he lifted her, holding her in arms as strong as steel bands. With a moan of surrender against his demanding mouth, she flung her arms up around his neck, laced her fingers in the silk darkness of his hair and gave herself up to the feelings that were sweeping like a tidal wave through every inch of her.

'*This* could never be denied, never forgotten,' Nairo muttered against her lips, tugging at her blouse so roughly that buttons pulled off and fell to the floor with a soft rattle.

'Never...' she echoed him, unable to find any other words in the flames that took her mind out of reality and into a world where there were only the two of them and the heat that melted every barrier between them.

Her hands were shaking as they slid from his hair, tracing the powerful lines of his face, fingertips catching on the day's dark growth of stubble that shaded his chin. She couldn't believe that she had the freedom to touch him, to kiss him once again as she'd been able to do in the past. It seemed that if she opened her eyes she might find that the immaculate modern kitchen had disappeared and they had been transported back to the squat. Dusty and dull and cold it might have been, but to her it had been a special place. Because she had been there with Jett and because she had already lost her heart to him, all her illusions still in place, no thought of the way they were soon to be shattered.

'Never, never, never...' she whispered, cradling his chin in her hands so as to draw him closer, tracing the shape of his lips with her tongue so that she tasted his mouth, the faint salt of his skin.

But suddenly Nairo snatched his hands from under her blouse, bringing them out to close around her arms, as he lifted her from the worktop where she had been sitting, let her slide down the hot hard length of his body.

'*No.*'

It was rough and hard and unbelievable.

'No,' he said again. 'Not like this—not here...'

'*Yes*—here—now...'

Here, now, anywhere, any time. He surely couldn't be thinking of stopping.

But then to her relief Nairo moved again, swinging her up into his arms as he turned, taking her towards the door.

'I swore to myself that the next time I did this, I would have a bed to take you to,' he murmured into the fall of auburn hair. 'A proper bed—not some damn shabby sleeping bag on a cold hard floor.'

She had been perfectly content in a shabby sleeping bag on a cold hard floor, Rose told herself as he carried her across the room. Because then it had meant so much to her. She had been lost in the way she felt about this man; she'd never paused to have second thoughts about it. All her thoughts had been of him.

So when he laid her down on the softness of a wide, wide bed, the fine cotton smooth and cool under her heated body, she knew a tiny hiccup of hesitation, a needlepoint of doubt puncturing her need. It lasted all of the space of a couple of uneven heartbeats, only surviving until Nairo came down beside her, his hands caressing the need back into her body, his mouth exploring her face, her lips, the skin that those hands exposed as he pushed aside her blouse, unhooked the delicate lacy bra underneath.

Within moments Rose was adrift again, throwing her

head back so that he could kiss his way down the lines of
her throat, across her shoulders. The warm, tantalising path
his lips and tongue traced over the slopes of her breasts
had her catching her breath in delight, arching her body
up to meet his touch, increase the pressure of his kisses
as the fire stoked up higher and higher inside her, throbbing at the hungry spot between her legs. When those
tormenting lips curved over one pouting nipple, drawing
it into his mouth where his teeth scraped gently over her
skin before the swirl of his tongue soothed the faint sting
in the same moment, it set up a whole new burn of need
along every nerve.

'Nairo...'

His name was a choking sound of hunger as her hands
held him closer, clutching at the powerful shoulders above
her, and then, impatient at the unwanted barrier of his
clothes, pushed their way between them to tug at the buttons on his shirt with as little care as he had shown hers
earlier.

'I want...I *want*...'

'I know, *querida*...'

His voice had an edge of raw laughter at the urgency
of her response, the words muffled against her skin as his
wicked mouth teased her to even further heights of need,
hunger burning out of control.

She didn't care that she showed it. Didn't mind what he
thought when her own hands joined his at the waistband
of her trousers as he eased the zip down, helping him to
slide the garment down to her ankles, where she kicked
it aside impatiently. She wanted to be naked with him,
touched by him—oh, dear heaven, possessed by him! In
her naïve foolishness she had lost all this ten years before
and having rediscovered it now she could barely wait until
Nairo made her his all over again.

Now she knew exactly why she had had to break off her engagement to Andrew. Why she had known all along that their marriage would have been the biggest mistake she had ever made. She had never felt like this, never known this all-consuming need with anyone but Nairo. And knowing that the mild affection she had only ever felt for anyone else, it was no wonder she had never been able to go through with taking their relationship any further.

'Red—Rose…*momento*.' The roughness of Nairo's voice betrayed the battle he was having with his self-control. Control that Rose didn't want him to hold on to.

'No…' She pouted her protests, her hands finding the buckle of his belt and flipping it open, sliding down the heated, swollen bulge of his erection, a smile curling her lips as she heard his groan of near surrender. But when she eased down his zip, sliding her cool hands into the heat underneath and feeling his long body buck in fierce response, she couldn't believe it when his hard fingers came down, closing over her wrist and holding her still.

'*Rose!*' It was a sound of reproach, the tightness of his jaw, his gritted teeth betraying the fight he was having with himself. 'We have to… We need…protection.'

Of course. If there was one thing Nairo had always considered whenever they had made love in the squat, it had been the need for protection. Somehow, in spite of the little money they had had, he had always made sure they had the condoms they needed, had never taken her to bed without them.

But there was something she needed him to know.

'Andrew…and I,' she managed as he levered himself up on one elbow, pulling out the drawer in the bedside table and reaching inside. 'I want you to know—we never…'

She couldn't complete the sentence. That tiny move

he'd made away from her let in a drift of air that cooled the mindless hunger just for a second.

But a moment later the heat and the need were there again as Nairo rolled back over her, covering her face with kisses that seemed even more ardent than before and that soon obliterated that moment of uncertainty. He tugged open the foil packet he'd grabbed, fingers uncharacteristically clumsy as he slanted his body away from her just for a moment.

'*Socorro.* Help me...'

It was a raw mutter of command, his hands reaching for hers as she aided him in sheathing the hardness of his erection, her fingers shaking as she felt his heat against her skin.

'Now...'

His impatience showing in the lack of finesse with which he pushed her back down onto the bed, Nairo's long body came over her, powerful, hair-roughened legs coming between hers, pushing them wide, coming so close to the hungry heart of her. Rose's eyes closed in anticipation, her head going back against the pillow, but even as she did so she heard his breath hiss in a sound of impatient dissatisfaction.

'No—*querida*—open your eyes. Look at me!'

His face was so close to hers when she obeyed him. His eyes glazed with passion, the high cheekbones streaked with red.

'I want you to remember this—to know who I am.'

'I know. And I remember...'

Her words broke off on a high wild cry of fulfilment as he thrust, hard and fierce, between her legs and up into the waiting, moist and yearning core of her body, making her close her hands over the powerful shoulders above her, her nails digging into the rigid muscles of his back.

When he began to move, she had no choice but to go with him. She rose to meet each thrust, sighed a release as he eased away, breath catching in her throat as she opened up more and more each time, giving everything she could, taking as much as she could get from him. It was hard and fast and ferocious as if the missing years had been stored up in the sexual hunger that now brought them both together in the wildness of their need. She welcomed the almost roughness of his passion, welcomed it and matched it as it took her higher and higher, pressure building and building until there was nothing left, nowhere to go but into the starburst eruption of total completion as they reached an explosive climax together.

Nairo woke early in the morning, as the dawn crept over the horizon and began to lighten the room, revealing the figure of the sleeping woman at his side, her auburn hair spread out across the pillow, her cheek cushioned on her hand.

His whole body ached in satisfaction in the same moment that just looking at her, at the soft swell of her breasts against the white linen of the sheets, the curve of her hips, the dark triangle of hair at the juncture of her thighs, sent a pulse thudding through him all over again. It roused a hunger that had been ten years building and from which nothing, not even the deep sleep of fulfilment that had finally swept over him, could distance him. He had Rose in his bed again after all this time and it had felt incredible.

It had been the best sex of his life, the sort of physical connection that he had been looking for all these years. It was what he had wanted ever since he had been with Red back in those days in the squat. Inexperienced as she had been then, she had been just a promise of what he now knew he had been searching for and why. Once he had found her again, he had had to keep her with him to anticipate just a moment such as this. To wake with her beside him, having taken her again and again until they had both tumbled into exhausted and satiated sleep.

At some point in the night, he had gone into the kitchen and fetched fruit and wine, a very belated replacement for the omelette that had never materialised. He had fed her grapes and peaches, licked the juice from her kiss-swollen lips. Then, when the shivering response of her body had made her spill some of the wine down onto her naked breasts he had lapped that up too, delighting in the way that her skin quivered under his tongue, the soft moan that escaped her mouth.

'So what happened to you after you left the squat,' he had asked at one point in the night when the darkness in the room hid their faces from each other, the expressions that might have betrayed more than their words could ever do. 'Where did you go? Surely not back to that bastard of a stepfather?'

He knew she'd reconciled with her mother, but surely she couldn't have gone back there. This time the shiver was far less sensual, far more a gesture of distress.

'Never! I couldn't have gone back there to save my life. But I got in touch with my mother—rang her when I knew he wouldn't be at home.' Her voice sounded bruised with the memories she was so reluctant to unearth. 'She was so unhappy—she realised just what this man she'd married was like and, like me, she was desperate to escape. We arranged to meet. But then she ended up in hospital.'

She paused, took a deep swallow of her wine as if finding strength to go on.

'She was bruised and battered. Broken ribs. We planned to get away together—leave him behind and make a new life for ourselves wherever we could. We had no money—

Mum wouldn't take anything from him and he'd controlled all the finances—but we didn't care. We contacted social services—they found a flat in another town, and we took whatever jobs we could find.'

Nairo levered himself up at her side, looking into her shadowed face. She had some courage, he had to give her that.

'And how did you end up with the designer's job?'

Rose tapped the edge of the glass against her teeth, gathering her thoughts.

'I found a job shelf-stacking in a supermarket—Mum and I worked in the same place. When I could, I started with evening classes—art and design—found I had a flair for that. When Mum found a better job I tried for college—won a scholarship. I worked in the evenings doing repairs and alterations at first, then I made a few dresses for people locally and I was lucky. People loved what I made. From that I got a place in a fashion house. I started at the very bottom, trained, worked hard…'

Her teeth flashed white in the shadows as she gave a slightly forced smile.

'I was lucky that I found some premises at an unbelievably low rent, and I seemed to get a reputation just by word of mouth. Then Mum found out she had cancer—and I met Andrew…and it all went downhill from there.'

'You never slept with him?'

He sounded as if he couldn't quite believe it.

'Never.' Suddenly she looked up at him, eyes shadowed in the moonlight. 'I never wanted to.'

Nairo's head went back sharply as he frowned his disbelief.

'But you wanted to marry him.'

'I said yes to his proposal.' Somehow she made it sound so very different from 'wanted to marry him'. 'I thought

Andrew offered me safety.' Her breath hiccupped on the word. 'But safety wasn't what I really wanted.'

It was supposed to reassure, but somehow it had a shockingly opposite effect.

'Safety,' Nairo repeated. 'As opposed to...'

Suddenly he slammed his wine glass down onto the cabinet at the side of the bed. Did she still think he was the dangerous one—the lawbreaker?

'If you wanted the bad boy...'

'Nairo, no! I had it all wrong. I was wrong. I should never...'

He couldn't stop himself from responding even though he knew his furious nod of his head had shocked her rigid.

'Yes, you should,' he growled. 'If you truly suspected that anyone—that I was involved with that filth, then of course you had to do something about it.'

'If I suspected...' She reached out, took hold of his hand as she leaned towards him. 'I did—but I was *wrong*. About you. And if you must know, I was wrong about Andrew as well.'

But that new mention of the man whose ring she'd worn was too much. He didn't want any thought of her past fiancé intruding into this night with her.

'Forget that man. He has no place here. All that matters is you and me.'

He'd taken the glass from her hand, placed it on the bedside table next to his own. Then he'd leaned over her, pressing his mouth against hers, kissing away the regretful words. As he'd known she would, Rose had returned his kisses, softly at first, then more hungrily, passionately, her mouth opening under his, her hands coming up to lace around his neck, pulling him down to her. She'd slid down on the pillows, taking him with her, the stroke of her hands turning from gentle to teasing to demanding in the space of a couple of heartbeats.

The next moment they had forgotten all about talking, or thinking, and had lost themselves in the wild, blazing passion that totally consumed them.

And now she was still here, beside him, naked and warm. All he had to do was to waken her...

But something stayed the hand he reached out to touch her, held it hovering over her body, so close that when she breathed in and out, slow and deep, the warm, flushed flesh of her breasts almost brushed against his palm.

If that happened, then he knew that so much else would happen too. He would not be able to control his response. Already his body was hardening in fierce anticipation of the pleasure it had known during the night and hungered to know again.

But know with *who*? Who was this Rose who had welcomed him into her warm and willing body so often in the night, and who lay there now, an open invitation to the heated oblivion he had known?

Was this the woman who had walked out on him without a backward glance, leaving him to face the police? They'd had nothing to convict him on, obviously, but the scandal of that raid on the squat and subsequent arrests had damn near destroyed every chance he had had of a reconciliation with his father.

Rose stirred, sighing softly, and Nairo pulled his hand back further, away from the temptation she offered.

Had she truly not known about the payment for information about the drugs that had taken Toby to his death? He had always believed that that had been her motivation for going to the police, and Jason, spitting fury at being found out, had vowed vengeance on her for exactly that.

Roughly he pushed himself up and out of the bed,

the jerky movement echoing the disturbed nature of his thoughts.

So what if Rose hadn't known about the reward? She'd claimed she loved him, but she hadn't trusted him. Like his father before her, she hadn't believed in him enough even to *ask* for the truth, going by what she'd seen, not by what she should have known of him. Then she'd seduced him into staying in the squat that night when he had planned to leave, to meet his father, to start the peace process that he had hoped might see him back in the family home.

But 'No—don't go…' Rose had pleaded, stroking his hair, his face, and pressing her gorgeous body softly against his, curling around him and doing that amazing little shimmy of her hips that had him hard and hungry in a moment, totally unable to resist her.

He was already burning erect now, just remembering it. So much so that it was uncomfortable and difficult to pull the zip of his jeans closed over his straining hardness. Every nerve in his body urged him to stop the crazy behaviour of pulling on his clothes—to throw them off and get back into that bed with Rose once again…

'Nairo…'

For a moment he wasn't sure if the soft voice he heard was in the past or behind him until the repetition of his name brought his head round to see where she had stirred in his bed, sleepy eyes only half open, a faint frown drawing her brows together.

'Where are you going?'

She levered herself up on the pillows, pale skin flushed from the warmth of the bed, the marks of his touch, the tumbled auburn hair falling over her face. Her mouth was still swollen from the passionate kisses he had pressed on her through the night.

'Don't...' was all she said and it was enough to stop him dead in his tracks.

'Come back here.' She held out a hand to him, regarding him through those half-closed eyes. 'Please.'

It was too much, and, with a groan of surrender that came close to a sound of despair, he tossed aside the tee shirt he had been about to pull on and threw himself down on the bed beside her. Gathering her slender naked body to him, he kissed her hard and let the waves of sensuality break over his head, taking him down, deep down under the surface until he was lost to the world.

CHAPTER EIGHT

It happened as she left Nairo's apartment.

That last time had been so very special, their lovemaking holding such an intensity, a sultry passion such as she had never known. Nairo's kisses seemed to draw her soul from her body, his touch leaving a trail of fire wherever it had caressed her skin until once again they had both fallen into a deep pit of exhaustion from which Rose had only just managed to wake before it was too late. After snatching at her clothes and pulling them on hastily, she made for the door.

She thought that she had slipped from the bed quietly enough not to be noticed, her bare feet silent on the thickly carpeted floor, but it was as she reached the door that she heard Nairo stir in the bed behind her.

'What are you doing?'

His voice was muffled by the pillow, but there was no mistaking the sharpness of the question.

'I have to go! You know I do. If I stay, I might be seen by one of the staff, perhaps even Esmeralda. Or, worst of all, one of Oscar's family, particularly Grand Duchess Marguerite. She always wakes early. Do you want people to know about…us?'

Was there an 'us'? Or had their time together just been

a one-night thing? Never to be repeated? To be kept hidden like a dirty little secret.

If she'd done this before—all those years ago on the night when she'd crept away from him in the squat. If she'd stayed, curled back beside him—or just *asked* him what was going on—might she have discovered then how different things had been, rather than the way she'd believed them to be? If she'd asked him, would he have told her...?

'Jett...'

The old name was just a whisper, a sliver of sound barely escaping her lips, and she was convinced he hadn't heard it. She heard him shift in the bed, turning his face on the pillow so that he was looking straight at her.

'No—you're right.' It was curt, dismissive. 'That would be a bad mistake. You have to go...'

A heavily indrawn breath signalled a darker change of mood.

'And the name is *Nairo*,' he said with brutal emphasis. 'Jett never existed in the same way that Red was just a fantasy.'

'Of course...'

Now she really did have to go—and not just for fear that someone in the main house might see her. She had completely lost control of her emotions and the burn of despair inside her was something she would do anything to conceal from him.

She had thought that she'd learned from the past. That she should talk to Nairo, ask him what he felt, what was happening, rather than just running away. So she'd asked. And the answer he'd given had made it plain that there was nothing special between them. Only the wild, blazing passion that had raged through them last night and killed rational thought. The hunger of desire that needed no explanations, no feeling, no *caring*.

That was all that Nairo had to offer her, and if she was going to be strong enough to take what he had to offer for as long as he offered it and not ask for more, then she had to hold herself in and never let anything of the true way she was feeling show. If he had wanted more than they had already, then he would have made it plain. She didn't dare to push it any further.

To do so was to risk blowing even this 'relationship' wide open and destroying it completely.

'I'll see you back in the house...'

Where she would show him the calmest, most unemotional face he could want. If this was all he had to offer her, then she'd take that and not ask for more.

Somehow she made it down the stairs, gripping onto the bannister with tight fingers, blinking hard to drive the tears away.

But still they blurred her vision, blending with the hazy light of the dawn to create a cloudiness that meant she could barely see as she made her way onto the path around to the main door of the *castillo*. So when a sudden bright, vivid flash came out of nowhere, blinding her, she thought it was more of the same distortion of her vision that resulted from the stinging moisture in her eyes.

Until it came again. And again, suddenly becoming a fusillade of sparks and flares blazing out around her into the silence of the morning.

It might have been ten years before, Nairo told himself as he watched the door settle back into its frame behind her. With Rose creeping from his bed to leave him without a word. Except that then he had barely stirred as she had slipped away from his side. He had never even suspected that she had gone for good.

Would she be back this time? Did he want her to stay?

Hell, he wasn't finished with her yet, that much was sure. The side of the bed where she had lain was cooling rapidly, but that wasn't the only reason why that space felt empty. He didn't want this night to end, didn't want Rose to leave. And not because he was concerned that the Schlieburgs would see her, though that seemed to be what disturbed Rose—what she seemed to expect that he would be troubled by.

Oh, he was quite sure that Marguerite wouldn't be too happy to find that he was sleeping with the hired help! But she would come round to it. Unless of course it affected the preparations for the wedding if the news got out, which, with what he'd seen of the reactions to Rose's past, it well might.

It was obvious that Rose wanted to keep it hidden, and expected that he'd feel the same way. He'd let her think that. Because the truth was that he wasn't ready to share this change in their relationship with the world. He knew that she believed that was because of a concern for the in-laws. That the prim and proper Schlieburgs were always in his mind whenever he acted right now. But the real truth was that it was less Esmeralda's new family that concerned him, but his sister herself. If he came out into the open about that fact that Rose was his mistress, then Esmeralda would read so much more into it. She would look into his face and see things that he didn't want her to see.

Or was there something more to it than that? The uncomfortable twist in his guts had him sitting up sharply, staring into the mirror on the wall, meeting his own eyes, searching to see just what was in the face he presented to the world now. He knew what had been there ten years before. The anger, the sense of betrayal, the loss.

Don't be long, he'd said and she'd promised him that she wouldn't be. But then she was gone and that was the last time he had seen her for ten years. Ten long, hollow years, he admitted now, acknowledging deep inside the emptiness he'd endured when she'd left him. He had been so sure that everything was going to be right. She had reached for him, had loved him—or so he'd believed—opening to him so warmly, so willingly, so generously, so heartfully.

But the truth was that she had used his desire for her to keep him right there in the squat until it was too late for anything else, until she had known that the police must have been on their way, and then she'd tossed that cool 'I won't be a minute…' at him and walked out of his life.

Or had she? Raking both hands through his hair, he forced himself to face the new thoughts that had intruded into his mind as he had come awake. There had been a difference, something close to desperation, in the way she had reached for him that long-ago night. Something that, recalling it now, had jarred so badly that he had reacted angrily when she had called him Jett. It had not been a comfortable experience being reminded of the man he had been then.

He'd still been smarting from his father's brutal dismissal of him, the way he'd been thrown out of the family home on the word of his lying stepmother. His judgement had been way off. He'd seen Rose as just another deceitful female who'd come between him and his family, ruining his good name all over again in his parent's eyes. That had been the final slash of the emotional knife that she had used to cut away every last trace of the connection they had shared, destroying the chance he'd thought he'd had of taking it further, making it work.

But he hadn't shared his plans with her. If he had asked her to stay that Christmas, told her about his plans to reconcile with his father, what would she have done?

He pushed himself upwards, throwing back the sheets as he reached for his jeans, pulled them on, dragging a black tee shirt over his head. This time there had been something else in her voice. A muffled, thickened sound that had made it seem as if she was upset.

Was it possible that there was more to it than he had suspected? he asked himself as he dashed down the stairs, out the door. Perhaps if he caught her up, made her talk to him... Perhaps there was something they could salvage...

He came to a violent, abrupt halt, the shaken, devastated realisation of just what was happening stopping him dead as he saw Rose some way off across the lawn...and the sudden frenzy of brilliant camera flashes filling the silence of the morning.

'Señorita Cavalliero...'

'Miss Cavalliero... Rose...'

The chorus of voices, some English, some speaking in Spanish, came at Rose out of the half-darkness, all firing questions at her. All the time the barrage of camera flashes went off right in her eyes until she threw up her hands to shield her face from their glare.

'Hey, come on, Rosie, give us a smile! Talk to us!'

'What do you want?'

She'd been through something like this when she'd broken off her engagement to Andrew, and that she'd understood. She'd left things to the very last minute and the plans for the wedding had been in the public eye for a few weeks. So she'd felt she deserved it when the paparazzi had descended on her shop, firing cameras in her direction, hurling questions she couldn't answer.

But now...

'When did this all start up, then, Rose? Been going on long?'

'How does it feel to be another notch on Nairo Moreno's bedpost—or is he a notch on yours? Is this why you dumped Andrew?'

'Will you be showing Señorita Moreno how to run out on her wedding at the last minute as you did?'

'No! Nothing like that!'

Rose kept her hands in front of her face as she tried to move forward, struggling to see her way along the uneven path. The reporters and cameramen were closing in on her on all sides, pushing and shoving, setting her off balance so that she stumbled awkwardly.

And would have fallen if strong arms hadn't suddenly come out to grab hold of her, haul her upright again and hold her tight against something warm and hard and supportive.

Nairo. Nairo's hands holding her. His arms keeping her upright, his powerful chest and long body providing the support she needed to stay on her feet. The heat and scent of his skin surrounded her and made her feel warm and safe, enclosed in a protective shell. She heard the buzz of excitement from the pestering reporters but couldn't bring herself to respond to it.

Luckily she didn't have to. She felt Nairo draw in a deep breath, then heard his voice, calm and strong, coming over her head to reach her tormentors.

'Gentlemen…'

She could hear the irony in his tone, feel the fight he was having with his own forceful nature to keep the control he clearly believed was necessary.

'Stop harassing my fiancée.'

No, she had to have heard that wrong, He couldn't have said… But even as the sense of shock reverberated through her she saw the same effect hit the reporters as they stilled, silenced, stared.

'I—' she tried, only to have Nairo squeeze hard where he held her. Then he bent his head to brush his lips against the side of her face.

'Let me get rid of them.' It was soft enough to be inaudible, especially when another thunderstorm of camera clicks and flashes drowned every other sound.

'Nairo…' Rose tried to protest, but he silenced her with another kiss, longer and more lingering this time, right on the lips she had parted to protest, creating a new frenzy of interest and making her mind whirl in confusion. Then he spoke over her head as he addressed the paparazzi.

Yes, the engagement was a recent thing—very recent. But not unexpected. Nairo had fallen for Rose from the moment he saw her, but he'd wanted to wait so as not to interrupt his sister's wedding and take the attention away from the bride-to-be. No, they hadn't even chosen a ring yet, though, in his family, tradition usually decided on that.

Rose heard his answers through what sounded like a thousand bees buzzing inside her head. The shock of the ambush by the reporters, the unexpectedness of Nairo's arrival, the solution he had adopted to explain their situation and that kiss had all combined to scramble her thoughts so completely that she couldn't be sure she was hearing anything right. The one thing she was sure of was that the reporters seemed happy with the story they'd been given. If she interfered now, contradicted anything Nairo said, then it would only make things so much worse.

So she managed to stand at Nairo's side, his arm around her waist, her body pressed close to his, and watch and listen as he appeased the scandal hunters by giving them what they obviously thought was a story worth a banner headline and a couple of the photographs they were still busy snapping as fast as they could.

'Spanish aristocrat to marry designer who ran out on her own wedding!' She could imagine the headlines now, and that made it a struggle to obey the hissed command

of 'Smile!' that Nairo gave her with a swift tightening of the arm that held her.

She knew what he was doing and why he was doing it even if the reporters didn't suspect. She recognised the defensive mode that Nairo had slipped into from the moment he had caught up with them and found her hounded by the pack of reporters. He was making the best of a bad job, putting a new spin on the fact that she had been caught sneaking from his apartment after what had obviously been a long night spent there with him. The very last thing that he would have wanted to happen before Esmeralda was married to her duke. This was his personal nightmare come true—the one he'd warned her he would be furious if it materialised. He was making sure that at least when his sister's soon-to-be in-laws heard about this—as now inevitably they must—they would not be appalled at the thought of a raging sexual affair but hopefully more tolerant of a couple who were secretly engaged but had held back from announcing it in consideration of the fast-approaching wedding.

'*Gracias, señores...*'

Nairo had obviously defused the problem for now because the reporters were packing up equipment, turning away, the story ready for filing for tomorrow's news.

Clearly Nairo thought so too because he grabbed hold of Rose's hand and almost dragged her in the direction of the main house. Yanking open the huge carved wooden doors, he pulled her into the tiled hallway and leaned back against the wall, letting his breath escape in a hiss of forceful relief blending with a sound of barely repressed fury.

'Hopefully that will hold them,' he muttered, releasing her at last.

'Hold them!' Rose spluttered, not knowing how to express the mixture of feelings that were curdling inside her. 'How can it hold them when you've just delivered a story that will run and run? They'll want more and more of this fiction…'

'I only said that we were engaged.'

Nairo looked down at her with an expression that made her wonder if she had suddenly grown an extra head. No wonder when the emotional battle going on inside her had made her voice tight and constricted like the control she was struggling to impose on the sudden rush of sadness that had swamped her at that 'I only said…'

Only. There was nothing only about this where she was concerned. The casual way that Nairo had dismissed the idea of an engagement between them—even a pretend one—as having any importance made it only too clear the size of the chasm between them on this.

It meant nothing to him but a pragmatic way of dealing with an unexpected problem and it didn't matter who else was involved or whether they agreed to his approach or not. While for her, the word *engaged* burned like a branding iron.

Add to that the fact that Nairo had only decided to bring their relationship out into the open because it had been forced on him. He'd used this way of explaining it because of the impact it might have on his beloved little sister. Rose might find herself on the pages of the gossip columns, Nairo might now have to tell his family about their relationship, but the truth was that she was really nothing more than his dark little secret, something he would have preferred never to let anyone know about.

'But *engaged*!' Rose echoed. 'Why did you have to say that?'

'It's the only thing the Schlieburg family will understand,' Nairo returned, his expression making it clear that she should have known that. 'If we are planning on getting married, they'll accept that. But a casual hook-up...'

His mouth twisted wryly and he shook his head.

'Not so good.'

'And what when this thing is over and we go our separate ways?' There was an awkward crack of her voice on the words.

A shrug of his powerful shoulders dismissed her question carelessly.

'Engagements break up.'

'But it will be too...complicated.'

It was the only word she could find. *Complicated* came nowhere near what she really meant. She had broken away from this man once before and it had been hell living with the memories. Those memories had even pushed her into the total mistake of her relationship with Andrew and got her the reputation as a heartbreaker when the truth was that it was her own heart that had been breaking at the thought that she seemed incapable of loving anyone else after losing Nairo.

So what did that mean for the way she felt about him now? She had ached with the loss of him even when she had believed that he was the drug dealer she had felt morally obliged to hand over to the police. Now that she knew more about that situation, recognising deep in her soul that she had made a bigger mistake in even suspecting him than giving him her heart, how did she feel about the man himself? She wanted him like hell, that much was obvious, but more than that?

Oh, it was pointless even questioning herself about it. He had made it plain that she was nothing more than a sexual fling for him. This affair was the leftover embers of the carnal passion that had flamed between them so powerfully all those years ago. They had never had a chance to allow that fire to burn itself out, and the bonds of passion that had tied them together had only frayed, not actually been broken. They were still there, still tangling round them, refusing to set them free until they allowed this hunger to burn itself out. The young, foolish adolescent love she'd once known for Nairo had never vanished. Now it had grown into a powerful full-blown adult passion. The love of a woman for a man.

But was Nairo only set on indulging the physical hunger he felt for her until at last, sooner or later, he was sated and could turn and walk away?

The cruel ache deep inside told Rose that she strongly suspected that would be sooner rather than later. He had only actually acknowledged her this morning because the paparazzi had forced his hand. Left to himself, wasn't it more likely he would have kept her hidden away?

'Complicated is not really what you mean,' he said now.

'Of course it is.'

Nairo shook his head, golden eyes locking with hers.

'I told you that you couldn't lie to save your life.'

Which lie did he mean? It caught on raw nerves that he might have guessed something of her feelings, reading too much from her face.

'You're afraid that when we split up they'll think you've done it again—run out on your husband-to-be so close to the wedding day.'

Rose hadn't been aware of holding her breath tight in her lungs, but the sudden inward rush of air snatched in a moment of release made her head swim.

'You're right. That's it.'

She grabbed at the chance to hide the whole truth. Surely there was enough of it in that to convince him on this at least.

Shockingly gently, Nairo reached out a hand, traced a

single fingertip down the side of her face until it came to rest along her jawbone. This time he actually did let the control over his expression melt into a sort of a smile.

'Don't worry, *querida*—I'll take the blame. When the time comes, I'll give you plenty of cause to break it off. Everyone knows I'm not the marrying kind, and you're unlikely to change that. All you'll have to do is to look like the broken-hearted fiancée. Everyone will be on your side in this.'

Even you. Rose dropped her eyes to the floor for fear he might see something she wanted to hide. So now he would be considerate when his thoughts were all of breaking up with her. Did he have to make it so blatantly clear that he just wanted to get her out of his system?

But then she should have expected this, shouldn't she? This was the same man who all those years ago had sent her running with his cold-blooded declaration of *I don't do love. I don't do commitment...I certainly don't do marriage.* And now he'd just reinforced that statement every bit as strongly, if perhaps a little less harshly.

Nairo Moreno or Jett, it didn't matter which incarnation of this man she was with, he'd stated openly that commitment was not in his vocabulary. While she seemed to fall in deeper with every breath she took.

'Great.'

She could have tried harder to make it sound convincing, Nairo told himself, but she hadn't even bothered to inject a note of resolution into her response. He had offered her a way out of the mess in which they'd suddenly found themselves, but she didn't appear to give a damn about it.

He'd come hurrying after her, wanting to talk. Willing to admit that the past had been full of mistakes, marked by emotional scars they'd both carried. That perhaps the present could be different. That had all been shattered in the moment he had seen her beset by the gang of reporters. He hadn't paused to think. Had only known that he couldn't let her be exposed to the scorn and ridicule that had been directed at her before by Geraldine and her type.

'Well, at least we won't have to get divorced or anything messy like that,' Rose said carelessly. 'That would really upset your prospective in-laws.'

The flippant response set his teeth on edge; the muscles in his jaw tightened so hard they actually ached.

'That is not going to happen.'

Things weren't going any further; he would just settle for what they had. Like a fool he'd tried to push things ten years ago, wanting to hold on to everything he thought he could have. So he'd rushed into telling his father that his life had moved onto a very different path. That he'd found the woman who would make him change. He'd wanted to show Raoul that he could settle down, become part of the family again, and he'd thought that Rose would come with him. But he'd moved too fast, assumed too much. He'd learned the hard way how wrong those assumptions had been.

Not this time.

'Our relationship is to be a tragic mistake. One we rushed into but then realised we couldn't live with. If the family ever think it was anything else…'

She actually recoiled from the intensity in his voice, her mossy-green eyes opening wide to reveal the dark shadows swirling inside them. She had looked like that once before. In the squat when he had told her that he had a way of getting them out of there, with money to support them both. At the time he hadn't realised that, believing so ill of him, she'd been horrified at the thought of any sort of future together. Just as now she couldn't make it plainer that all she wanted was a sexual fling. Time to—what was it she had said?—get this thing out of her system. *This thing!* Little Red had grown up—she had no fear of saying exactly how she felt.

'You're really over the top about looking after Esmeralda, aren't you? What created this obsession?'

She was getting uncomfortably close to memories he didn't want to probe.

'Is it an obsession to want your sister to be happy and cared for?' he growled. 'Surely that's a normal brotherly feeling.'

'Happy, maybe,' Rose acknowledged. 'But you seem prepared to do anything for her.' Even tie himself into a fake relationship he didn't want so that her in-laws would be happy. 'Don't you think it's OTT?'

Something flared in those amber eyes. Anger? Rejection? Or something else?

'She was only a kid when I left home—and she needed me. When I went back—when my father finally let me in—I promised myself I'd never let her down again.'

'Let her down?'

She'd seen the way he looked at his young sister—and, more importantly, the way that Esmeralda looked at him. Those weren't the looks between someone who had been let down and the person who'd upset her badly. The truth was that Rose had envied Esmeralda's close connection with her brother, the obvious complete trust she had in him.

'How did you do that?'

But that was obviously a question too far. His jaw set tighter, his face seeming carved from granite. Hardly surprising when she had touched on that all-important word *trust*. The one thing he had wanted from her—and the way she had failed him. The bitter twist of her conscience was nasty and sharp, making her suddenly need to sidestep this particular subject.

'So what do you mean, when your father let you back in? I was the one who had to get away—escape from having anything to do with my stepfather. So I couldn't risk going back home. You told me you were the one who just walked out. So, presumably you could walk back in?'

No response. Not a word or a change in his set, taut features. Suddenly she wanted to provoke him. Wanted the truth from him.

'It was OK for you, surely. You had a comfortable home, a business, family wealth just there for you.'

'Walk back in! Hah!' His tone was so cynical it could have flayed a layer of her skin away. 'You have to be joking.'

'Why? Wasn't it like that?'

'In my dreams. How could it be with—'

'With what?' Rose questioned when he broke off, turning his head sharply to stare out across the garden, where the sun was now beginning to burn through the dawn mist, refusing to meet her eyes. 'What happened? Nairo—tell me.'

CHAPTER NINE

'NOTHING TO TELL.'

The face he turned back to her was bleak and so ruth-lessly controlled that it seemed as if his cheekbones might slice through the skin where it was pulled taut and white against them.

'It no longer matters. It's done with.' He bit the words off with a brutal snap. 'In the past.'

If he expected her to believe that, then he needed to be more convincing. All that his expression conveyed right now was the fact that he was cutting himself off from whatever had happened, and his body was so rigid that it made her want to ease some of the tension away from his muscles.

'It might be in the past, but it's pretty obviously not done with. Not when it makes you look like this.'

With careful fingers she traced the drawn shape of his cheeks and jaw, feeling the muscles bunch under her touch. She wanted to soften it even more, perhaps risk a kiss, but she didn't dare. Every instinct told her that if she pressed her lips to his, then he would respond with that searing hunger that flared between them so fast. Light the blue touch paper and stand well back.

Even if she welcomed the thought of being taken to his bed again, of giving herself up to the passion that stormed her body, sent her brain spinning, she knew that if she did so, if she let him take her out of the here and now and throw her into the wildness of pleasure he could give her, then he would never let her go this way again. He would snatch at the opportunity to distract her totally, and so never tell her the truth, never let her into this particular dark space inside his mind.

'Tell me,' she urged softly.

'I told you. Back then.'

'Oh, come on!' Rose mocked. 'You told me only as much as you wanted me to know. Why do you think…?'

But that was treading on dangerous ground, going back to the confrontation they'd had the previous night. She hadn't trusted him. She'd been a naïve fool to think she could say she loved him when she had never really known him. But the man she was getting to know now, the man who cared for his sister, had worked so hard to regain his father's respect… Who, face it, had come to her rescue just now even if he had used his own pragmatic way of dealing with things, and so had trapped them both in a situation that he must hate. One that tore at her heart for the lie that it was.

'You told me that you had a row with your father and walked out.'

He'd made so little of it then that she had believed it had been nothing like the fear she had fled from in her own home. It seemed that in that, as well, she'd been badly mistaken.

'He threw me out.'

Suddenly he flung up his hands in a gesture of surrender and it was as if she had pressed the right button, and the stream of words couldn't be held back.

'My parents' marriage was toxic. She married him for his money and thought her duty done when she provided one heir—me. Two children were not in the contract, so she didn't stay around after Esmeralda was born.'

'She left when you were—what—nine?'

The sharp nod of his dark head held all the anger he wasn't prepared to express.

And his sister just a baby. It was no wonder that he had always felt so protective to Esmeralda as her big brother.

'We had nannies of course—and my father had plenty of women, but none of them stayed around very long. They just helped him spend his money and then moved on. But later *Papá* married again. My stepmother—my *much* younger stepmother—tried to seduce me. She came on to me one night, hot and heavy. I'd had a drink and, stupidly, didn't quite realise just what she was up to. But then when we were found in a compromising situation— she had half her clothes off and was starting on mine—she claimed I'd been the one who had started it all. My father told me to get out.'

The stark control was back, giving away only the most basic of facts. That in itself told Rose more than she wanted to know about what had actually happened.

'He cut off my allowance, threatened to disinherit me totally, said he never wanted to see me again. I can't say I wanted to see him either if he believed her word against mine.'

Rose flinched away from the flat coldness of that statement, knowing how much lay behind it. No wonder he had been so darkly angry at the way she hadn't trusted him either. With his father's betrayal behind him—both his parents' really—he would find that so very hard to forgive.

She wanted to reach for him again, bridge the gap between them with a touch, but even though they were barely inches apart the emotional chasm seemed too great to overcome.

'So I came to London, ended up in the squat.'

The look he turned on her actually had a glint of dark humour in it, an unbelievable smile tugging at his mouth.

'It wasn't just any old squat—it was actually once my family's London house. One my father had let become so run-down because he'd been spending all his money on women. To tell you the truth I quite enjoyed the thought of squatting in the family home. After all, *Papá* had left it to go to rack and ruin. At first it gave me some satisfaction to know my father would hate my being there—but later I had a crazy idea of standing guard over the property, making sure it wasn't totally destroyed by the others.'

His bark of laughter was cold and brutal so that she winced inside just to hear it.

'I should have realised then how bad things had got—how fast my father had gone through his fortune—and that was before Carmen divorced him and took half of what was left. But then, that Christmas, I decided it was time to try to build bridges. I contacted my father—offered an olive branch. He was hard work—I almost didn't make it.'

Another shrug of those powerful shoulders, another controlled, obvious understatement, hiding so much more. And her behaviour must have made it so much worse. She didn't need to be told; she could fill in the blanks for herself. His father had heard about the drugs bust and the police raid. He'd also learned that someone had died and had blamed Nairo for that.

'I'm sorry.' What else could she say? 'So sorry.'

His eyes were dark, shuttered as he looked down at her, but astonishingly he shook his head in rejection of her apology.

'What else were you supposed to do if you wanted to stop that awful trade that Jason was involved in? It was what I was going to do as soon as I got you out of there.'

For a moment she'd been so rocked by that 'what else were you supposed to do?' that she almost missed the final throwaway sentence. But even as she registered it, he was speaking again and that dreadful, flat, controlled tone allowed for no interruptions.

'When I was allowed back home, I found that the stepmother had left. She'd abandoned Esmeralda—who was only nine. That was the second time she'd lost a mother.'

Bitterness twisted the word into an appalling sound.

'The woman who gave birth to us walked out when she was only a baby. Now this one. And my father was busy with a new woman. I promised myself I'd take care of Esmeralda, but he said he wouldn't have me in the house unless I went to work on the *estancia* in Argentina—to "earn my place in the family".'

'Esmeralda told me you revived the *estancia*. You proved yourself with a vengeance.'

Nairo nodded sombrely.

'What did you do there?'

For the first time his face lightened. There was even a curve to his lips, a light in his eyes.

'I turned the place into a profitable venture by making it a popular holiday destination—horse riding, wine tasting. I even set up an arts trail—there are some brilliant new painters out there. My father must have hated the way it had become so commercial—but he couldn't deny how it started paying its own way. Especially when it ended up out of the red and completely into profit.'

'He'd have had to admit you did the right thing. And he must have let you come back home.'

'Yeah—but when I did Esmeralda had changed out of all recognition. She'd felt so out of control for too long. There was nothing she could do about the family situation, so she started to impose a ruthless control on something she could govern—herself.'

'I wondered if she'd had an eating disorder,' Rose put in on a gasp of shock. 'Was she anorexic?'

It was obvious when she thought about it. Esmeralda was so delicate, so bird-like. She almost looked as if a touch would snap her in two. And if this was what she was like now, some time since the events Nairo was describing, then what must it have been like back then?

'She almost died.' Again, the flat, toneless voice expressed the horror of that time.

'I understand,' Rose said, knowing she meant more than his sister's story. It was no wonder he was now so totally focussed on propriety and the family's reputation. That he wanted Esmeralda to be happy.

But he had lost his mother too. When she'd walked out she'd left both of her children, and Nairo, at nine, had to have been more aware of her abandonment than his baby sister.

No wonder he'd reacted with such ferocity when she'd told him her story, declaring that her mother should have been there for her, to defend her. That she hadn't deserved the—in *his* mind—too easy forgiveness Rose had given her. But for Esmeralda's sake *he* had been prepared to hold out an olive branch to his father, to work his 'penance' in Argentina.

And not just for his sister, a sad little voice in her thoughts reminded her. *As soon as I got you out of there.* He had thought of her too then, but she had let her fears swamp her and had run into the night. Had she really been fool enough to lose something that could have been so valuable because she'd been afraid she was like her mother?

Some cold, cruel little witch who stamped on his heart and then betrayed him without a care.

Esmeralda's words sounded over and over in her head, making her feel worse with every repetition. What if Nairo's sister had really not been mistaken? What if *she* was the one who had betrayed Nairo in this way?

What if he had once truly cared for her—all those years ago? And she had destroyed that caring by not trusting him so that now all he wanted was the blazing physical passion that had brought them together this time.

A passion that he had felt obliged to cover up by announcing their fake 'engagement' to the world. So that now he was tied into a relationship with her that he had never chosen or wanted.

'I can't do this,' she muttered, knowing from the sharp turn of his head, the dark, assessing glance down at her, that he had caught her words and knew exactly what she meant.

'You have to.'

'No, I don't—I can admit the truth, tell everyone that this engagement is a lie. Move out...'

At least that would free him. So why didn't he look pleased—relieved even?

'But that would break our contract.' His frown darkened dangerously. 'I can still take this commission from you, get someone else in to finish the dress.'

'You wouldn't!' Stark horror rang in Rose's voice. 'Not when Esmeralda's wedding is so close.'

'I would,' he returned, hard and sharp. 'If it meant stopping you from ruining her day by letting her know that what I've just told the press is a lie and so opening up a new sort of scandal that will have the paparazzi feasting on it like vultures for weeks.'

He would too, Rose realised. There was no doubt on that. He felt he had to make up to his sister for her losses—for what he saw as his abandonment of her when she needed him—and to do that he would pay any price. Even letting himself be bound into a fake relationship that he hated the idea of.

'I can't let you do that to her.'

And she couldn't do it either. She had grown so fond of Esmeralda over the past weeks, come to care for her.

'All right, then,' she agreed heavily.

It was only—what? Another couple of weeks and then she could...

Her mind flinched sharply away from the thought of what would happen then.

'Be assured you will still have the wedding commission and all that goes with it.'

He made it sound as if that were all that mattered, but then that was how he believed she felt. It was what she had set out to make him think she felt. The twist of pain in her gut had to be ignored if she was to go on. And she had to go on.

'OK,' she said slowly. 'I'll do it.'

'For Esmeralda?'

Of course, in his mind it could only be for Esmeralda. There was no one else who mattered.

'Of course for Esmeralda,' she said sharply. 'She and Oscar make a lovely couple and, like you, I'd hate it if anything prevented them from having their perfect day.'

Now what had she said that made his jaw clamp tight like that, the muscle at the side of his mouth clenching in uncontrolled response?

'Don't you believe me?' she asked uncomfortably.

For a long moment he looked down into her face.

Then, 'Oh, yes,' he said slowly. 'Yes, I believe you.'

It was the answer she wanted, but somehow it didn't give the reassurance she was looking for. There seemed to be so much behind the simple comment. With a brusque nod of agreement he turned and walked away down the hall, leaving her staring after him wondering why, when he'd said he believed her, he had left her feeling that he actually felt the exact opposite.

'And for you,' she suddenly found herself saying, the words escaping before she had time to think.

She would have caught them back if she could, but then she saw the way his long back stiffened as if a bullet had hit him between the shoulder blades and he came to an abrupt halt. Slowly he swivelled on his heels to turn round to face her.

'What?'

Too late to go back now, and, besides, she didn't want to withdraw the declaration even if he was glaring at her from beneath black brows drawn sharply together.

'Just what does that mean?'

'That I hope that when you've seen Esmeralda married to the man she loves, you'll finally feel that you've done your duty. That you'll have repaid whatever debt you feel you owed your sister—and even your father...'

'You think that's what all this is about?'

'I know it is.'

Though she had to admit that the deepening of that frown made that certainty falter badly.

'And I hope that maybe my part in all this will make up for the mistake I made in believing that you were involved in dealing drugs. I thought that was where you were getting the money you said would change our lives.'

'You didn't trust me enough to ask!'

There was something in his voice that tore into her heart and ripped it open. She deserved it, she knew, and she stiffened her spine to take the accusation that should have been made all those years ago.

'But I didn't trust you enough to tell you.' Nairo supplied the words she had hesitated to say.

'No, you didn't.' It was just a sigh. 'I thought I loved you, but I didn't know what loving someone really meant.'

She did now, and it was tearing her apart not to be able to say it. This time it was not a matter of trust, but knowing that this was not what he wanted from her. That the blazing heat of passion that they shared in bed was all that she meant to him.

'You can't really love where you don't really trust.'

'We were young—foolish—' Nairo's tone almost threw the words away. 'We had a lot of growing up to do.'

Rose could only nod mutely as she clamped her mouth shut on any thoughtless words she might let spill out and ruin the emotional truce they had reached. If this was the best she could have with Nairo, then she would take it.

'Now all we have to do is to see Esmeralda married,' Rose blurted out. Anything to remove that dark frown from between his eyes, lift the tension that held his jaw so tight. 'And then break off our fake engagement. That can't come soon enough.'

She couldn't keep him trapped longer than she was absolutely forced to.

'You promised...'

'I promised that no one would blame you for our breakup,' Nairo inserted, cold and steely. 'And you needn't worry—I'll keep that promise.'

'Good.' She even managed a smile to go with the word, though she prayed it didn't look as unconvincing as it felt. 'And then we can go our separate ways, knowing we owe each other nothing.'

Say no, she begged him in the privacy of her thoughts. *Tell me, just this once, that you don't want it to end this way.* If he even offered her an affair, for as long as it took to burn itself out between them, she would take that. She'd take anything if he'd just make her feel that she mattered to him, in this way at least.

Nairo's silence seemed to drag on and on, drawing out and out until she felt as if her already overstretched nerves might actually snap under the strain. But then at last he moved, nodding slowly.

'That would be the best way to handle this.'

'Then we'll keep to that business deal.'

Rose forced a smile onto stiff lips, though agreement was the last thing she felt. She even held out her hand as if she were still making the business deal he had first proposed to her. Her throat closed tight as Nairo took her fingers in his, her eyes blurring so that she missed the sudden change in his expression.

'No,' he shocked her by declaring sharply, his hand clenching around hers, holding tight as he whirled her towards him, right up against the warm, hard wall of his chest.

'There's more to it than that and you know it. There's this…'

His kiss plundered her mouth, crushing her lips back against her teeth, his tongue sliding along the space he had opened to him, tasting her, tormenting her.

'We've locked ourselves into this fake engagement now, the least we can do is to take advantage of it,' he muttered, rough and raw. 'I want you, and if you try to say that you don't want me, then I'll out you for the liar you are.'

'I— You…'

She tried to speak, but there was nothing to say. She'd told herself that if he had nothing to offer other than his passion, then that was what she would take for as long as it lasted. She wouldn't ask for anything more, knowing he had nothing to give.

So she gave up all attempts to think or to speak and sank into the warmth and strength of his embrace with a sound that was a sigh of acceptance and surrender and encouragement all in one.

'Yes,' she managed. 'Yes—I want you. I want this.'

For as long as it lasted.

CHAPTER TEN

'THAT LOOKS BEAUTIFUL…'

The voice in her ear made Rose start in surprise. With her head bent over the soft pink silk, her hands busy folding and pinning to get the perfect length for the skirt, she hadn't even been aware of the fact that Nairo had come into the room where she was working on the fitting for one of the bridesmaids' dresses. She didn't notice his arrival until he bent his head down to hers and pressed a kiss against her cheek.

Unable to look up at him, or find any words to respond, she simply nodded her head and focussed even more intently on the material in front of her, even though she knew that was not what was supposed to happen. Not when she was meant to be greeting her fiancé on his return after too long an absence away on business.

The feelings were there, it was just that she found it impossible to show them. He'd been away from the *castillo* for some days and she'd missed him more than she could imagine. It was a feeling that had been made all the worse by the knowledge that as the time drew closer to the actual date of Esmeralda's wedding, then so too the days of their 'engagement' must be counting down until the moment when the need for the pretence would be over and the break-up Nairo had promised he would choreograph would have to be set in motion.

When that happened she would have to pack her bags and leave. For good.

'Don't you agree, Marguerite?'

Nairo stunned her even more by turning nonchalantly away towards Oscar's stern matron of a mother, who had taken to supervising the preparations for the wedding, making sure that everything had her seal of approval before it was finalised, smiling easily.

'The dress is spectacular, isn't it? Your daughter will look wonderful in it.'

It was impossible not to contrast that easy question—and the duchess's equally relaxed agreement—with the way things had been just ten days ago. Before Nairo had announced their fake relationship to his family. After that, it had been as if the heating had been turned on in the house and the atmosphere had warmed steadily, even when Nairo wasn't there. Esmeralda, of course, had been overjoyed that her adored brother and her newfound friend had apparently fallen head over heels in love, and the Schlieburg family, even Duchess Marguerite, had thawed noticeably.

Not that this had made life any easier for Rose herself. Quite the opposite. The truth was that every moment was more uncomfortable, every glance, every smile, a torment when she knew they were all based on a lie, one she had to maintain because of her promise to Nairo. She was supposed to pretend that she was madly in love with him, a pretence that, deep inside, was frighteningly easy. Too easy, so that she felt she was in real danger of giving herself away to him while she knew that the softening of his voice when he spoke to her, the gentle touches on her arm

or her waist and, worst of all, the softly lingering kisses
that he drifted across her cheek or her lips, were just part
of the act he had determined to play. One that he seemed
better at playing, when there was nothing real in his feelings, than she was when her emotions were tearing her to
pieces inside, making her feel as if she were bleeding to
death from a thousand little cuts.

What made matters worse was the fact that she couldn't
talk to anyone about their relationship.

Relationship! Hah! Rose let the pink silk drop from her
hands as she lifted her finger to suck at the spot where a
pin had gone in sharply and a tiny bead of blood had risen
to the surface.

This was no *relationship*. The real truth was hidden
away like a dark and dirty secret while every day she was
treated with growing affection and welcomed into the family as if she really belonged there. But only for as long as
Nairo would allow that to last.

'Careful! You don't want to mark it.'

He had seen the tiny damage she had inflicted on herself and he moved swiftly to ease the silk away so that
there was no risk of her staining the beautiful material.
But at the same time there was the touch of his other hand
at the back of her neck, tracing over the knots of her spine
where it was exposed by the way her head was bent over
her work. The warmth of those strong fingers lingered,
moving softly, stroking, circling over the bone at the nape
of her neck, sending delicious shivers of response through
her whole body.

'Come to me tonight,' he murmured against her ear,
soft and low. 'Eleven o'clock…'

Another whisper meant for her alone and already Nairo
was moving away, taking his caressing hand from her so
that she felt a cold sense of loss that was a shadow over

her heart. One that she couldn't help but contrast with Esmeralda's glowing happiness. Nairo's sister could bring her
love for Oscar right out into the open for everyone to see,
while Rose could only hide the truth of hers away. Holding it close to her heart while Nairo thought the way she
was behaving was as much an act as his own performance.

It was a bitter irony that in those past days, when she
had thought that she'd loved him, she had run away from
revealing that love, not having the strength to hold on to
it for better or worse. Now she knew how hard real love
was to handle, she was strong enough—or did she mean
weak enough?—to hold on as hard as she could until the
day that this dream would come crashing down around her.

Perhaps it was that thought that made all the difference, or the days of his absence on a business trip were
what made Nairo particularly passionate that night. She
had barely arrived in the apartment before he snatched her
up in his arms and carried her into the bedroom, dropping
her down onto the bed with little ceremony. Then he proceeded to strip every item of clothing from her, giving her
no time to feel the chill of the night air on her exposed
flesh as he kissed and caressed his way down her, leaving her burning and tingling where his lips had touched.

By the time his hard body slid into her welcoming
warmth she had been floating on a heated tide of hunger,
yearning and open to him. The pulse that throbbed at her
temples made her head swim so uncontrollably that she
was thankful to be supported by the soft downy pillows.
Her whole body felt as if it had dissolved into a pool of
molten wax, lost, adrift, blind with her need for him.

That night her orgasm was so sharp, so overwhelmingly
powerful that it seemed to split her mind in two, sending
her spinning into the wildness of a world where nothing

existed but herself, this powerful, passionate man and the exquisitely raw sensations they had created between them.

It took a long, long time for her to come back to reality. She had no idea how long she lay there, oblivious to everything but the man whose hard, warm chest cushioned her head, his ragged breathing slowly easing and his heart slowing from its frenzied race under her ear.

'That was special.' She couldn't hold it back even if it was the least she could tell him. 'So special.'

She felt the change in his mood in the way it affected the long, lean body lying beside her. From a sweat-sheened relaxation that came with intense sexual fulfilment, every muscle suddenly tightened, holding taut against her in a disturbing silence that pushed her to defiance.

'Oh, I know I would be a fool to think that you agreed with me.'

'It was special to me,' he said at last, his voice slow and dark. 'How could it not be? I've known the best sex I've ever had with you.'

If it was meant to be a compliment—and obviously that was the way that he intended she should take it—then it didn't have the desired effect. If sex was all it was, then it meant too little, nothing like the feelings she found herself longing for. Besides, it couldn't be true. No matter how she might long for even that little satisfaction.

'That's not really true,' she managed, unable to hold the words back.

'What?'

This time he pulled away from her, lifting himself up until he was propped against the carved wooden bedhead. Coldly searching eyes raked over her face.

'Just what the hell are you talking about?'

Could she, like him, tell the difference? Nairo wondered. The very thought rocked his sense of reality. *Noth-*

ing could ever match the way he had once felt about her. The searing burn of that long-ago innocence he had thought they had shared. From the first time, she had made everything make sense, made him want to change his direction in life, to change his world.

For her.

His head spun at the thought that she might even have sensed any feeling like that. Was there something in what he had done—the way he had kissed her, touched her, taken her body—that had risked exposing that hidden part of him to her? A part that not even his father, nor Esmeralda, had ever seen.

'Tell me,' he demanded. 'What the devil is that supposed to mean?'

She shifted in the bed beside him, lifting herself up till she was kneeling close, sitting back on her legs. She pulled the sheet with her, covering the pink-flushed delights of her body from him. It was that change in her mood, the need for concealment, that alerted him to the fact there was no room for dreams in what they had now. She still held her essential self apart from him, even when she had given him her body so willingly and openly.

'That there was someone very special once... No?' Rose questioned as she saw his head move in adamant denial.

'No one.'

'But Esmeralda said...'

The beautiful mouth that had just given her so much pleasure twisted sharply, giving her his response without him having to speak.

'My sister is a hopeless romantic. Besides, she was only a child at the time and she knew nothing. And now, all wrapped up in the fairy-tale details of her upcoming wedding, she still knows nothing of the truth of the basic facts of how it can be between a man and a woman.'

His tone formed the words into ice, making Rose shiver as they landed on her exposed skin, pulling the sheet closer round her for protection from their impact.

'And how is that?'

'Do you have to ask? You were there. You know what it was like.'

'Tell me,' she said, needing to know exactly what she was dealing with. 'How was it?'

That was almost a smile, she noted. But a smile that did nothing to warm the chills that had shuddered over her skin. Instead it made her shiver even more, deeply and inwardly.

'Couldn't be simpler,' Nairo stated. 'I had the hots for you and you had the hots for me.'

He reached out a hand, let his fingers trail across her shoulders and down to where the white sheet formed a tight but impossibly fragile barrier against his touch, his eyes darkening noticeably as they locked on to hers. She managed to control her response but only just.

'I still do—more so now you've grown up.'

Something in Nairo's face changed, sharpening that stare till it felt like the scrape of a blade across her skin.

'That was how it was for you too, wasn't it?'

Somewhere in the back of her mind, Rose acknowledged the death of the wild, foolish hope she had let half form.

'Oh, yes...'

Fearful that that probing gaze might discover more than was safe, she affected a tone of total nonchalance, even managing a sort of a smile, though it couldn't have been as careless as she had hoped for.

She'd prayed he'd forgive her for going to the police and that wish had been fulfilled. It was a long time ago he'd said, a third of a lifetime. So he'd shrugged off her foolishness, her naïveté in suspecting him. But behind that was the real, darker truth that he could shrug it off so easily, not because it hadn't mattered but because *she* hadn't mattered. Because he had never cared about her as she had cared about him.

'That was exactly how it was for me,' she managed even though the lie burned on her tongue like acid, threatening to make her stumble over the words.

Needing to protect herself from the way he made her feel, the way she was tempted to lay her soul open to him, she pushed herself out of the bed, wrapping the sheet round her and taking it with her.

'I'm starving,' she tossed over her shoulder at him, knowing she meant a very different form of hunger than the one that could be appeased with any amount of food. 'Want anything?'

'You know what I want,' he growled behind her, but to her surprise he snatched up his black towelling robe and followed her into the kitchen.

'So where did you go this time?' she asked a short while later, curled up on the settee and nibbling on the edge of some slices of apple, which were all that she could manage to prove her claim of hunger without them choking her.

'London. I had business there.'

Nairo fetched a glass of wine for them both, placing hers on the table before her while he lounged in one of the big dark red chairs, stretching his long legs out in front of him.

'Your mother's looking better,' he added unexpectedly.

'You went to see her?' Rose found it hard to believe, but he nodded easily.

'It seemed wrong to be so close and not check she was OK. And yes, she's doing fine. And she and Margaret are even better friends than before. She sends you her love.'

'Thank you! That means so much!'

It meant even more that he had put aside his own belief that she had forgiven her mother too easily in order
to do this.

'I never thought...' she began, but Nairo was shaking
his head, anticipating what she was about to say.

'I would never have been able to live with myself if I
hadn't made peace with my father before he died,' he said,
his voice rough and low. 'All I wanted was to be part of the
family again. That's why I swallowed my pride...'

The way he tilted his glass, swallowed down some wine,
revealed his feelings more than any words.

'Me too.' Rose dropped the apple slice down onto her
plate, unable even to make a pretence at eating it. 'And I
think I should say that's what Mum was looking for all
her life—a sense of belonging.'

Something changed in Nairo's face, not exactly a softening, but his muscles lost some of their tension, the tautness of his jaw easing just a little.

'I brought you something.' He indicated with his glass,
waving it in the direction of the dresser near the door. 'A
gift.'

'You didn't need to...'

'Now what sort of a fiancé would I be if I didn't bring
my betrothed a present to compensate for being away from
her for so long? It's over there...'

Getting to her feet, the sheet wrapped round her trailing
along in her wake, Rose moved as he directed.

'Here?' She let her fingers rest on the top of the briefcase he'd obviously deposited there as he arrived back
home.

'Open it. It's not locked!' he added as she hesitated.
'Look inside.'

'I'm looking—' Rose stared into the open case. 'But
what...?'

'In the bag—from the art gallery.'

He was watching intently as she picked up the cream paper bag with the name of a London art gallery on it in an elegant script. It was thin and flat as if there were nothing in it.

'This?' She frowned her confusion. 'But…'

There was just a single sheet of card inside the bag, a glossy postcard that shook in her grip as she tried to focus on it. It was an abstract design, glowing with colour. A splash of scarlet and gold and a deep clear turquoise that was her favourite colour ever.

'Lovely!' she managed, knowing there was something she was missing. 'It's gorgeous, but…'

When had he got up and come close to her? She hadn't seen him move and yet suddenly he was behind her, the heat of his body reaching her through the thin covering of the sheet.

'Turn it over.'

As he spoke he reached out to capture the fingers clasped on the edge of the card, lifting her hand to turn it over as he instructed, so that she could see the words written on the back: *Rosa in tramonta.*

'It means rose in sunset,' Nairo was explaining when she saw the rest of the inscription and knew exactly what he'd done. Why he'd done it. The room seemed to spin round her, everything blurring wildly.

'Enzo Cavalliero…' she managed through the tears that were streaming down her face. 'Enzo… My father…'

Twisting in his arms, she could only rest her damp face against his chest and weep out the tidal wave of emotions that had overwhelmed her.

'Hey…' His voice sounded odd, shaken. 'It was meant to please you.'

'And it does…' Rose drew in her breath on an unsteady hiccup. 'So much.'

'Bueno' was all he said. And then he just held her loosely, supporting her until the storm of emotion was over. At last, dashing a hand across her eyes and sniffing inelegantly, she regained some control and lifted her head to smile up into his watchful dark eyes.

'Thank you.' It was low and heartfelt. But she was surprised to see that no answering smile lit his face.

'I'm only sorry…'

Gently he lifted the card again, pointed to the dates. It took a moment, but then she realised what he was trying to tell her. Enzo Cavalliero had died very young.

Before she'd been born.

It took some long moments and a lot of hard swallowing before she could respond, nodding her head and managing at last to say in a whisper, 'No wonder my mother could never find him.' Her voice strengthened as she swallowed again. 'But at least she can know that he didn't abandon her…and me. Did you tell her?'

His rough shake of his head dismissed that idea.

'I thought you'd want to do that.'

He was so right about that. She couldn't wait to tell Joy, show her the postcard.

How different would her mother's life had been—and her own—if Enzo hadn't died so young? Perhaps she would never have run away from Nairo as she had if she'd had a family of her own, more reason to trust. But then there came the inevitable realisation that she would never have had to run from Fred Brown and so she'd never have met Nairo at all and that splintered her thought processes completely. All she could do was hold on to his hand, and the beautifully coloured card, and repeat sincerely, 'Thank you for this.'

It was when her mind and her eyes cleared as she turned back to close the briefcase that she stopped in astonishment as she saw what now lay on the top of it that had been hidden under the gallery bag at the start.

'What's— This is the house,' she said, picking up the photograph. 'The squat.'

It was no longer a squat. The large town house had been renovated, fully restored to its original elegance.

'What's this?' There was a large plaque at the side of the door. The words on it set her mind reeling again.

'Esmeralda House—a clinic…?'

'For anorexic girls,' Nairo supplied with obvious reluctance.

He didn't look at her but kept his gaze fixed on the photograph. Was he, like her, looking at that first-floor window as if it were possible that the ghosts of the people they had been ten years before might appear behind the glass?

'I didn't want the house for myself and I wanted to put it to good use. They can get medical and psychological help there. They can even live there under supervision until they get well.'

'What a wonderful idea!'

This time when she flung her arms round him it was with real delight and enthusiasm and she felt the stiffness of his long body hold for a moment, then slowly ease against her.

'I'm glad you think so.'

It was another moment before his hand came up to rest on her back, long fingers splayed out against her shoulder blades. The warmth of his touch set a whole new rush of sensations flooding through her. Not sexual but that sense of belonging that she had enjoyed since she had come to be part of the household here. The feeling of being part of a family in a way she'd never known before.

'Nairo,' she said quietly. 'Do you have a photo of her?'

She didn't explain who she meant and she knew she didn't have to. Already Nairo was reaching for his phone, scrolling through photographs until at last he held it out to her.

'That's Esmeralda?' She couldn't believe it—could barely recognise the bird-like creature she knew in the small, sturdy little girl with the huge dark eyes and the curling black hair. 'How old…?'

'Nine. Just before…'

Before he'd been driven out of the house by his lying stepmother, his angry father.

She knew what she wanted to say and suddenly, in this new atmosphere, she felt she could say it.

'Did that woman—Carmen—tell her she was fat?' She read the answer in the set of his face, the way that his jaw had clenched tight. 'How dare she?'

But he didn't want her to go any further, that much was obvious. So instead she took his hand and led him back to the big settee, pulling him down beside her, and leaning against him softly.

Taking his hand in hers, she stroked along his fingers, tracing the muscles, the veins.

'You can't blame yourself for Esmeralda's illness, you know.'

His hand jerked under hers, but she tightened her grip, holding him still.

'Your parents, your stepmother—they all did their part.'

'If I'd been here…'

'If your father had believed you, you would have been here.' Her voice rang with the confidence of knowing that was the truth. 'Nothing else would have stopped you.'

For a long, long moment he was silent and still, but when he spoke his lips were just against her temple.

'Gracias,' he said. *'Muchas gracias.'*

He didn't need to thank her, Rose thought. It was enough that he was here, holding her like this. She could stay here all night. But even as the thought crossed her mind she felt Nairo stir and he turned her hand so that now he was the one holding her fingers in his, the one stroking her hand.

Until he stopped dead, his touch and his focus resting on just one spot. At the bottom of the third finger of her left hand. Instantly she knew what was on his mind.

'No! I don't need a ring—I don't *want* a ring.' She prayed it sounded definite rather than desperate.

'Esmeralda asked about it. It's expected,' Nairo growled.

She couldn't bear it if he went any further. She already felt bad enough, fighting the urge to turn tail and run.

'It might be expected, it might be tradition, but this is a *lie!*'

Twisting in his hold, she came halfway across him, almost on his lap, as she set about distracting him the only way she knew how.

'An engagement ring should be about commitment,' she managed, pressing a kiss against his stubble-shadowed jaw and then moving up, one kiss at a time, towards his beautiful, sensual mouth, feeling the instant reaction in him and breathing a silent prayer of thanks for it. 'About togetherness—about love. But there's none of that here.'

Her hands stroked over his skin, caressing, teasing, awakening the need she wanted him to feel. His groan was a sound of surrender, one that told her she'd succeeded, even if deep down that was the last thing she wanted. She welcomed the hunger and demand of his response in the same moment that it tore her heart in two.

With only the slightest tug he released the derisory protection of the fine cotton sheet, letting it fall to the side, exposing her nakedness to him once more.

Nairo's hand smoothed over her skin, along the curve of her hip and sliding upwards over her ribcage to curl around and cup the heaviness of one breast. He let one finger trail over the darker-toned nipple and watched as if hypnotised the way that the skin puckered and pouted under his touch. His smile was a slow, lazy curl of his lips before he bent his head and let his tongue circle the raised bud. The warm breath of his laughter made her draw in her own air on a gasp of delight before he took the sensitised skin into the heat and moisture of his mouth, tugging on it softly in a way that sent the burn of desire flashing along every nerve in her body.

'I've never known love,' he murmured against her, making her quiver and squirm against the softness of the white linen sheet. 'Never wanted it, but, *infierno, querida*, when things are this damn good, then who needs love?'

'No…one,' Rose managed on a gasp. 'No one could want anything more.'

Even the deep-down knowledge that she was lying, that she desperately longed for so much more, couldn't enforce the restraint she knew she should impose on herself. Restraint had nothing to do with this—it was all sensuality. The glorious wild storm of passion that was swamping her, driving away every other thought from her mind.

She wanted so much more than this. Needed more from this man than the feelings he had brusquely described as 'the hots'. She wanted things that were a lifetime, an eternity, away from what he was prepared to give her. But she wanted *him* so much that she couldn't bear to drag herself away and turn her back on the little he did have to offer her.

So she let him pull her down beside him, felt the rest of the sheet torn away and tossed aside, her pulse thundering rough and raw as he moved to come over her, the heat and hardness of his body searing over hers. His mouth took hers, his hair-roughened legs coming between hers, nudging them aside to let the blunt heat of his erection push at the moist core of her being that so longed for him.

She was open to him already. Lost to herself, given up entirely to him and oblivious of anything else. She was all sensation, all heat. All longing, all need. And that was all that mattered right now.

'Oh, yes,' she told herself, whispered against his ear as she pulled him closer, adjusted her body so that he could feel the need she had for him. 'Yes!'

Tomorrow would come soon enough and she would have to face what tomorrow would bring. But for here and now, for tonight—if only for tonight—as Nairo had said, when things were this damn good, then who needed love?

If she said it often enough, then she might just come to believe it.

CHAPTER ELEVEN

'I'VE HAD A wonderful time, Rosalita! Everyone said how absolutely beautiful my dress was.'

Esmeralda accompanied her joyful words with an enthusiastic hug, squeezing all the breath out of Rose and taking away her ability to answer at the same time.

'Just think—next time it will be your big day!'

But that was a step too far. With its scenes of joy and promise, the declarations of love and commitment, it had been inevitable that Esmeralda's wedding day would be an ordeal, but two things had combined to make it even worse than she had anticipated.

The fake engagement was bad enough and she had struggled to accept the congratulations of so many of the guests at today's event. Her head had pounded, her jaw muscles had ached from the effort of forcing a fake smile onto her lips. But the last twist of the knife had arrived in the shape of a letter that had been delivered to her room only that morning. She had discovered it lying on her dressing table when she had crept back into the house from Nairo's apartment, just in time to help Esmeralda prepare for her wedding, and the memory of its contents had haunted her all through the day.

She couldn't meet Esmeralda's wide brown eyes, knowing the questioning look that would be in them. So she stared fixedly over to the side of the room to avoid it. But that only made matters so much worse when she spotted the tall, darkly elegant figure of Nairo making his way towards them.

Knowing that he believed she couldn't lie to save her life, she had hoped that she would be able to keep away from him today, at least until she got some control over her face and her thoughts. But she had forgotten that Esmeralda had wanted her to be waiting at the door of the cathedral, ready to make any last-minute adjustments to the dress before she began her walk up the aisle.

'I can't wait for you to become my sister!' she had said.

Rose had hated having to lie to Esmeralda and the knowledge that very soon she would have to disillusion the girl who had become such a close friend to her was more than she could bear. Now that Esmeralda was happily married, and Nairo had achieved his stated aim, then surely the end couldn't be long in coming, and the report in the newspaper cutting that had been in that envelope, with the photograph that brought such bittersweet memories along with it, must surely mean that she was already living on borrowed time.

'We don't want to rush into anything,' she managed painfully, aware of the fact that Nairo was prowling nearer.

'Don't want to rush!' Esmeralda laughed up into her brother's watchful face. 'Oh, come on, Nairo—what do you call rushing? I mean, you haven't even given dear Rose a ring.'

This time Rose couldn't hold her feelings in check as her gaze flew to Nairo's face, clashing with the hard stare of his bronze eyes with a sensation like slamming into a brick wall. Were his thoughts too filled with the memories of the night she'd told him she couldn't bear to wear such a symbol of the lie they were living?

'I don't need a ring,' she put in hastily. 'Really I don't…'

But Esmeralda was not to be diverted. 'I don't understand you, *hermano*…' She shook her head at her brother. 'Now that you've finally found someone you can love, wouldn't you want to let the world know about it? I know I would!'

'But you, little sister, just want everyone to share in all the fripperies and the fancies that make up your idea of a romantic wedding.'

As always when he spoke to his sister, Nairo's tone was warm and indulgent, making Rose struggle against the bitterness of knowing that she would only ever share in that warmth as an act put on to present a false image of their relationship.

Desperately she lifted the beautiful crystal glass she was holding to her lips, hoping that a swallow of champagne would at least ease the painful dryness in her throat. She felt as if she had been struggling to breathe through the tightness in her heart since the moment she had watched Nairo take his sister's arm in order to lead her down the aisle to her groom.

This might be his sister's wedding, but that image of Nairo, sleekly elegant in the fitted formal wear, was the way that he would look at his own marriage, with the slender figure of a bride at his side in a dress of beautiful white lace, with a delicate veil cascading down from her head. She had no idea who that future bride might be. She only knew that it would never be her.

'But I came to tell you that your new husband is looking for you—and I need to claim my fiancée. Rose and I need to talk.'

He hadn't needed to add the second half of his comment; the mention of Oscar had been more than enough to have Esmeralda turning and setting off in his direction before Nairo had even finished speaking. Leaving Rose alone with the man whose looming presence sent uncomfortable shivers of nerves skittering up and down her spine.

'Talk about what?' she asked sharply, knowing immediately it was the wrong thing to say and the wrong way to say it.

'Not here,' he responded, his voice as flat and expressionless as his face. 'Come with me.'

His grip on her hand was hard and tight, and he set off in the opposite direction to his sister without looking back to see if Rose was following him. Of course she was; it was either that or be dragged along in his wake.

How many difficult and life-changing conversations had begun with the words *we need to talk*? Rose asked herself as she stumbled after Nairo. Once out in the hall, with the doors closed behind them, the buzz of conversation died away to just a low hum and the house seemed suddenly cold and silent, alien somehow. Only now did Rose realise how much she had come to love living at the *castillo.* Not because of its size and luxuriousness but because over the past weeks it had felt like home to her too, she realised, living there in security and peace for perhaps the first time in her life. The nights she had spent with Nairo had been the glorious icing on the cake that was the sense of coming home, so much so that she had pushed away to the back of her mind the realisation of the fact that before too long, she would no longer belong here.

But wasn't the truth that she had never actually *belonged* here?

The time with Nairo was ticking away too, and she'd known this moment had to come. She just hadn't expected it to come quite this fast. The ink was barely dry on Esmeralda's wedding certificate, but it seemed her brother was already looking for his freedom. Well, she wasn't going to beg for more time. She'd gone into this with her eyes open, and if this was what had to be, then she'd face it with as much dignity as possible.

Don't worry—I'll take the blame... All you'll have to do is to look like the broken-hearted fiancée.

There would be no hardship there. When she left here she wouldn't need to pretend that her heart was shattered. She would leave it behind her, in Nairo's keeping, and would have to try to find a way to live without it.

'In here...'

The library was as far as possible away from the ballroom, and it had a door that locked. Perhaps that would guarantee them the privacy he needed, Nairo told himself as he led her into the room he'd decided was the best place for this. If there was such a thing as a 'best place' for this. Just as there was never going to be a 'best time' for it either.

The truth was that this was probably going to be the worst possible time to have this confrontation with Rose. But he had been living a lie for too long now and he couldn't let the situation continue a moment longer.

Today had been the last straw. He had had to watch Esmeralda light up like a brilliant star, her joy blazing in her eyes. He had felt the tremors of emotion run through the fingers that rested on his arm as he walked her down the aisle. Tremors that had vanished in an instant as she had seen Oscar turn to face her, his own smile mirroring hers.

It had been that smile that had shaken him out of the reverie he had slipped into. Just for a moment, wildly, crazily, dangerously, he had actually found himself imagining that *he* had been the one heading for the altar—with Rose as his bride...

Coming back to reality had been like being slapped hard

in the face, and it had forced him to acknowledge there was no way he could let this situation continue as it was.

He was in danger of finding himself back in the same sort of mess as he'd faced ten years before if he wasn't careful. Had he really learned so little in the intervening time? That was when he had known that he had to speak to Rose, and as soon as possible.

But now that he was here, in this quiet room, turning the key in the door against intruders, it seemed that all words had deserted him.

'Is this going to be so bad that you have to lock me in?'

Rose's voice was high and rather tremulous, though she flashed a smile that was clearly meant to make him think she had used the line as a joke.

'I'm keeping others out, rather than locking us in.'

Though he didn't think she'd stay around long once he'd told her what he had to say. She'd been reluctant to come here from the start and now it seemed that she was positively itching to get away.

When all he wanted to do was to keep her with him.

He'd known he was in trouble in the moment that she had moved forward to help Esmeralda arrange her dress when they had stepped out of the limousine onto the stone steps of the cathedral. Everyone who had seen his sister in her wedding finery had exclaimed in delight at the vision she presented. But for Nairo there was only one woman in the whole of Spain in that moment.

Her dress was an old gold colour, silky and close-fitting, with touches of lace at the shoulders and hem. Her auburn hair had been gathered up under a ridiculous frivolity of a hat, nothing more than a couple of feathers in a colour that exactly matched that dress, and just the way those feathers nodded and danced in the breeze made his heart clench on a clutch of need. He had rarely seen her wearing much make-up at any time, but today the subtle use of shadow made her hazel eyes seem huge and dark, and her lips looked full and soft, touched with a shimmer of colour. How he had stopped himself from giving in to the hunger that burned through him, tilting up that determined little chin and planting a hard, demanding kiss on that luscious mouth, he would never know. He'd had an ugly fight with his most primitive needs right there in the porch of the cathedral and he was having exactly the same battle right now.

Especially when she reached up and unpinned the perky little hat, tossing it onto a nearby table and shaking back her hair in a gesture that spoke of relief and freedom. One that almost broke his resolve to hold on to his control.

'I know what this is all about,' she said, her voice sounding as uneven and jerky as the pulse that was battering at his temples.

'You do?'

He had thought he had managed to hide his true feelings throughout the day.

But then he realised that she had opened the small boxy clutch bag she carried and was pulling something out of it. A creased piece of newspaper.

She unfolded the paper, slapped it down on the table in front of him. But he didn't need to see it. He knew exactly what she was trying to show him. It was the same photograph that had hit him right between the eyes when he had opened the paper that morning.

'Ah…' he said flatly. 'That.'

'Yes—that.'

Narrow fingers tipped with soft rose-pink polish reached for the paper again, and, intriguingly, he noticed that they shook a little as they did so.

She touched the photograph briefly, then looked up at

him, green-brown eyes dark like the water in the depths of a bottomless, shadowed pool.

'That was what you wanted to *talk about*, wasn't it?'

The emphasis on the two words made him wince inwardly. She was sounding altogether more challenging than he had expected. Had he got this all wrong?

'Partly.'

He wasn't giving anything away, Rose reflected. The single-syllable answers told her nothing, and surprisingly she couldn't see the anger she'd expected in his face. Or was he just better at hiding it than she'd imagined?

She flattened the newspaper again, so that the face in the picture stared up at her from the photograph.

Her own face.

It was a tiny, tatty old passport-style photograph. The sort that was taken in a photograph booth, four prints for a few pounds. It showed every day of its ten years of age, and she knew that age to the exact day. It was one copy of the photograph that she and Nairo had taken in a rare moment of indulgence. Nairo was laughing into the camera while she had her lips pressed tight against his cheek in a playful kiss.

The photo had been published in the UK papers as well as the Spanish ones and the headline in the copy she had read: 'Hola de Nuevo! *Long-Lost Lovers Reunited.*'

The story below it told how 'billionaire Spanish entrepreneur Nairo Moreno knew his beautiful fiancée, designer Rose Cavalliero, many years ago'. The whole story of their life in the squat had been dragged up again, even with a photograph of the once near-derelict building as it was now repaired and restored to its former glory. But no mention of the use to which it was now being put.

The story of the drugs raid had been excavated too, the report of the police investigation repeated over again. Only right at the bottom did it say that Nairo had been found completely innocent.

She knew what seeing this report must have done to Nairo, the anger he must have felt. Surely he would believe there could only be one person who had provided the information to the press. All day she'd been expecting the volcano to explode at any moment; she was just stunned to find that his anger was such an icy, controlled response rather than the eruption she'd been expecting.

'Tell me about it,' Nairo said, and there was a subtle change in his voice. No anger. No recrimination. Instead she might almost have said that he sounded as if he had lost something very important. It was strange because that was the exact way she was feeling too.

Swallowing hard, she had to draw on all the courage she could find inside. She'd sold him short ten years before by not talking to him openly; she wasn't going to do it this time.

'The photo—' she began, her mouth so dry that she found it hard to form the words. 'I didn't...'

'No—you didn't. But I kind of wish you had.'

'You—what...?'

Coherent thought deserted her. She could only stand and stare into the clouded golden eyes that had turned opaque and hidden.

'You didn't give the photo, the report, to the papers. I know you didn't. You couldn't. You would never hurt someone you love that way.'

A rush of relief was blended with another very different strain of emotion. How did he know? How had he guessed? What had she done to give herself away? And how was she supposed to cope with the fact that he'd guessed and yet he looked so uninvolved—so *disappointed*?

'You would never do that to Esmeralda on her wedding day.'

Now her head was really spinning. She had come in here expecting the outbreak of war, to be told to pack her bags and get out, but instead she was confronted by this deadly quiet man with the almost colourless face, the deep dark eyes, and suddenly she didn't know who Nairo was or what he wanted from her.

'I don't understand.'

Her legs felt weak as cotton wool so that suddenly she plumped down into the nearest chair, grabbing hold of the arms for support. But that just made things so much worse. Nairo's dark figure towered over her, making her feel very small and vulnerable.

'What has Esmeralda to do with this?'

That made his face change at least, but the way it brought the frown back to between his dark brows didn't help at all.

'Surely it's obvious. I've seen you with Esmeralda. I know that you care for her. You wouldn't do this to her.'

She wanted to smile, she wanted to laugh, she wanted to break down and bury her head in the cushions on the chair, weeping her heart out. She wanted to do all three at once. Shockingly, it was laughter that won and she heard the strangled, slightly hysterical sound echo round the elegant room.

'You know I didn't do this—for Esmeralda?'

His frown this time was one of genuine confusion.

'Of course—who else?'

'Oh, Nairo, don't you know?'

As soon as she asked the question the stab of a shard of ice right in her heart gave her her answer. Of course he didn't know. He could see the way she felt about his sister, but to the way she felt about him he was totally blind.

Either because he just couldn't see, or because he didn't *want* to.

It was then that something hit her like a light bulb going on inside her head. Of course! She was the one who couldn't see. He had promised to give her a reason to break off their engagement. One that everyone would understand, and this…

'Look. I know you want this over and done with!'

She pushed herself to her feet again, unable to hold back, not caring if she let him into the way she was really feeling. It was too late to worry about that.

'But really, don't you think you could have waited—that you could have had a bit more consideration? Today was supposed to be Esmeralda's perfect day. She's so happy… What do you think she'll feel when she realises that our engagement has broken up—today of all days?'

'It has to be today,' Nairo flung at her, his voice raw with emphasis. 'There's no other way. Because I can't live like this. I can't live this lie any longer.'

CHAPTER TWELVE

SHE COULDN'T KNOW what it had done to him to lie all this time, Nairo admitted inwardly. To fake the feelings or, rather, to show the feelings and know that she believed they were faked, put on for show to convince everyone else and meaning nothing.

What was that saying 'fake it till you make it'? Hadn't the last weeks been such hell because he had been *making* it for so many days now while all the time the person he most wanted to persuade was convinced that he was doing the perfect job of faking it as they'd agreed? That was what he couldn't bear to live with any longer.

The truth was that he'd hoped for something else, he admitted bitterly. He'd hoped that when he let Rose know that he trusted her, totally sure that she hadn't been the person who had sent the photograph and the story to the press, then things would change. He strongly suspected he knew who had done that and it wasn't her. It had all the hallmarks of Jason's nasty-minded tricks and schemes to make a profit out of someone else's upset. Though how he'd got hold of the photo in the squat he had no idea.

But the real culprit didn't matter. What mattered was the fact that he believed in Rose. For perhaps the first time in his life he had put all his trust in a person—a woman— who wasn't part of his family. He had brought her here to demonstrate that trust and deep down he'd hoped that when he'd done so she might rethink the idea of breaking off this false engagement, going their separate ways.

That had failed miserably. Bitter laughter caught in his throat, making him cough, and he was grateful for the way that needing to cover his mouth with his hand gave him a chance to hide what he was feeling, to hold back the words that he came so dangerously close to letting slip. The ones she clearly didn't want to hear.

'No more lies!' he managed, forcing the words out so that they sounded as cold and as brutal as her *I know you want this over and done with!* Anything else would have stuck in his throat.

No more lies. Rose had to struggle to catch the words because they seemed to get tangled up in the cough that shook Nairo's throat—or was it a laugh? She couldn't see what there was to laugh about.

But then she remembered how just a few minutes before, she had let go and laughed herself, when laughing was the last thing she felt like doing. When she really wanted to just break down and weep.

Thinking back, she knew he had said something…but she couldn't make it make any sense.

She didn't give the photograph to the press, she had said, and he had replied…

'No—you didn't. But I kind of wish you had.'

She only realised that she had repeated the words out loud when she saw him nodding along with them, a strange little smile curling at the corners of his mouth as he raked both his hands through the darkness of his hair, ruffling it impossibly.

'I'm a fool, aren't I?' he stunned her by responding. 'A blind, crazy fool. But I did hope.'

The tousled effect of his hair falling softly over his forehead gave him an impossibly young and boyish look that tugged on something vulnerable in her heart. She hardly dared to ask, but she had to take the risk because if she missed this chance it might be the only one she would ever get.

'Why would you…?' Her voice shook with disbelief. 'How could you ever *hope* that I'd sent the photo to the papers?'

Nairo sank back against the huge polished oak table in the middle of the room, staring down at his feet, shaking his head as if in disbelief at his own behaviour.

'So that then I'd know you kept the photo.'

'Do you *still* want proof?'

Had she been a fool to let herself hope? She couldn't believe how close she had come to letting him in and now it seemed that she had been blindly led along by what she most wanted rather than what he had actually meant.

'Rose—no…'

His movement towards her was rough, almost desperate, his hand coming out to her. But she was already reaching into her purse, yanking out the small photograph and tossing it down onto the table. That would show him she hadn't parted with her copy of the picture to any reporter.

'I don't need any proof at all. I know exactly what you mean.'

'You do?'

It was meant to sound unconvinced, totally sceptical. But there was something in his tone and in his face that shook the conviction she needed so that instead her words were only questioning, suddenly uncertain.

'I do. Because of this…'

Nairo's hand slid into his pocket, pulled out a black leather wallet and opened it. The small piece of paper he took out and placed on the table beside the one she'd just tossed down had a black-and-white image on it just the same.

Except that on this one it was Rose who was looking straight into the camera, her mouth stretched wide in a smile. And Nairo was the one who had his lips pressed against her cheek.

'You…' It was all that Rose could manage, the sight of the two photographs side by side taking any other words away.

It was the fact that he waited, silent and still, that got to her in the end. It gave her a strange sort of hope, one that she would never have found in any words he might say.

'You kept the photograph—but why?'

'Because I never wanted to forget you.'

Forget her or forget what she'd done? The way she'd treated him.

'When I saw the photo in the paper I hoped that was what it meant to you too. That you had kept your copy, perhaps for the same reason.'

Shockingly, Rose saw that the fingers that reached for her copy of the photograph were not quite steady.

'But I knew you would never have done that. You just couldn't.'

The revelation of his total trust was so huge, so important, that it rocked her mind and for a moment she had to turn off onto a mental siding, another topic, while she gathered her thoughts.

'Who do you think did that?'

'Who gave it to the press?' Nairo asked. 'Jason, I expect. That night he vowed he'd have his revenge on you—on both of us. He must have decided this was worth a try to come between us.'

'Come between us,' Rose echoed. 'But was there ever an "us" to divide?'

'Can you doubt it? Look at those pictures—'

A long forefinger dropped onto the one he had pulled from his wallet. The one where he was kissing her cheek, his eyes closed in an expression of absolute happiness.

'The day we took those felt like a whole new beginning for me. That was the day I first contacted my father, told him I was prepared to apologise.'

That rocked Rose's sense of reality.

'But you'd done nothing wrong—why apologise?'

'If that was what it took. I wanted to turn my life around—make a fresh start. I wanted to have more to offer you than a dreadful room in a scruffy squat. I wanted to take you to Spain—bring you here. Give you a home—with me.'

'Instead I messed it all up for you.'

And for herself. She'd lost her chance to make that new start in life with Nairo. The pictures of the two of them blurred through the film of bitter tears.

'It was my fault as much as—more than—yours,' Nairo said urgently. 'I didn't trust you enough to tell you. Didn't trust you with my real name or my hopes to reunite with my family. I was never honest with you about my feelings. I haven't been even now.'

'Even now?' What did she take from that? Rose had no idea at all and she was afraid to hope.

'When I saw how the paparazzi were hounding you, I thought it would be too much for you. You wouldn't be able to take the press attention all over again and you'd leave.'

'You came to my rescue.'

'No.' It was hard, forceful. 'I couldn't let you go, but I was a coward and didn't tell you why. So I pushed you into an engagement, hung it on the importance of Esmeralda's big day. I had to keep you here until we had a chance to try again. But why would you want to try again if I was never honest with you about my feelings?'

'And what are those feelings?'

It was the question she had to ask, but he would never know how much courage it took her to make it. A direct question demanded a direct answer, but what if the response was not the one she longed for?

Nairo drew in a long, ragged breath, reached out to touch the photographs again as if they were some sort of talisman.

'I wanted to get the wedding out of the way so that then maybe we could have our own time.'

Our own time sounded wonderful, but what she needed was a future. She'd tried to tell herself that she would accept what they had for as long as he let her, but watching Esmeralda today she had known that just wasn't enough. It was all or nothing. She couldn't accept anything else.

'Nairo—we agreed.'

'I know we agreed.' It was dark, raw, vehement. 'And I'll keep to that if I have to. If you still want me to give you an excuse to break us apart and let everyone know this engagement is over, then I promised and I'll keep that promise. But don't ask me to make it look as if I want someone else—as if I love someone else. I can't do that. I once told you that you couldn't lie to save your life and on this neither can I. It would be a lie to make it look as if I care for anyone else. Even for you.'

This time his shake of the head was more violent, sending his already impossibly tumbled hair flying until it fell back in even more disarray than before.

'I can't lie like that even to give the one person I really love her freedom.'

The one person I really love. Rose's heart was thundering, her pulse racing. Had she heard right? Had he really said…?

'In fact I can't let you go at all.'

Again he pushed both hands through the now wildly ruffled black hair, the gesture expressing so much more than his carefully controlled words.

'I know you stayed for Esmeralda…'

'It wasn't just for Esmeralda. How could it be when I—'

'You love her,' he inserted, and the odd shake in his voice did more to convince her than anything else he had done or said.

'I love her—for herself of course,' Rose told him softly. 'But perhaps even more than that I love her because she's a part of the family of someone who means the world to me. Because she loves and is loved by someone I love more than life.'

'Who?'

It rasped from a throat that sounded constricted as if he was having to fight to get it out. But there was no fight left in his eyes. Their bronze depths were clear and unshadowed, totally open to her, hiding nothing of the way he was feeling. That feeling gave her heart such a lift that she felt almost as if her feet had left the floor as she smiled at him, straight into those eyes, everything she dreamed of sharing showing in her own face.

'Oh, Nairo—do you have to ask? I love you with all my heart.'

She needed to make the first move now, stepping forward, reaching out to him. But he met her more than halfway, gathering her up into his arms and crushing her against him as his mouth came down hard on hers.

It was all that Rose had ever dreamed of. All she had hoped for but never believed it would come true. She was here, in Nairo's arms, and to him she was *the one person I really love*. She couldn't ask for anything more.

But Nairo, it seemed, had one more thing he needed to say. Slowly, softly, reluctantly he released her, searching in his jacket pocket for something. The leather box he pulled out was obviously old, worn, slightly battered.

'Esmeralda said I'd never given you a ring. I know how you feel about that—but this is different.'

'How *I felt*,' Rose inserted gently, needing to put every last misunderstanding behind them.

He looked down at the box in his hand, closed his fingers around it, then opened them again.

'I brought this with me because I wanted to ask you to marry me properly. To do me the greatest honour of being my wife—but now…'

He frowned, tightened his hold on the box again and shook his head.

'This is the ring I'm supposed to offer. It's tradition— the family ring—one handed down from generation to generation and so it's the ring I'd want you to have. But my father gave it to my mother—and look how that worked out. I didn't think you'd want something that came with that shadow over its history.'

'Oh, Nairo…'

The fact that he cared, that he'd even stopped to consider that, told her more about his feelings than any more flowery declarations of love and devotion. He wanted her to have his family ring—but he wanted it to be right for her. He didn't want them to end up at war, separated like his parents, who had scarred the family so badly.

'But there were others who wore it, weren't there?' she said softly.

He nodded slowly, dark eyes locked with hers.

'My grandfather gave it to my grandmother and he and

Abuela were married for almost sixty years. And their parents before them.'

Rose couldn't hold back her smile. He needed that and she wanted to give it to him.

'So its history is not all bad, my love. There was just that one blip—and we can break away from that. We can make it a ring of love and happiness all over again.'

It was as if a light had been switched on behind his eyes. His head came up, his long body straightening as if a huge weight had been lifted from his shoulders. His own lips curved into an echoing smile as he flipped open the box, displaying the magnificent diamond ring it enclosed.

'We can—and we will, *mi amor*,' he declared in a voice that resonated with confidence and, more importantly, with a newfound happiness. 'I could ask for nothing more than to spend the rest of my life making you, my beautiful wife, the happiest woman in the world, if you'll let me.'

'Oh, yes—yes, please!' was all that Rose could manage before he caught her to him again and crushed her lips in a kiss that sealed his promise for the rest of their days together.

* * * * *

AN ENTICING DEBT TO PAY

ANNIE WEST

For dearest Claire
whose hard work, exuberance
and sheer talent are an inspiration.
With love.

CHAPTER ONE

'I'M AFRAID THE latest audit has thrown up an...irregularity.'

Jonas looked across his wide, polished desk and frowned as his Head of Finance shifted uncomfortably in his seat.

What sort of *irregularity* could make Charles Barker palpably nervous? He was the best. Jonas made it a policy only to employ the best. He didn't have patience for underperformers. Barker ran his part of Jonas' business enterprise like a well-oiled machine.

'A significant irregularity?'

Barker shook his head. 'Not in overall financial terms.'

Since the company's total assets figured in the billions, Jonas supposed he should be relieved, but watching Barker loosen his tie, Jonas felt a prickle of foreboding.

'Spit it out, Charles.'

The other man smiled, but it turned into a grimace as he passed his laptop across the desk.

'There. The top two lines.'

Jonas noted the first entry—a transfer of several thousand pounds. Below it another, much larger entry. No details were provided for either.

'What am I looking at?'

'Withdrawals against your original investment account.'

Jonas' frown became a scowl. He used that account now only to transfer personal funds between investments.

'Someone accessed my account?' But the answer was obvious. Jonas hadn't made these withdrawals. He managed day-to-day expenses elsewhere and, though large by normal standards, the withdrawals weren't significant enough to match his usual personal investments.

'We've traced them.' Of course, Barker would make it his business to have an answer before he fronted Jonas with the problem.

'And?' Curiosity rose.

'You'll remember the account was originally set up as part of a family enterprise.'

How could Jonas forget? His father had given him chapter and verse on how to run a business, pretending he, as head of the family, was the senior partner in the enterprise. But they'd both known it was Jonas' talent for spotting a sound investment, and his ruthless hunger for success, that had turned the floundering investment company around. Piers had simply been along for the ride, revelling in the novelty of success. Until father and son had parted ways.

'I remember.' Memory was a sour tang on his tongue.

Barker shifted again. 'The withdrawals were made using an old cheque book—one that had supposedly been destroyed.' Jonas looked up, catching a faint flush on the other man's cheeks. 'The records show they were accounted for but this one of your father's…'

'It's okay, I get the picture.' Jonas let his gaze drift across the unrivalled view of the City of London.

His father. Jonas hadn't called him that since childhood when he'd discovered what sort of man Piers Deveson was. Despite his bluster about honour and the family name, Piers had been no model of virtue. It shouldn't surprise Jonas to learn the old man had found a way to access his son's assets illegally. The wonder was he hadn't used it earlier.

'So Piers—'

'No!' Barker sat straighter as Jonas turned back to him. 'I'm sorry, but we've reason to believe it wasn't your father. Here.' He passed some photocopied pages across.

Jonas scanned them. Two cheques with his father's familiar flourishing signature.

Except they *weren't* Piers Deveson's signature. They were close enough to fool a stranger but he was familiar enough with that scrawl to spot the differences.

'Look at the dates.'

Jonas did and to his surprise felt a punch to the gut that winded him.

Bad enough to think the old man had pilfered funds. But this was—

Jonas shook his head, his lungs cramping as unexpected emotion filled him.

'The second one is dated a day after your father died.'

Silently Jonas nodded, his heart slowing to a ponderous beat. He knew the date, and not just because it was recent.

For years his father had been a thorn in his side, a blot on the family—living in gaudy luxury with his scheming mistress. They'd flaunted themselves among the rich and notorious, uncaring of any hurt they'd caused. When Piers died Jonas had felt nothing—neither regret nor an easing of the tension that had gripped him since Piers' defection had taken its ultimate toll. He'd expected to feel *something*. For weeks there'd been nothing, just an emptiness where emotion should have been. Yet now—

'Not my father then.' His voice was calm, belying the raw emotions churning in his gut. Beneath the desk his hands clenched.

'No. We've traced the perpetrator. And she's not too clever, given the obvious anomaly with the date.' Barker spoke quickly, obviously eager to get this over. 'It was a Ms Ruggiero. Living at this address in Paris.'

Barker handed over another paper. It bore the address of the exclusive apartment Piers Deveson had shared for the last six years with his mistress, Silvia Ruggiero.

Jonas paused before reaching out to take the paper. His fingers tingled as if it burned him.

'So.' Jonas sat back. 'My father's whore thinks she can continue to milk his family even after his death.' His voice was devoid of emotion, but he felt it deep inside like the burn of ice on bruised flesh.

How could the woman think she'd get away with this after all she'd done to the Devesons? Surely she wasn't stupid enough to expect mercy?

His pulse thudded as he thought of the woman who'd destroyed so much.

He remembered Silvia Ruggiero as clearly as if he'd seen her yesterday, her voluptuous figure, flashing eyes and froth of dark hair. Sex on legs, one of his friends had said the first time he'd seen Silvia, who was then the Devesons' housekeeper. And he'd been right. Not even a drab uniform had doused the woman's vibrant sexuality.

That had been mere weeks before Jonas' father had turned his back on family and responsibility, let alone respectability, by running off with his housekeeper to set her up in a luxury Paris apartment.

Four months later Jonas' mother was found dead. An accidental overdose, the coroner had said. But Jonas knew the truth. After years spurned by the man she'd loved, his public repudiation had finally been too much. His mother had taken her own life.

Jonas breathed deep, pulling oxygen into cramped lungs. Now the woman responsible for his mother's death had struck again. She had the nerve to think she could continue to steal from him!

The paper in his hand crackled as his fist tightened slowly, inexorably. Fury surged, tensing every sinew. His jaw ached as he clenched his teeth against a rising tide of useless invective.

Jonas never wasted energy on words when actions were so much more effective.

For six years he'd spurned the idea of revenge. He'd risen

above that temptation, burying himself in work and refusing any contact with Piers or his gold-digging mistress.

But now this—the straw that broke the camel's back.

The blood raced hot and sharp in his veins as for the first time Jonas allowed himself to contemplate fully the pleasures of retribution.

'Leave this to me, Charles.' Jonas smiled slowly, his facial muscles pulling tight. 'There's no need to report the fraud. I'll sort it out personally.'

Ravenna surveyed the apartment in despair. Most of the furnishings she knew now were fake, from the gilded Louis Quinze chairs to the china masquerading as period Limoges and Sèvres.

Mamma had always been adept at making ends meet, even through the toughest times.

A reluctant smile tugged Ravenna's lips. Life in a swanky apartment in the Place des Vosges, one of Paris's premier addresses, hardly counted as tough, not like the early days of Ravenna's childhood when food had been scarce and the winters cold without enough blankets or warm clothes. But those early experiences had stood her mother in good stead. When the money began to run out she'd methodically turned to replacing the priceless antiques with copies.

Silvia Ruggiero had always made do, even if her version of 'making do' lately had been on a preposterously luxurious scale. But it was what Piers had wanted and in Silvia's eyes that was all that mattered.

Ravenna tugged in a shaky breath. Her mother was far better off in Italy staying with a friend, instead of here, coping with the aftermath of Piers' death. If only she'd told Ravenna straight away about his heart attack. Ravenna would have been here the same day. Even now she could barely believe her mother had kept that to herself, worrying instead about disturbing Ravenna with more trouble!

Mothers! Did they ever believe their children grew up?

Silvia had been barely recognisable when Ravenna had arrived in Paris from Switzerland. For the first time her gorgeous mother had looked older than her age, worn by grief. Ravenna was concerned for her. Piers might not have been Ravenna's favourite but her mother had loved him.

No, Mamma was better off out of this. Packing up here was the least Ravenna could do, especially after Piers' generosity when she most needed it. So what if it meant facing creditors and selling what little her mother had left?

She returned to her inventory, glad she'd organised for an expert to visit and separate any valuable items from the fakes. To Ravenna they all looked obscenely expensive and rather ostentatious. But since her home was a sparsely furnished bedsit in a nondescript London suburb, she was no judge.

Jonas pressed the security buzzer a second time, wondering if she was out and his spur of the moment trip to Paris had been an impetuous waste of time.

He didn't do impetuous. He was methodical, measured and logical. But he also had a razor-sharp instinct for weakness, for the optimum time to strike. And surely now, mere weeks after Piers' death, his father's mistress would be feeling the pinch as creditors started to circle.

Static buzzed and a husky, feminine voice spoke in his ear. 'Hello?'

Yes! His instinct had been right.

'I'm here to see Madam Ruggiero.'

'Monsieur Giscard? I was expecting you. Please come up.'

Jonas pushed open the security door into a marble foyer. He ignored the lift and strode up the couple of floors to what had been his father's love nest. Suppressing a shiver of revulsion, he rapped on the door of the apartment.

It swung open almost immediately and he stepped past a slim young woman into a lavishly furnished foyer. Through an open door he glimpsed an overfull salon but no sign of the woman he'd come to see. He moved towards the inner room.

'You're not Monsieur Giscard.' The accusation halted him.

He swung round to find eyes the colour of rich sherry fixed on him.

'No. I'm not.'

For the first time he paused to survey the woman properly and something—surprise?—rushed through him.

Slim to the point of fragility, she nevertheless had curves in all the right places, even if they were obscured by ill-fitting dark clothes. But it was her face that arrested him. Wide lush mouth, strong nose, angled cheekbones that gave her a fey air, lavish dark lashes and rather straight brows framing eyes so luminous they seemed to glow. Each feature in her heart-shaped face was so definite that together they should have jarred. Instead they melded perfectly.

She was arresting. Not pretty but something much rarer. Jonas felt his pulse quicken as heat shot low in his body.

He stiffened. When was the last time the sight of a woman, even a uniquely beautiful one, had affected him?

'And you are?' She tilted her head, drawing his gaze from her ripe mouth to the ultra-short sable hair she wore like a chic, ruffled cap. Another few weeks and she'd have curls.

He frowned. Why notice that when he had more important matters on his mind?

'Looking for Madam Ruggiero. Silvia Ruggiero.' It surprised him how difficult it was to drag his gaze away and back to the apartment's inner rooms.

'You don't have an appointment.' There was something new in her voice. Something hard and flat.

'No.' His mouth curled in a smile of grim anticipation. 'But she'll see me.'

The young woman strode back into his line of sight, blocking his way to the salon. Jonas catalogued the lithe grace of her movements even as he told himself he didn't have time for distractions.

She shook her head. 'You're the last person she'd see.'

'You know who I am?' His gaze sharpened as he took in her defiant stance—arms akimbo and feet planted wide, as if she could prevent him if he chose to push past! She was tall, her mouth on a level with his collarbone, and she stared up at him with complete assurance.

'It took me a moment but of course I do.' A flicker of expression crossed her features so swiftly Jonas couldn't read it. But he watched her swallow and realised she wasn't as confident as she appeared. Interesting.

'And you are?' Jonas was used to being recognised from press reports, but instinct told him he'd met this woman before. Something about her tugged at half-buried memory.

'Forgettable, obviously.' Her lips twisted in a self-deprecating smile that ridiculously drove a spike of heat through his belly.

Jonas blinked. She wasn't smiling at him yet he reacted.

Annoyance flared. He drew himself up, watching her gaze skate across his shoulders and chest.

'She's not here.' The words tumbled out in a breathless rush that belied her aggressively protective stance. 'So you can't see her.'

'Then I'll wait.' Jonas stepped forward, only to come up against her slim frame, vibrating with tension. He'd expected her to give way. She surprised him with her determination to stand her ground. But he refused to retreat, no matter how distracting the sensation of her body against his. His business with Silvia Ruggiero was long overdue.

He looked down and her golden brown eyes widened as if in shock.

'I'm not going away,' he murmured, suppressing an inexplicable desire to lift his hand and see if her pale face was as soft as it appeared. The realisation threw him, making his voice emerge harshly. 'My business won't wait.'

Again she swallowed. He followed the movement of her slim throat with a fascination that surprised him. The scent of her skin filled his nostrils: feminine warmth and the tang of cinnamon.

Abruptly she stepped back, her chest rising and falling quickly, drawing his attention till he snapped his eyes back to her face.

'In that case you can talk with me.' She turned and led the way into the salon, her steps a clipped, staccato beat on the honey-coloured wood floor.

Jonas dragged his gaze from the sway of her hips in dark trousers and followed, furious to find himself distracted from his purpose even for a moment.

She settled herself on an overstuffed chair near a window framed by cloth of gold curtains. Hoping to put him at a disadvantage with her back to the light? It was such an obvious ploy. Instead of taking a seat Jonas prowled the room, knowing that with each passing moment her unease increased. Whoever she was, she was in cahoots with Silvia Ruggiero. Jonas wouldn't trust her an inch.

'Why should I share my business with a stranger?' He peered at an over-decorated ormolu clock.

Was there nothing in this place that wasn't overdone? It reeked of a nouveau riche fixation with show and quantity rather than quality. His cursory survey had revealed the best pieces in the room to be fakes. But that had been his father—all show and no substance. Especially when it came to things like love or loyalty.

'I'm not a stranger.' Her tone was curt. 'Perhaps if you stopped your crude inventory you'd realise that.'

To Jonas' surprise unfamiliar heat rose under his skin. True, his behaviour was crass, calculated to unnerve rather than reassure. But he felt no need to ingratiate himself with his father's mistress or her crony.

He took his time swinging around to meet her eyes.

'Then perhaps you'll do me the courtesy of answering my question. Who are you?'

'I thought that would be obvious. I'm Ravenna. Silvia's daughter.'

Ravenna watched shock freeze Jonas' features.

You'd think after all these years she'd be used to it, but still it struck her a blow.

She'd been a gawky child, all long limbs and feet and a nose it had taken years to grow into. With her dark, Italian looks, exotic name and husky voice she'd been the odd one out in her English country schools. When people saw her with her petite, ravishingly beautiful mother, the kindest comments had been about her being 'different' or 'striking'. The unkindest, at the boarding school her mother had scrimped to send her to—well, she'd put that behind her years ago.

But she'd thought Jonas would remember her, even if she'd worn braces and plaits last time they'd met.

True it had taken her a few moments to recognise him. To reconcile the grim, abrasive intruder in the exquisitely tailored clothes with the young man who'd treated her so kindly the day he'd found her curled in misery behind the stables. He'd been softer then, more understanding. To her dazed teenage eyes he'd shone like a demigod, powerful, reassuring and sexy in the unattainable way of movie stars.

Who'd have thought someone with such charm could turn into a louse?

Only the sex appeal was unchanged.

She looked again into those narrowed pewter-grey eyes that surveyed her so closely.

No, that had changed too. The softness of youth had been pared from Jonas Deveson's features, leaving them austerely sculpted and attractively spare, the product of generations of aristocratic breeding. He wasn't a chinless wonder of pampered privilege but the sort of hard-edged, born-to-authority man you could imagine defending Deveson Hall astride a warhorse, armed with sword and mace.

From his superbly arrogant nose to his strong chin, from his thick, dark hair to his wide shoulders and deep chest, Jonas was the sort to make females lose their heads.

How could she find him attractive when he oozed disapproval? When his barely veiled aggression had kept her on tenterhooks from the moment he stalked in the door?

But logic had little to do with the frisson of awareness skimming Ravenna's skin and swirling in her abdomen.

Steadily she returned his searching look. No matter how handsome he was, or how used to command, she wasn't about to fall in with his assumption of authority.

'What's your business with my mother?' Ravenna sat back, crossing one leg over the other and placing her hands on the arms of the chair as if totally relaxed.

He flicked a look from her legs to her face and she felt a prick of satisfaction that she'd surprised him. Did he expect her to bow and scrape in his presence? The thought shored up her anger.

'When will she be back?' No mistaking the banked fury in those flashing eyes. For all his outward show of calm his patience was on a short leash.

'If you can't answer politely, you might as well leave.' Ravenna shot to her feet. She had enough on her plate without dealing with Piers' privileged son. Just confronting him sapped her already low stamina. The last thing she needed was for him to guess how weak she felt. He'd just railroad her into doing his bidding—he had that look about him.

She was halfway to the door when his words stopped her.

'My business with your mother is private.'

Slowly she turned, cataloguing the harsh light in his eyes and the straight set of his mouth. Whatever his business it spelled trouble and Mamma wasn't in any state to deal with him. She was floundering, trying to adjust to the loss of the man she'd loved so ardently. Ravenna had to protect her.

'My mother's not in Paris. You can deal with me.'

He shook his head and took a pace towards her. It ate up the space between them alarmingly, bringing him within touching distance.

Did she imagine she felt the heat of his body warm her?

'Where is she?' It wasn't a request but a demand. 'Tell me now.'

Ravenna curled her fingers into tight fists, her nails scoring her flesh. His high-handed attitude infuriated her.

'I'm not your servant.' By a miracle she kept her voice even. She knew the guilt Silvia had suffered for years because of this man's refusal to reconcile with his father. 'My mother might have worked for your family once but don't think you can come here and throw your weight around. You have no power over me.'

Anger pulsed between them, so strong she felt it throb hard against her chest wall.

At least she thought it was anger. The air between them clogged with tension that stole her breath and furred the nape of her neck.

'But I do have power over your mother.' The words were silky soft, like an endearment. But it was suppressed violence she heard in that smooth baritone, a clear threat.

'What do you mean?' Alarm raised her voice an octave.

'I mean your mother's in serious trouble.'

Fear clawed at Ravenna's throat and she swallowed hard, taking in the pitiless gleam in his silvery eyes.

Understanding hit. 'You're not here to help, are you?'

His bark of laughter confirmed the icy foreboding slithering along Ravenna's spine.

'Hardly!' He paused, as if savouring the moment. 'I'm here to see she goes to prison for her crimes.'

CHAPTER TWO

RAVENNA LOCKED HER knees as the room swirled sickeningly.

She reached out a groping hand to steady herself and grabbed fabric, fingers digging claw-like as she fought panic.

The last few months had been tougher than anything she could once have imagined. They'd tested her to the limits of endurance. But nothing had prepared her to confront such pure hatred as she saw in Jonas Deveson's face. There was no softness in his expression, just adamantine determination. It scared her to the core.

Shock slammed into her and the knowledge, surer with every gasping breath, that he was serious. He intended to send her mother to prison.

A hand covered hers to the wrist, long fingers encompassing hers easily, sending darts of searing heat through her chilled flesh.

Stunned, Ravenna looked down to find she'd grabbed the only thing near—the lapel of Jonas Deveson's tailored jacket. Now he held her hard and fast.

'Are you all right?' Concern turned his deep voice to mellow treacle. She felt it softening sinew and taut muscle, easing her shocked stasis enough that she finally managed to inhale. The spinning room settled.

She tugged her hand away. Worryingly, she felt cold without that skin-to-skin contact.

Ravenna spun on her foot and paced to the window. This

time when she clutched fabric it was the heavy gold swag of curtain. It was rich and smooth under her tingling fingers, but not as reassuring as the fine wool warmed by Jonas Deveson's body.

She shook her head, banishing the absurd thought.

'Ravenna?'

Her head jerked up. She remembered him calling her by name years before, the only time they'd really talked. In her emotionally charged state then she'd imagined no one but he could ever make her name sound so appealing. For years her unusual name had been the source of countless jibes. She'd been labelled the scrawny raven and far, far worse at school. It was disturbing to discover that even now he turned her name into something special.

'What?'

'Are you okay?' His voice came from closer and she stiffened her spine.

'As okay as you can expect when you barge in here threatening my mother with gaol.'

For a moment longer Ravenna stared out of the window. The Place des Vosges, elegant and symmetrical with its manicured gardens, looked as unchanged as ever, as if nothing could disturb its self-conscious complacency.

But she'd learned the hard way that real life was never static, never safe.

Reluctantly she turned to find him looming over her, his eyes unreadable.

'What is she supposed to have done?'

'There's no *suppose* about it. Do you think I'd come *here*—' his voice was ripe with contempt as he swept the salon with a wide gesture '—if it wasn't fact?'

Ravenna's heart dropped. She couldn't believe her mother had done anything terrible, but at the same time she knew only the most extreme circumstances would bring Jonas Deveson within a kilometre of Silvia Ruggiero. There was hatred in his eyes when he spoke of her.

'You're too angry to think straight.' At her words his lowering dark brows shot up towards his hairline. Clearly this was a man unused to opposition.

She drew another, slower breath. 'You've despised my mother for years and now you think you've found a way to make her pay for the sin of falling in love with your father.'

The sizzle of fire in his eyes told her she'd hit the nail on the head. Her hands slipped onto her hips as she let righteous indignation fortify her waning strength.

'I think you've decided that, without Piers here to defend her, she's easy prey.' Her breath hitched. 'But she's not alone. You'd do well to remember that.'

'What? She's moved on already?' His voice was contemptuous. 'She's found another protector to take his place? That must be some sort of record.'

Ravenna wasn't aware of lunging towards him but suddenly she was so close she saw his pupils dilate as her open hand swung up hard and fast towards his cheek.

The movement came to a juddering halt that reverberated through her as he caught her wrist. He lifted it high so she stretched up on her toes, leaning towards him. Her breasts, belly and thighs tingled as if from an electric charge as the heat of his body, mere centimetres away, burned hers.

His eyebrows lowered, angling down straight and obstinate over eyes so intent they seemed to peer into her very soul.

His scent—clean male skin and a hint of citrus—invaded her nostrils. Abruptly she realised she'd ventured too far into dangerous territory when she found herself inhaling and holding her breath.

A shimmy of reaction jittered through her. A reaction she couldn't name. It froze the air in her lungs.

Instinct warned he was dangerous in ways that had nothing to do with her mother.

Ravenna tugged hard but he refused to release her hand. Leaning up towards him like this, almost touching along the length of their bodies, Ravenna became fully aware of the raw, masculine power hidden beneath the designer suit. The clothes were those of an urbane businessman. The burning stare and aura of charged testosterone spoke instead of primitive male power, barely leashed.

She breathed deep, trying to douse rising panic, and registered an unfamiliar spicy musk note in the air. Her nerves stretched tighter.

Never had Ravenna felt so aware of the imbalance of physical power between male and female. Of the fact that, despite her height, she was no match for this man who held her so easily and so off balance.

'Nobody slaps me.' His lips barely moved, yet Ravenna felt his warm breath on her face with each terse word.

'Nobody insults my mother like that.'

Even stretched taut against him, her mind grappling with a multitude of new sensations, she refused to back down. She stared into those glittering, merciless eyes and felt a thrill of fear, realising he was utterly unyielding.

'Then we're at an impasse, Ms Ruggiero.'

Did he tug her closer or did she sway towards him? Suddenly keeping her balance was almost impossible as she teetered on the balls of her feet.

'In which case there's no need for the macho act. You can let me go.' She paused, deliberately going limp in his hold. 'Unless you feel you have something to prove.'

Relief gushed through her as he released her.

Rather than let him see it, Ravenna bent her head as if examining her wrist for bruises. There wouldn't be any. His touch hadn't been brutal, but its implacability had scared her.

'Let's get one thing straight,' she said finally, looking up into his arresting, aristocratic face. 'My mother loved your father.'

'You expect me to believe that?' Jonas shook his head, his lips curling in a sneer. 'I'm not some callow kid who believes in fairy tales. She was on the make—out to snare a rich lover. It was obvious to everyone.' He raised a silencing hand when she would have spoken. 'She flaunted herself every chance she got.'

'My mother never—'

'He was years older, with a wife, a home, a family. He had an extraordinarily comfortable lifestyle, the respect of his peers and a social life he revelled in. You think a man of my father's disposition would give all that up unless he'd been lured into it by a clever gold-digger?'

Ravenna hesitated, as ever torn by the knowledge of how many people had been hurt by Piers and her mother. But loyalty made her speak up.

'You don't believe in love, then?'

'Love?' He almost snorted the word. 'Silvia pandered to his desires in the most obvious way. I'm sure he loved flaunting her just as he loved showing off his other possessions.' His gaze raked the room, lingering on a Cézanne on the far wall that Ravenna knew for a fact was a copy of an original sold just last year. The derisive twist of Jonas' lips told her he knew it too.

'And as for her...' Wide shoulders shrugged. 'He was just a meal ticket. They had nothing in common except a love of luxury and an aversion to hard work. Why should she toil on as a housekeeper when she could be kept in style for simply letting him—'

'That's enough!' Bile blocked Ravenna's throat and she swallowed hard, forcing it down. 'I don't want to hear any more of your poison.'

His brows rose. 'You're hardly a schoolkid any more, Ravenna.' This time when he said her name there was no lingering warmth and no frisson of subtle reaction. 'You can't pretend.'

'Leave it!' She put up her hand for silence. 'We'll never agree, so leave it.' She hefted in a deep, steadying breath. 'Just cut to the chase and tell me why you're here.'

* * *

Fury still sizzled in Jonas' blood so he took his time slowing his breathing and finding his equilibrium. It wasn't like
him to lose his cool. He was known for his detachment, his
calm clarity of vision even in the most potentially dangerous of commercial ventures.

And in his personal life…he'd learned his lesson early,
watching his father lurch from one failed love affair to another. He'd seen the ecstatic highs of each new fixation, then
the boredom and disappointment of each failure.

Jonas wasn't like his father. He'd made it his business to
be as different from the old man as humanly possible. He
was rock steady, reliable, controlled.

Except right now his hands shook with the force of his
feelings. He swept the gilded room with a contemptuous
glance and assured himself it was inevitable his father's
flashy love nest would evoke a reaction.

'Well? I'm waiting.'

At her husky voice he turned to survey her.

Ravenna Ruggiero. He'd never have recognised her as
the tear-stained girl he remembered. Then she'd been lanky
with the coltishness of youth, her features still settling and
her hair in ribbons, as if to remind him she was still a child.
Only her mouth and her stunning eyes had hinted at beauty.
And the low register of her voice that even then had unsettled him with its promise of sensuality to come.

It had come all right.

Silvia Ruggiero had been a stunning woman in her prime.
But her daughter, even dressed in sombre, loose clothes, out-
shone her as a flawless diamond did a showy synthetic gem.

There was something about Ravenna. Not just a face that
drew the eye as a magnet drew metal so he'd had to force
himself not to stare. But an elegance, a grace, that contrasted
with yet magnified the earthy sexuality of her voice, and that
sassy attitude of hers…

The feel of her stretched up against him, her breasts almost grazing him as she panted her fury in defiance of his superior strength, had stirred something long dormant.

Suspended in a moment of sheer, heady excitement, he'd revelled in the proximity of her soft curves and lush mouth. There'd been a subversive pleasure in her combative attitude, in watching the sparks fly as she launched herself at him.

For the first time in his life Jonas, who preferred his pleasures planned, wondered about being on the receiving end of such unbridled passion. Not just her anger, but—

'Did you hear me?' Fingers clicked in the air before him, dragging his attention to her flushed face.

The colour suited her better, he realised, than the milky pallor he'd noticed earlier. Then he cursed himself for the stray thought.

'You want to know what your mother's been up to?' It was easy to thrust aside his unsettling distraction and focus on familiar ire. 'She's stolen money. My money.'

He had the satisfaction of seeing Ravenna's eyes widen.

It galled him that she'd had the temerity to defend Silvia when they both knew the truth about her mother. Like a magpie with an eye for a pretty, expensive bauble, she'd feathered her nest with his father's wealth.

Jonas recalled the day he'd come home unexpectedly to Deveson Hall from London and found the housekeeper in his mother's suite, in front of a mirror, holding an heirloom choker of sapphires and pearls to her throat. Instead of embarrassment at being caught out, she'd laughed and simply said no woman could have resisted the temptation if she'd found the necklace lying there. Without turning a hair she'd put it down on the dressing table and turned to plump the cushions on a nearby settee.

'No.' This time Ravenna's low voice sounded scratchy as if with shock. 'She wouldn't do that.'

'Wouldn't she?' He looked around the over-stuffed room, wondering how many of the pieces were what they appeared.

Money had obviously been tight enough for his father to cash in the more valuable pieces.

'Of course not.' Ravenna's certainty tugged his attention back to her. No longer flushed but pale and composed, she stared back with infuriating certainty.

'Then how do you explain the fact she forged my father's signature in a cheque book she shouldn't even have had access to?'

'Why blame my mother?'

'No one else had access. Piers would have kept it safely by him, believe me.' He let his gaze rove the room. 'I'm sure if we search the apartment we'll find it.'

'There'll be no searching the apartment. And even if it was here, what's to say it wasn't Piers' signature? His handwriting could have changed when he got ill.'

Jonas shook his head. 'That would have been convenient, wouldn't it? But it won't wash. Unless you can explain how he managed to cash a cheque the day after he died.'

Her eyes widened, growing huge in her taut face.

'I don't believe you.' It was a whisper but even that was like a flame to gunpowder. How could she deny her mother's wrongdoing even now?

'I don't care what you believe.' It was a lie. Her blind faith in the gold-digging Silvia was like salt on a raw wound. Perhaps because he'd never known such loyalty from his own parents. Why should she lavish it on a woman so patently undeserving?

Piers had been an absentee parent, finding plenty of reasons to stay in the city rather than at the Hall. As for his mother—he supposed she'd loved him in her own abstracted way. But she'd been more focused on her personal disappointment in marrying a man who loved not her but the wealth she'd brought with her.

Jonas slipped a hand into his jacket pocket and withdrew the photocopied cheques.

'Here.' He held them out, daring her to take them. 'I

never lie.' His father had been an expert at distorting the truth for his convenience. As a kid Jonas had vowed never to do the same.

He watched Ravenna swallow, the movement convulsive, then she reached out and took the papers. Her head bowed as she stared at them.

The sound of her breath hissing in told him he'd finally got through to her. There was no escaping the truth.

The papers moved as if in a strong breeze and he realised her hands were trembling.

In that instant guilt pierced his self-satisfaction. Belatedly it struck him that taking out his anger on Silvia's daughter was beneath him.

His belly clenched as he reviewed their encounter. Even given his determination to make Silvia pay for her crime, he'd behaved crassly. He'd stalked in, making demands when a simple request for information would have done. Worse, he'd been too caught up in own emotional turmoil to spare a thought for the shock this would be for Ravenna.

'Do you want to sit down?' The words shot out like bullets, rapid and harsh with self-disgust.

She didn't say anything, just stood, head bowed, staring at the papers in her shaking hands.

Hell! Was she in shock?

He leant towards her, trying to read her expression.

All he registered was the stiff set of her jaw and the scent of warm cinnamon and fragrant woman.

And the way she bit her bottom lip, pearly teeth sinking deep in that lush fullness.

Jonas breathed in slowly, telling himself the heat whirling in his belly was shame, not arousal.

The idea of being turned on so easily by any woman was anathema to a man who prided himself on his restraint. When she was the daughter of the woman who'd destroyed his mother... Unthinkable!

'Ravenna?' His voice sounded ridiculously hesitant, as if the ground had shifted beneath his feet.

She looked up, her eyes ablaze as they met his. Then her gaze shifted towards the window.

'You're mistaken.' Her voice sounded wrong, he realised, tight and hard. 'Silvia had nothing to do with this.'

'Stop denying, Ravenna. It's too late for that. I've got proof of her forgery.'

'Proof of forgery, yes. But not Silvia's.' She shifted, standing taller.

Jonas shook his head, weary of the unexpected emotional edge to this interview. 'Just tell me where she is and I'll deal with her.'

Those warm sherry eyes lifted to his and he stilled as he saw how they'd glazed with emotion.

'You don't need to deal with her. She had nothing to do with it.' Ravenna tilted her chin up, her gaze meeting his squarely. 'I did it. I took your money.'

CHAPTER THREE

RAVENNA'S PULSE KICKED as Jonas stiffened. Her throat dried so much it hurt to swallow. But she didn't dare turn away. Instead she met his stare unflinchingly.

She feared if she showed even a flicker of the emotions rioting inside, he wouldn't believe her.

He had to! The alternative, of pinning the theft on her mother, was untenable.

With Jonas' revelation so much fell into place—Piers' remarkable generosity in not just covering her medical costs these last months, but funding the long convalescent stay at an exorbitantly expensive Swiss health resort.

Only it hadn't been Piers making that final, massive payment, had it? It must have been Silvia—breaking the law to help her daughter.

Ravenna's heart plummeted as she recalled her mother's insistence that she needed total rest to recuperate. That without the health resort there was a danger of the treatment failing. Ravenna, too weary by then to protest when all she wanted was to rest quietly and get her strength back, hadn't put up much resistance.

She'd never sponged off Piers' wealth, and had silenced her protesting conscience by vowing to pay back every last euro. It was only when she'd arrived at the Paris apartment the other day that she realised they were euros Piers and her mother could ill afford.

Guilt had struck Ravenna when she saw how much they'd sold off. But she'd never for a moment thought her mother had purloined money that wasn't hers!

Oh, Mamma, what have you done?

Through the years Silvia had gone without again and again so Ravenna could have warm clothes and a roof over her head. And later, so she could go to the respected school her mother thought she needed. But to take what wasn't hers…!

'You're lying.' Jonas' frigid eyes raked her face and a chill skimmed her backbone.

Ravenna smoothed damp palms down her trousers and angled her chin, trying to quell the roiling nausea in her stomach.

'I don't lie.' It was true. Maybe that was why she hadn't convinced him. Her muscles clenched as desperation rose.

She couldn't let him guess the truth. Already a broken woman, Mamma would be destroyed by the shame and stress of gaol.

For a moment Ravenna toyed with blurting out the whole truth, revealing why her mother had stolen the funds and throwing them both on Jonas Deveson's mercy.

Except he didn't have any mercy.

That softer side he'd once shown her years before had been an aberration. In the six years Silvia and Piers had been together, Jonas hadn't once condescended to acknowledge his father's existence. He had ice in his veins rather than warm blood, and a predilection for holding a grudge.

Now it seemed he had a taste for vengeance too.

That might be ice in his veins but there was fire blazing in his eyes. It had been there since he shouldered his way into the apartment, prowling the room with lofty condescension as if his father's death meant nothing to him.

His hatred for her mother was a palpable weight in the charged atmosphere.

He blamed Silvia for his father's defection. He'd sided

with the rest of his aristocratic connections in shunning the working-class foreigner who'd had the temerity to poach one of their own.

Ravenna had to keep this from her. If Mamma found the theft had been discovered she'd come forward and accept the penalty. Ravenna couldn't let her do that, not when she saw the violence in Jonas Deveson's eyes. She couldn't condone what Mamma had done but could understand it, especially since she must have been overwrought about Piers.

'You haven't got it in you to do that, Ravenna.' He shook his head. 'Theft is more your mother's style.'

Fury boiled in her bloodstream. She didn't know which was worse, his bone-deep hatred of her mother or that he thought he knew either of them when at Deveson Hall family hadn't mixed with staff.

His certainty of her innocence should have appeased her; instead, tainted as it was by prejudice, Ravenna found herself angrier than she could ever remember. Rage steamed across her skin and seeped from her pores.

'You have no idea of what her style is or mine.' Her teeth gritted around the words.

His damnably supercilious eyebrows rose again. 'I'm a good judge of character.'

That was what Ravenna feared. That was why she had to work hard to convince him.

Maybe if her mother had a spotless reputation she'd ride out a trial with nothing worse than a caution and community service. But sadly that wasn't the case.

Years before, when Silvia had been young and homeless, kicked out by her father for shaming the family with her pregnancy, she'd resorted to shoplifting to feed herself. She'd been tried then released on a good behaviour bond. That had terrified the young woman who'd been until then completely law abiding.

Much later, when Ravenna was nine, her mother had been accused of stealing from the house where she worked.

Ravenna remembered Mamma's ravaged, parchment-white face as the police led her away under the critical gaze of the woman who employed her. It didn't matter that the charges had been dropped when the woman's daughter was found trying to sell the missing heirloom pieces. Silvia had been dismissed, presumably because her employer couldn't face the embarrassment of having accused an innocent woman.

Mud stuck and innocence didn't seem to matter in the face of prejudice.

Look at the way Jonas already judged her. If she went to trial he'd dredge up her past and every scurrilous innuendo he could uncover and probably create a few for good measure. His air of ruthlessness that chilled Ravenna. His lawyers would make mincemeat out of her mother.

Ravenna couldn't allow it. Especially since her mother had stolen to save her.

Hot guilt flooded her. How desperate Mamma must have been, how worried, to have stolen this man's money! She must have known he'd destroy her if he found out.

Which was why Ravenna had to act.

She stepped forward, her index finger prodding Jonas' hard chest. It felt frighteningly immovable. But she had to puncture his certainty. Attack seemed her best chance.

'Don't pretend to know my mother.' Furtively she sucked in air, her breathing awry as her pulse catapulted. 'You weren't even living at home when we moved to Deveson Hall.'

'You're telling me you masterminded this theft?' His tone was sceptical. 'I think not.'

'You—' her finger poked again '—aren't in a position to know anything about me.'

'Oh, I wouldn't say that.' Warm fingers closed around her hand so that suddenly she was no longer the aggressor but his captive. Tendrils of sensation curled up her arm and made her shiver. 'I know quite a bit about you. I know you hated school, especially maths and science. You wanted to run away but felt you had to stick it out for your mother's sake.'

Ravenna's eyes widened. 'You remember that?' Her voice faded to a whisper. She'd assumed he'd long forgotten her teary confession the day he'd found her wallowing in teenage self-pity.

'You hated being made to play basketball just because you were tall. As I recall you wanted to be tiny, blonde and one of five children, all rejoicing in the name of Smith.'

It was true. Living up to her mother's expectations of academic and social success had been impossible, especially for an undistinguished scholar like Ravenna, surrounded by unsupportive peers who treated her as a perennial outsider. For years she'd longed, not to be 'special' but to blend in.

'And you didn't like the way one of the gardeners had begun to stare at you.'

Ridiculously heat flushed her skin. That summer she'd been a misfit, neither child nor adult. She hadn't known what she wanted.

But she hadn't minded when Jonas Deveson looked at her or, for one precious, fleeting moment, stroked wayward curls off her face.

Ravenna blinked. She wasn't fifteen now.

'You remember far more of that day than I do.' Another lie. Two in one day had to be a record for her. Maybe if she kept it up she could even sound convincing.

Did she imagine a slight softening in those grey eyes?

No. Easier to believe she'd scored her dream job as a pastry chef in a Michelin-starred restaurant than that this steely man had a compassionate side.

'You haven't changed that much.' His deep voice stirred something unsettling deep inside.

'No? You didn't even recognise me.' She pulled back but he didn't loosen his grip. He held her trapped.

For a moment fear spidered through her, till she reminded herself he had too much pride to force himself on an unwilling woman. His hold wasn't sexual, it was all about power. The charged awareness was all on her side, not his.

She had no intention of analysing that. She had enough to worry about.

'You've changed a lot.' Her tone made it clear it wasn't a compliment. At twenty-one he'd been devastatingly handsome but unexpectedly kind and patient. She'd liked him, even more than liked him in her naïve way.

Now he was all harsh edges, irascible and judgemental. What was there to like?

'We're not here to discuss me.' His eyes searched hers. Stoically she kept her head up and face blank. Better to brazen out her claim than show a hint of doubt.

Yet inside she was wobbly as jelly. The past days had taken their toll as she saw how grief had ravaged her mother, making her seem frail. Ravenna had sent her away from the apartment so ripe with memories of Piers. She'd offered to pack up the flat and deal with the landlord, but even those simple tasks were a test of Ravenna's endurance. Now this...

'We're here to discuss my money.' Jonas' fingers firmed around her. 'The money stolen from my account.'

Ravenna swallowed hard at his unrelenting tone.

Just what *was* the penalty for theft and forgery?

Jonas felt her hand twitch in his.

A sign of guilt or proof she lied about being the one who'd ripped him off?

Her soft eyes were huge in her finely sculpted face, giving her an air of fragility despite her punk-short hair and belligerently angled chin.

Jonas wasn't sentimental enough to let looks mar his decision-making. Yet, absurdly, he found himself hesitating.

He didn't *want* to believe Ravenna guilty.

Far easier to believe her rapacious mother had organised this swindle. After years keeping his emotions bottled up he'd almost enjoyed the roaring surge of fury against his father's mistress that had borne him across the channel in a red-misted haze.

But what bothered him most was the recognition he didn't want it to be Ravenna because he remembered her devastating innocence and honesty years ago. He didn't want to reconcile that memory with the knowledge she'd become a thief.

Jonas' lips twisted. Who'd have thought he still had illusions he didn't want to shatter? He'd been too long in the cut-throat business world to believe in the innate honesty of mankind. Experience had taught him man—and womankind were out for all they could get.

Why should this revelation be so unwelcome?

'You say you wrote the cheques?'

Again that jerk of tension through her. Her pulse tripped against his palm and he resisted the absurd impulse to caress her there.

She nodded, the movement brief but emphatic.

'How did you get access to the cheque book?' Piers would have been canny enough to keep it close at hand, not lying around. 'Were you living here with them?'

'No, I—' She paused and her gaze shifted away. Instinct told him she hid something. 'But I visited. Often. My mother and I have always been close.'

That at least had the ring of truth. He remembered her misery in her teens, not simply because she hated school and the vicious little witches who made her life hell there, but because she didn't want to disappoint her mother by leaving. She cared what her mother thought.

Enough to learn her mother's ways in seeking easy money from a man? Had she modelled herself on Silvia?

The notion left a sour tang of disappointment on his tongue.

'You're hurting me!'

Jonas eased his grip, but didn't let her go. He was determined to sort this out. Until then he'd keep her close.

'Why did you need the money?'

Her eyebrows arched and she tilted her head as if to inspect him. As if he weren't already close enough to see the rays of gold in the depths of her eyes.

'You're kidding, right?' Her tone of insouciant boredom echoed the attitude of entitlement he'd heard so often among wealthy, privileged young things who'd never worked a day in their lives. Except something in her tone was ever so slightly off-key.

Suspicion snaked through him.

He pulled her closer, till her body mirrored his. He felt the tension hum through her. Good! He wanted her unsettled.

'A girl needs to live, doesn't she?' This time there was an edge of desperation in her tone. 'I've had…expenses.'

'What sort of expenses? Even shopping at the top Parisian fashion houses wouldn't have swallowed up all that money.'

Her gaze slid from his. 'This and that.'

A cold, hard weight formed in the pit of Jonas' belly. He was surprised to feel nausea well.

'Drugs?'

She shook her head once, then shrugged. 'Debts.'

'Gambling?'

'Why the inquisition? I've admitted I took your money. That's all that matters.' Her gaze meshed with his and a jagged flash of heat resonated through Jonas. It stunned him.

How could a mere look do that? It wasn't even a sultry invitation but a surly, combative stare that annoyed the hell out of him.

Yet aftershocks still tumbled through his clenching belly and he found himself leaning closer, inhaling her warm cinnamon and hot woman scent.

This couldn't be happening.

He refused to feel anything for the woman who'd stolen from him. Especially since she was Silvia Ruggiero's daughter. The thought of that family connection was like a cold douche.

Deliberately he chose his next words to banish any illusion of closeness. 'Why steal from me when Piers would have indulged a pretty young thing like you? I'm sure he'd have been amendable to *private* persuasion.'

'You're sick. You know that? Piers was with my *mother*. He had no interest in me.' She drew herself up as if horrified. Either she was a brilliant actor or she drew the line at men old enough to be her father.

'In my experience he wasn't discriminating.'

Ravenna yanked her hand to free it from his grasp but Jonas wasn't playing. He wrapped his other arm hard around her narrow back, drawing her up against him.

Just to keep her still, he assured himself.

It worked. With a stifled gasp she froze. Only the quick rise and fall of her breasts against his arm where he still held her hand revealed animation.

'Speaking from personal experience, are you, Jonas?' Her voice was all sneer. 'What are you doing now? Copping a feel?'

His jaw ached with the effort to bite back a retort.

Unlike his father he'd never been a sucker for a pretty face and a show of cleavage. Sure, he appreciated a sexy woman. But he was discriminating, private in his affairs and loyal to whomever he was with. His intellect and his sense of honour took precedence over cheap thrills.

When he married there'd be no shady liaisons on the side, no whispered rumours and knowing looks to embarrass his family. None of the pain to which Piers had subjected them.

Jonas stared down at the firebrand who'd managed to tap into emotions he'd kept safely stowed for years. In one short interlude she'd cut through years of hard-won self-control so he teetered on the brink of spontaneous, uncharacteristic, dangerous action. He almost growled his fury and frustration aloud.

He wanted to lean down and silence her sassy mouth, force those lush lips apart and relieve some of his frustrated temper in steamy passion and a vibrant, accommodating woman.

She'd be receptive, despite that accusatory look. That was what made the idea so tempting. Ravenna might hate him for making her face what she'd done. But it wasn't merely anger she felt for him—not by a long chalk.

'Oh, I choose my women very carefully, Ravenna.' His voice was a low, guttural burr. 'And I never take anything from a woman that's not offered freely.'

Dark satisfaction flared as he assessed her reaction with a knowing eye.

He read her rapid breathing and the flush that began at her cleavage and highlighted her cheeks. The way her tongue furtively slicked her lower lip. The indefinable scent of feminine arousal.

'Really?' Her breathless challenge didn't convince. 'Well, keep that in mind. I'm not offering you anything.'

Jonas was torn between wanting to kiss her senseless and wanting to put her over his knee. He leaned in a fraction and heard her soft exhale of breath. A sigh...of surrender or triumph?

Suddenly it hit him anew that he was in danger of succumbing to the allure of a Ruggiero female. Of an unprincipled thief who threw her crime in his teeth.

Who enticed with her soft body and tell-tale physical signals.

'Is that so?' he murmured, knowing he had her measure.

She'd use any tactic to thwart his retribution. Did she aim to play him for an easy mark, as her mother had targeted Piers?

The realisation stilled his impetuous need to taste her. Yet he couldn't draw back. He was trapped by a hunger sharper and more potent than he'd known in years.

That infuriated him even more than the missing money. He burned with it, the fire in his belly white hot with a virulent mix of lust and self-disgust at his weakness.

Keeping one arm around her back, he released her hand and let his fingers drift. She didn't flinch, didn't move, her eyes daring him to do his worst. Because she thought herself immune or because she assumed he wouldn't rise to her challenge?

His fingers brushed her soft, high breast and moulded automatically to that sweet ripeness. The hard nub of her nipple pressed into his palm and arousal seared his groin. A spasm of something like electricity jerked through his body.

For a breath-stealing moment she stood rigid as if about to lambast him for groping. Her eyes widened in shock, then dropped in heavy-lidded invitation. Her lips parted on a silent sigh. A moment later she shifted, melting against him.

'Tell me to stop and I will.'

He prayed she wouldn't.

She opened her mouth but no sound emerged.

The weight of her in his palm, the press of her body, the heady sense of promise thickening the air between them, sapped his resolution.

He was ready to take her up on her unspoken invitation. His body was rock hard with a hunger that was all the stronger for being unexpected. Why not take a little something for himself after she'd taken so much from him? Clearly she expected it, wanted it, if the tremors in her pliant body were any indication.

But that smacked of history repeating itself. The little thief would think he kept his brain between his legs, as his father had when he'd run off with her mother, leaving his responsibilities behind.

Jonas couldn't let Ravenna enjoy the illusion of triumph. He had too much pride.

He was nobody's gullible mark.

As she'd learn to her cost.

Gently he squeezed her breast, just enough to elicit a delicate shudder in her fine-boned body and a throaty sigh of delight.

The hairs on his arms prickled and his blood rushed south at the sound of her pleasure. But he refused to respond to the urges of his suddenly intemperate body.

'You like that, do you, Ravenna?'

Slitted now, her eyes had a glazed look that told its own story. She swallowed convulsively, drawing his attention to the slim length of her pale throat. The collar of her dark jacket sat loose, giving her an air of fragility at odds with the pulse of vibrant life he felt as she arched against him.

He'd pull back soon. In a moment. When he'd allowed himself a single taste...

Cinnamon and feminine spice filled his nostrils as he dipped his head, nudging aside her collar and nipping gently at the sensitive spot where her neck and shoulder met. She shook in his hold, her hand grasping his between them as if for support.

'No. Please I—'

Her words cut abruptly as Jonas laved the spot, drawing in the sweet taste of her warm skin.

Too late he realised his error, as he angled his head hungrily for a better taste, pressing kisses up her arching throat, past the throbbing pulse to the neat angle of her jaw.

She was addictive. Scent or taste or the feel of silky soft flesh, or perhaps all three, had Jonas ignoring the voice of reason and losing himself in the moment. In the luxury of caressing Ravenna.

He'd never come across a woman who tempted him so easily.

Her free hand cupped his neck, holding him close, and he pulled her tight against him, enjoying the slide of her body as she bowed back to give him free rein.

He stroked his tongue along the scented skin behind her ear and had to tighten his hold when she slumped against him as if her knees had given way.

She was so responsive, inciting a surge of arousal that swamped all else. Blood roared in his veins, primal instinct taking over. His focus blurred, his mind racing frantically with the practicalities of getting her horizontal as soon as possible.

He nipped lightly at her ear lobe and she turned her head restlessly as if seeking his lips.

Triumph hummed through him as he pressed a kiss to the corner of her lush mouth.

One quick taste then he'd find that preposterous gilded sofa and treat them both to sexual release so intense it would shatter them. Already he was hard as a rock. Carrying her across the room would be torture but he wasn't letting her go till he'd had his fill. Till they were both limp and the urgent hunger gnawing at his vitals was appeased.

His ears rang with the force of his blood rushing. He ignored it and tilted his head to take her mouth.

Except her eyes were open now and that dreamy expression had faded. Stark horror flared instead in those dark gold depths.

Jonas frowned. She wanted him. He knew it. He felt it with every muscle and sinew as she pressed herself against him. Yet—

The ringing sounded again. This time he realised it came from somewhere outside his head—the front door.

'Let me go.' Her voice was so hoarse he read her lips rather than heard her. Jonas blinked, trying to make sense of the abrupt shift in mood.

She pushed against him with both hands. 'I said, let me go!' Her gaze slid from his as if she couldn't bear to look at him. Because he'd made her forget her little game of temptation? Because she'd been the victim of unexpected lust this time instead of the temptress?

Something soured his belly. Memory. Disillusionment. The realisation that despite his vaunted immunity he'd fallen hard and fast for what she offered: hot sex with a gold-digging opportunist.

Just like his father before him.

He released her so quickly she wobbled and he reached out a hand to steady her.

'Saved by the bell,' he murmured and watched heat flush her cheeks. Not for the life of him would he let her see how she'd knocked him for six. That was his private shame.

She knocked his hand away, rubbing her palm over the place he'd held her as if to erase his touch. But he wasn't fooled by her show of antipathy. She'd lost control too. It was that latter truth that cut him to the core, tapping the long-dammed reservoir of fury so it finally broke free.

He watched her spin away from him, her steps uneven as she headed for the foyer. With each step he cursed himself for his weakness. He'd seen what she was. She'd *told* him. Yet he hadn't been able to resist her.

'If that was you being unaffected,' he drawled, 'I look forward to seeing what you're like when you put a little effort into sex.' He drew a slow breath, watching her stumble to a halt. 'I was willing to test the waters to see how far you'd go. And I wasn't disappointed.'

Her shoulders hunched but she didn't turn around.

For a moment something like sympathy hovered. Jonas had a ridiculous urge to cross the room and pull her close to comfort her.

He shook his head.

What was it about Ravenna Ruggiero that got under his skin despite what she'd done?

Was there a family weakness after all? Something in the Deveson genes that made them putty in the grasping hands of the Ruggiero women?

He gritted his teeth against a howl of fury and, worse, disappointment that now he'd never have her in his arms again. He couldn't trust himself with her. How sick was that?

He buried the knowledge behind a wall of disdain.

'Do let me know, if you decide you have something to offer me after all. I might even consider being a little less *discriminating* just for the novelty of it.'

CHAPTER FOUR

RAVENNA STARED AT the mellow wood of the floor, wishing the old boards would part in a yawning void and suck her away into nothingness. Anything to escape the sarcastic lash of Jonas Deveson's contempt.

As if she should be so fortunate! This past year there'd been no good luck in her life. Except the unexpected gift of the rest cure in Switzerland. But now it turned out that had an awful catch. An enormous debt to be paid.

And a big, ruthless debt collector to make sure she paid in blood.

She shivered, cold to the bone, yet her skin crawled with a clammy heat that matched the nausea twisting her insides. She fought it, refusing to be ill in front of him.

Could anything be more humiliating than this?

She felt sullied by him. It was far worse than facing a dressing-down by the head chef at work, whose explosive tirades were legend. As for the torments of her school years—they'd been nothing to this excruciating shame.

For this time every word was deserved. She'd behaved like some slut, eager for the touch of a man who despised her. For the first time she hadn't behaved like the sensible, careful, self-contained woman she was.

She'd acted like a hormone-riddled stranger with no scruples or self-respect.

The doorbell rang again and she dragged herself into the

foyer, propping herself against the wall with a shaking hand as she pressed the intercom.

'Monsieur Giscard?' The words were so faint she cleared her throat to try again. The response from below was garbled in ears that still thrummed with the pulse of arousal.

Nevertheless, she pressed the button to let the visitor in downstairs. Whoever it was, he couldn't be more devastating than Jonas Deveson.

She felt his eyes on her. Her skin prickled and heat drilled her spine. She could pinpoint the exact place between her shoulder blades where that penetrating gaze scored her. If she found later that his laser-sharp gaze had scorched a hole in her jacket she wouldn't be surprised.

Ravenna struggled to swallow the hard knot of emotion blocking her throat.

What had got into her to behave so utterly out of character?

Taking a deep breath, she tried to centre herself but instead inhaled the remnants of his tangy, hot citrus scent. It had impregnated her very pores.

Never in her life had attraction been like that—instantaneous and absolute. Consciously, to her thinking mind, there'd been no attraction—just fear and shock at his revelations, and a determination to divert his thunderous anger from her mother.

But something had happened when he'd touched her. Something unheralded.

She'd heard of animal attraction. She had some experience of desire.

But this… This had been a tsunami obliterating reason and doubt and anything like resistance. She'd stood like a rabbit spotlighted by a hunter, watching his eyes cloud with desire as he touched her. Excitement had stormed through her.

Part of her brain had screamed for her to move, to slap his hand away, but she'd stood, rooted to the spot, eager for more. When he'd bitten her neck in that delicate tasting, she'd gone up in flames.

How was it possible?

Brushing off male attention had never been hard. Yet she'd practically begged for more from him as carnal heat melted her insides and left her a quivering, pathetic wreck.

Where was her backbone? Her sense of self-preservation?

The doorbell rang and she stumbled forward. Her legs felt like melted wax and she fumbled at the door with shaking hands.

On the threshold stood a man of middle years, exquisitely dressed and sporting a rosebud in his lapel.

'Mademoiselle Ruggiero?' He pronounced her name with the softened consonants of the French.

'Monsieur Giscard.' She held out her hand. 'It's a pleasure to meet you. I appreciate you coming so quickly.' She led him into the apartment, carefully keeping her gaze from the far side of the salon and Jonas' watchful presence.

If she could she'd eject him from the premises, but he wouldn't leave till he was good and ready. They had too much to discuss.

At least having the antiques expert here gave her something else to concentrate on, and a chance to regroup after that devastating embrace.

Despite her best intentions her gaze slid across the room to lock with eyes the colour of impenetrable mist. Jonas' face was blank but his words echoed in her ears, making heat scorch her throat and cheeks.

Beside her the dapper Frenchman started forward eagerly, his arm outstretched as he introduced himself to Jonas Deveson. For a moment Ravenna thought the two must have met before but it appeared Monsieur Giscard simply recognised him from press reports.

Ravenna spun away on the ball of her foot. Jonas Deveson even managed to usurp the position of authority now, without trying. Her visitor was fawning over him like a long-lost son. Or a wealthy potential client.

'I have an inventory of furnishings here, Monsieur Giscard.' Reluctantly he turned towards her, and then nodded.

'Perhaps, Mr Deveson, we could meet later today to conclude our discussion?' She had a snowball's chance in hell of fobbing him off but she had to try. The idea of him watching them trail around the apartment, sizing up her mamma's possessions, made her skin crawl.

'I think not, Ravenna.' He deliberately dropped his voice to a pseudo caress on her name. To her consternation and shame she felt her skin tingle and her nipples harden.

It was as if she were programmed to respond sexually even to the cadence of his voice!

'I'm afraid Monsieur Giscard and I will be busy for some time—'

'Don't let me disturb you.' His open wave of the arm, as if graciously giving them permission to continue, made her grit her teeth. 'I'm happy to wait.'

As if to emphasise his point he sank onto a gilded chair and nonchalantly crossed his legs, his hands palm down on the arms in a pose that screamed authority. His tall frame in that delicate chair should have looked ridiculous. Instead he looked...regal.

For a second Ravenna toyed with the idea of calling for the police to eject him as an unwanted intruder. Until she realised the police were the last people she wanted. Her mother's crime loomed over her like a leaden storm cloud.

Fear sank talons deep into her vitals. This impossible situation could only get worse, given this man's implacable thirst for vengeance. Her body stiffened, adrenalin surging and heart pounding in an unstoppable fight-or-flight response. Chaotic thoughts of disappearing out of the front door and not coming back raced through her brain.

But she couldn't do it.

Ravenna was hardworking, dutiful, responsible. It was

the way she was made, reinforced no doubt by watching her mother slave so long and hard to support them both.

Besides, if she disappeared, Jonas would go after Mamma.

Drawing a slow breath, she squared her shoulders. If there was one thing the last months had taught her it was that she had the power to endure more than she'd ever thought possible. She'd pay the debt somehow, save her mother from his destructive fury, then get on with her life.

'As you wish. Feel free to make yourself comfortable.' She shot him a dazzling smile and had the momentary pleasure of seeing him disconcerted. Then she turned to Monsieur Giscard, gesturing for him to precede her from the room. 'I thought we might start in the study.'

Why Piers had needed a study was beyond Jonas. The old man hadn't worked for years, merely living off what was left of his investments.

Jonas had been at the helm of what had begun as a Deveson family investment company. He'd cut the old man from his life and manoeuvred him from the business when he'd left and destroyed Jonas' mother, never once expressing regret.

Shifting in the uncomfortable chair, he cast a scathing look around the room. It didn't improve with familiarity. The few good pieces were overwhelmed by the clutter of showy ornamentation.

Piers had been a magpie, attracted by the bright and shiny, displaying his wealth in the most obvious way. That went especially for women.

Jonas raked his hand through his hair. Had Ravenna Ruggiero's dismay been genuine when he'd suggested she should have used her feminine wiles to get money from Piers?

More important—what on earth had possessed him to touch her?

He was appalled by his reaction to her, but fascinated. He

couldn't remember being fascinated by anything other than an exciting investment opportunity in years.

Jonas shot to his feet, unwilling to sit on the sidelines.

He found them in a large room dominated by a massive desk. They were examining ornate snuffboxes.

'This is a passably good piece. You might manage a hundred euros for it.'

The antique dealer, Giscard, had his back to the door so Jonas couldn't see what he held. But Ravenna's disappointment at the words was clear. Her shoulders slumped and her whole body sagged.

'Really? I'd thought perhaps this at least might be worth more.' Her voice had an edge of desperation.

Giscard turned and Jonas watched him hesitate, his brisk manner softening as he took in her barely concealed distress.

'Well, perhaps a little more. I tend to err on the side of caution, Mademoiselle Ruggiero.' He turned back to the item in his hands. 'After a closer look I think it possible we could do better. If you like I can undertake the sale personally. I have some contacts who might be interested.'

'Really?' Ravenna's eyes shone hopefully and she leaned towards him. 'That would be wonderful, Monsieur Giscard.' Her voice was soft with hope and Jonas felt his skin contract as if she'd brushed her fingertips over him.

He clenched his jaw, furious yet intrigued at the power of that throaty voice.

'It is the least I can do in the sad circumstances.' The dealer moved closer as if drawn by her tremulous smile. 'Perhaps, in the circumstances, you should call me Etienne.'

Jonas' grip tightened on the doorjamb as the pair continued their conversation, oblivious to his presence.

Distaste was a pungent note on his tongue as he watched the older man respond to Ravenna's artful show of vulnerability. That was what it was, he realised, his lips thinning in a grim smile.

The woman who'd made such a point of confronting him

with her crime was no innocent. She was brazen and un-repentant.

From the moment she'd revealed her identity, flouncing about the astronomically expensive apartment as if it were hers, he'd wondered why she'd dressed as she had. The dark trouser suit was tailored but it hung on her, making her look like a child dressing up, especially with the gamine haircut accentuating her exquisitely pared features and huge eyes.

There'd been nothing childlike about her when he'd ca-ressed her. She'd been all needy woman. Yet with her navy jacket hanging loose around her neck, she exuded an air of fragility that intrigued him.

Now he knew why. That vulnerability, enhanced by the sedate cut of clothes that hinted at mourning, was a deliber-ate act to aid her dealings with the antique dealer.

Look at Giscard! He ate her up with his eyes, like a dog slavering after a bone.

She'd prepared carefully for the interview to play on the Frenchman's sympathies.

And Jonas had doubted she was capable of thieving!

She was as conniving and dangerous as her mother.

More so. He remembered Silvia as having a blatant sensu-ality that made her stand out like a Mediterranean sex god-dess with her flashing eyes, swinging hips and earthy laugh. But her daughter... He narrowed his eyes as he watched the woman so easily manipulating the Frenchman. She had an arresting face, the sort of eyes that a less pragmatic man could lose himself in, and a body that, though slim, made him want to haul her close and discover its secrets.

But there was more. An aura of banked passion and quick intelligence that melded into something that drew him at the most primitive, male level.

He wanted her.

The realisation hit him a solid blow to the belly.

He didn't like or admire her. She was the sort of woman he'd learnt to despise.

And still he wanted her.

He dragged in a deep breath, ignoring the anticipation fizzing his blood at the thought of bedding Ravenna Ruggiero.

It wasn't going to happen. His standards were higher than that.

Instead he would make her pay for what she'd done. He'd make sure she learned the value of the money she'd taken, and when he'd finished with her she'd understand the value of hard work too. She'd repay her debt in full. There'd be no easy escape if she tried batting those long eyelashes at him.

There'd be no police, no trial. He'd looked forward to branding his father's mistress publicly as a thief. But for reasons he didn't want to investigate, that didn't seem appropriate now Ravenna had revealed herself as the culprit.

Yes, he could throw her to the mercy of the courts. But having seen her, touched her, he wanted a much more personal recompense.

She'd stolen his money but the insult carved deeper than the loss of mere money, which, after all, was easily replaced.

Jonas told himself his decision had nothing to do with the heat haze of desire still drenching his skin as he watched her flirt with another man.

Or the feeling she'd somehow bested him in their first confrontation even though he held all the winning cards in this contest.

For there *was* a contest. Of wills. Of strength and, above all, of pride.

Somehow she'd breached the fortress he'd long ago built around his emotions. He was disappointed to discover she'd gone the way of her mother, intent on easy money rather than working for it like any decent woman. He'd expected better of her. It was as if she'd betrayed his memory of her.

His lips twisted as he reviewed his decision to give her a chance to avoid a criminal record. It was almost altruistic of him. Facing the consequences of her crime in the form of hard work might be the making of her.

Jonas' eyes narrowed as she batted those lush lashes at the besotted Frenchman. Something cold and sharp solidified in his belly.

No matter what the outcome, he looked forward to collecting on his debt.

'Now these,' purred Monsieur Giscard, 'are in a different class altogether.' He stood in front of a cabinet displaying a collection of old glassware.

'Really?' Ravenna stepped closer, her hopes rising. So far they'd come across little that could be sold to pay off Mamma's debts, let alone set her up with a nest egg for the future. 'You think they may be valuable?'

She had little expectation of finding anything to cover the money her mother had taken from Jonas Deveson's account but scraping together enough to pay Mamma's immediate bills would be an enormous relief.

'I need to examine them properly, but this appears to be a fine collection of early glassware.' He paused, excitement lighting his face. 'Really, a very fine collection…' His voice trailed as he bent to view a goblet with a long, thick stem of twisted glass.

Ravenna held her breath as he opened the cabinet and reached for the goblet.

'I'm afraid those pieces aren't for sale.' The deep voice came from just behind her and she jumped. She hadn't heard Jonas Deveson approach.

'Do you have to sneak up like that?' As soon as the words snapped out she regretted them, seeing his raised brows and knowing smirk. Maybe it was petty given the enormity of what lay between them, but she'd rather not reveal how thoroughly he unsettled her.

He didn't answer, instead turning to Monsieur Giscard, who held the glass cradled reverentially in his hands.

'C'est magnifique!'

'It is, isn't it?' Before Ravenna could stop him Jonas reached out and took it from the Frenchman, holding it up to the light for a moment, before putting it back in the cabinet and shutting the door. 'But it's not for sale.'

'Now look here—!'

He cut her off as if she hadn't spoken. 'It seems this inventory of yours is flawed.' He took the clipboard from her and glanced down at it. Before Ravenna had the presence of mind to snatch it back he'd taken a gold pen from a pocket and begun slashing lines through her list.

'You'll find the contents of this cabinet are old family pieces. They belong to my father's estate—in other words, to me.' He looked up, his silver gaze skewering her. 'Unless you'd like to try stealing this as well?'

Ravenna's breath hissed in and blood scalded her cheeks. In her peripheral vision she was aware of Monsieur Giscard's sharp, curious look.

'I didn't—'

'No?' Jonas' mouth curled up in a superior smile she'd give anything to wipe away.

'No. And it's strange that your father's solicitor hasn't been in contact about collecting anything entailed. I understood the furnishings belong to my mother.'

'Who is conveniently not here.' His voice was velvet with a razor-sharp edge. 'And who was conveniently not available when lawyers tried to contact her.'

Ravenna shook her head, denying his implied accusation. 'She's upset, grieving. She wasn't ready to handle this.'

'Which is why she installed you with your special...*capabilities,* to wrap up the estate?'

The air between them thickened and Ravenna felt fire spark in her blood. He spoke so contemptuously, as if she were a conniving thief.

Which is exactly what you want him to believe. For your mother's sake.

Caution battled fury as she swallowed a furious protest. She was battered by the intensity of his disapproval, and her need to submit.

Finally she broke eye contact and looked away. Instantly her cramped lungs eased as she sucked in sustaining oxygen.

'Monsieur Giscard.' She turned to the dealer with an apologetic smile she hoped masked her desperation. 'As you see things are not as clear cut as I'd thought. Would you mind—?'

'Of course, *mademoiselle*.' He looked only too happy to go, glancing nervously at Jonas who stood glowering like a disapproving idol, his face carved from unforgiving granite.

'I'll call you when I've sorted this out.'

'Of course, of course.' The Frenchman almost scurried out of the door and he didn't meet her eyes when she farewelled him at the entrance to the apartment.

Ravenna's skin crawled with embarrassment, reliving that moment when Jonas had spoken with such calculated cruelty about her stealing. Her stomach plummeted and she leaned against the wall for support. She'd have to get used to it if she was going to carry this off. She had a disturbing feeling it wasn't just public humiliation Jonas Deveson had planned.

He wanted more. He wanted his pound of flesh.

She shivered, remembering his strong teeth nipping at the erogenous zone in her neck. And that she'd done nothing to stop him.

'Alone at last.' His low voice curled around her like a phantom and wholly misleading caress. She should have guessed he wouldn't let her out of his sight.

Ravenna didn't bother replying. Nor did she have any intention of meeting those judgemental eyes. She turned abruptly and walked away.

'Where are you going?' His tone sharpened in surprise. Obviously he wasn't used to anyone turning their back on him.

'I need a drink.'

Of course he followed her and even in the spacious kitchen she felt that claustrophobic sense of the air thickening. She had the unnerving suspicion that even beneath a wide blue sky she'd feel hemmed in by what Jonas made her feel.

Refusing to acknowledge her burgeoning panic, she busied herself filling the kettle and getting out the cafetière.

'How very domestic.'

She shrugged. 'Well, I *am* the housekeeper's daughter.' She filled the coffee grinder and vented her feelings cranking the old-fashioned grinder.

It didn't make her feel any better.

'So, Jonas. What are your plans? Have you called the police? Am I going to be led off in handcuffs?' Her voice was so brittle the words came out in hard little bites.

'The scenario does have a certain charm.'

Ravenna stiffened, the hairs on her arms rising as she paused in the act of emptying the grinder.

'But?' There was a but in there. At least she hoped there was. Unable to pretend indifference any longer, she swung round. Predictably he lounged against the doorjamb, filling the one and only exit with his broad shoulders and athletic frame.

Ravenna licked her lips as her mouth dried. Fear rather than pride prompted her next words. 'I'll pay you back. I promise.'

'You promise?' He paused as if considering. 'And how will you do that?' He straightened and prowled across the room. She had nowhere to go and stood her ground, but the countertop bit into her back as the space between them closed. 'I'm curious. Do you have a job?'

She opened her mouth to confirm she had, then snapped it shut. She'd been a junior in the restaurant, had only worked there a few months. She'd lost her job when it became obvious she'd need months off work and that she might never return.

'No. I don't have a job at the moment.'

'Somehow that doesn't surprise me.'

'And so?' She refused to be baited. 'What are your plans?'

For the space of four heartbeats he said nothing, then his mouth turned up in a smile that didn't meet his eyes. It made him look lethally dangerous, and, to Ravenna's horror, sexy with it. If you were a woman who liked to live on a knife edge of peril. She told herself she didn't.

'Plans?' He paused. 'Oh, you mean about the theft?'

She clenched her hands. She wouldn't take another swing at him, no matter how tempted. She had no intention of getting close enough again to touch him. 'The arch air of disingenuousness doesn't suit you.'

He shrugged. 'And the wide-eyed air of innocence doesn't suit you.'

She crossed her arms so he wouldn't see how they shook. Behind her the kettle whistled and stopped but she fixed her attention on the man who held her future in his hands.

'I intend to ensure you pay back your debt. It's that simple.'

'Nothing with you is simple.'

This time there was a flicker of appreciation in his smile. 'Ah, you're a quick learner.'

When she said nothing he finally continued. 'I'm reopening Deveson Hall. It's been shut since my mother's death with no one to look after it but a caretaker for the grounds.'

Ravenna frowned. A stately old home like that needed constant attention and upkeep. Not just cleaning but maintenance and ongoing repairs. One of her mother's jobs as housekeeper had been to know exactly who was working where on the rambling old place.

'I'm advised it needs considerable attention.' An undercurrent of emotion coloured his words and, to her surprise, Ravenna saw him scrub his hand around the back of his neck as if to ease sudden tension. His lips pursed and she could have sworn she read concern in his features.

It was the first indication she'd seen today that Jonas Deveson was capable of feeling anything softer than bitterness or contempt.

From the way he spoke he hadn't mourned his father, yet the neglect of his family home moved him?

He was more complex than she'd thought. She'd pegged him as a man who cared for nothing but his own pride.

Ravenna opened her mouth to ask why he hadn't bothered to do something about the house earlier but the answer was obvious. He'd only just inherited the place.

Piers had spent most of the last six years out of England and hadn't visited the estate since his wife's death. Ravenna wasn't surprised to discover he'd decided to spend his money maintaining his lavish lifestyle rather than on the upkeep of a mansion he preferred not to visit.

'That's where you come in.' Jonas' slow smile chilled her anew. 'As well as the renovation work, the Hall needs to be cleaned from top to bottom. Scrubbed till it shines.'

'You want me to be part of the crew that—?'

'Not part.' He shook his head slowly, his smile growing. 'You'll be *it*. Personally responsible for getting the place ready for the ball I'm hosting to celebrate the Hall's reopening.'

Ravenna couldn't prevent herself gaping. Deveson Hall had been built centuries ago when the family employed an army of servants. It was gorgeous, precious, sprawling and the complete opposite of the low-maintenance residences being designed now. It was three floors of steady toil for the team her mother had overseen. Four floors if you counted the attics. Five with the cellars.

She had no doubt Jonas would include the cellars.

'*One person* to do all that? It's impossible!'

'There will be builders working to fix what needs repairing. You'll be responsible for getting the place ready to live in again.'

A flash of something showed in his steely eyes and

Ravenna realised he was waiting for her to refuse, to toss away what she knew instinctively would be her only option apart from prison.

'Is that all?' Somehow she choked the words out.

His smile faded.

'No. If your work is of a high enough standard then you can stay on and work off the rest of your debt as my house-keeper. That's my offer. Take it or leave it.'

The dreadful irony of it didn't escape her. Her mother might have escaped Jonas Deveson's wrath but she wouldn't. He began with putting her firmly in her place, as his servant.

Her insides twisted. She'd vowed never to be anyone's servant after seeing the way her mother had been treated by so many employers. There were wealthy employers who believed service was akin to bonded slavery. Even the sheer hard work of a commercial kitchen was preferable.

Childhood taunts echoed in her ears. Her peers had viewed sharing a classroom with a servant's daughter an insult. They'd made her pay for that insult.

Ravenna had thought she'd escaped all that.

It would take years to pay off the money. Yet she had no choice. She didn't want a criminal record or a stint in prison.

She drew a breath, trying to slow her frantic pulse.

Jonas would make her time at Deveson Hall hell, but she was strong enough to cope. He couldn't throw anything at her that was worse than what she'd already faced. She pushed her shoulders back and looked him in the eye, ignoring the sizzle of heat arcing between them.

Before she could say anything he spoke again. 'Don't get ideas of history repeating itself.' His voice was glacial. 'I don't have a weakness for the hired help like my father.'

Her chin went up. With every word he degraded what her mother and Piers had shared.

'That's a relief.' Ravenna forced the words through numb lips. 'You're not my type.'

His stony face tightened. Yet he said nothing as he waited

for her to reject his preposterous scheme. Then he'd call in the police.

'How could I refuse such a generous offer? You've got yourself a housekeeper, Mr Deveson.'

CHAPTER FIVE

THE BLEAK WEATHER did nothing to brighten Ravenna's mood. Deveson Hall was as imposing as she recalled, sprawling across what seemed acres, its blind eyes reflecting no light on this dreary, damp day.

Ravenna shuddered and wrapped her arms around herself as the drizzle-laden wind tugged her coat.

She wasn't afraid of hard work but this… She swallowed, her throat dry as the enormity of it sank in. He expected the impossible.

No sane man could expect one person to care for all that. Even if the Hall hadn't been neglected for years it needed a team of staff. He couldn't seriously think—

Of course he didn't. Jonas Deveson was no fool. He expected her to throw up her hands and surrender. He wanted to watch her admit defeat before he subjected her to the humiliation of the justice system. He'd shred her of her self-respect and rub her nose in the fact she was at his mercy.

She shuddered at the memory of his merciless gaze.

Again the furtive temptation to run sneaked into her brain. But that would solve nothing. The money had been stolen and if she didn't accept the consequences Mamma would. She was in no condition to do that. Besides, it was Ravenna who'd benefited.

She sent up a prayer of thanks that her mother was in Italy. Face to face Silvia would have known Ravenna lied when she said all was well, explaining she'd left Paris for a promising job in England.

Mamma had been so excited for her, seeing this as a chance to get her interrupted career back on track. She probably thought Jonas with his billions wouldn't miss the money. If she guessed Ravenna had accepted her guilt…it didn't bear thinking about. Ravenna felt sick to the stomach lying in their regular phone calls but she had no choice. She wouldn't leave her mother to Jonas Deveson's mercy.

Reluctantly Ravenna delved ice-cold fingers into her pocket and dragged out the key. Picking up her bag, she stepped through the weeds and up to the back door.

On the step was a carton of supplies. She ignored it as she dealt with the lock and the keypad of the state-of-the-art security system that matched the new high-security perimeter boundary.

There might be no one at the Hall but there was a full-time presence at the gatehouse security centre.

She'd been warned not to try leaving the estate lest she set off an alarm. The implication being that she was a prisoner. The shiver scudding through her turned into a full-blown shudder as she recalled the curious blaze in Jonas Deveson's pewter-hard eyes.

'Prisoner' sounded Dickensian, but that was what she was.

There would be a camera trained on this door now, eyes monitoring the entrances. Apart from keeping the place safe from intruders, Jonas probably suspected her of trying to steal the antique silver.

Was that his game? To tempt her into another theft so he'd be absolutely certain she'd get a prison sentence as a repeat offender? It seemed likely.

She grabbed her bag and entered, eager for privacy.

The flagstone hall was so gloomy she flicked on the light. The place was drear and freezing, far different from her memories. The rest of the Hall had been off limits but she'd been allowed free access to the back of the house.

She made her way to the suite of rooms Mamma had used. Rooms Ravenna had called home during summer holidays. For a weak moment she let herself wish her mother were here. She could do with her trademark optimism and determination.

Ravenna pushed open the door and slammed to a stop.

The smell hit her. A pungent aroma of damp and mouse and something rotting. Her nose wrinkled as she stared at what had once been a cosy sitting room. A breeze eddied and she turned, seeing the half-closed curtains stir as air funnelled through a broken pane.

The caretaker employed by Piers hadn't done much of a job if he'd missed something so obvious.

But the damp wasn't just from rain soaking through the hole. It streaked the walls from the ceiling. The wallpaper had green-brown smears no scrubbing could clean.

Putting down her case, she stepped forward. Debris crackled underfoot as she headed for the bedroom. The smell was worse there and the stained walls too.

Steadfastly ignoring the sound of tiny, scurrying feet, Ravenna headed back to the corridor.

Had Jonas realised the damage was this bad? No wonder he'd looked smug as he offered her this chance.

The place didn't need a cleaner. It needed ripping down and starting again! Except in a heritage-listed building things weren't so simple.

It would be a nightmare to restore, she decided as she opened door after door and found similar damage. She guessed a water pipe had burst upstairs or a drain had become blocked and these rooms had borne the brunt of the damage.

It was criminal that it had been neglected. How could Piers have been so irresponsible?

She thought of the laughing, garrulous man she'd known. He'd loved Mamma as she'd loved him. Ravenna had seen it in his eyes and in his readiness to please her mother.

But she'd also seen his self-indulgence. The way he changed the subject whenever anything unpleasant cropped up. He preferred gaiety and good times to responsibility. He'd had the look of a man who'd indulged himself for decades and he'd been a connoisseur of fine food and wine—one of the reasons he'd approved her career choice.

He'd lived a life of casual luxury. According to Mamma there was only one thing he'd been firm about and that was in having nothing to do with his family or the entailed estate he'd left behind in England.

No wonder there'd been murder in Jonas Deveson's face when he'd talked of the work that needed doing here.

Finally she came to the kitchen and hope kindled. In the grey light from the grimy windows it looked neglected rather than damaged. Ravenna released a breath she hadn't known she was holding.

At least this room was habitable. She cast a professional eye over the outdated range and badly laid out cupboards. She'd worked with worse.

The trip had exhausted her. The enormity of what faced her made her want to curl into a ball and hide.

But Ravenna had learned that the worst had to be faced. Ignoring bad news didn't make it go away.

Imagine Jonas Deveson's delight if she gave up before she'd begun! Squaring her shoulders, she turned and went to get the box of supplies.

'What's the meaning of these?' Jonas let the pile of bills flutter onto his PA's desk.

Unflappable as ever, Stephen turned from his computer. 'You said anything to do with Ms Ruggiero or Deveson Hall should come straight to you.'

'But this?' He poked a finger at the top invoice. 'Glazing?' He stirred the pile. 'Boiler repairs? Why are they coming here?'

He should have known she'd find a way to niggle at him, reminding him of her presence even though she was out of London. She should be busy scrubbing the Hall from top to bottom, too exhausted to do more than worry if he might change his mind and hand her to the police. Instead she had the temerity to interrupt him at work.

Jonas shoved aside the fact that she'd been interrupting him ever since Paris. Too often he relived the cinnamon-scented sweetness of her skin and the arousing sound of her sighs as he tasted her.

The tightness in his belly exacerbated his anger.

'Explain!'

Stephen looked at him in surprise and Jonas realised he'd raised his voice. He never raised his voice. Ever. His calm was renowned.

The only exception had been in Paris. With Ravenna Ruggiero.

He palmed the back of his neck, massaging tight muscles. What was it about her that made him lose it?

Before he could apologise Stephen spoke. 'The building project manager has been held up in Singapore. He can't start yet. I sent you a memo about it two days ago.'

He had, and Jonas, wanting only the best on the delicate job of restoring his family home, had preferred to wait a little longer to get the best in the business.

'But this?' He picked up another bill. 'Twenty mouse traps? What on earth is she doing?'

'Fighting a plague?' Stephen grinned.

Jonas rifled through the invoices again. He'd thought he could leave her to stew in her own juices for a while. But without anyone to supervise her... 'Clear my diary from tomorrow. I'm going to Deveson Hall.'

* * *

Jonas stood at the bottom of the wide front steps, a curious, hollow sensation in the pit of his stomach.

It yawned wider as his gaze crossed the weeds choking the gravel and sprouting in the litter edging the stone steps. An ornamental urn leaned drunkenly near the front door and a couple of window panes were haphazardly boarded with rough planks and even, if he wasn't mistaken, cardboard.

The emptiness in his belly became an ache and then a hard churning that riveted him to the spot. His nape prickled and something snaked through him. A searing hot sensation that wound tight around his vital organs, squeezing mercilessly till the force of it threatened to poleaxe him.

Emotions, turbulent and powerful, rose in a potent, poisonous brew.

Six years since he'd been here.

Six years since his mother took her life and his father—

Jonas clamped a lid on those thoughts, horrified at what he felt.

For six years his life had been satisfying, productive, with challenges, triumphs and pleasures. There'd been no place for emotions in his ordered, busy world.

He didn't waste time on regrets or any other pointless feelings that might distract him from his purpose. Instead he'd focused on moving forward, taking the company to even greater success.

He dragged in a slow, sustaining breath.

That was better. He had himself in hand now.

But that moment of sickening weakness, of horrible vulnerability disturbed him.

For six years there'd been nothing like it. Nothing to shake him to the core of his being. Not until Ravenna Ruggiero. Her theft, her brazen guilt, the conflicting mix of sensations she'd aroused, had unsettled him.

She was to blame.

It was as if she'd opened the sluice gates on a dam of emotion he'd walled up long ago.

He didn't like it one bit.

Another reason to have his revenge and be done with her. Surely now, seeing the magnitude of the task facing her, she'd admit defeat. There would be no more flashing eyes, no sassy comebacks, no dredging up unwanted responses.

Jonas firmed his lips and strode up the stairs.

The past hit him in a rush as he opened the massive door. A sense of long-forgotten familiarity, of childish memories and days gone by.

Of homecoming.

His hand tightened on the old wood as he fought back emotion.

There was nothing welcoming about the dimly lit room. Frigid air misted his breath as he surveyed the vast, lifeless space. Jonas absorbed the scent of dust and old wood, his gaze raking the darkened recesses, as if expecting the spectres of his past to rise up before him.

With a huff of self-disgust he strode to a window and yanked back the wooden shutters. Light spilled across the worn flagstones to the foot of the massive staircase. Overhead the shadowy beams of the high vaulted ceiling were just discernible.

Another few paces and another window, and another. Till the great hall, once the heart of the house, was revealed in its grimy glory. No sign anyone had been here in years. It looked soulless despite the faded tapestries and ancient furniture.

Jonas flung open the doors into a drawing room. More modern than the Hall, this had a fine Regency fireplace, decorative plasterwork and a massive mirror that reflected the wraith-like forms of furniture concealed beneath dustcovers.

Temper rising, he yanked open more shutters and curtains. Daylight revealed no evidence of recent habitation. His hands were grimy from the dust everywhere.

Damn it! Was she even on the premises?

He strode from room to room, letting doors slam wide to reveal neglected spaces of damp, dusty decay.

By the time he'd stalked back to the great hall that strange, unsettling feeling was gone. Instead anger burned bright and hard.

Anger against the woman who couldn't be bothered to lift a finger even to pretend to do the job he'd held out to her as an alternative to gaol.

Anger for the greedy woman who'd stolen from him.

For the woman whose mother had stolen his father, broken up his family, such as it was, and destroyed his mother.

Like mother, like daughter. Both out for an easy life. Well, not any more!

He took the stairs two at a time. If she couldn't make an effort to work on the beautiful reception rooms he knew there was no chance she'd be below stairs.

He found her three doors along, in one of the family bedrooms.

She didn't even stir at the sound of his approach. He slammed to a halt at the foot of the four-poster bed, heart beating double time as his gaze raked her.

She lay on her side, hands tucked beneath her cheek and legs curled—looking the picture of innocence.

Suspicion surged.

Was she aware of him watching? It would be remarkable if she hadn't heard him slamming through the downstairs rooms then marching up here.

His eyes narrowed but he saw no change in her breathing, no giveaway flutter of lashes.

Slanting light traced her features, throwing delicate shadows beneath her eyes and cheekbones. Tiny frown lines marred her brow as if even in sleep something troubled her.

Probably dreaming of a way to escape justice!

Jonas' gaze dipped to her mouth, softly pink and slightly

parted as if in invitation. He remembered the sigh of her sweet breath as he caressed her, the hunger to taste more.

Jonas caught himself leaning closer, hand raised as if to gentle her awake. Jerking back, he grasped the carved bed-post, anchoring himself.

He was no gullible mark like Piers. Jonas had her measure. He knew what she was, as she'd discover to her cost.

'I said it's time to get up.' The deep voice wound its way into Ravenna's sleep-fogged brain and she snuggled into the soft pillow. Just a little longer. It felt so good to let her exhausted body relax, weightlessly floating.

'Much as I appreciate the Sleeping Beauty tableau, it's not working.' The rich voice lost its mellow timbre and turned harsh, yanking her out of her hazy dream of warmth and well-being and the delicious scent of spiced citrus. In her dream strong arms had held her tight and close. Now she was alone, her skin chilled and legs cramped.

Ravenna opened her eyes and swallowed a scream as she saw him looming above her, all but blocking the light.

'You!' It was a strangled gasp, torn from tight lungs as she struggled up, scooting back against the carved headboard.

'You were expecting someone else?' Dark eyebrows slashed down in a ferocious scowl that turned his proud face into that of an avenging angel. He didn't seem to move but she had the impression he stood closer, keeping her within reach.

Panic flared and her heart beat a tattered rhythm as she read the sizzle in those narrowed eyes. Not pewter now, but the luminous silver-grey of lightning. Ravenna remembered his fury in Paris, his lashing tongue and hard, unforgiving hands that turned gentle as they curved around her breast and stroked her nipple till she all but swooned.

Fear sliced her. It had nothing to do with the taut anger in his face and wide, masculine shoulders and everything to do with the yearning that softened her traitorous body. Liquid heat rushed to her womb as she met his gaze and felt again that juddering vibration, like an unseen explosion radiating through the air between them.

Despair filled her. She'd convinced herself it had been a one-off. Some horrible aberration, never to be repeated. She *couldn't* be attracted to him. She *wasn't!*

In a tumble of limbs Ravenna scooted to the other side of the bed and off the side.

But she'd underestimated her exhaustion. No sooner did her feet hit the floor than her knees crumpled. Only her hold on the high bed stopped her collapsing.

A split second later he was there, arms outstretched as if to support her.

If she'd needed anything to galvanise her failing strength that was it.

'Don't touch me!' It came out high and breathless, choked with emotion.

Instantly he reared back, his mouth a thin line and eyes unreadable.

Dragging in a rough breath, Ravenna braced herself and stood straight. She had herself in hand now. Her legs shook like jelly but that was to be expected after the hours she'd been on her feet. It had nothing to do with Jonas Deveson.

'What are you doing here?'

His eyebrows arched high. 'I think that question is my prerogative. What are you doing sleeping *here* of all places? And in the middle of the day?'

Ravenna glanced at her watch. Two o'clock. No wonder she felt wobbly. She'd only lain down fifteen minutes ago, desperate for a restorative nap.

Since arriving she'd forced herself to her limits, ignoring earlier advice about taking things easy and allowing her body time to recuperate.

Terror was a fine motivator, allowing her to push beyond the boundaries of exhaustion day after day, knowing Jonas

Deveson would leap at that chance to accuse her of not being up to the impossible job he'd set.

And here he was. Just as she'd feared.

Ravenna swiped suddenly clammy palms down the worn denim of her jeans, vowing not to let him best her.

'I started early this morning so I was having a short... break.'

'Most people take a break over a cup of tea and a biscuit, not stretched out on a valuable antique bed.'

He was accusing her of damaging the furnishings? She might not be some delicate, petite woman, but she was hardly a heavyweight, especially after her recent illness.

Her gaze swept the bed. It was huge enough to sleep four and she'd barely wrinkled the coverlet. The rich, embroidered coverlet she'd carefully cleaned along with the full-length curtains that just a week ago had been caked in dust.

'If you're waiting for me to tug my forelock you can give up now.' She stuck her hands on her hips in a confrontational pose she hoped hid the way her legs shook. 'If I'm good enough to clean the damned thing, I'm good enough to sleep in it.'

His features tightened. 'Spoken like your mother's daughter. She must have had the same view of Piers' bed whenever she *serviced*...his room here.'

Ravenna felt the blood drain from her face at his crude implication. That Mamma was some greedy tart, using sex to her advantage.

'You b—'

'Now, now.' His voice was maddeningly superior as he raised his hand. 'Don't say anything you'll regret.'

'Believe me,' she bit out between quick breaths, 'I wouldn't regret it.' But the warning hit the mark. She couldn't afford to get him even further off side. It was only at his whim that she wasn't in police custody.

Ravenna drew a shaky breath as the surge of adrenalin dissipated, leaving her feeling ridiculously fragile. 'But since you have such archaic views on class differences, I should warn you that this is my bedroom.'

That shocked him.

Swiftly she surveyed the room she'd so painstakingly brought back to mint condition, from its plaster-decorated ceiling to its delicately shaded carpet. Old wood gleamed after multiple applications of beeswax, the soft furnishings had been painstakingly cleaned and even the crystal drops in the overhead light had been polished till they shone. He hadn't even spared it a glance.

For some reason that galled her almost as much as his high and mighty attitude.

'The housekeeper's accommodation wasn't good enough for you?' His eyes glinted a warning she refused to heed.

'The housekeeper's accommodation wasn't weatherproof or dry.' She watched shock freeze his face and knew an unholy pleasure that she'd punctured his self-satisfaction. Then her mind processed a little further, realisation dawning. 'You didn't know, did you?' Ravenna stared at his still face. 'How long since you've been here?'

Predictably he ignored her question.

'If this is your room then we'll go elsewhere for our discussion.'

It was on the tip of Ravenna's tongue to riposte with some barbed retort when she realised the sense of his words. The last thing she needed was to imprint the memory of him here, in her personal space. As it was the sight of him looming over her in the bed would haunt her for too long.

Abruptly she spun around to lead the way out. But she'd reckoned without her lingering physical weakness. Her limbs still felt like wet noodles, wobbly and uncoordinated, and for one horrible, slow-motion moment she felt herself sway dangerously and begin to topple, her arms flailing.

He grabbed her elbows, his long fingers hard and hot through the wool of her ancient cardigan.

Ravenna stared at the charcoal knit of his cashmere pullover mere centimetres away, rising and falling with each breath. Her nostrils twitched as his scent reached her, the tang of lemon and hot male skin that conjured images of long, powerful limbs, naked in warm Mediterranean sunlight.

A shudder ripped through her and she closed her eyes in denial. *No, no, no.* She was weak from what her body had been through recently, but she wasn't weak for him.

She'd have to be sick in the head to desire *him*.

'Are you all right?' No mistaking the reluctance in his voice. If he'd had time to think rather than act on instinct he'd probably have let her drop to the floor.

Slowly Ravenna lifted her gaze, past the strong contours of his jaw, up to his grim mouth, bracketed now with disapproving grooves that somehow emphasised the leashed passion in those surprisingly soft lips. She remembered the tender way they'd caressed her neck and shivered as that betraying heat swirled and swooped low in her belly again, settling and spreading at the core of her.

A tingling started up between her legs. An edgy sensation that made her want to snuggle up against him and—

'I'm fine.' Her voice was hoarse and she ducked her head rather than meet his scrutiny. Instead she felt it graze the contours of her face.

How she wished she still had her long hair. She could use it as a shield, obscuring herself from his sharp eyes.

Ravenna shook her head. Of all the things to regret, the loss of her hair was the least of them.

She stepped back, moving carefully, giving her body time to adjust. His hands dropped away instantly, as if he was only too eager to let her go.

Ravenna told herself that was a good thing. If he realised the power his physical presence had over her, he'd be sure to use it to his advantage.

They were on the landing when she spoke again. 'You haven't told me why you're here.'

'To check up on you, of course.' The words came from too close behind her. She imagined his warm breath on the back of her neck and hurried down the stairs.

'In case I was stripping the place of valuables?'

'I'm sure security would put a stop to that.' His tone was complacent. 'No, I decided you needed supervision and from what I've seen I was right.' Familiar disapproval coloured his voice. 'That's why I've decided to stay.'

Ravenna clutched the banister as the world reeled.

She'd thought this nightmare couldn't get any worse. How naïve she'd been!

CHAPTER SIX

JONAS SCANNED THE large kitchen. Old-fashioned and functional, it held a homely warmth he hadn't expected to find when Ravenna had led him to the servants' domain.

Bright sunlight revealed a huge, scrubbed table, old-fashioned wooden cabinets and a collection of brass moulds and pots hanging on one white wall. It looked like something out of the past.

His past.

He remembered having cocoa and fruitcake here, presided over by Mrs Roberts, the motherly woman who'd ruled the kitchen in his childhood. He'd often sneak in for a sample of the exotic meals she prepared for his parents' sophisticated dinner parties. She regularly patched up his scrapes and let him help roll out pastry or stir a pudding.

Until his mother had found out and put a stop to it, insisting he had more valuable things to do with his time than hobnob with servants.

Jonas blinked and turned his head, ignoring the sharp, twisting sensation deep inside and the metallic tang on his tongue. He catalogued the scrupulously clean room, the vase of evergreens on the old Welsh dresser and the way Ravenna bustled around the vast space, with an economy of movement that told him she was at home here.

The housekeeper's daughter.

She'd flung that in his face, hadn't she?

But she was far more than that.

Jonas ran a hand through his hair, watching her loose-fitting jeans pull tight and tempting as she bent to get something out of a cupboard.

His pulse thudded into overdrive as he watched her supple body. Gone was the vulnerability he'd seen earlier in her startled dark gold gaze and her clumsy movements.

Her weakness had worried him. She'd almost collapsed and it had been no act. He'd felt the tremors race through her. He'd seen the frustration in her not-quite veiled eyes and watched her work to hold herself upright, moving as if each step was an effort.

He didn't want to feel sorry for her. He didn't want to desire her either! But he'd done both. Every time he came within sight of her his hormones roared into life.

Whatever the problem it was gone now. She moved gracefully, snaring his gaze so he couldn't look away.

Jonas scrubbed his hand over his face and round his neck, massaging the stiffness from his muscles. Fat chance it would erase the stiffness elsewhere!

This wasn't supposed to happen. Not for her.

'Here.' A cup and saucer appeared on the wood before him with a plate of biscuits. Shortbread, perfectly formed and, if he wasn't mistaken, home-made.

'You're feeding me? Should I check for poison?'

She didn't answer, merely settled at the far end of the table and sipped from a cup that matched his own.

Blue and white willow pattern. It had been Mrs Roberts' favourite, brought out whenever he visited.

A jagged splinter sheared off from the twisting screw in his belly and jabbed hard.

Reacting blindly, he reached for a biscuit. It dissolved in his mouth, pure buttery comfort, like those special treats he'd devoured here long ago when his parents' blistering arguments had driven him to seek refuge in the warm kitchen.

A roaring rush of ancient memory sprang to life. Ruth-lessly Jonas blanked it out.

'What's the plan? To distract me with your culinary skills?' He sounded boorish, but the alternative, letting the murky past swamp him, wasn't an option.

She didn't even look fazed, though her jaw tightened as if keeping tight rein on her temper.

That only fuelled his anger. Jonas didn't like feeling in the wrong. It was a new and unsettling experience for a man who ruled his world with confidence and authority.

'I thought for once we could have a civilised conversa-tion. Clearly I was mistaken.' She drew a breath that lifted her breasts. Jonas' hands curled, a reflex to the memory of touching her there.

'Come on.' She shoved her chair back. 'Let's get this over with. You're dying to inspect what I've haven't done, aren't you?'

She was right. He'd stormed down here, intent on putting her firmly in her place—under his heel. Yet since arriving he'd been on edge, feeling curiously *full,* as if he barely kept a lid on emotions he'd long pushed aside. His brain teemed with unwanted memories.

Venting his spleen on Ravenna Ruggiero was the perfect antidote to those disturbing feelings.

Except now, following as she marched through the house, flinging open doors on room after room of criminal neglect, he couldn't do it.

He'd read the building report but still hadn't imagined how severe the damage was. It cut him like a blade to the heart. Anger and self-recrimination scored deep.

He'd refused to visit while Piers was an absentee land-lord. He'd told himself the Hall wasn't home. Home was London, New York or Tokyo, wherever there was money to be made. He'd avoided the past and concentrated on building Devesons into the country's premier investment company.

Later, receiving the building report, he'd chosen to stay

away till refurbishment started. There'd been no reason for his personal presence.

His mouth twisted. It had been easier to stay away than remember those last months when his mother had been in such despair. He'd almost hated the place then and all it represented. Their failure of a family. His father's betrayal. His mother's depression. His inadequacy. Nothing he did or said could make things better.

He'd failed her. He hadn't been able to save her.

'Well?' The word yanked him into the present. Sherry-gold eyes sparked at him in the gloom of the damp cellar. 'Aren't you going to accuse me of slacking because I haven't fixed this yet?'

Jonas cast a cursory look over the puddles, the evidence of recent flooding, the bulging wall, and knew the sooner he got his building expert on the premises, the better.

He turned back to see her braced for confrontation. The light in her eyes challenged him to do his worst.

'It will take a team of experts to deal with this. There's nothing you can do.'

His response was utterly reasonable yet Ravenna looked stunned. More than stunned, she looked suspiciously annoyed, as if, despite her earlier words, she'd *wanted* another confrontation.

His gaze bored into hers, trying to read her thoughts, and a flush climbed her cheeks. Abruptly she looked away, lashes dropping, hiding her expressive eyes. She looked… discomfited.

Could it be that she too found it easier to trade barbed insults? And if that was a defence mechanism, what was she hiding from?

'Okay. You've shown me the worst, now show me what you've done. Or did it take all your time to clean up the kitchen and bedroom?' Given the state of the other rooms he wouldn't be surprised.

Ravenna's jaw sagged, her mouth gaping as if she'd never seen him before.

Finally he'd stemmed her flow of snarky comments. He'd fantasised about doing just that. But in his imaginings he'd silenced her with his lips fused to hers, his tongue in her mouth, finishing what he'd started in Paris.

The image erupted out of nowhere, of her melting into him as incendiary sparks ignited their bodies. It was so vivid his hands twitched, ready to reach for her. Heat drenched him despite the cellar's chill and blood roared in his ears.

His response was so sudden, so profound, it made a mockery of all the reasons he'd told himself he'd never touch her again. Upstairs, holding her steady lest she fall, Jonas had been abundantly aware of Ravenna Ruggiero as a woman. Not a thief or a parasite. Not kin to the woman who'd destroyed his mother. But as desirable.

Even in faded jeans and an oversized cardigan, Ravenna fascinated him in a way he didn't understand. He liked his women sophisticated and ultra feminine. Ravenna was feminine all right, but with a sharp tongue and prickly attitude that should have been a turn-off.

Instead—

'All right.' She spun away, turning the movement into a flounce of disapproval. 'This way.'

He got under her skin.

At least he wasn't the only one.

By the time they finished the tour Ravenna didn't know what to think. Reading Jonas Deveson when he was in a temper was easy. But now she hadn't a clue what he thought.

'*You* did that?' There'd been surprise in his voice when she showed him how she'd boarded up the windows as best she could, and the new panes the glazier had begun installing.

Did he really think she'd ignore the damage as if it didn't

matter? Deveson Hall was a beautiful old place. It deserved better than what Piers had dealt it.

She'd shown Jonas the attic bedrooms she'd cleared and scrubbed, with some notion of starting at the top and working down. But the rest of the vast attics had defeated her, filled as they were with what looked like several hundred years' accumulation of family memorabilia.

Instead of berating her for giving up on the top floor he'd merely nodded and gestured for her to move on.

She'd shown him the gallery where she'd spent the morning on a ladder, carefully cleaning ornate picture frames, aware all the time of rows of haughty Devesons looking down their superb noses at her as if outraged anyone so lowly should dare enter their presence.

Now they surveyed the bedrooms. Only one other than hers was finished, where they stood now.

'You've done a good job.'

Again he'd robbed her of speech. Praise? From Jonas Deveson?

Ravenna swung round to find him watching her. She should be used to it—that piercing regard so sharp it could scrape off skin. Or carve a needy hollow deep inside.

She blinked and tried to tear her eyes away.

'It's come up well,' she agreed. 'But I'm surprised you admit it.' What was he up to?

He shrugged. 'It's the truth. Besides, if we're going to be here together, I'd rather not have you glaring daggers at me all the time.'

'This isn't about the way *I*—'

'See what I mean?' He was frustratingly superior, as if the thickened atmosphere between them were down to *her!*

'There's no need for you to stay.' The words shot out. 'You've seen what you came to see. You know I'm not trashing the place.'

'No,' he mused, frowning, 'you're not. You're actually making a difference.'

Ravenna's hands clamped her hips. 'No need to sound surprised!'

Again that shrug. It emphasised the broad planes of his shoulders and chest and the way he blocked the doorway, making the spacious room seem too small.

'In the circumstances—' he stepped towards her '—I can be excused for doubting that. You gave the impression of a woman who's never worked in her life.'

Ravenna shuffled back, away from that keen gaze. She walked a knife edge with the truth. If she revealed too much about herself she might inadvertently let the truth slip—that it was Mamma who'd stolen his money.

'I have hidden depths.' She stopped abruptly as her legs came up against the edge of the bed. Something dark and un-tamed skittered through her belly at the feeling he'd trapped her there.

He paced closer, a dangerous light in his eyes. Ravenna gulped down rising tension and told herself he wasn't in-terested in her. That…caress in Paris had been simply him illustrating how vulnerable she was.

He stood so close she saw the beginning of dark stubble on his jaw. She remembered the soft scrape of it against her skin and sucked in a breath warm with the scent of his skin.

Flurries of sensation raced across her flesh as she met grey eyes that now looked anything but cold.

'I'll enjoy sleeping here.'

He moved and she stiffened, but instead of touching her he reached out and prodded the mattress. 'A nice, big bed,' he murmured approvingly. As easily as that Ravenna could think of nothing but how it would feel to have that long, strong body flush against hers, naked on the king-sized bed.

'You can't sleep here!' It was too close to hers, connected by a bathroom.

One ebony eyebrow arched and to her amazement she saw amusement in his face. It turned his strong aristocratic features into something potently seductive. 'It's either that or in your bed, Ravenna.'

'I didn't mean…'

He straightened and she sucked in a breath as the distance widened between them. 'Forget it, Ravenna. I'm staying. The place can't be left like this.'

Not in *her* untrustworthy hands. That was the implication. In the circumstances she could hardly blame him, yet his prejudice rankled.

'But you've got a business to run.'

Steely eyes pinioned her. 'You really are desperate for me to leave, aren't you?'

Ravenna tilted her chin. She was sick of lying. 'You can't be surprised. You're hardly pleasant company.'

Instead of glowering as expected, Jonas flummoxed her by laughing. It was a deep, rich sound that eddied and swirled around her like a liquid embrace. Ravenna shivered and rubbed her arms, scared of how much she liked it.

'That's rich coming from the woman who thieved from me.'

Ravenna flinched. She couldn't help it. And she regretted it instantly, when Jonas' eyes narrowed on her face. What did he see there? How much did he guess?

'I propose a truce,' he murmured. 'We'll behave like civilised people while we're under the same roof. Agreed?'

What other option was there? Her nerves were shredded after an hour with him. She'd be a gibbering wreck if he chose to prolong the animosity.

Ravenna nodded but she pretended not to notice his outstretched hand. Touching Jonas Deveson again was right up there on her list of never-to-do experiences, like swimming with sharks and sleeping on a bed of nails.

Two hours later Ravenna emerged into the high street of the nearby market town, arms full of provisions. Jonas had insisted he accompany her since her meagre supplies wouldn't cater for them both.

He's making sure you don't do a runner, a sour voice inside her head insisted. After all, once off the estate there was nothing to stop her disappearing except fear of what he'd do when he caught her again.

A little shiver raced through her. For Jonas *would* find her if she ran. She couldn't imagine him failing at anything he wanted. And he wanted her under his thumb.

He walked beside her, carrying the bulk of the shopping. But it wasn't his role as gaoler that unsettled her so much as his physical presence. Big, bold and aggressively male, his testosterone-charged presence challenged her in ways she didn't like to examine.

He'd been as good as his word—a perfect gentleman during their outing yet that only unbalanced her more. She could cope with his temper, even his disapproval. But there was something ridiculously intimate about the simple act of shopping together, having him insist on carrying the heavy items and even opening doors for her.

Realising how much she liked it made her edgy.

Her eyes lit on the dark red Aston Martin across the street, magnet for a bunch of admiring boys.

'You've got a very showy car.' Conveniently she ignored the fact that she adored its sleek lines and the delicious sense of being cocooned in comfort as they'd driven here.

'You think I should drive something that blends in?' Infuriatingly she heard laughter in his voice. 'A discreet dark Bentley or a battered Land Rover?' He strode towards the car. 'I worked hard for everything I've got, and I'm not ashamed of enjoying it.'

Ravenna huffed as she hurried after him, stopping as he opened the boot and unloaded his purchases. 'You were born with a silver spoon in your mouth. I hardly think—'

He turned and his expression clogged the words in her throat. She almost heard ice crackle at the look he shot her.

'Frankly, I don't care what you think.' He reached for her packages and stowed them with the rest of the food, then closed the boot. 'But for the record, I may have been born with a silver spoon in my mouth but the rest of the family silver was hocked. Piers only married my mother for the much-needed money she brought the failing family coffers. With his spectacularly unsuccessful investments and his skill at spending that disappeared soon enough.'

He leaned towards her. 'Do you know *why* I got a reputation as a *wunderkind* investor?' His breath was hot on her face but she couldn't step away. She was mesmerised by what she saw in those remarkable eyes—passion and, if she wasn't mistaken, pain.

'It was because by the time I was finishing school there was no money left. If I wanted to go to university I had to fund myself.' He shook his head. 'Hell, if I wanted to keep a roof over my mother's head I had to fund that too, since your precious Piers was incapable of doing it.'

'He wasn't my Piers.' The words came out automatically, Ravenna's mind whirling. All these years she'd imagined the Devesons living in easy luxury.

'No.' Jonas invaded her space, head thrust forward. 'He was your mother's. Did she know it was my hard-earned money she lived off all these years? Or didn't she give a damn?'

'Yours?'

His laugh had a razor edge. 'Devesons may have started as a family company but the most Piers did was act as front man. He loved that—preening publicly at our success. At *my* success. Not that he'd admit that. Easier for him to talk of the company's spectacular profits than admit it was his teenage son taking the risks and doing the work.'

'I'm sorry. I didn't know.'

With the knowledge something shifted subtly, like a kaleidoscope on the turn, pieces sliding and settling in an almost familiar yet totally different pattern. It revealed Jonas in a new light.

He'd been the breadwinner all those years, keeping Deveson Hall running and funding his parents' lifestyle? Jonas had striven to accumulate the fortune that supported Piers and her mamma?

What had it been like carrying that weight of responsibility and expectation so young?

Ravenna's teenage problems paled by comparison.

Jonas lifted his shoulders, the movement shrugging away everything but the pair of them, standing close. 'No, you didn't, did you?' he mused. 'How could you know?'

His breath ruffled her hair and suddenly his grey eyes looked soft as mist. Ravenna felt herself heat from the inside as warm treacle spilled and swirled deep in her belly. That skittering sensation was back, drawing her flesh tight.

A whirring sound intruded and Ravenna turned, startled to find a massive lens trained on them.

'Who's the girl, Jonas?'

For a startled moment Ravenna thought it must be a friend asking. But the man with the camera was backing away, camera still trained on them, as if aware of Jonas' big body tensing.

Jonas' hand encircled her arm, drawing her abruptly away and into the car.

'Damned paparazzi,' he muttered under his breath.

'Paparazzi?' Ravenna stared at the man, now two car lengths away. 'Why would they want a photo of us?'

Jonas shrugged. 'Slow news day.' Reading her frown, he added, 'Don't worry. The photo probably won't get used. And if it is—' again that wide shrug '—it's hardly damaging.'

He closed her door and got into the driver seat, apparently unfazed by the press intrusion. Which left Ravenna pondering what it was like to be so influential that even a shopping expedition was newsworthy.

They really were from completely different worlds.

It was imperative Ravenna remember that. Especially as there was unfinished business between her and Jonas Deveson, and she sensed it wasn't all to do with stolen money.

It was easier sharing a house with Jonas than Ravenna had believed possible. They avoided each other.

Yet she was hyper-sensitive to his presence. The rich murmur of his voice through a half-closed door as he spoke on the phone. The spicy scent of damp male skin that clung to the bathroom, evoking heady images of what that solid, athletic body might look like naked.

She found herself cataloguing facts about him. He made his own bed—because he was neat or because he didn't like the intimacy of her touching his bed? His weakness for shortbread and fruitcake. His habit of leaving half-empty coffee mugs about when work distracted him.

Jonas worked ridiculously long hours, running his business from a distance in between a continuous schedule of meetings with conservation officials, builders and others.

Occasionally a young man with a thin, intelligent face and a ready smile arrived, with laptop and briefcase, and the pair closeted themselves for hours. Ravenna took pity on the assistant, Stephen, and supplied refreshments. Jonas never noticed but Stephen would grin and thank her. Ravenna told herself she was glad Jonas never looked up.

She didn't want his notice. She wanted—

A betraying twist of sensation between her legs reminded her of what she'd wanted from Jonas in her dreams last night. What she'd *demanded,* and what he'd so willingly supplied.

Heat suffused her and Ravenna made herself concentrate on the next stack of leather-bound books to be lifted from the shelves.

So she had a libido. She should be glad. It meant her poor battered body was getting back to normal after the long stint of treatment.

She just wished her libido hadn't fixed on the man who'd made it his mission to wreck her life!

Ravenna laid the books on the desk and wiped her brow. It really was warm in here. She'd filled the study with every heater she could find, laying open damp-damaged books to air. But the number of books needing attention was enormous.

If only Jonas would get in staff to help her. She hadn't suggested it again, preferring to avoid him. But that hadn't worked. He was in her head all the time.

Grimacing, she yanked off her pullover. She'd worn extra layers since Jonas arrived as if they would somehow protect her. Ridiculous since he kept to himself. She could work in her underwear and he'd be none the wiser.

Grinning at the thought, Ravenna climbed the library ladder to finish clearing the top shelf.

'Careful up there!' Jonas' deep voice sounded from below, furring her arms and nape with what felt far too much like anticipation. 'I don't want you injuring yourself.'

'Afraid I'll sue for damages?' Gripping the rail, Ravenna turned. Her insides tightened at the picture he made, legs apart and arms folded, hair rumpled.

She'd thought him formidable in bespoke Italian tailoring. In a casual white shirt and faded jeans that clung to heavy thighs, he looked like a pirate. He hadn't shaved and the shadow on his sculpted jaw gave him a dangerous air. Or maybe it was the glitter in his silver gaze.

Sensation scudded through her. Something she preferred not to name. It made her feel hot and achy, needy.

She narrowed her eyes. 'Or afraid I'll squash you if I fall?' She was one of the tallest women she knew.

His mouth quirked in a sexy curl that did devastating things to her. His voice was a deep purr. 'I'm sure I'm up to your weight, Ravenna.'

He moved into the room, his gaze raking from her bare feet, cotton trousers and T-shirt to her flaming face.

She clamped her mouth shut but it didn't stop the shimmer of awareness charging the atmosphere.

'What have you got here?' He stopped by the table and picked up a small volume. Instantly the feeling of pressure in her lungs eased and she drew a slow breath.

'Those were in the small writing desk by the window. And the bigger ones are from up here.'

Jonas stood stiffly as if braced, head bent to the pages of the small book. Colour leached from his face, leaving it starkly pale, skin stretched taut over strong bones. He was so still he didn't seem to breathe. Then the pages began to flutter in his suddenly unsteady hand.

Alarm knifed her. 'Jonas?'

He didn't even look up.

By the time she climbed down he was slumped in a chair and his face was a sickly, greenish hue that made her stomach clutch. He looked as if he was going to keel over.

CHAPTER SEVEN

JONAS WAS STARING.

Ogling was probably a better word, since he couldn't tear his gaze from Ravenna's slender body. With her arms raised, reaching for an upper shelf, her white T-shirt moulded to her breasts. Her enticing, braless breasts.

Damn. He planted his feet wider, needing to ground himself, assert control over his wayward, yearning body.

He'd avoided her all week, telling himself his fascination with her would fade.

That had been a spectacular miscalculation. Every time she entered a room he lost his train of thought. He found himself staring blankly at the computer screen while she traded banter with Stephen, and his PA, still inexperienced in the ways of women, lapped up the attention.

Jonas' mouth set grimly and he yanked his gaze away, turning to the giant desk in the centre of the room. Anything other than Ravenna's distracting body.

'What have you got here?' He grabbed the first book he saw, opening it at random.

As the pages came in focus the world eclipsed.

His skin tightened. A curious ripple raced down his spine as he recognised the handwriting and the import of the words at the top of the page.

He hadn't known she'd kept a diary.

His mother had never struck him as the sort to pen her

thoughts. In later years she'd found solace and company in alcohol. But then—his gaze flicked to the date—this was an old book. Almost as old as him.

His gaze fixed on the line that had caught his eye.

Now I know it's true. Piers is having an affair.

How can he when I love him so?

Jonas couldn't help but read on, scanning the pages where the young woman who'd been his mother had poured out her despair at finding Piers with another woman. A woman who was vivacious, beautiful and confident. All the things Jennifer Deveson felt she lacked.

Jonas' stomach churned. So early in the marriage? He'd thought at least there'd been a honeymoon period. But as he read he realised Piers had had no compunction about pretending affection once the knot that bound him to his wife's money was tied.

Bile soured Jonas' tongue as he read, unable to stop. A pattern emerged. Of Piers seeking out the most gorgeous women and flaunting them. Of his wife retreating into her shell, only emerging to row with her faithless spouse.

Memories rushed back. Scenes he'd witnessed and pretended to forget. The raised voices, the threats, the undercurrent of despair. Despair so profound his mother hadn't wanted to live once Piers left her for good. What sort of sick love was that, clinging on even when it was rejected?

He'd been conceived in such a relationship?

His gut wrenched. His one dream had always been the same. To turn Deveson Hall into what it had never been in his time—a true family home. He'd fantasised about family, a real family, all his life. One that cared and shared and gathered together to celebrate the important things in life. The things his family never did.

Since he was a kid he'd imagined the Hall filled with laughter and companionship. Filled with the family he'd never had but had vowed to acquire. The gorgeous, supportive wife, the brood of happy kids. A generous-hearted matron like Mrs Roberts presiding over the kitchen. A muddle of pets, like the ones he'd never been allowed, to complete the picture.

His lips stretched mirthlessly. His imagination was as corny as a greeting card ad. Yet wasn't that why he was here? Overseeing the refurbishment ready to marry and start that family? Piers' death had been a wake-up call.

Tradition was important to Jonas in a way it could never be to a child who'd known love. He'd absorbed the legends of the house and the Devesons with an enthusiasm honed by his determination to escape the emptiness of real life. He needed heirs to fill that vacuum and share those traditions.

Now, reading his mother's despair, he felt again the helpless emptiness of his childhood.

He hadn't been important enough for her then. Nor had he been able to save her at the end.

Who was he fooling, thinking he could achieve the impossible and create a genuine family? That he could rise above the past that had moulded him? With his family history he was a foreigner to the softer things in life like love and caring. The truth smashed his long-held illusions.

'Jonas?' A hand touched his and he realised the book had fallen from his hold. He watched slim fingers mesh with his. Hers felt warm, roughened by work, but supple and capable. Feminine. She smelt of cinnamon and honey, mouth-watering. 'Are you all right?'

He opened his mouth but no sound emerged.

What could he say? That Jonas Deveson, the man who ran a multibillion-dollar business, whose views were canvassed by investors and leaders worldwide, who lived a life envied by many, was a hollow shell?

There'd been such *pain* in his mother's words. It pierced him in a place that even after all this time was raw and vulnerable.

Guilt swamped him. He hadn't been able to make things

right for her. For all his skill and corporate savvy, he'd never been good at that. He'd failed her.

'Jonas!'

His head whipped up and he saw Ravenna's concern.

He must look as bad as he felt if *she* worried about him!

Her touch was gentle as she hunkered before him. He swallowed, feeling something unravel within. Some of the tightness binding his chest slackened.

'What's wrong?' She leaned closer and he lost himself in the dark gold glow of her eyes. He focused on that rather than the darkness within.

'Nothing.' His tongue was thick and his speech slurred. 'Just an old book.'

'It's obviously upset you.' She looked down as if to reach for it and he snapped his hands around her wrists.

'Leave it. It's just history.' He couldn't believe his reaction—how long-buried emotions had rushed to engulf him as if he were some callow youth.

'I've never seen a history book affect someone like that. You look…ill.'

He felt it. Though the swirling nausea had abated a little with her touch. His hold tightened.

'I really think—'

'No!' He yanked her close, bringing her to her knees before him so she couldn't delve for the book.

'It's my mother's diary.' The words shot out, harsh and uncompromising. 'About Piers' first extra-marital affair. And the next. And so on.' He paused, listening to his blood hammer in his ears. 'Not a book I'd recommend.' He tried for casual but his voice betrayed him, emerging gruff and uneven.

Her eyes widened. 'I see.' And she did, damn her. She read him as easily as he'd read those pages for there was more than sympathy in her eyes now. There was pity.

Pity for *him!*

Everything in Jonas revolted at the idea. He'd spent a

lifetime taking on the world and winning, proving himself stronger, better, triumphant. His name was synonymous with success. He didn't need her pity.

Fury sparked, rising in a searing, seething flood.

There she was, kneeling between his legs, her expression solemn, her lips soft and desirable, the perfume of her skin tantalising and her nipples dark smudges of promise budding against her thin T-shirt. Anticipation was so strong he could almost taste her.

Lust swooped, tightening his groin, urging his legs in hard to trap her where she knelt. He welcomed it, a distraction from emotion.

This he could handle. *This* he welcomed.

Ravenna froze, her expression morphing into disbelief.

'I think I'd better get up.' Her voice was husky.

'I thought you wanted to make me feel better.' He leaned close, meeting those huge sherry-gold eyes.

He didn't want her looking at him like that, as if she could read his secrets.

'I don't think that's possible.'

'Oh, but it is.' Triumph coloured his voice as he cupped her jaw and felt her pulse hammer. Yes! That was what he wanted. Not pity or sympathy. He'd settle for something simpler and far more satisfying. And when they were done he'd feel whole again. Not like some pathetic, wounded...victim.

He slipped his hand round the back of her neck and tugged her to him, planting his mouth on hers before she could speak. And there it was, that raw spiral of heated need, spinning between them, dragging them under.

Her lips were soft as he'd known they'd be. Yet despite a week of anticipation he wasn't prepared for the delicate taste of her. Delicious. Addictive. Perfect.

Using both hands, he pulled her close, locking his thighs against her hips, imagining how it would be with her legs wrapped around his waist.

Heat shot through him and his groin was in agony, constricted by too-tight denim.

He needed her. Now.

Ravenna's head spun as Jonas dragged her into his arms with a ruthless economy of movement that spoke of practice. If she'd been in any doubt about his experience with women, his fierce certainty abolished it.

He knew women. The graze of his hard palm over her budding nipple told her that.

Yet nothing could hide his uneven breathing, or erase the pain she'd read in his face. It was his pain that had lured her close, casting aside caution.

But it was something else that kept her here. Not the taut clench of his thighs that stoked delicious awareness of his masculine strength. Nor the arm wrapped possessively around her back.

Despite the overwhelming sense of Jonas' superior size and power, despite the implacable hunger she'd read in his face as he plastered his mouth over hers, Ravenna had no fear he'd force her. Instinct, and the knowledge she'd gleaned of his pride and self-possession, told her she was safe. *If she wanted to be.*

Her mind whirled as her body responded to his urgent demands.

The truth struck her like a flare of lightning, illuminating what she'd tried to hide.

She didn't want safety. Not with his mouth reducing her to willing compliance, his body flush against hers and that heady rush of arousal in her veins. It didn't matter that they were enemies.

Maybe her response was an outlet for pent up emotions that had weighed on her too long.

Maybe she needed this rush of life-affirming pleasure after coming so close to death mere months before. She felt so *alive* in his arms.

Or perhaps she simply responded to the sheer wanton thrill of being desired by such a man: devastatingly attractive and potently charismatic, if you forgot that cutting tongue.

Right now his tongue was doing things that turned Ravenna's bones to butter.

She clawed at his shirt, relishing the taut, hot muscle beneath, and kissed him back. He tasted like last night's erotic dreams: spicy, delicious and unique. No matter how she worked she'd never create a dish with such a wonderful flavour.

Large hands slid below the drawstring of her trousers, beneath her panties to splay over her buttocks and brand her with his searing touch. He tugged and Ravenna found herself plastered against a solid ridge of denim and rampant male.

For a dizzying moment caution vied with pleasure. But her need was too strong. She thrust her hands through his hair, tugging glossy dark locks then clamping hard on his skull as she ground her hips against his.

Fire shot through her veins and the world juddered.

'Again.' The word was a hoarse rasp in her ear.

Ravenna obliged. How could she not, when the stranger who'd taken possession of her body craved Jonas as if her life depended on it?

Again she tilted her hips. They came together in a move that would have left her impaled on him but for their clothes. Light burst in the darkness of her closed eyes and she shivered at the myriad sensations bombarding her. His body, his touch, the clean smell of aroused male, even the friction of their clothes was erotic.

Ravenna tugged at his shirt buttons, whimpering with frustration when she couldn't get her fingers to work. She needed her skin against his.

'Yes, touch me.' Did she hear the words or just taste them in her mouth?

His shirt disappeared, ripped by strong hands, leaving her free to palm his torso. Blindly she traced the contours of Jonas' chest, the broad weight of hair-fuzzed pectorals, the smoother planes and ridges lower down.

She'd just reached a barrier of taut denim when abrupt movement widened her eyes. She was falling. No, not falling—Jonas' strong arm was at her back, cushioning her as she landed on the floor.

She lay on the rich antique rug as Jonas ripped open the drawstring at her waist and tugged her trousers and underwear down.

A surge of indignant anger would have given her the strength to slap his face and cover herself. But it wasn't anger she felt.

It was excitement.

Her breath came in raw gasps as she watched him wrestle the clothes off her feet and toss them aside. His eyes glowed pure silver, almost molten, and his gaze, raking her from top to toe, was incendiary. Rivers of fire ignited in her blood, searing through anything like caution.

The way he looked at her, as if there were no one and nothing else in the world, as if he'd die if he didn't possess her...she revelled in it. For she felt the same.

She traced his powerful frame with possessive eyes, rejoicing in the heavy rise and fall of his chest and the pulse hammering out of control at his throat.

'Jonas.' His name was an aphrodisiac on her tongue. 'Come here.' She reached out and he planted a brief, fervent kiss on her palm then turned aside.

Ravenna opened her mouth to protest then realised he was tearing open a small packet he'd grabbed from his wallet. Undoing his jeans with the other hand, he moved swiftly, economically. A glimpse of his erection made her inner muscles tighten in a mix of anticipation and doubt. She was tall but—

The weight of his half-naked body on hers obliterated any doubts. He was big, his bare torso burning up, and she revelled in the way he imprisoned her, propped on his elbows to protect her from his weight.

He lowered his head, suckling her nipple through her T-shirt and she arched high, a moan of pleasure throbbing in her throat. The movement produced friction lower, where he waited at the juncture of her thighs, and lower still where her calves slid against the jeans he still wore.

Ravenna clutched his head, holding him to her breast. 'Please.' It was all she could manage, words failing her. She wanted his mouth on her but she wanted far more. She needed—

He must have understood for with one quick movement he centred himself and thrust hard and fast, right to the core of her. It was shockingly perfect, the feel of them joined so completely. For a trembling moment Ravenna felt she hung suspended from the stars, quivering in awe.

Then one large hand pushed her T-shirt up and cupped her breast. Jonas sucked on her other breast, hard and insistent, as he withdrew then surged in again, higher this time.

As easily as that she shattered. Not in delicate ripples of delight but in a cataclysmic upheaval that made her buck and scream beneath him, hands clinging and voice hoarse as she rode out a storm of pleasure so exquisite, so intense, it must change her for ever.

She was floating in ecstasy when he said her name in a voice so deep it rumbled through her, right to her bones.

Eyes snapping open, she was snared by Jonas' hot, silver gaze. In her confused state she wondered if she'd wear the brand of that intense look for life. She felt it like a touch, heavy and erotic, strong enough to mark her.

His face was austere, pared to bone and taut flesh. Then he moved, short, sharp thrusts that sent shock waves through her, re-igniting desire though it should be impossible now. It was his look that held her captive, that intense connection, the throb and push of his body in perfect sync with hers, the raw pleasure and something more, something huge and full of emotion.

Ravenna slid her hands around his hot, damp torso and down, clamping hard on the taut muscle of his backside, pulling him in, needing to share.

'Ravenna!' His voice was a roar, his eyes shocked as he bucked hard, pulsing frantically and she shattered again. This time she wasn't alone. They rode the whirlwind together, gazes enmeshed. His ecstasy was hers. Every throb and quake of delight was shared. Every gasp and groan. Every delicious shudder and squeeze of loosening muscle.

Still he held her gaze and Ravenna held him close. She reached up to those wide shoulders, tugging.

'I'm heavy.' His voice wasn't the clipped, sure one she knew. It burred soft enough to make what was left of her insides melt.

'I know.' She tugged again. 'Come here.'

He let her pull him down so they lay chest to chest, his heart pounding against hers. It felt so right, as if she'd waited all her life for this.

She'd known a man before. Just one. He'd been attractive, fun, nice. Yet she hadn't experienced anything like this feeling of completion with him. As if all was right with the world and at long last she'd found her place in it, not an outsider any more. It was as if with Jonas she was home.

Ravenna took a shallow breath, inhaling the musky scent of sex and the sharp tang of Jonas' flesh. She was barely aware of the trickle of tears down her cheek as she hugged him close.

Ravenna was limp in his arms as he carried her upstairs.

For a tall woman she didn't weigh much. There was a delicacy about her that tugged at him, made him want to keep her close.

His stride lengthened as he marched to his bedroom. Still she didn't stir. The cynical side of him wanted to assert she was playing him, trying to stir protectiveness. But he'd seen her stunned expression as she'd climaxed not once, but twice. He'd felt her convulse around him in great waves of pleasure that shook him to the core.

Jonas had never experienced anything so intense. It was as if her passion had turned him molten and forged him into someone new. He felt...different.

His arms tightened. Was it like this with her every time?

He'd known Ravenna was passionate. Her vibrancy, whether in fury or indignation, had fascinated from the first, drawing him despite himself. If he'd known how that translated to erotic passion he'd have followed through on that kiss in Paris instead of waiting all this time.

Satisfaction stirred as he nudged open the bedroom door. *This* was what he wanted from her. Sex. The sort of passion that drove out anything as corrosive as pity. He didn't need her feeling sorry for him. He was no charity case.

Jonas laid her on the bed, taking in the beguiling curve of her full lips and those lustrous, long dark lashes that fanned her rosy cheeks. Something unfamiliar skated through him as he looked down at her. Tenderness. The need to look after her.

The realisation slammed into him, catching his breath. Already his hand had reached out as if to trace Ravenna's cheekbone, the pure angle of her jaw, the delicate pulse at her throat. His heart skipped a beat as he remembered the look in her eyes as they'd climaxed together. The wonderment and joy. A joy so strong it had branded him.

Jonas snatched his hand back.

Even asleep Ravenna was dangerous.

He assured himself this wasn't different from what he'd experienced with other lovers. It *couldn't* be different. If he felt altered it was only because of the depth of his arousal. He couldn't remember ever needing any woman with such a primitive urgency.

Jonas nodded, satisfied with that explanation. He knew

what he wanted from Ravenna and it wasn't emotion. He'd never felt emotionally bound to a lover and he wasn't about to start with her of all women.

When the time came for feelings they would be for his wife. The perfect woman who would fit his requirements and his world, who'd excel at being a mother, a gracious hostess, a social success and a loyal, supportive spouse.

Jonas frowned. For the first time his vision of the perfect wife to create his perfect future didn't fill him with anticipation.

He looked at Ravenna, noting the graze of stubble rash on her cheek where his unshaved jaw had rubbed and how the damp patch on her T-shirt clung to her nipple where his tongue had laved.

He felt a primitive satisfaction that he'd marked her as his.

His chest tightened and a frisson of doubt snaked through him. No! This was lust pure and simple. Not to be confused with his longer-term plans. Those plans had been all that kept him sane in a world where no one cared for him except as a pawn in the game of his parents' disintegrating marriage or, later, as the goose that lay the golden eggs. His family, his women—all had only wanted what he could give them. They hadn't wanted *him*.

So he'd learned to take.

He let his gaze rove Ravenna's slim legs, bare and supple, to the V of dark hair between her thighs. His sex stirred, eager for more.

That was what he wanted. Physical pleasure and release. He could seduce her awake or have her again while she slept. But he did neither.

His gaze caught on a red mark on her hipbone. It was where he'd gripped her hard as he came. White-hot memory of that glorious cataclysm rocked him. And more, of the soft light in her eyes when she'd tugged him to her and wrapped him close in trembling arms. She'd had nothing to gain from that embrace. It had been about giving, sharing, and he couldn't remember anything better than those moments in her arms, not even that spectacular orgasm.

Silently Jonas shucked off his jeans and climbed onto the wide bed, careful not to disturb Ravenna. The bed shifted beneath his weight and she rolled towards him. Automatically he put his arm around her, tugging her close, her head on his shoulder, her hand at his hip. His breath snared at the innocently erotic pleasure of her touch but he made no move to wake her. For now this was enough.

He wrapped his other hand around her thigh, dragging it over his belly, and sank back into the mattress.

It seemed hours later that she woke. Her lashes tickled his chest as they fluttered open. Her fingers twitched as if testing the surface she lay on. Instead of rearing back in horror she nuzzled closer as if drawing in his scent. All his senses went ballistic.

She blinked sleepily up at him, her lips widening in a smile that knocked a chunk of granite off the corner of his heart. Her gaze was warm and for the first time he saw her smile reach her eyes. They glowed.

Jonas felt something shift deep inside. Something he had no name for. He felt it again when her hand skimmed up and around and he found himself being cuddled.

Hugs weren't common in his experience, even after sex. He discovered he liked them. They made him feel...good.

Who'd have thought 'good' could be so satisfying?

'Thank you.' Her voice was low, shivering through him like a caress.

Another first. How many lovers thanked him even though he put their pleasure first?

Guilt pummelled him. He hadn't been careful with Ravenna. He'd taken her with a savagery that bordered on uncontrolled. Look at the way he'd bruised her.

'Are you okay?'

She blinked at his rough tone and moved as if to prop

herself up to see him better, but he kept her clamped to him. He liked her right where she was.

'Okay? I feel fantastic.' Her smile turned secretive and her lashes lowered as her cheeks coloured.

A woman who blushed and thanked him for taking her with the finesse of a horny teenager? Ravenna was far from the woman he'd imagined.

'I didn't hurt you?'

She shook her head. 'I told you I enjoyed it. Didn't you?' Ravenna's voice was like warm whisky spilling through his veins and pooling low in his belly. She looked him square in the eyes and Jonas' heart give a great thump.

'Absolutely.' *Enjoy* didn't come close to describing what he'd felt. 'But I should have been more careful. I've bruised you.' His hand drifted to her hip, caressing the spot where he'd held her.

Her lashes dipped, hiding her eyes as she shrugged. 'I bruise easily. But it doesn't hurt.'

'Good.' Jonas told himself he should end this, get up and walk away. But he couldn't. His fingers feathered the soft skin at her hip and he heard her hiss of indrawn breath.

'In that case,' he murmured, slamming a door on the voice of caution crying out in his head, 'perhaps we might do it again.' He watched her eyes widen with anticipation and felt satisfaction flare. Satisfaction at the thought of having Ravenna again, of taking his time to pleasure her slowly. Of sharing that oneness again.

'I never thought I'd say this, but you have some good ideas, Jonas Deveson.' Her smile was sexy as she trailed a finger up his throat to his ear.

Arousal jolted through him. Swiftly he rolled her onto her back, capturing her wrists and dragging them above her head. At her moue of disappointment, he leaned in and tasted her mouth, shocked yet pleased to discover her as delicious as before.

'Let me, Ravenna. I want to do this slowly.' He feathered

tiny kisses down her neck, then moved down and licked the underside of her breast, unbearably turned on just by the taste of her and by her uneven breathing.

'I'm not sure I can bear it.' But the look in her eyes belied her words. It was warm like a caress as it locked with his. Again he felt that unfamiliar clenching in his chest.

In that moment it was far more than sex that he wanted.

CHAPTER EIGHT

RAVENNA WOKE IN Jonas' bed. Smiling, she rolled on her side, reaching for him. He wasn't there.

Her stomach dipped. She'd never imagined herself insatiable but an afternoon with Jonas had taught her things she'd never expected.

That she had erogenous zones she'd never known.

That she could make Jonas lose his cool.

That ecstasy made her noisy. Her face flamed at the way she'd screamed his name over and over. But he hadn't minded, encouraging her as if he enjoyed hearing her shout his name.

That she had a weakness for silvery eyes, a broad chest and clever hands that knew exactly how to touch her.

That she had a weakness for Jonas Deveson.

Her breathing quickened. Jonas wasn't the frigid enemy she'd thought. He had his own difficult past. He'd been the one supporting his family and her mother, from the day he left school. Was it any wonder he'd had no time for Piers or Silvia, who'd kept their distance yet lived off his hard work?

As for his mother… Ravenna bit her lip, remembering his wretchedness as he read that diary. Whatever else Jonas might be, he wasn't unfeeling. He'd been raw with pain. It had hurt to see him so.

When he'd made love to her it hadn't been a cheap little wham, bam, thank you ma'am, no matter how fast and furious the first time. She'd felt so much. They had shared more than mere physical coupling. And his tenderness here in his bed—

Ravenna wriggled under the sheets. The next time he'd been gentle, utterly devastating with those careful caresses, until the white-hot urgency overtook them again.

It had been wonderful, far beyond her imaginings.

The explosion of passion had been inevitable. She'd been too inexperienced to understand the frisson of sexual tension from the moment he'd stalked into the Paris apartment. All she'd known was that around Jonas she was on edge, as if her skin didn't fit. She'd put it down to hatred, not attraction.

Ravenna watched the door. Jonas would be back soon. Their relationship had changed irrevocably and they needed to work out where they went from here.

It wasn't so much sex that had changed their relationship, but the sense of intimacy. She knew him for a more complex, feeling man than she'd imagined. And he knew she was more than the grasping thief he'd believed, or he wouldn't have let her get so close. He was too proud to open himself to a woman he disdained. The knowledge buoyed her.

Tantalisingly, Ravenna felt on the brink of understanding Jonas. Not completely, but she realised his original antipathy came from the harsh realities he'd faced. She'd seen a hint of the scars he'd carried since childhood.

In that moment she despised Piers. He'd been good to Silvia and she was grateful, but to ignore his own son...!

Whatever difficulties Ravenna and her mother faced, they'd had each other. She couldn't imagine growing up so alone. Jonas hadn't spoken much of his relationship with his mother but she guessed it hadn't been easy. What she knew of Piers' wife made her seem self-focused rather than maternal.

A shiver passed through Ravenna. She and Jonas still had a long way to go. The money was an almost insuperable barrier. Ravenna couldn't simply blurt out the truth.

Jonas detested her mother and would love a chance to make her suffer if he learned it was she who'd stolen from him.

But surely now Ravenna could make him listen and he'd be more understanding. Things weren't black and white any more. Behind the lord-of-the-world façade was a man she wanted to know better.

Given time they'd work things out. It wouldn't be easy, or immediate, but eventually he'd understand.

Through the bathroom door her mobile phone rang. The insistent ringing grated, high pitched like nails clawing her sensitised skin. Maybe because she'd faced such bad news in the last year she couldn't ignore it—had to check it wasn't something important.

Scurrying to her room, she snatched up the phone and draped a rug around herself, chilled after leaving Jonas' bed.

'Ravenna?'

'Mamma? What is it? Are you all right?' Her stomach curdled at Silvia's tone. They'd spoken only yesterday. What had happened since to put the fear in her mother's voice?

'I'm fine. It's you I'm worried about. What has that man done to you?'

Ravenna stilled in the act of shrugging the rug closer.

'What man?'

'Oh, *Ravenna!*' It was a wail of horror. 'So it's true. I can hear it in your voice.'

'What's true? What are you talking about?' It was impossible Mamma had guessed she was with Jonas. Yet, standing naked, aching in unfamiliar places after his thorough loving, Ravenna felt as if she'd been caught out.

'Don't pretend, darling. I know you're with Jonas Deveson.'

Ravenna sank onto the bed. What on earth was going on?

'I saw it in a magazine. You and him shopping together.'

'A magazine?' It must have been the paparazzi shot that had so surprised her.

'The press have labelled you his secret girlfriend. They

'say the pair of you are holing up in a love nest.' Her voice rose in panic. 'Tell me it's not true. Tell me you wouldn't be stupid enough to fall for him.'

Ravenna opened her mouth then shut it again. Everything was moving too fast. She felt dizzy.

'Ravenna?' Her voice was sharp. 'Has he hurt you?'

'Of course he hasn't hurt me, Mamma. You're overreacting. There's nothing to worry about.'

'Nothing to worry about?' She could almost see her mother roll her eyes. 'You're such an innocent when it comes to men. There's nothing innocent about the way he's looking at you in that photo. He looks like he wants to eat you all up.'

Heat scorched Ravenna from her toes to the tips of her ears. That was precisely what Jonas had done, using his mouth on her body to reduce her to quivering desperation.

'Ravenna.' Her mother's voice, now quiet, vibrated with worry. 'Tell me you didn't fall for his lies.'

'Jonas isn't a liar, Mamma.'

'Oh, Ravenna! You did, didn't you?'

Ravenna squared her shoulders. 'I'm twenty-four, Mamma, not a little girl. Jonas hasn't hurt me.' Given her mother's response to that innocent photo, now wasn't the time to reveal the whole truth. Her mother would hotfoot it to England and that would set the cat among the pigeons. Much as Ravenna wanted to see her, Silvia was safer in Italy. 'I'm…working for him, as a temporary housekeeper.'

'That's the job you were excited about?' Silvia was disbelieving. 'You vowed never to work in service.'

It was true. Ravenna had determined never to be anyone's servant after years of being made to feel inferior at school.

But that was before her mother had stolen and put her in a situation where she had to swallow her pride. Mamma had taken the money for *her*. This was her responsibility.

'Jonas is hosting a ball to reopen the Hall and I'm doing the catering. It will be a great opportunity to showcase my skills.' Ravenna was babbling but couldn't stop. Maybe because she was naked, her body tingling from his touch. 'I hope it will be a stepping stone to other jobs.'

Her mother sighed. 'Promise me you'll keep your distance. He hates me and he'd do anything to hurt me. You have no idea how ruthless he is—' her voice dropped '—or how much he despises me. He blames me for his mother's death. But I swear I had no idea she still cared about Piers. While I was at the Hall all she did was snipe at him. Poor Piers—'

'I know.' Ravenna had heard it before, how Piers had fallen in love for the first time ever with her mamma. How happy they'd been. 'But Jonas can't hurt me.'

He already had his retribution. What more could he do?

'Don't be too sure. Even when he was young he had a way with women, a magnetism that drew them even though it was obvious they were expendable.'

Ravenna bit her tongue rather than snap that if he had, he'd probably got that from his father. Her mother hated hearing anything negative about Piers. He was one of the few subjects they didn't see eye to eye on.

'I wouldn't put it past him to seduce you, just to settle the score. He's charismatic and persuasive but beneath the charm he's cold and calculating.'

'Maybe there's more to him than you think. Besides, it was Piers, not Jonas, who ripped that family apart.'

Silence greeted her words. It was the closest she'd come to criticising Piers to her mother. He'd been good to Silvia and he'd loved her in his own way, but she'd never been comfortable with his irresponsible take on life.

'I know.' Her mother's misery caught at Ravenna's heart.

'I'm sorry, Mamma. I—'

'No, don't apologise. It's just I'm worried about you. No matter what you think you know about Jonas Deveson, remember this: he's an aristocrat through and through. He's not easy-going like his father. He's a perfectionist who only settles for the best. To him that means a woman from the right family, with the right connections, the right accent, the right look. You'll never be that woman. To him you'll always be the housekeeper's daughter. Worse, you're a permanent reminder of me and Piers.'

A weight crushed Ravenna's chest as she heard her mother say all the things she'd told herself. But that was before—

'You'll find the right man one day, Ravenna. But it won't be Jonas Deveson. At best he'd offer a brief affair. At worst—well, you only have to look into his eyes to understand the meaning of revenge.'

Ravenna swallowed. She'd seen that look. That day in Paris it had transfixed her with a fear she dared not show.

'I'm sorry, Mamma,' she said quickly. 'I have to go. But don't worry. I'm perfectly able to look after myself.'

So why, when she ended the call, did Ravenna feel shaken to the core? Jonas didn't love her—she wasn't that naïve. But there was something between them stronger than prejudice. Something drew them despite the reasons they shouldn't be together. It was worth exploring.

Tossing aside the rug, Ravenna went to her wardrobe. It was time she squashed those poisonous tendrils of doubt.

She reached for a pair of trousers and paused. Call it feminine pride but she wanted him to look at her with desire. Ravenna pulled out the one decent dress she'd brought.

It felt disturbingly as if she donned protective armour.

Ravenna was back in his bedroom when he returned. At the sight of her tucking in sheets with swift movements, he almost wondered if he'd imagined the last, passionate hours when they'd driven each other to ecstasy again and again.

His gaze dropped to the length of her legs, revealed as she leaned across to plump up the pillows, and the sweet curve of her bottom against the clingy orange dress.

Jonas swallowed over sandpaper as his body stirred.

Then she turned and he saw what she wore. Not the nondescript work clothes he'd fantasised about stripping off her all week. The dress was held in place by a single, provocative tie at the waist. A V neck hinted at her delicious cleavage, but it was the way the dress clung that made his heart hammer. Like lover's hands it cupped, caressed and flowed over proud breasts, the swell of her hips and a waist that he could almost span with his hands.

She was blatantly sexy. Her gaze collided with his and that white-hot blast of connection shimmered in the air.

Hunger slammed into him as if he hadn't already had his fill of her several times. Instead of sating desire, an afternoon spent in bed had turned him into a randy teenager, driven by his libido, not his brain.

It unsettled him. He ruled his world through logic and careful planning. Yet he'd lost a precious afternoon's work and all he could think of was how many moves it would take to have Ravenna naked beneath him again.

He raked his hand through his hair. He'd left her to seek refuge downstairs, needing to gather himself, yet just one look shattered him all over again.

'Jonas.' Her voice had a low, throaty quality that would make him think about sex even if she were wearing a sack. 'I was just coming to look for you.'

She approached then halted as if having second thoughts.

'I was busy downstairs.' Busy revisiting that diary. When that got too much he'd taken refuge in thoughts of Ravenna coming apart in his arms, more radiant and alive than any woman he'd known.

'Oh.' She wiped her hands down her dress, instantly dragging his gaze to her thighs and flat belly.

Jonas drew in a breath redolent with the tang of feminine arousal. He'd yanked his clothes on without bothering to shower. Till this moment he hadn't admitted it was because he revelled in the scent of her on his skin.

He frowned. Why? What made her different from other women?

He hadn't even come back here in the hope of more sex.

She'd been so exhausted he'd expected her to be asleep. He'd simply returned to be with her—she made him feel good.

That was a first. An unsettling one.

'Why did you want me?' It came out gruffly but for once Jonas was incapable of charm.

Ravenna shrugged but the movement was jerky, betraying nerves. 'I thought we should talk.'

He nodded and prowled further into the room. 'Go ahead.'

Her eyes widened before she looked down, lashes veiling her eyes. Silently Jonas cursed the loss of even the most basic courtesy. No morning after had ever been so awkward. He had a horrible suspicion it was because none had ever felt quite so important. He was ridiculously on edge.

'We need to talk about us.'

Every male instinct Jonas possessed hummed to alert.

'Yes?' He noted the way her gaze skated over his shoulder then to a spot below his ear.

'About this afternoon.'

Suddenly her uncertainty made sense. He'd been careful about protection, as always, but that last condom had torn. He hadn't realised she'd noticed and had told himself the chances of it leading to anything were slim.

'Are you on the pill?'

'No.' Her gaze jerked to his. It wasn't worry he saw in her face but something indefinable. Instinct told him it was something she didn't want him to notice.

'I see.' That complicated matters. Suppose she got pregnant? It wasn't what he'd planned, but he'd never walk away from a child of his.

The idea of Ravenna being pregnant with his seed shafted possessiveness through him. 'If there's a child—'

'There won't be a child.' Her expression was shuttered.

'It's possible.'

She shook her head and he read obstinacy in her jaw. 'You don't have to worry about it.'

His belly twisted hard. His mother's diary had revealed

with brutal clarity why he was an only child. After him there'd been an abortion and she'd ensured she didn't have another baby to the man who'd betrayed her. Jonas had thought he'd plumbed the depths before, but that revelation had torn a gaping hole somewhere in the vicinity of his chest.

'Why?' The word shot like a bullet. 'Because you'd terminate it?'

Ravenna's face froze. 'No! Because I know my body and you don't have anything to worry about.'

Air escaped his tight lungs and he realised he'd been holding his breath. 'I see.'

Ridiculous to feel a pang of regret.

'So what did you want to discuss?' He stepped closer but made himself stop at arm's length.

'Us.' She waved one arm in a gesture that encompassed the bed. 'I mean, what happens now?'

Jonas could think of several things he'd like to happen. All involved Ravenna naked. He moved forward but stopped, seeing her draw herself up stiffly. He remembered how demanding he'd been. She could be sore. Jonas tried to feel guilty but couldn't bring himself to regret what they'd done.

'Things aren't the same now.' She fixed him with a keen gaze. 'Are they?'

What did she want? An admission that she'd turned him inside out with her sexuality, indomitable spirit and devastating generosity? That moment in the study when she'd offered comfort had undone him. He was so unused to anyone's concern, he'd repudiated it even as secretly he coveted it.

He hadn't managed to fathom what it was he wanted from Ravenna, except more. Until he understood he'd admit nothing.

'Jonas?' Her tone sharpened.

'What happens now?' He shrugged, not liking the sensation of being cornered. 'We both have work to do.'

Her stare grew fixed. 'Is that all?'

'No, of course that's not all. I want to take you back to

bed.' His gaze dropped to the V of her neckline. 'Hell! I don't even want to wait that long.' Heat surged in his blood and his lower body grew heavy and hard. 'But given the fact you're up and dressed I'm assuming you don't feel the same.'

Jonas enjoyed the fiery colour slashing her cheeks. It reminded him of her full body blush when he made love to her.

'I'm not talking about that.'

'No?' He jerked his brain back into gear. 'What else is there?'

Her eyes widened and he felt a moment's regret. But he refused to be railroaded into discussing *feelings,* if that was what she meant.

'I see.' Ravenna's jaw tightened and she crossed her arms. Did she realise how that plumped up her breasts? 'So as far as you're concerned we'll go on as before, except for bouts of hot sex when the fancy takes you.'

'It's an improvement on what went before.'

She didn't respond to his smile.

He wondered how long it would take to seduce her into breathless compliance. His body stirred. He'd always enjoyed a challenge and despite her frosty attitude Ravenna would welcome him. Look at the way her nipples budded and her pulse throbbed in her throat.

'Let me get this straight.' She unfolded her arms and stepped into his space, her eyes glinting gold sparks. 'After what we shared you think nothing has changed, except you get rights to my body whenever you want?' She shook her head. 'You're in the wrong century, Jonas. The droit du seigneur vanished ages ago.'

He stiffened. 'No one forced you, Ravenna.' Her sceptically raised brows grazed his pride, for he hadn't been gentle that first time. But nor had she been forced. Ravenna had made a choice. She could have refused. 'You wanted me.'

'I did,' she finally admitted. 'But that doesn't mean you can expect me to slave away here under your Draconian con-

ditions and be your sex toy as well. You can't have it both
ways. I deserve better.'

Jonas surveyed her defiant face, her pouting lips, fuller
from his kisses, her reddened cheek where his stubble had
marked her. Anger flashed in her eyes and something like
disappointment.

His gaze dropped to the seductive flame-coloured dress
designed to bring a man to his knees.

His belly curdled as finally, and far too late, realisation
struck. Jonas almost staggered under the impact.

How had he been so blind? Disappointment carved a
hollow through his vitals. Disappointment and fury at his
naivety. Him, naïve! You'd think with his history he would
have expected this. Yet he felt sick with the shock of it.

Just like her mother, Ravenna aimed to sell her body for
a rich man's favours. She saw him as an easy target and
wanted to buy her way out of debt. She thought sharing her
body wiped out her crime.

That put what they'd done together in a new light.

Anger and resentment swamped Jonas—that he should
have responded, wanted so much, when all the time it had
been a tawdry transaction by a conniving woman.

Ravenna watched storm clouds gather in Jonas' eyes. That
leaden stare sent a chill scudding down her spine. It was as
if they were back to the animosity of Paris.

Stoically she forced down rising bile. Had she deluded
herself? Had the man she'd begun to feel for been an illusion? Had his vulnerability and his easy charm been as her
mother had warned—a ploy to make her lower her guard
so he could wreak revenge on her family?

She didn't want to believe it.

'What did you have in mind, Ravenna?' His voice was a
low purr, but instead of soothing it made her hackles rise.
He sounded like a hungry lion inviting her to dine.

She lifted her chin. 'I was hoping to talk. Get to know

each other better.' The words sounded lame in the face of his cool regard but she plunged on. 'I thought we might come to a better arrangement too about the work to be done here.'

'Really?' One saturnine eyebrow rose in lofty surprise.

'Yes, really.' His condescension sliced through her caution. 'If you want this place put in order I'll need help.'

'You don't think you should dirty your delicate hands now you've slept with the boss?'

That sarcastic tone scraped her skin raw. She felt sullied, pressing a hand to her stomach as nausea rose. Familiar exhaustion struck, dragging at her limbs, making her panic she wouldn't be able to stand up to him physically.

Not now. Not in front of him!

'In case you hadn't noticed my hands aren't delicate.' They were firm and capable, bearing nicks from her apprenticeship in a commercial kitchen.

Jonas shifted, looming over her by a head, making Ravenna feel every inch of the difference between them. From his chiselled, aristocratic features to his elegant handmade clothes and designer watch he was the epitome of wealth and authority. She, with her shorn hair and cheap, chain-store dress didn't fit his world. She'd never been ashamed of being poor, but she'd always hated condescension.

This was worse, far worse.

'You know what I mean,' he said, his voice low and lethal. 'You think because we had sex I'll forget your crime? Or are you setting your sights higher? Do you think I'll keep you in luxury now I've had a taste of what you're bartering?'

Ravenna rocked back at the force of his contempt.

'All I *want*,' she ground out between her teeth, 'is a little respect.'

'Is that what you call it? And there was I, thinking you were simply whoring yourself like your mother.'

Ravenna's hands clenched as she fought the urge for violence.

'You really are a self-satisfied bastard.' He didn't even flinch, whereas she felt as if she were crumbling.

'And I'm sorry to say you're every inch your mother's daughter. I warned you, I don't share my father's weakness for the hired help.' His smile killed something fragile inside. 'But that doesn't prevent me taking what's on offer.' His eyes stripped her bare and she shuddered.

'There's *nothing* on offer.' Not any more. Not when he'd taken her caring and her concern, and, yes, her body, and reduced them to nothing with a few slashing words.

'Let's get one thing straight, Ravenna.' He leaned closer, invading her space. 'If you're aiming for something permanent you're barking up the wrong tree.' His voice was rough, reminding her of the sharp emotion she'd seen in him when he talked of his family. Yet his eyes had the blank look of someone who'd shut himself off from feelings.

She wished she could do the same.

She wished her mother had been wrong and Jonas was even half the man she'd begun to believe him. Mamma had been right—Ravenna had confused sex with caring. Now she paid the price as pain sliced her.

'Don't worry. I get the picture. As far as your family is concerned the Ruggiero women are good enough to be mistresses but never wives.' From some inner reserve of strength Ravenna summoned a shaky smile. 'Frankly, a long-term relationship hadn't occurred to me. I'd like to respect the man I live with. But thanks for the clarification.'

Ignoring his glare, she turned away, careful to keep her balance on wobbly legs. When the door shut behind her it was with a snick of finality.

CHAPTER NINE

JONAS TOSSED THE design portfolio onto his desk and sat back, rubbing eyes gritty from lack of sleep. He couldn't concentrate. He hadn't been able to concentrate since that scene with Ravenna.

Ruggiero women are good enough to be mistresses but never wives.

The look on her face as she'd thrown what he was thinking straight back at him! Defiance, hauteur and a pain that cut to the bone. It was that anguish, etched in her eyes and taut frame, that had dragged him from blind fury long enough to recognise he might have overreacted.

Might have? He'd jumped down her throat without hearing her out.

Because it was easier to dismiss Ravenna as a gold-digging opportunist than believe she could be something more.

Yet it was the something more he'd responded to, not just her sexuality. It was the woman who'd comforted him, her enemy. The woman who, without being asked, catered cheerfully for those working around the Hall, even him, the man set on making her life hell. The woman who had rolled up her sleeves and taken on the ridiculously impossible task he'd set her, revealing a grit and determination he'd not thought possible. The woman who'd fought him tooth and nail but never shied from the consequences of her actions in thieving from him.

He shook his head. Something didn't add up, but he was too befuddled to work it out.

Jonas looked at his half-empty mug and the scatter of crumbs on the plate she'd left on his desk and felt remorse.

Good enough to be mistresses. The pain in her words made him feel two inches tall.

No woman deserved to think that. Especially the woman who'd shared herself so unstintingly while he'd behaved with the finesse of a Neanderthal.

In Paris he'd thought her a consummate liar, a woman totally changed from the earnest, engaging teenager he'd met. But that scene in his bedroom proved him wrong. Ravenna couldn't hide her shame and anguish as she faced him down.

He felt like scum.

As if he'd taken advantage of her.

For the first time he wondered how Ravenna had reacted to her mother's affair.

The teenage Ravenna had seemed heartbreakingly alone in a world that judged merit on status and money. She'd suffered at the hands of bullies who despised her lack of wealth. Yet she hadn't envied their money, just hated their shallowness.

How had she felt when her mother took up with Piers, revelling like a self-satisfied potentate in the furore over his gorgeous mistress? Had Ravenna enjoyed the ride?

Or, the thought struck hard, had she cringed at the gossip about her mother leeching Piers for cash?

Ravenna had developed that shell of pride for a reason.

Once the thought lodged he couldn't shake it. Especially as he recalled the wretchedness she'd tried to hide when he'd accused her of sleeping her way out of trouble.

Guilt smote him. Perhaps it was true. Perhaps not. But the memory of that haunted look discomfited him.

Jonas shoved back the chair and strode across the room.

He halted when he saw Ravenna talking with his garden designer, Adam Renshaw. The man's auburn head was bent towards hers and fire seared Jonas as if he'd been skewered on a spit. He couldn't breathe.

It took a moment to identify the unfamiliar feeling as jealousy.

His jaw tightened. He wanted to stomp out and haul Ravenna away.

As if he had a right to her.

As if she wouldn't simply ignore him after what had passed between them.

Jaw gritted, Jonas admitted that no matter what he wanted, no matter what Ravenna wanted, this wasn't over. They had unfinished business.

His mouth twisted mirthlessly as he registered something like relief at the knowledge.

The women in his life had always been expendable. Even the Honourable Helena Worthington, the blonde beauty with impeccable bloodlines and a sweet disposition whom he'd half decided on as a future bride. She hadn't been important enough to stop him taking Ravenna to bed.

Yet with Ravenna, for the first time in his life a woman seemed infuriatingly *necessary*.

He had to discover why.

Then find a way to free himself.

Jonas swung away, almost knocking over the easel of samples his interior designer had set up. His gaze slid over dark paint and patterned fabrics. He'd wanted traditional but this was… He shook his head. Too predictable?

Then he noticed the sheet of paper Ravenna had brought with his coffee. Concise bullet points listed matters needing attention. Every day she presented him with another list of problems—from damage to wainscoting to cracked tiles, usually with suggestions on how to deal with them. She had an eye for detail and a flair for organisation. Qualities that didn't sit well with his original judgement of her.

Jonas looked from the list to the design portfolio. They

were talents he could use. And they would keep her out of the garden and in here, where he wanted her.

'Sorrel, chervil, sage, fennel.' Adam Renshaw smiled. 'There must be at least three dozen herbs on this list.'

'Too many?' When he'd asked Ravenna, as interim house-keeper, for input to his garden design, enthusiasm had over-come her bitterness about Jonas.

How could she resist the opportunity to help plan what promised to be a superlative cook's garden? She daydreamed about having such a place, with space for not only herbs and vegetables but fruit trees and berries. Just walking in this garden with its mellow stone walls and gnarled apple trees lifted her spirits. Something she needed badly.

The alternative, dwelling on Jonas, was untenable.

'Not at all. It's good to have your input.' Adam moved closer. 'We'll fit them in easily over there. I just need to check the final design with Mr Deveson.'

'Did I hear my name mentioned?'

Ravenna froze as that familiar, rich voice curled around her like velvet on bare skin. Her lips compressed. How could she react that way when the same voice had lacerated her just days ago?

Adam swung round to face their boss. Ravenna took lon-ger, bracing herself before she met his gaze. Would it be coolly dismissive or would he ignore her as he'd done this morning when she'd brought coffee and he'd been absorbed in a huge portfolio?

Neither, she realised with a jolt as she turned. His gaze was as intent as ever but with none of the chill she expected. Nevertheless she moved half a step closer to Adam, aware of those dark pewter eyes narrowing.

She lifted her chin, reminding herself she didn't care what Jonas Deveson thought.

She'd been naïve to believe she could bridge the chasm between them. He'd used her and made a mockery of what she'd felt. The knowledge kept her chin high and her gaze steady.

'Of course,' Adam was saying, when she finally tuned in to the conversation. 'Ravenna and I were plotting the herb beds, but I think we've got it now.' Warm brown eyes smiled at her approvingly and she wished she could summon a spark of excitement for this pleasant, talented man.

Instead her attention focused on Jonas, standing preternaturally still, just watching the pair of them.

Her mouth flattened in self-disgust. No matter how hard she tried she couldn't ignore him.

'Excellent. In that case I'll just borrow Ravenna.' Jonas turned to her. 'If you have a few minutes?'

She raised her eyebrows. Jonas was requesting, not ordering? Suspicion rose but she forced herself to nod, bidding Adam a warmer than necessary goodbye. This was the first time Jonas had sought her out since that scene in his room and her stomach knotted. What did he want?

'You two seem to get on well,' Jonas said, holding open a door for her to enter.

'Adam is good company.' And attractive. And clearly interested. But Ravenna's pulse didn't quicken when he was around. Yet now, walking beside the man who despised her, she couldn't control her racing pulse.

'Do you have a lot in common?'

She swung around to face Jonas, livid at his feigned interest and at herself for being so weak. 'Why do you ask? You're not interested in my personal life. Only my ability to scrub floors or spread my legs.'

A flush coloured those high cheekbones. 'I deserve that.'

His admission did nothing to mollify her indignation or self-recrimination. She took a deep breath and looked away. 'What do you want, Jonas?'

She was so weary. Her chores had been almost beyond her lately as she fought an exhaustion she hadn't known for some time. At the back of her mind lingered the worry that perhaps her illness had returned. That worry gnawed at her, keeping her awake at night. That and thoughts of Jonas.

'In here.' He gestured to the open study door.

Squaring her shoulders, she entered, studiously averting her eyes from the dark carpet on the far side of the room where they'd come together in such urgent passion.

Cheeks flushed, she took a seat by the desk. If he was going to tell her he'd finally decided to call the police to deal with the theft she'd rather be sitting.

'I'm sorry.'

It was the last thing Ravenna expected. She jerked her gaze up to find Jonas standing over her, as tense as she'd ever seen him.

'I beg your pardon?'

'I said, I'm sorry.' He waved one arm in a gesture of frustration. 'I'm no good at this, but I'm trying to apologise for what I said. What I did.'

Ravenna blinked and stared. 'For what exactly?'

Jonas rubbed his jaw and she heard the faint scratch of bristles. Her skin heated as she remembered that roughness against her skin. Just looking at his unshaven jaw made her stomach tighten as erotic recollections filled her head. She shivered. Her thoughts were dangerously self-destructive.

His lips twisted ruefully and despite everything she couldn't help the little tug of attraction deep inside.

'Not for the sex. I can't regret that.' His smile disappeared. 'But for later. The way I acted, what I said about you.' He breathed so deep she watched, fascinated, as his chest expanded. 'I was crass and hurtful.'

Ravenna stared. 'You're saying you don't think I tried to buy my way out of trouble with my body?'

'I'm saying I don't know enough about you to judge.'

It wasn't what she wanted to hear but at least it was honest.

Yet did she want to wait while he took his time learning to judge her on her merits? Why should she?

Because she had no choice. She was trapped here.

More importantly, despite everything, she couldn't turn her back on Jonas.

That spark of fire between them had morphed into something that tied her to him, no matter how she tried to sever the connection. As if she still believed the half-formed hopes she'd harboured when she'd met him, passion for passion, as an equal rather than a bonded servant.

That scared her more than anything.

'I behaved badly, accusing you the way I did.' His voice was deep with regret. 'I should have listened. Especially after...' he shrugged and spread his hands in a gesture that seemed curiously helpless '...after your concern for me.'

He looked as if he were swallowing hot coals. As if he wasn't used to anyone's concern. Or being seen as vulnerable.

That realisation dried the caustic response forming on Ravenna's lips.

As her gaze meshed with his it wasn't the heat of anger or lust she saw there, or his familiar stonewalling expression. She read uncertainty in those grey depths, as if he'd lowered the shutters to let her glimpse the man behind the façade of authority. The man she'd discovered the day they'd shared passion so fierce it had burned away everything else and left her feeling raw and new.

'And so?' Ravenna forced herself not to trust the regret she thought she read in Jonas' features. Only days ago she'd been duped into believing he felt something for her.

'And so I regret what I said.'

Ravenna nodded. He watched her as if expecting a response but she said nothing. Words were easy. It was actions that counted.

'And I've decided to make some changes.'

Here it comes. Ravenna clasped damp palms together. *He's calling in the police.*

'I'm bringing in extra staff. Not just the builders but some local people to help with the cleaning and heavy work.'

Ravenna searched his face for some hint of a catch.

'But you said—'

'I know what I said. Looking after the Hall was to be your penance.' His lips compressed as his gaze swept her. 'I was unreasonable.'

Her jaw sagged as he met her eyes almost defiantly. She couldn't believe her ears.

'There's no need to stare as if I've got two heads.'

'Are you feeling all right?'

Jonas gave a bark of laughter. 'I should have known you wouldn't just say thanks. You wouldn't let me off easily.'

Let *him* off? He was the one in control. Ravenna stared, bemused, as laughter softened the grooves around Jonas' mouth and eased the severity of his austere features.

She swallowed, fighting fizzing awareness.

'And what about me? Are you pressing charges? Is that it?'

Jonas' expression sobered. 'No. Not for now. You'll stay and work as my housekeeper.'

Not for now. He still held that over her. What had she expected? That without evidence of her innocence and in the teeth of her admission of guilt he'd let her go? Impossible!

'But I'm hoping we can continue in a more…civilised way.'

Ravenna sat straighter. 'If by civilised you mean sharing a bed because I'm supposed to be grateful you've brought in staff—'

Jonas' raised hand stopped her. 'I've never had to buy my way into a woman's bed, Ravenna. I won't start now.'

Heat scored her cheeks. Once had obviously been enough for him. Once with the hired help to satisfy his curiosity.

'It's time to take some of the heat out of this situation.' He looked at her long and hard, as if attempting to read her mind. 'I'm trying to be reasonable, Ravenna. We can't continue as before.' He sighed. 'Contrary to what you might think I'm not prone to outbursts of temper.'

She did believe it. She'd learned all she could about her nemesis and there had been plenty. The consensus was that Jonas Deveson was one of Europe's most eligible bachelors, wealthy, charming and urbane. He was known for his incisive mind, impenetrable calm and careful planning. Employees and competitors respected him and his generosity was renowned. As was his drive to succeed. There was no mention anywhere of a temper or strong passions.

Which left her wondering why, with her, he'd been anything but calm and controlled.

A tremor whispered down her spine.

Perhaps it had something to do with the way her emotions undercut caution and good sense when he was around.

'So you'll treat me as your housekeeper and I'll treat you as my employer?'

After what had passed between them was it even possible? The strain of the last couple of days had almost broken her.

'That's the idea.' He nodded. 'To step back from the rest.' His wide gesture encompassed all that had gone before: the animosity, the flagrant desire and the illusion of closeness that had betrayed Ravenna into believing they shared something special.

'How can I refuse?' That was safest. No more dangerous, incendiary desire. No fireworks. She should be thanking her lucky stars, not feeling dissatisfied, as if a rug had been pulled out beneath her.

'Thank you, Ravenna.' Their eyes met and she felt a now-familiar jolt of heat. The awareness hadn't gone away.

Jonas turned away and she breathed deep, searching for equilibrium. He offered a truce and this time she was determined nothing would break it. If she had to stay here with him, it would be strictly on a boss-employee basis.

'In the circumstances I thought you might help me with this.' He turned, the large portfolio in his hands.

'What is it?'

'Come and look.' He put it on the desk.

Ravenna stared from the album to his broad back in charcoal cashmere. She didn't want to stand beside him. It was easier to maintain her poise if she kept her distance.

'Ravenna?'

Reluctantly she crossed to the desk, keeping as much distance as she could from Jonas. He turned the pages, revealing swatches of colour and design, all rich but rather ponderous and dark.

'I told my designer I wanted a traditional feel. But it's not working.'

He stopped at a page showing one of the drawing rooms. There were fabric swatches in deep, rich hues, heavily decorated, and photos of imposing antique furniture. It would be like living in a museum.

'You see what I mean?'

Ravenna straightened, realising she'd been leaning over the page, imagining the finished room and disapproving.

'Why show me? I'm just the housekeeper.'

'You know this house better than anyone, apart from me.' He picked up a sheet of paper and tossed it on top of the portfolio. Ravenna saw it was a list she'd made of repairs. 'You've got a good eye for detail and a feel for the place.'

She raised her eyebrows. 'Where are you heading, Jonas?'

'I thought you might have some thoughts on what would suit the old place.' His eyes met hers then shifted to the portfolio. Because he was up to something or ashamed of his earlier behaviour? Ravenna wished she could read him.

'I'm the housekeeper, remember? This is what you pay a designer for.'

'Most women would jump at the chance to plan a redecoration.' His tone was persuasive.

'I'm not most women.' Her hands crept to her hips. Despite his apology, his earlier accusation still rankled.

'No, you're not. Most women would have run screaming from Deveson Hall the moment they saw how much work it needed. But you didn't.' His deep voice was rich with what sounded like admiration. 'Others might have made a mere token effort at the job, but not you. You've been boarding up holes and drying out damp books on top of everything else. You make lists of repairs. You've even sourced local suppliers so work can begin quickly.'

Jonas paused. 'You've betrayed yourself, Ravenna.'

She started, horrified that somehow she'd given away her mother's secret.

'You've shown yourself to be a woman who cares and takes pride in what she does. I'd like to have you work with me. If we could set aside our differences I believe we'd deal well together.' He spread his hands in a gesture of openness. 'Of course, I'd take your assistance into account when it came to determining how long it takes to pay off your debt.'

Ravenna braced herself on the polished desk, her pulse hammering. She told herself it was relief that her mother's guilt was still secret. Or disappointment that he still held that debt over her head.

The alternative, that it was reaction to Jonas' praise, wasn't an option.

'When you put it like that, how can I refuse?' She tore her gaze away and made a show of concentrating on the samples. 'So long as you don't hold it against me if the result is a disaster. I have no decorating experience.' Furnishing her bedsit with second-hand pieces hardly counted.

'Don't worry, I'll still use the decorator. I just want another opinion on some things. Like this.' His finger jabbed a page showing the study.

Ravenna took in the handsome, heavy furnishings in the design, the deep green colour and the use of dark wood. She guessed nothing in the proposed design was less than a hundred years old. Even the light fittings were modelled on old lamps. Just looking at the page made her feel claustrophobic.

'What do you think?'

She shrugged. 'You said you wanted traditional.'

'But?'

'How honest do you want me to be?'

'I've never had a problem with honesty, Ravenna.'

She met his bright gaze and knew an almost overwhelming temptation to blurt the truth. To explain about the money and her mother's desperation. To resolve the lurking tension between them so she could be free of the burden of secrecy and Jonas' bad opinion. But love for her mamma stopped her. Ravenna couldn't leave her to his not-so-tender mercies.

'It's like something out of Dickens.' She waited, trying to read his expression. 'Or a movie set of what an old-fashioned gentleman's residence should be.'

'My feelings exactly.'

'Really?'

He nodded. 'I couldn't work in a room like that.'

'What *do* you like?' Her curiosity stirred.

Jonas waved his hand towards the long windows. 'Light. Space. A comfortable chair built to take a man's weight and a desk high enough for my knees.'

Ravenna surreptitiously scanned his big frame. She'd never thought of Jonas' height being an issue. He always looked supremely comfortable whatever his surrounds.

'So keep this desk. It's a bit battered but the wood is lovely. I'm sure an expert could restore it beautifully.'

Jonas' mouth turned up at one corner and Ravenna felt a little tug as if someone pulled a string through her insides. 'That's one decision I'd already made. The desk stays. But what about the rest?'

'What colours do you like?' She forced the words out, mesmerised by that half-smile. It evoked intimate memories she'd tried and failed to bury.

'Gold,' he murmured, his voice low as he leaned close,

looking straight into her eyes. 'Old gold, something like the colour of a good aged sherry.'

Ravenna felt his breath on her face like an elusive caress. Her skin drew taut and the tugging sensation in her abdomen became a heavy thrum. Her pulse sounded in her ears as she swayed.

Blinking, she stepped back, wary of the way his low, masculine purr resonated through her. Once bitten...

Deliberately she turned. It was ridiculous to imagine Jonas had been describing the unusual colour of her eyes.

'Tell your designer you want gold.' She surveyed the walls. 'Or maybe lighter. What about a soft straw? Something more neutral so the woodwork doesn't overpower the room?'

'That could work.' From the corner of her vision she saw him finally look away towards the walls. 'What else?'

'You said a comfortable chair. What did you have in mind? Do you mean for working at the desk or a sofa?'

'Both. I like the chesterfields.' He waved a hand at a couple of sofas that needed reconditioning. 'But there's a young German designer who does brilliant ergonomic chairs in minimalist design.' Jonas frowned. 'But would that clash?'

Ravenna read his abstracted look and realised Jonas really wanted her opinion. When he'd suggested getting her input she'd thought it some ploy. Instead he was genuine.

Something softened inside. She hoped it wasn't her defences.

He met her eyes, a hint of familiar impatience in his expression. 'Well? What do you think?'

Ravenna shook her head. 'That's for your designer to advise. How about I make a list? Can you pass me a pen and paper?'

CHAPTER TEN

RAVENNA PULLED HER jacket close and stepped out briskly. Even after a couple of months getting used to the bustle of building work, she preferred early morning solitude.

She surveyed the house, its stones mellow in the early sun, its new glazing glittering. Despite its size the Hall felt welcoming, maybe because she'd come to know it intimately. She'd delved its crannies, supervising cleaning and small repairs, and helped Jonas plot the refurbishment of what would be a marvellous home as well as historic treasure.

Turning, she crunched her way along the gravel path, wishing she could turn her mind as easily from thoughts of Jonas. His presence pervaded the place, even though he spent half the week in London. From London he rang regularly to check progress, his deep voice never failing to send a thrill of pleasure through her.

Life had fallen into an easy, if busy, routine since his apology. A routine Ravenna found a little too easy given Jonas still held her future in his hands.

Surely it wasn't right that she cared so much for a place she'd leave as soon as her debt was paid? Or enjoy Jonas' company? She laughed too often at his dry humour over the restoration's inevitable mishaps and delays.

He was patient, flexible and understanding. All the things she once thought him incapable of. Plus he appreciated her efforts, thanking her when she catered for emergency meetings with contractors and heritage officers, or when she helped him sift decorating suggestions.

She enjoyed the latter most of all. She told herself it was because she loved having input to the way the grand old house would look. It had nothing to do with the camaraderie that had developed between them as equals, rather than boss and servant.

Jonas had never come on to her again—he kept his distance. It was as if that day they'd spent exploring each other's bodies had been a dream.

Except her body remembered the pleasure he'd bestowed so lavishly. It quivered in anticipation when he approached, or when she inhaled his scent of citrus and warm male.

There were times when she'd swear she saw heat in his polished silver gaze. A heat that reflected all the things she told herself she shouldn't feel for Jonas. Since his apology the vicious, vengeful man she'd met in Paris had disappeared, replaced by one she liked far too much.

Ravenna quickened her pace, passing a drift of spring flowers, only to pause at the sounds from the newly restored stable block. Jonas had mentioned animals being delivered yesterday.

The stables had been empty while Silvia worked here and Ravenna had never seen thoroughbred horses up close. She followed the path to the nearest door.

'There now, Hector. That's better, isn't it?' Jonas' voice halted her in mid stride. 'That's my beauty.' The words were a slow thrum of approval. Obviously he was gentling some highly strung stallion, but, even knowing his words weren't for her, Ravenna felt the murmur like a caress on her skin.

Her heart dipped. Most of the time she coped with her situation, telling herself she was almost over the feelings Jonas evoked. But coming upon him suddenly, unprepared for the impact of those deep baritone cadences, her instant response told its own story.

How long before she could shake off this volatile attraction?

'Tim, you're in the way. There will be time for you in a moment.' Jonas laughed and she couldn't resist inching closer.

The sight that greeted her stopped her in her tracks.

There was Jonas in scuffed boots, worn jeans clinging to bunching muscles and a plain black T-shirt that stretched across a torso that was all hard-packed strength and perfect proportion. His dark hair was tousled and his skin glowed. He looked like a pin-up for the outdoor lifestyle.

But it wasn't just his breathtaking male appeal that sent the air scudding from her lungs. It was the joy in his expression. Unadulterated happiness that turned his strong features into something so powerfully appealing it wrapped tight fingers around her heart.

Ravenna had seen him smile, heard his wry humour, had even heard him laugh, but she'd never seen him look so happy.

And the cause of his happiness? A sway-backed draught horse that nudged him as he brushed it and a chocolate Labrador that lurched between man and horse, its tail waving.

'Watch out!' Ravenna darted forward as the horse shifted and the dog wandered into the path of its massive hoof.

Man, dog and horse all turned to stare. An instant later the hoof descended harmlessly as the dog hobbled towards her with a ruff of pleasure.

'He's only got three legs.' No wonder the dog had wobbled so badly. She dropped to her knees so it could sniff her hand then lavish a rough-tongued caress on her wrist.

'Timothy! Back here.' Jonas moved towards them. 'I'm sorry. He's a bit too enthusiastic.'

Ravenna laughed as the dog tried to lick her face. 'No, don't worry. That's fine. I like dogs.' She looked up into silver eyes and felt a jolt right to her core.

'So I see.'

Ravenna blinked, telling herself she couldn't feel Jonas' gaze. As for the way her lungs had constricted… It was as well she was booked for a medical check-up soon.

'Look out!' she warned.

But it was too late. Jonas staggered towards her after being nudged by the draught horse's massive head. He braced himself before her, legs planted wide as she looked up into his laughing face.

'Obviously Hector doesn't like his routine being interrupted.'

'Hector?'

A large square hand reached down to her. Automatically she took it, letting Jonas pull her up. For an exhilarating moment they stood toe to toe, then he let go and moved back.

'Meet Hector.' He raised a hand to the massive animal's neck and the horse whinnied as if in response.

At Ravenna's feet the lopsided Labrador looked up expectantly, tongue lolling.

'I suppose this is Timothy.' The dog barked at the sound of its name.

Bemused, she looked around the stables. The stalls were deserted but for this one.

'*These* are the animals you brought in? They're not yours?'

Jonas shook his head. 'I'm giving them temporary accommodation as a favour to a neighbour. Part of her stables burned down due to an electrical fault and she put out an SOS for Hector. Where Hector goes, so does Timothy.'

The dog hopped over to the big horse, which lowered its head and gusted its breath over the Labrador.

'That's…very nice of you.'

'But not what you expected?' He didn't miss her surprise.

She shrugged. How could she say caring for a lame dog and an old horse wasn't how she saw him spending his spare time? She hadn't known he *had* spare time.

'I thought you'd bring in thoroughbreds to ride.'

'Later. For now Hector needs a home.' He patted the horse. 'Didn't you, old fellow?'

'You know him?' There was familiarity in his tone.

Jonas nodded. 'Hector was saved from the knacker's yard when I was a kid. Vivien, my neighbour, finds homes for unwanted animals—donkeys, goats, ponies, even a three-legged dog and a blind draught horse.'

'He's blind?' Ravenna stepped closer and saw Hector's eyes were cloudy.

'Pretty much. But he's got Timothy, who leads him where he wants to go. Together they make a good team.' He ruffled the dog's ears then picked up the brush he'd been using.

'I spent a lot of time at Vivien's when I was young. She taught me to ride and help out. Hector was venerable then.' Absently Jonas rubbed the horse's neck and it struck Ravenna she'd never seen him so relaxed, except for the day they'd spent sprawled in his bed, boneless and spent from ecstasy.

Fire seared her cheeks and she bent to pat Timothy, who'd hobbled back to her. 'I'd imagined you learning to ride here.' She waved her hand around the enormous stables.

Jonas turned away to brush the big horse, but not before she saw the shutters come down, eclipsing the laughter in his eyes. 'My mother didn't ride and Piers had other things to do with his time.' Wide shoulders shrugged. 'He spent most of his time in the city and when he was here he had interests other than teaching me.'

The edge to Jonas' voice made her think instantly of comments he'd made about Piers chasing women. Not much of a father then.

'So you spent a lot of time at your neighbour's?'

'Enough to learn to ride and to care for animals.' His words were matter of fact but his tone confirmed the experience had been precious.

'Didn't you have animals here at the Hall?' She stepped closer, needing to know more.

* * *

Jonas flicked a warning look over his shoulder. He didn't welcome prurient curiosity. But the sight of her, bent to scratch Timothy behind the ears, even while she looked up at him with serious eyes, gave him pause.

'Pets weren't allowed. My mother wasn't an animal person and Piers…' Jonas shrugged. Piers had rarely been around long enough to express an opinion. As for teaching him to ride! His father had never taken time out from his own pursuits to be with him. Even on those occasions when his parents had temporarily made up, Jonas wasn't a priority.

Jonas watched Ravenna's expressive eyes flick from him to Hector. 'You like horses?'

'I don't know. I've never met one up close.'

Jonas remembered the first time he'd visited Vivien's stables, the excitement tinged with fear that had turned to delight. 'Come and meet Hector. He's very gentle.'

She hesitated for so long he thought she wouldn't come. Why it was important that she did, Jonas had no idea. But it felt good when she approached, as if she trusted his word.

'Here.' He took her hand, fishing in his pocket for one of the sugar lumps he'd brought. He dropped it onto her open palm and drew her in front of him.

Sensing a treat in store, Hector snuffled at her hand. Instantly Ravenna stepped back, her curves enticing even through her jacket.

'No, don't drop your hand.' He held hers up and flat. 'Hector won't bite.'

'He's so big.' She leaned back, her shoulders pressing into his chest, her riot of newly grown dark curls tickling his chin. She smelled of cinnamon and sugar, and beneath them was the scent of her pale skin, an unnamed but heady perfume that he greedily inhaled.

He'd missed her, missed the right to touch her. Every day was a battle not to reach for her, to palm her soft skin, taste her, draw her close and have his fill.

'Oh, you beautiful boy,' she crooned as Hector lipped up the treat then nodded as if in thanks. 'Did you see that? How he took it from my hand?'

'Mmm, hmm.' Jonas strove to suppress the arousal that fired as Ravenna whispered her delight to Hector. She wasn't even talking to Jonas yet the low thrum of her voice and the press of her body almost made him forget his promise to keep his hands off.

'Here.' He found the curry comb he'd been using and sidestepped, taking Ravenna along with him till she stood at the horse's shoulder. 'You can groom him.'

'Can I? How?'

The best way to demonstrate was to put the comb in her hand and cover it with his, moving them both in slow sweeps.

Hector shifted and Ravenna shrank back. Jonas smiled as he wrapped his other arm around her waist to hold her steady. Or perhaps it was a grimace, given the exquisite torture of holding her and not revealing his needy reaction.

'You're safe. Hector is a gentleman.' Their joined hands traced a wide arc across that broad equine shoulder and side.

'And you're here to protect me.'

Had he heard right? The indomitable Ravenna needing protection?

'Did you visit your neighbour and her animals often?'

'As much as I could. It was so *alive* there, always something happening.' He watched their hands move in tandem, telling himself he'd step away soon.

'I'd have thought the Hall would have been busy too. I seem to remember quite a few servants and tradespeople when I visited.'

Jonas dropped his hand, letting her continue alone. 'As son of the house I was kept separate from that.' And he'd hated it. 'My early memories of the Hall were of solitude. There never seemed enough people to fill it and a house like this needs people. When there were visitors it was for formal dinner parties to which small boys weren't invited.'

'You make it sound like you were on the outside, looking in.' Ravenna half turned then seemed to think better of it, leaning in to comb Hector with a long stroke that moved her backside temptingly against Jonas' groin.

He should move away, should drop the arm wrapped around her waist, before she sent him over the edge. But he couldn't shift his feet.

'Not all the time.' He didn't want her sympathy. 'The kitchen was always welcoming and then there was Vivien's and the animals.'

'It still sounds lonely.'

He watched the curry comb slow almost to a stop.

'I was no lonelier than lots of homes.' He had no intention of sharing exactly how bleak his childhood was. 'I remember you here, just behind this stable block, crying your eyes out because someone named Pamela had made your life hell at school. Because you were excluded.'

Ravenna's hand slid to her side. 'You remember *that?*' She'd never thought he'd recall in such detail.

'I remember feeling sympathy for someone else who felt like an outsider.'

Ravenna stiffened as the memory of ancient pain surfaced. He saw too much. Then it hit her he'd made it sound like something they had in common. Both outsiders.

She spun around. Jonas was so close her pulse thudded in response. She saw deep into his eyes, could even count his spiky dark eyelashes.

He was so near one tiny move would bring them together. A half-step, a tilt of her head, and they'd be kissing. The air between them crackled and heat saturated her skin. Her fingers tingled, anticipating the feel of his smooth-shaven jaw. Surely he'd moved closer?

Her breath hitched audibly and suddenly there was distance between them.

Ravenna blinked. Had she imagined that moment of intense expectation? The way their bodies swayed together?

Hurriedly she gathered her scrambled thoughts.

'But you fitted in. Your family has been here for centuries. You were born to all this. You *belonged*.' She waved her hand wide. 'I never did.'

Move back, she told herself. *It's too tempting, too dangerous. You're too close to Jonas.*

But her body wouldn't listen. She stood, looking expectantly into his dark face.

His mouth curved in a half-smile that was poignant rather than amused.

'You belonged, Ravenna. You had your mother, remember? You were close. Even now I can't help feeling that she's mixed up somehow in the reason you're here.'

Ravenna opened her mouth to protest but his raised palm stopped her. 'I'm not asking for your secrets, Ravenna,' he said, surprising her. 'I'm just saying you always had her on your side. She loves you.'

She nodded. That went without saying.

'Then you were lucky. Luckier than a lot of kids.'

Like Jonas.

'Who did you have, Jonas?' The housekeeper he'd spoken of so warmly now and then? His neighbour, Vivien? Everything he *hadn't* said about his parents confirmed what had been lacking in his family: warmth and love.

'I had myself.' Not by a flicker of an eyelid did his expression change. He looked strong, proud and sure of himself. All the things she'd seen in Paris when she'd thought him arrogant and self-opinionated.

But now Ravenna realised there was much more to him. The man who'd lost himself in her body. Who, in his grief, had needed her with a desperation that scorched through every barrier. Who now distanced himself again.

With a fervour that surprised her, Ravenna wished for a return of the intimacy they'd shared. She wanted—

This wasn't about what she wanted.

'Was that enough?' Suddenly it struck her that Jonas' sometimes superior air, his confidence, his determination to get things right, no—perfect, every time, might be traits he'd learned in his youth to overcome loneliness and doubt. Had they been defence mechanisms for a little boy desperately in need of love? Mechanisms that had become habit in the man?

His dark eyebrows rose. 'Every child wants to be at the heart of a big, loving family, don't they? But I was luckier than a lot. I had food and warmth. I had an excellent education.' His stare dared her to feel pity for him. 'And I had this—Deveson Hall. I knew one day it would be mine and then I'd make it right.'

'Right?'

'Absolutely.' His eyes shone. 'I had a lot of time to dream as a boy. I spent my days exploring the Hall, absorbing its history and traditions and planning how it would be when it was mine. The old place became my family in many ways. It was my mainstay.'

'So that's why you're here through the renovations.' Ravenna had wondered why he didn't stay in London and leave the detail to his project manager. She'd thought at first it was because he wanted to keep a close eye on her.

'I want the job done properly.'

There was that perfectionist streak again. Everything had to be done just right before Jonas would be satisfied.

'You wanted it furnished in a traditional style to match what you'd known when you were young?' Or more probably, from what he'd said, to bring it up to a standard he'd never known as a child when money had grown shorter each month.

Jonas shrugged. 'Maybe. Though my tastes have changed. Traditional with a modern twist perhaps.' He strode to the open stable door to gaze at the Hall, automatically stooping to pat an adoring Timothy, who shadowed him.

'When it's done I'll hold a ball. That's a Deveson tradition that got dropped over the years. This year it will be a turning point.' Jonas turned and she read anticipation in his face. 'I'll want you there, Ravenna.'

Her heart fluttered, till she reminded herself the housekeeper had a vital role in any big house function.

'Of course. I'll supervise the catering.'

He nodded. 'It will be a big job but we'll do it.'

Ravenna felt a tiny jolt of pleasure at his 'we'. They worked well together, perhaps because of the unspoken boundaries they'd been careful not to cross.

'But I don't want you behind the scenes.' His gaze collided with hers and her skin tingled at the approval she saw there. 'After all your hard work I want you at the party, not in the kitchen. You deserve to celebrate too.'

Ravenna blinked, a tiny trail of fire flaring in her blood. It was the closest he'd come to hinting he'd forgiven her for the money. Would the celebration signal the end of her servitude? The weight she'd borne so long lightened a little.

Working in service reinforced all the insecurities of her youth. Despite the ease of the past couple of months, it still stuck in her craw to be a servant, especially here.

'Ravenna?' Jonas watched her expectantly. 'You'll come?' So it wasn't an order. It was an invitation. Ravenna smiled.

'Of course. How could I miss celebrating you achieving your dream?'

He shook his head. 'Not quite. This place is my heritage, a part of me. But the refurbishment is just the first step.'

'Really? What else is there?' She reached up to stroke Hector's cheek as he snuffled at her pocket, searching for treats. She could get used to the warm, comfortable smell of horse and hay. In fact, she could get used to life at Deveson Hall with an ease that surprised her.

Jonas surveyed the mansion that had come to life under his supervision.

'I loved this place as a kid but even I could see it wasn't a home. It was cold and unloved, despite the best efforts of our housekeeper.' He paused so long Ravenna thought he wouldn't go on.

When he spoke again it was in a low, musing voice that made her wonder if he talked more to himself than her.

'That's what I want. A home. Something more than the apartments in London and New York. A place with heart.' He shoved his hands in his pockets and rocked back on his feet. 'A place for a family. A wife who'll love the place as I do. We'll fill the old place with children.' He bent to pat Timothy as the Labrador bumped his leg. 'And a muddle of dogs and other animals. I'll make it a real home.'

Ravenna clutched Hector's mane.

Home. A family.

It shouldn't surprise her. Why else renovate Deveson Hall? Jonas wouldn't want to live there alone.

Fill the old place with children.

Her stomach dipped in an abrupt roller-coaster curve that hollowed her insides, turning them queasy.

She'd listened to Jonas' plans for the Hall with an approving smile. Wistfully she'd almost seen herself as part of that, despite her resolve to keep her emotional distance. In a hidden chamber of her heart had lurked the hope that one day they could put the past behind them and start again—pursue that connection she still felt to him just as strongly as the day they'd shared their bodies.

Then he'd mentioned children.

Her hand crept to her cramping belly, over the womb she knew was barren.

Months ago, shocked at the news of her cancer diagnosis and the need for early action, she'd told herself infertility was a small price to pay for the treatment that would give her a chance to live.

She'd always wanted children but she was young, yet to find a man with whom she wanted to spend her life.

Ravenna had concentrated on being grateful she'd survived, refusing to regret what couldn't be cured—the chance to bear her own children.

But now the void within yawned wide and pain poured in.

She was crazy ever to have imagined she could build a relationship with Jonas. Everything stood against it. Their history. The theft. Her background and social status. She didn't fit in his world. She never would.

And she could never give any man children. She was strong, capable and worthy of a good man's love. But she lacked—

Hot tears prickled her eyes and she blinked. She hadn't cried through months of treatment. She wouldn't start now.

Quietly, leaving Jonas to his dreams, she turned and slipped out through the other door.

CHAPTER ELEVEN

JONAS MANOEUVRED THE Aston Martin through the city streets on autopilot. His attention was all for Ravenna, sitting pale and subdued beside him.

These last weeks she'd changed. They still worked well together but that spark of camaraderie, that sense of being *comfortable* together had gone.

Perhaps it was his fault for not addressing the question of how long he expected her to work for him. The money she'd taken was substantial, but the effort she'd put into Deveson Hall had been remarkable. Without her organisational skills, eye for detail and hard work there'd be no celebratory opening ball next week.

Who could blame her for wanting to end their arrangement?

Yet he'd avoided the issue. He couldn't imagine the place without her.

The realisation made him frown.

No one was indispensable in his life. No one except the wife he'd marry once the Hall was ready.

He'd spent the last couple of years considering potential brides, taking his time sorting through likely candidates before settling a few months ago on Helena Worthington. Beautiful, gracious and warm-hearted, she'd make an excellent spouse and mother. Born and bred on her family's vast country estate, she lived in London, working at an exclusive gallery. She had the skills to make him an excellent hostess.

One of the reasons for the ball was to see her in his home and check he'd made the right choice before finalising his plans. They'd been out a few times in the past and she was definitely interested, but he'd kept things light till he was sure.

Beside him Ravenna shifted. He really should talk to her about the future.

He could offer her top dollar to stay permanently as housekeeper. She'd run the Hall with the brisk efficiency and empathy for the place that he required.

But keeping an ex-lover on his staff? It went against every instinct. No matter that they'd proved they could work together and put those few hours of weakness behind them.

Almost behind them.

Jonas set his jaw and confronted the truth. Not a day passed when he didn't remember in glorious detail the incandescent pleasure of sex with Ravenna. He enjoyed being with her. Her quick wit, her indomitable attitude, her pleasure in so many things he enjoyed, like seeing the gardens come to life, celebrating the completion of each room, even smiling over the antics of Timothy and Hector.

Until a few weeks ago. Something had changed and he couldn't work out what. He only knew he didn't like it.

'Where exactly is it you're going?' Jonas asked as she pleated her skirt with restless fingers.

'Just a few streets away. You can drop me anywhere here. I would have been quite happy catching the train. You really don't need to go out of your way.'

Which was the most she'd said on the whole journey. If he didn't know better he'd think she was babbling.

Ravenna never babbled. She was articulate and composed. Except that day they'd been naked together and ecstasy had stolen her voice. Predictably, arousal stirred at the memory, and a deep-seated satisfaction.

Hell! He shouldn't feel anything like this for Ravenna. Not now, not when he was planning to marry. But the sexual attraction between them hadn't yet dimmed, no matter how hard he tried to ignore it.

Jonas forced himself to concentrate on the traffic rather than the past.

Yet something was wrong and he couldn't ignore it. Over the months at the Hall Ravenna's colour had improved—she wasn't pale and fragile as when they'd met in France. But now that healthy glow had faded.

'Where will I collect you?'

Her head swung round, her eyes large and startled. 'There's no need. I'll catch the train.'

'My business won't take long so I can pick you up whenever you like. Just give me the address.'

'Really, I—'

'Unless you want me to wait now?'

'Up here.' She pointed abruptly at a café. 'If you come by and I'm not here, then just go on without me and I'll find my own way back.'

Jonas suspected she had no intention of meeting him and fobbed him off with a place chosen at random. Once he'd have suspected she was plotting to run away and escape the consequences of her crime but now he knew better. Concern filled him.

'Very well.' He manoeuvred the car into a recently vacated spot and watched her fumble with the door. 'I'll meet you in an hour or so.'

Ravenna nodded and got out, walking away without looking back.

Jonas watched her go, telling himself it wasn't his business she kept secrets. She had a right to a personal life. But the tension in her rigid body was palpable.

He waited till she'd rounded the corner before he got out and followed.

* * *

Ravenna pushed open the clinic door and emerged into the open air. She breathed deep, filling her lungs with the city scents of wet pavement and exhaust fumes. It was better than the not-quite-neutral smell she associated with hospitals and doctors' waiting rooms that dredged up bleak memories.

She grabbed the railing at the top of the few steps to the street and gathered herself, feeling the adrenalin still coursing through her system after the nervous wait to hear the results of those recent tests.

Her hands clamped the metalwork as emotion hit.

'Ravenna?'

She lifted her head to find Jonas on the step below, his face level with hers. She blinked moist eyes and drew in a breath redolent with that tangy scent she always associated with him.

'What are you doing here?'

'Waiting for you.' His voice was harsh and his expression grim. 'Come on.' He took her elbow, his grip surprisingly gentle given his expression. 'Let's get away from this place.'

She followed his gaze to the sign beside the door, proclaiming exactly what branch of medicine the staff practised.

He led her down the street and into the sort of exclusive restaurant in which she hoped one day to work.

She hesitated on the threshold. 'There's no need for this. I'm ready to go now.'

'Well I'm not.' He swept her into the beautifully appointed dining room and secured a quiet table before Ravenna could do more than blink owlishly at the expensive furnishings.

'A drink?' he asked as she seated herself.

'Nothing, thanks.'

'Cognac for me,' Jonas said to the waiter before turning back to her, his eyes steely. 'Don't tell me you wouldn't like something after visiting that place.'

He was right. She *was* on edge and had been all day with that appointment looming. At least it was over. She sank back in her seat with a sigh. 'A sauvignon blanc if you have it, please.' Ravenna smiled at the waiter who nodded and passed over two leather-bound menus before leaving them.

'Are you all right?' Jonas leaned towards her across the fine linen tablecloth, his gaze intent.

'Fine, thanks. Just a little tired.' Yet tension eddied in her stomach. He'd seen where she went, which meant she couldn't fob him off with vague answers. She'd have to explain, which meant revealing what she'd kept hidden all these months.

It would be a relief, she decided. It had been a strain, lying all this time.

She opened her mouth to speak but halted when he leaned across and took her hand in his. It was the first time he'd touched her since—

No. She wouldn't go there.

'Why didn't you tell me you were ill?' His voice was hoarse and Ravenna read intense emotion in his silvery gaze.

'I'm not.' She shook her head, her heart lightening. When she'd left the clinic she'd still been numb, just coming to grips with the news, but now she felt happiness surge. 'I'm healthy.' Her mouth widened in a smile that felt wonderful. She'd been so worried her remission might be short-lived, perhaps because she'd felt so depressed these last weeks.

'Thank God!' His fingers squeezed hers. 'When I saw you go in there…' He shook his head.

'You followed me?'

'You were anxious. I knew something was wrong.'

Ravenna stared. Jonas Deveson had followed her because he *cared* about her? Her heart leapt and she had a struggle to keep calm.

It made no difference that he'd been concerned. There wasn't anything between them. There could never be.

'So it was a false alarm? You thought you had cancer?' He sat back in his seat, still holding her hand. She should pull away, but she liked the sensation and it was probably the last time he'd touch her—he was so adept at keeping his distance now.

Ravenna drew a slow breath. 'No, not a false alarm. I had cancer. I don't now.'

'Ravenna?' Shock lined his face.

'I'm in remission. I have been for a while. This was just another check-up to make sure nothing had changed. I've had several, but this time I thought the results might be—' She shrugged, not wanting to admit she'd been so down lately that she'd half convinced herself her illness had returned.

The waiter arrived with their drinks and, at a signal from Jonas, left without taking their order for food. Jonas reached out and grabbed the glass of cognac, his eyes not leaving hers. He tossed the liquid back in one quick movement then put the empty glass down.

Guilt stirred. Not because she hadn't told him about her illness. That was private. But because he'd obviously been worried.

'I'm sorry, Jonas.'

'Don't be.' His voice was gruff. 'That's excellent news. I'm just…surprised to know you've been ill.' He paused, his fingers threading hers. 'How long has it been?'

Ravenna hesitated. But she was sick of lying. Surely now, when he heard her out, Jonas would give up his idea of revenge against her mother. He'd already had his pound of flesh after all.

She hoped she was right.

'Ravenna?'

'Last year I was diagnosed with leukaemia.' She saw his eyes widen. His firm grip tightened. 'I was advised to have treatment straight away. The cancer was aggressive but potentially curable. And they were right. I'm well now.' Joy made her smile again.

'How long before I met you?'

Ravenna's gaze dropped to her untouched glass of wine then up to the flat line of Jonas' mouth.

'When we met in Paris I'd just come from a Swiss sanatorium. I'd been there, recuperating.'

'I see.' His expression didn't change but his gaze turned laser sharp. 'Why didn't you tell me when we met?'

Ravenna tugged her hand but his grip didn't ease. It kept her anchored within his warm grasp. Could he feel her pulse trip faster?

'It wasn't relevant. It's not the sort of thing to share with strangers.'

'I was hardly that, Ravenna.' His tone made her nape prickle. 'Could it be because you didn't want to admit you needed my money to fund the health resort?'

She sighed. 'You're sharp, aren't you?' Not that it mattered now. He'd have to know it all. She'd just have to do her best to protect her mother.

'Sharp enough to realise if you were recuperating in Switzerland you weren't in my father's Paris apartment, forging his signature.'

Jonas felt his gut plunge hard and fast, like a stone in deep water.

He remembered Ravenna in Paris—proud and defiant, throwing her guilt in his teeth. To deflect him? Of course. And he'd been so wrapped up in his hatred of Piers and Silvia that he hadn't stopped to question.

He'd seen how pale Ravenna was, how delicate her wrist as he shackled it and pulled her to him. He recalled how fragile her body had seemed compared with her in-your-face attitude.

Because she'd been ill.

Too ill to fight back?

Guilt was a raw slash of pain to his belly. He'd bullied her when she was vulnerable. What did that make him?

Jonas dragged his free hand through his hair. No wonder her clothes hadn't fitted. She must have lost weight in therapy. He'd been sure she'd dressed to project waif-like vulnerability for that antiques dealer. He'd been so ready to make snap judgements, hadn't he?

Bile seared his throat as he reviewed that day. He'd stormed in, all violent temper and attitude, and nearly ripped her head off when she'd dared stand up to him.

'Your hair,' he croaked, his windpipe tight. 'That's why your hair was so short.'

Ravenna lifted a hand to the sable curls clustering like a dark halo around her face. 'I'm growing it now.'

'I remember it before. It used to be long.' For months after meeting the teenage Ravenna Jonas had wondered why so many women cut their hair short. There'd been something deliciously appealing about long female tresses.

'Another drink, sir? And something to eat?' He hadn't noticed the waiter approach.

'Another cognac.' He didn't drink much but today he needed it. Confronting the truth had never been so unpalatable. 'Ravenna? Something to eat?'

She looked up and after a moment's hesitation engaged the waiter in a discussion of the day's specials. When she'd ordered he said he'd have the same and finally they were alone.

'It wasn't you who stole my money, was it?' Jonas spoke through gritted teeth. How could he have fallen for her story? Hadn't the evidence pointed to Silvia from the first?

After a lifetime keeping a lid on his feelings, they'd finally erupted with the news of the embezzlement, undercutting his usual clear thinking. Why hadn't he questioned her more closely when she admitted the theft?

Because his blistering anger had needed a target and she was handy. Because she was the daughter of the woman he'd spent years blaming for his father's defection, despite knowing Piers had always sought his own pleasure rather than embracing his responsibilities.

It had been easier taking out his long-simmering fury on Ravenna than dealing with the fact that the person who'd been at the root of so much pain—Piers Deveson—was finally beyond either reproach or reconciliation.

'It was Silvia, wasn't it?'

'Please don't hurt her, Jonas.' Ravenna's hand twisted in his, her fingers grasping with reassuring strength. The shock of seeing her entering that clinic still reverberated through him.

'Jonas?' Solemn eyes of old gold fixed on him. 'I know it was wrong. She had no right to the money. Nor had I.'

'Did you know where it came from?'

'Not till you confronted me in Paris.' Her quick gesture discarded that as a minor issue. But it wasn't. Ravenna had been innocent from the first. She'd claimed responsibility only to protect her mother and then she'd worked like a slave to pay off a debt for which she had no responsibility.

Jonas was torn between admiration for her and deep-seated nausea at what he'd done. He'd used and abused her. He'd taken out his ire on an innocent woman.

'Mamma was desperate. She'd been selling off assets for ages, just to live the way Piers expected. She had no money of her own.' Ravenna shook her head. 'Piers had expensive tastes and in the past he'd bought Mamma extravagant gifts, but he'd never spent money on me. I should have known his generosity to me was out of character.'

'You were sick.' Even now the thought of it smote him a hammer blow to the chest.

'But I should have realised.' Her mouth firmed. 'Maybe I didn't want to think too much about it. Maybe—' His finger to her warm lips stopped her words.

'Stop beating yourself up.' He let his hand drop to the table, noting how she slid her hands into her lap, away from him. Who could blame her after what he'd done? 'You weren't to blame.'

Ravenna leaned forward, the subtle, sweet perfume of her skin enticing. 'You have to understand my mother was desperate. She shouldn't have stolen from you, but she was convinced I needed time and care to recuperate fully. She was terrified I'd have a relapse.'

Jonas nodded, his stomach churning in sympathy with Silvia Ruggiero for the first time. He understood her fear too well. He still felt sick from the shock of believing Ravenna ill.

'Please, Jonas. Please be lenient with her.'

'She should have stayed. Not left you to carry her guilt.' That stuck in his craw.

Ravenna's slim fingers closed over his hand, startling him before sliding away. 'She didn't. She has no idea you'd discovered the loss. I suppose she hoped the money wouldn't be missed or you'd write it off as money to your father.'

'So naïve.' When he started out Jonas had risked every penny to invest then invest again. He never took money for granted, given how he'd worked to acquire it.

'Jonas, what are you going to do to her?' The fear in Ravenna's voice brought him up sharply.

'Nothing.' He watched her exhale on a sigh that left her looking limp. 'Here, drink this.' He lifted her wine glass to her lips, waiting till she held it herself and took a sip.

'Nothing? Really?' She looked dazed. He really *had* been an ogre. And now he felt about two feet tall. 'You won't prosecute?'

'There'll be no gaol, no prosecution. I've had enough of revenge.' Jonas grimaced on the word, its taste souring his tongue. 'How could I prosecute a mother for trying to save her daughter?'

'But I would have been all right without the funds.' It was as if still she didn't believe him—had to test him.

Jonas raised his eyebrows. 'Piers would have looked after you?'

'No. He was unwell by that stage, but no one knew how unwell.' Ravenna's eyes dipped to the pristine cloth. 'I'd have come back to London to work.' She lifted her head. 'I'm a chef. I had a promising position before...' She waved her hand vaguely and Jonas' anger fired. She'd lost her job when she got sick?

'So you were going to return straight to work after cancer treatment, doing long hours in a commercial kitchen?' He knew how gruelling that would be. He'd worked as a waiter in his university years. He'd vowed then to make his living the comfortable way—at a desk rather than on his feet doing split shifts till all hours.

The full brunt of what Ravenna had borne hit him. The illness. The slow convalescence. Dealing with her mother's financial crisis on top of what must be worry about her own finances and career. Then facing down an irate idiot hell-bent on vengeance. How had she coped?

He remembered that first day at the Hall, finding her asleep in the middle of the day and assuming she was lazy. His gut twisted as he realised she must have been exhausted.

'I'm sorry, Ravenna.' The words were too little, too late. 'What I've done to you, what you've been through…I had no right to threaten and take out my anger on you. I should never have forced your hand the way I did.'

'You didn't know.' She smiled wearily. How much she'd borne. The knowledge shafted home his guilt.

'I should have made it my business to know.' Instead of jumping in boots and all.

How could she take it so calmly? He winced, remembering his harsh words and actions. 'I said things I had no right to.' Her pain when he'd accused her of being a gold-digging opportunist like her mother! 'I'm sorry, Ravenna—'

'It's all right.' She looked over his shoulder. 'Here's our lunch.'

The waiter didn't linger but served them swiftly, providing another large cognac for Jonas. He reached for it, wanting that quick burn of fine brandy in his throat, then stopped. His father had always avoided the consequences of his actions and responsibilities. His mother had escaped reality in her own world of gin-fuelled disappointment.

Jonas put the glass aside.

'It's *not* all right, Ravenna.' It was all wrong, in so many ways.

'It is if you're not going to make Silvia pay.' She paused as if waiting for him to confirm it.

'Forget the money. There *is* no debt.' He breathed hard, still grappling with the knot of self-disgust in his belly. 'It was put to good use.'

Her eyes flashed pure gold and Jonas' breathing hitched. 'Thank you, Jonas.'

'Stop being so gracious!'

Her eyebrows arched. 'You'd prefer if I made a scene?'

'You think I'm being melodramatic?' Was any woman so infuriating?

Ravenna smiled and something fizzed in his veins. 'We were both at fault. We both jumped to conclusions and said things we regret. Can't we wipe the slate clean?' Her stomach growled. 'Especially as I'm starving. I was too anxious to eat this morning.'

'Then eat.' He gestured to her plate.

'And we're all sorted?' Her gaze searched his face.

'Absolutely.' What else could he say? She didn't want his apologies. He felt…frustrated.

'Thank you, Jonas. That's very generous. My mother will appreciate it as much as I do when she hears.'

He didn't care what Silva thought. It was Ravenna who concerned him.

'You'll want to leave Deveson Hall.' The thought struck abruptly as she lifted her fork to her mouth.

She took her time chewing. 'You want me to leave straight away?'

'No!' The word shot out with more force than necessary. He didn't want her gone. Not yet. 'I'd like it if you stayed on. Not to work,' he assured her quickly. 'But for the ball. You've worked too hard to get the place ready. It would be a shame to miss it. If you want to stay on.'

Ravenna kept her eyes on her plate. What was she thinking? Tension crawled down Jonas' spine, one vertebra at a time.

He was working on blind instinct. He had no plan in the aftermath of the truths that had rocked his complacent world. He only knew he'd feel bereft if she left now. He needed time to adjust. Time to replace her, his sensible self reasoned.

'Thank you.' Still she didn't look up. It was as if, having his promise that the theft had been written off, she didn't want to connect with him. 'I've never been to a ball and I'd love to see the Hall with the renovations complete. I'll stay till then.'

CHAPTER TWELVE

SHE SHOULD NEVER have agreed to stay. She should have left the same day. But the shock of her sudden freedom hadn't been as welcome as she'd expected.

Ravenna strode up the staircase as if expending energy could erase the dreadful weakness she harboured.

Despite Jonas' assurances that she didn't have to, she'd put long hours into getting the Hall ready. But they'd done nothing to extinguish what she felt for him. If anything her feelings were stronger since his apology and the sight of his horror when he realised she'd been innocent.

Jonas was essentially a decent man despite his plot to make her pay for the stolen funds. And who could blame him for that? His prejudice against Piers and Silvia was understandable, and to have Mamma then steal from him... Ravenna guessed it had been the final straw.

She walked along the corridor, checking all was in order. It was easier to focus on the busy work of housekeeping than think of the future. The ball was tomorrow and then she'd leave. She had no reason to stay.

Except she didn't want to leave Jonas.

Ravenna blinked at an arrangement of roses gracing a hall table. Reaching out to a velvety red petal, she was reminded of Jonas' touch, exquisitely tender as he brushed his fingers over her naked body, his gaze luminous as he'd watched her shiver with delight under his ministrations.

Sharply she sucked in her breath. This couldn't go on.

There was no future for them. She'd gone from being the enemy to a reminder of an episode he'd rather forget. She saw the shadow of guilt in his face whenever he looked at her.

Ravenna pushed open the door to her bedroom then halted as she saw the flat box on the counterpane. Only one person could have left it there.

Her heart seized then leapt to a gallop, gaze riveted on the distinctive embossed name on the box. Every woman in the western world knew that name. It belonged to one of the grandest Parisian couture houses, one whose young chief designer had taken the world of fashion by storm.

Ravenna's hands trembled as she moved closer, lifting the lid to pull back layer after layer of finest tissue.

Her throat closed. The dress was a delicate filigree of bronze shot with blue and amethyst as the light caught it. Ravenna had never seen anything so ravishingly beautiful in her life. She lifted it out—full length, with a wide skirt and tiny, jewelled shoulder straps, it was a modern Cinderella fantasy. Wearing this would make any woman feel special.

Twirling, she hugged it close and surveyed herself in the long glass. The woman staring back didn't look like Ravenna Ruggiero. She was a princess. The belle of the ball.

Except she *was* Ravenna Ruggiero. She'd never be the belle of any ball, especially Jonas Deveson's. Pain tugged her insides and her fingers crushed the sumptuous fabric.

The dress was a generous, extravagant gesture, borne of guilt and shame. Jonas wanted to put the past behind him and tried to make it up to her like this. He thought an expensive dress for his expensive party would make everything okay.

The gift was the embodiment of his guilt. He'd been too gracious to insist she leave immediately. But every time he looked at her in this gown he'd be reminded how he'd treated her.

And she'd remember he thought to buy her forgiveness.

She stiffened, her hands dropping.

That was what rich men did, didn't they? Bought what they wanted? It was what Piers had done with Mamma. Her mother had fallen for Piers hook, line and sinker and in his own way he'd fallen for her. But he'd begun by lavishing outrageously expensive gifts on her, blinding her with his generosity, because that was how the system worked.

Rich men married rich women. They only offered poor women expensive treats in return for—

No! That was not what Jonas was doing. He didn't want her in his bed.

But he did want her silence, her forgiveness, a sense of closure over what had happened between them.

The dress dropped from Ravenna's numb fingers and she turned from the mirror. She wasn't for sale. Just touching the dress brought his earlier accusations about her selling herself rushing back.

She didn't need Jonas' gift. Gorgeous as it was, she'd feel worse for accepting it, as if she'd let herself down. Besides, did she want this stunning gown hanging in her meagre wardrobe? It would be a constant reminder of a time, and feelings, she needed to forget.

Swiftly she scooped up the froth of fabric and tucked it back into its box.

'It's delightful, Jonas. You've done a marvellous job restoring Deveson Hall.' Helena smiled up at him, her china-blue eyes bright with approval and her perfectly sculpted lips curving in an enchanting smile.

He held her close but not too close as they danced. The ballroom glittered as the antique mirrors down one wall reflected the brilliant chandeliers, opulent gowns and lavish jewellery.

Over Helena's shoulder he saw Vivien dancing with a cabinet minister, while the local vet stood in earnest conversation with a sheikh in pristine white robes and a minor royal, no doubt discussing horses, given all three were passionate about them.

Everyone was enjoying themselves. He alone was dogged by a sense of anti-climax.

'Thank you, Helena. I'm glad you approve.' He smiled and pulled her a little closer.

This was the woman he planned to marry. Why couldn't he feel more enthusiasm? The Hall was just as he'd hoped, better, even. Nothing stood in the way of him reaching out and making his dream a reality.

Helena's eyes were as bright as the platinum-set sapphires at her throat. She was interested, expectant. He sensed it with the instinct borne of experience.

'What are your plans, Jonas, now you've completed work on the Hall?' Her voice was warm and appealing. She was intelligent, generous, good company.

And holding her in his arms he might have been waltzing with an aged great-aunt. Where was the spark of attraction he'd once felt?

'Plans?'

She tilted her head to regard him better and he inhaled the subtle designer perfume she favoured. It was like her—elegant, appealing—just right.

Except she wasn't. Not tonight. Something had changed.

'Now you've finished will you move in full time? Commute from here to the city? Perhaps allow the public in for viewings?' Her smile made light of the question, but he read her anticipation.

It was a perfect opportunity to talk of the future, *their* future. Except looking down at her he felt none of the satisfaction he'd felt before.

'I'm not sure yet.' Where those words came from he had no idea. 'But, yes, I'm considering opening the gardens once they're established. I've had heritage and horticultural groups already badgering me about open days.

Apparently my designer has done something quite special with the grounds.'

'They look marvellous already.' Helena took his lead, chatting about landscaping. Only the puzzled expression in her eyes hinted she'd expected something else. Jonas was grateful she was intelligent enough not to press.

For suddenly, on the brink of achieving his long-held goals, he found himself hesitating.

The music ended and they pulled apart. 'Let me get you a drink.' He took her arm and led her through the throng to the end of the room where drinks were being served.

At the vast double doors more people were clustered, mainly men, their dark formal clothes contrasting with the slim form of a woman in a dress of soft, buttery gold.

Jonas stiffened, every sense alert as she nodded and half turned. No wonder half the men in the place where there. Ravenna's smile was enough to stop any man in his tracks.

Jonas' chest tightened, squeezing his heart into a racing beat. The arousal he hadn't felt when embracing Helena surged hard and fast in his groin, betraying the need he hadn't been able to banish.

Ravenna looked good enough to eat. Heat swamped him and suddenly his bespoke tailoring seemed too tight. He wanted to rip his collar undone and shrug out of his jacket.

Then what? Stalk across and haul her to him so her audience knew she wasn't available?

To hell with the crowd, he wanted to hold her for the sheer satisfaction of having her where he wanted her.

The realisation hit in a blinding flash.

She turned again and her skirt belled out. Unlike most of the gowns hers ended at the knees, revealing smooth, shapely calves. She wore no jewellery except glittering earrings, but she didn't need any. She looked graceful and gorgeous with her cap of dark curls and pale gold skin.

Jonas frowned. That dress! What had happened to the one he'd bought? He surged forward.

'Jonas? Is everything all right?'

Helena's voice recalled him to sense. He slammed to a halt and turned, fixing on a stiff smile.

'Of course. I just wanted a word with my housekeeper but it can wait.' Though the effort of holding back almost killed him.

'Is that her? In the brocade? That material is just gorgeous. I've never seen anything like it.'

Unaware of their gaze Ravenna left the group and crossed the room only a few feet away. She was deep in conversation with one of Jonas' business associates, who looked far too suave and smug as he separated her from the crowd.

As they passed the light caught the material of her dress. Jonas blinked, not believing what he saw.

'I believe it's quite unique,' he muttered.

Damn! It *was* unique. It had been woven especially to a design by his artist great-grandmother. Until a couple of weeks ago it had hung in one of the massive state rooms.

Ravenna had rejected his gift—the best Paris fashion had to offer—and instead swanned around his home wearing discarded curtains!

His hands clenched in fists that shook with outrage. So much for his conciliatory gift! Did she deliberately try to provoke? And the way she flaunted herself, monopolising the unattached men!

'I should go and congratulate her,' Helena said. 'She's done a fantastic job here.'

'Later, Helena.' With a mighty effort Jonas unclenched his teeth. 'Let's get you that drink first.'

Ravenna paused in an alcove off the ballroom, catching her breath. It had been months since she'd mixed with more than a handful of people at a time. The London restaurant kitchen with its frantic pace seemed light years ago.

She'd enjoyed herself tonight. When she'd admitted she was the housekeeper many had congratulated her on her work and plied her with questions about the restoration. One or two men had even been a little too attentive, which, while awkward, had done wonders for her bruised ego.

There'd been raised eyebrows among the society women though, and pointed looks at her home-made dress and extra height. Those stares reminded her of childhood peers who'd claimed she'd overstepped the line, presuming to socialise with them.

But Ravenna was no insecure child now. She'd responded with cool courtesy and moved on, refusing to let prejudice spoil the only ball she'd ever attend. Yet the experience reinforced everything she'd known. Jonas moved in a different world. She was an outsider here and always would be.

Her gaze zeroed in on the couple at the top of the ballroom. He was tall and commanding while she, in figure-hugging midnight satin, was the epitome of cool, English beauty.

Jonas Deveson and Helena Worthington, looking the perfect couple. Her hand was on his sleeve as she leaned in, wearing a private smile.

A hot knife of jealousy sliced Ravenna's breast. Was that the woman Jonas would marry? The press thought so and guests had speculated about an engagement announcement.

Ravenna couldn't even dislike the woman. She was pleasant and charming, with a down-to-earth friendliness. Ravenna could imagine her here with Jonas and their brood of children. Helena would probably even take to Hector and Timothy.

Ravenna lifted her glass of vintage champagne, trying to wash away the sour tang on her tongue.

What had she expected? That after all that had gone wrong between them, Jonas would feel the same unsettling yearning Ravenna did? That he'd want her over the woman who was patently perfect for him?

She took another sip of the effervescent wine, letting it fizz on her tongue then slide down her aching throat.

Across the room Jonas turned and unexpectedly their

eyes locked. Ravenna's breath stopped as lightning arced through her veins. Her toes curled as if she'd touched a live wire. Her whole body hummed with awareness.

His dark eyebrows came down in a straight line of disapproval.

He couldn't know how she felt. He couldn't! So why was he annoyed? The answer was easy. The sight of her discomfited him. The sooner she left, the better.

Her breath caught on something suspiciously like a sob. She turned abruptly to find herself against a solid chest.

'Ravenna?' It was Adam Renshaw, the horticulturalist. His friendly smile was balm to her tattered soul. 'I've been looking for you. Would you like to dance?'

'Thank you, Adam.' Ravenna was fed up with herself—pining for what she could never have. She had to move on with life. Defiantly she drained her glass and put it down with a sharp click, ignoring the slightly foggy feeling of a little too much champagne. 'I'd love to dance.'

Ravenna switched off the last of the lights and stood in the vast, empty ballroom, revelling in the silence. The ball had been a huge success and she'd enjoyed it, she assured herself, ignoring the pain clutching her chest.

She'd danced for hours and instead of being relegated to the kitchens she'd indulged in champagne and caviar, in a midnight supper on the terrace with Adam and then more dancing. She smoothed her hands down the heavy silk of her skirt, trying to focus on the evening's pleasures rather than the dragging feeling of disappointment that weighted her.

'You've been avoiding me.'

Hand to her throat, she spun towards the door.

A shadow detached from the inky gloom of the wall and blocked her path. Ravenna's heart lurched then thumped against her ribs in a too-familiar needy rhythm.

'You startled me.'

'Did you really expect to keep your distance all night?'

She couldn't read Jonas' expression in the dark but his voice had an edge that cut.

'Why not?' Pride lifted her chin. 'You were busy with your guests. And I didn't need looking after.'

'So I noticed.' He stepped closer, his form growing in bulk as he approached. Even in her heels she felt dwarfed by him, weakened, as if he sucked the energy from the air between them. 'You let Renshaw monopolise you.'

Ravenna stood straighter. 'Adam and I have a lot in common.'

'He'll be moving on to the next job, Ravenna.' Was that a warning in his stern tone? 'He won't stick around.'

'Nor will I.' She'd leave as soon as it was daylight. Seeing Jonas and Helena together had been the impetus she'd needed.

He raised an arm as if to touch her then let it drop. 'You're going together?'

Ravenna frowned, hearing an unfamiliar note in his voice. 'I thought we'd agreed that what I do from here on is my own business, not yours.'

Jonas' breath hissed between his teeth. 'I see.' There was a wealth of disapproval in those two syllables. 'So that's why you didn't wear the dress I gave you.'

'Sorry?'

'If you and Renshaw are an item he'd wonder why you wore clothes bought by another man.'

Jonas' words confirmed her decision not to accept his gift. There was something far too intimate about accepting such a present.

'Adam had nothing to do with my decision. He and I aren't "an item" as you put it.' Pride wouldn't let her hide behind such a deception.

Jonas stalked closer, a hint of his male scent making her nostrils flare.

'You could have fooled me, the way he kept touching you.'

'We were dancing! That's what people do when they

dance.' He was a fine one to talk. She'd seen the way he held Helena. 'I'm going to bed now.'

'Alone?' He moved in front of her as she tried to sidestep and her heart slammed against her ribs. Ravenna sensed tension in him, an aggression that made her neck prickle.

'My movements have nothing to do with you.' Why did that hurt so much, even now? She had to get over this... obsession.

Still he stood unmoving, his bulk blocking her exit.

Ravenna tried to tell herself it was anger stirring butterflies the size of kites in her stomach. 'Instead of giving me the third degree why don't you go to bed? Helena will wonder what's keeping you.' The words shot out on a burst of bravado that left her feeling hollow.

'Helena's gone.'

'Gone? But she was with you, farewelling the guests.' Ravenna had tried not to notice how the blonde beauty had lingered. She'd headed to the kitchens to supervise the packing up so she didn't have to watch the pair.

'Nevertheless, she's gone.' His tone had a ring of finality.

'I should go too.' The air was fraught with tension that sent quivers through her body. Jonas was so close she saw his eyes gleam. If she leaned in they'd touch. She felt his proximity from her tingling lips to her budding nipples and lower, where desire spiralled deep.

His arm snapped out and long fingers circled her bare arm in a bracelet of fire.

'Let me go.' She tried to keep her voice even but it came out in a rush of breathless energy.

'Not till you tell me what's going on. Why aren't you wearing my dress?'

Ravenna tried and failed to tug her arm free. Desperation rose. She needed to get away.

'Because it would mark me as yours, bought as easily as any other commodity.' She shook her head, trying to find her voice in a throat choking closed on a rush of emotion.

'I know you didn't do it because you *want* me. Only because you want to be *rid* of me. But—' she drew a ragged breath and met his eyes '—I am not for sale. You don't need to *buy* me with anything. I told you we were quits. I won't wear your guilt.'

His hand slid up her arm to close on her shoulder. Hard fingers spanned her bare flesh, warming it against the chill inside her.

'You're wrong.' His voice was a low throb, brushing like velvet across her skin and making her shiver. Ravenna squeezed shut her eyes. He only had to speak and she weakened! And his touch...this was impossible.

'Let me go, Jonas.'

For answer he lifted his other hand and cupped her face, his hand engulfing her jaw, imprisoning her so she had no option but to lift her head towards his.

'You're wrong,' he said again and this time she heard a tremor in that deep, rich voice. It mirrored the shiver in his long fingers. 'I do want you, Ravenna. I've never stopped wanting you. Seeing you tonight only confirmed it.'

Stunned, Ravenna stared up at him.

Jonas stared back, committing every detail of her face to memory, his mind supplying the detail the darkness hid. He knew her features as well as his own.

His hand at her shoulder slid down, shaping the supple curve of her back and dragging her in against him.

'That's impossible.'

His bark of laughter was short and humourless. Jonas pulled her closer, higher, cupping her buttocks in an act of flagrant carnality that set his mind spinning. He'd wanted this so long.

'Impossible? Surely this—' he thrust his hips forward, melding them in a move that made his head spin '—proves it.'

Her hands clamped his shoulders. To push him away or

tug him close? He tightened his grip. No way was she waltzing off to her gardener tonight. Not now. Not when her yielding body told him she wanted him too. A sigh escaped her parted lips and it was music in his ears.

Fire coursed through his veins. He burned up with need. Touching her, imprinting her against him stoked the flames.

'Ravenna.' He dipped his head and kissed her neck, triumph filling him as she arched, giving him access to her throat. She tasted sweet as honey, soft and alluring. Impossibly tempting. 'You want me too. I feel it.'

Her hands clutched him. One thigh lifted to slide restlessly along his, inflaming his libido. He shook with the force of standing firm, doing no more than taste.

'No. This isn't right.' But her voice lacked force. It ended on a sigh when he scraped his teeth along the base of her neck and she shivered voluptuously. 'What about Helena?'

'I sent her away.' How could he even think of marrying her when he was consumed by thoughts of Ravenna?

'Away?' Ravenna stirred in his hold and Jonas squeezed his eyes shut, trying to withstand the excruciating delight of her body moving against his.

'It's you I want, Ravenna. All night I've watched you, wishing I was with you. Wishing we were alone so I could do this.' He bent his head and traced the neckline of her dress down to the delicious swell of her breast, fuller now that she wasn't so waiflike. Her gasp of pleasure as he suckled her through the fabric set his blood roaring. He remembered the taste of her naked breast and needed it now.

In one urgent move Jonas backed her against the wall.

'You want me too. Don't you?' Her body responded to his, arching into his touch, but he needed to hear it. 'Ravenna.' His voice shook with the force of holding back. He was on the edge, never so inflamed by desire as now, holding Ravenna's slim form, tasting the musky note of arousal on her skin. 'Tell me.'

'I can't.' Her voice was a thready whisper.

Jonas blinked and lifted his head to look down at the woman he wanted—no, needed. A sliver of moonlight pierced the gloom, revealing confusion on her fine features. But it also showed the slumberous warmth in her eyes.

'Can't or won't?' He let one hand drop to her leg, drawing her dress inch by inch up her thigh, watching her eyes widen then narrow to hooded slits. Her tongue darted out to slick her bottom lip in unconscious invitation.

His groin was tight and hard, needy for her. Only her. He pressed close, imprisoning her against the wall, revelling in the way her thighs parted for him. Yes! She wanted him as much as he did her.

Jonas slid his hand beneath the rucked-up skirt to touch silk stockings then cool flesh. His rough fingers felt clumsy as he circled her inner thigh, drawing another gasp from her.

'Say it, Ravenna.' She drove him crazy! He stroked up to the apex of her thighs, to brush hot silk and feel her quiver. His ears clogged as his blood pounded. His nostrils filled with the scent of arousal. His body grew rigid with the force of holding back.

Fear held him. He didn't trust himself to touch her again. He was too close to losing control.

The brush of her hand against his shirt came out of nowhere, making him start. Her fingers trailed lower and he was stone, set solid with desperate anticipation.

Her voice was a ragged whisper that sounded as if it had been torn from her. 'I shouldn't but I do. I want you, Jonas.'

An instant's shocked stillness then restraint ripped away. Jonas' fingers tangled with hers, fumbling to undo his trousers. The feel of her nimble hands wrenching open his zip almost tipped him over the edge. And when her cool fingers touched his hot flesh…

With a hungry growl he planted his hands at her hips and hiked her up against the wall. Her legs came round his waist in a quick, clumsy movement as between them they hauled her skirt up out of the way. Her breath came in pants that matched his tortured gasps.

Their eyes locked. Jonas never wanted to look away. When Ravenna looked at him like that he could do anything, be anything she wanted.

Unsteadily he reached for her, tracing the lace edge of her underwear, pulling it aside. But he couldn't manage gentle; his hands were too clumsy. He heard tearing and her panties came away in his hand.

Something flared in her eyes. Something that told him she was excited, not afraid. Her legs tightened around him, and suddenly it was too much. He thrust high and hard, burying himself in her heat. She was all around him, hot silk against his erection, long legs circling his waist, hands cupping the back of his neck.

'You're mine.' The words slid through gritted teeth as he thrust again, anchoring her, probing as deep as humanly possible, making her his in the most elemental way.

'Mine,' he growled, feeling tremors begin deep inside her and knowing a fierce, possessive joy that *he* did this to her. He brought her bliss. He saw it in her radiant face, heard it in her hoarse voice, shouting his name, felt it in the pulsing climax that rocked her from the inside out. She came so hard and fast he had no time to think before it took him too, overtaking him with a rush of such force, such violent ecstasy, he doubted he'd survive.

Bracing himself, Jonas rode out a storm of pleasure that wrung every ounce of energy he'd once possessed. It was all he could do to stand. Yet from somewhere he found strength to hold Ravenna. Nothing could have pried her from his possessive grip.

She was his. Nothing in his life had ever felt so right.

CHAPTER THIRTEEN

AFTER ANOTHER URGENT coupling, this time on the newly re-upholstered sofa, Ravenna lay, pulse racing, weighed down by Jonas' solid form. He held her close. His head pillowed on her bare breasts, the dark spill of his hair tickling, and his hand splayed possessively at her hip.

Her heart tumbled in a rush of amazement and pleasure.

Ravenna cradled him as his breathing began to slow, the hot puff of his breath deliciously intimate on her skin.

She couldn't believe what had happened despite the evidence of her own sated body. She could lie here for ever.

But already she saw the sky lighten through the French windows on the far side of the ballroom. Dawn was on its way.

How long had they been here, lost in each other?

Too long. Shocked, she remembered today was the day she left Deveson Hall for good. Left Jonas.

Pain cramped her chest, constricting her breathing.

Jonas stirred. Languidly he licked the underside of her breast, then took her nipple into his mouth, suckling gently. Immediately a fine thread of tension pulled from her breast to her womb, tugging her senses into tingling awareness. Molten heat filled her, turned her boneless all over again.

Her breath caught at the sight of him there at her breast and the thread of pleasure snapped to vibrating tautness.

Yet it was the emotional connection, rather than the physical, that undid her.

How could she bear to walk away?

She had no choice.

The metallic tang of despair filled her mouth. She blinked and looked away, forcing her arms to her sides. They felt empty without him.

'We need to move.' The words rushed out.

'Ravenna?' He lifted his head, silver eyes piercing in the gloom. 'You regret this?'

How could she not?

Yet it was an exquisite memory to hoard for later. Instinctively she knew forgetting Jonas would be impossible.

'This wasn't supposed to happen.' She put her hands on his sturdy shoulders but he didn't budge.

'No. But it was inevitable.'

'Nothing is inevitable.' Except perhaps her weakness for Jonas. The full import of what she felt for him had hit her hours earlier as she'd swayed in Adam Renshaw's arms, trying not to stare at the glamorous couple at the centre of the throng. Trying to tell herself she was mistaken—she could never care for Jonas *that* much. But the hollow in her heart told its own story.

'You're going to marry her.' She saw the shock in his eyes and knew the rumours were true. Pain stabbed.

Again she pushed his unyielding shoulders. 'You need to get off me.' She couldn't bear to look at him now he'd silently confirmed the truth.

'We need to talk.' Still he didn't move.

Ravenna's fingers clawed at his bare flesh, trying to shift him. How could she think when they lay naked together?

'Please, Jonas. Let me up.'

For a moment longer he lay there, then abruptly he was gone.

She'd never touch him again, she realised with a tinge of desperation. Slowly, avoiding his eyes, she sat up, naked but for her suspender belt and silk stockings. Frantically she scanned the floor but couldn't locate her clothes. She couldn't even recall where she'd lost them.

'Here.' Jonas draped something around her shoulders. It was his dinner jacket, she realised as it enveloped her and the scent of his body engulfed her. She wrapped it close, prolonging the moment she had to trust her jelly legs and look for her dress.

Jonas tugged on his dress trousers then turned to her, barefoot and bare-chested. One furtive glance confirmed he looked sexier than ever. And more dangerous, his jaw set stubbornly.

'First up, you're wrong. I'm not marrying Helena.'

Her gaze collided with his, a ripple of shock filling her. 'You're not?'

A frown wrinkled his high brow. 'I'd thought about it.'

Again pain knifed her. 'But you've changed your mind. You've found another bride.'

Slowly he shook his head. 'No. I just realised I couldn't marry her.' His polished pewter stare pinioned her. 'Because of you.'

Elation mixed with disbelief in a potent brew that made her light-headed. Ravenna clutched the lapels of his jacket with stiff fingers.

'I don't understand.' She wanted to hope but something held her back. Maybe the confusion in Jonas' face.

He shoved his hands in his pockets and her gaze dragged down over the bunched muscles in his arms and chest. He'd used that power tonight to pleasure her, taking her with a fervent passion and raw strength that had made her feel positively petite against him. She'd never felt more feminine.

He spread his arms. 'I'd planned to marry Helena. She'd make an excellent wife and mother.' He ticked off points against his fingers. 'We mix in the same spheres. She's intelligent and attractive. Warm-hearted too.'

With each point Ravenna's belly squeezed hard over a

knot of pain. It was one thing to realise she'd been right, but quite another to hear Jonas spell out all the reasons Ravenna would never be right for him.

'I get the picture,' she said before he could continue. 'You want the perfect wife for your perfect life at Deveson Hall.'

'It's not that simple.' He inhaled, his impressive chest rising mightily. Ravenna remembered the feel of it, hot and slick, rough with a smattering of hair that tickled her sensitised breasts.

'No?' She jerked to her feet, unable to sit, listening to his marriage plans. On still-wobbly legs she crossed to one of the French windows, preferring the grey pre-dawn view to Jonas' sharp gaze.

'No.' His voice came from behind her. 'Give me credit for some scruples. How can I marry her when I'm fixated on you? All night my attention kept wandering to you flirting with Adam Renshaw, driving me quietly insane.'

Stunned, Ravenna whirled to find him a few paces away. Big, bold and surly—he was the most intimidating male she'd ever met.

'But you and I aren't…we weren't—'

'Lovers?' His eyebrows drew together. 'Think again, Ravenna.' His look scorched her skin and she pulled his jacket close, as if to hide her wanton eagerness at his possessive stare. He kindled an excitement that turned her bones to water.

'I want you,' he murmured in a voice of rough gravel that abraded her senses. 'I've wanted you from the first and I want you now. I tried to keep my distance, especially when I discovered how wrong I'd been about you. The truth about you only made me want you more.'

He took a step towards her but stopped as she held her palm out.

'That's why I can't marry Helena.' His look was grim. 'Because I want you here, Ravenna, with me. Will you stay?'

His words knocked the breath from her lungs, leaving her

dizzy from shock and lack of oxygen. She put a hand to her thumping heart to stop it catapulting right out of her chest.

He wanted her with him?

He wanted her to replace Helena as his bride?

For a fleeting moment Ravenna pictured herself with Jonas, not just sharing her body, but her life. The picture was so alluring it almost blinded her to reality. For she loved him. She'd fallen for him despite her caution. Fallen for him hard as she learned the sort of man he really was.

Then she remembered what he wanted from life.

She couldn't give him that.

She could never be the woman he needed.

Her knees loosened and she reached out blindly, steadying herself on the window pane, cool from the night air.

Besides, she'd asked if he'd found another bride and he'd said no.

Sheer willpower made her straighten and face him. 'What exactly is it you want from me, Jonas?'

Jonas tried to lock his eyes on her face but they kept straying. Never in his life had he seen a woman so sexy. His jacket hung loose and long on her, but now she'd forgotten to clamp it closed it parted to reveal her satiny skin, a hint of one lush breast and the shadow of her pubis, a dark arrow between her legs. She shifted, inadvertently revealing the suspender strap that secured one of her stockings and his blood thundered in a storm of need.

Twice hadn't been enough. Would he ever have enough of this woman who so intrigued and innocently seduced? From the look on her face she had no idea he fought arousal all over again.

'I want you, here, with me.' The words felt good. *He* felt good, admitting the truth he'd avoided too long. Relief filled him and his mouth tugged up in a smile. He saw emotion flare in her eyes and knew it would be all right. Ravenna wanted him too.

Jonas stepped in, lifting his hand to stroke her cheek. She turned her head and shifted away, making him frown.

'Ravenna?' What was she playing at? 'You feel it too—I know you do. After tonight you can't deny it.'

She swung to face him, her expression guarded. 'In what capacity do you want me, Jonas?'

He shrugged. Lover? Girlfriend? What did words matter?

'As your housekeeper?'

He hesitated. He'd thought about asking her to stay and keep the Hall running as she'd done so admirably, but it didn't seem right.

'Or as your mistress?'

'That's a word I prefer not to use.' It implied payment for services. Ravenna would stay because she wanted to, not because he'd shower her with gifts. He'd been wrong earlier, believing her driven by mercenary motives.

'Or maybe both?' Her husky voice rose half an octave. 'Housekeeper and mistress together? Keeping up the family tradition?'

Jonas shook his head, her words like a smack in the chest. What they shared had been wonderful, incandescent. Why did she twist things?

'I refuse to do to your fiancée what Mamma and Piers did to your mother.' Ravenna planted her hands on her hips, anchoring his jacket wide and inadvertently displaying her nakedness. Jonas' blood pressure soared but he dragged his gaze to her face.

'I'm not Piers.' Her expression remained accusing and he felt anger stir. 'Besides, I told you I have no fiancée. Helena and I have never even discussed marriage.'

Still Ravenna didn't look impressed. What did he have to do to make her admit what was between them? Didn't she realise what a huge decision he'd made, ditching his planned proposal? Had she no inkling of what a momentous concession this was for him, pushing aside his long-held plans? All because of her?

'But you will have a fiancée at some stage, won't you?' Ravenna stepped into his space. She poked an accusing finger into his sternum.

Jonas grabbed her hand, flattening it against his chest. He breathed deep of her sweet cinnamon scent, letting it steady him.

'I want you, Ravenna, and you want me. It's that simple.'

He lifted his free hand to her jaw then let it slide slowly down her throat, between her breasts, to her navel. He felt her skin twitch and she sucked in a huge breath. Pleasure filled him at her responsiveness but he kept his eyes locked with hers. His hand drifted down her belly then slid between her legs to the damp core of her where he'd lost himself so recently. Where he wanted to lose himself again.

Need juddered through him and his body grew rigid. Still she didn't move.

'Remember how good we are together?' His demand emerged gruffly but somehow it sounded more like a plea. Why the defiant look in her eyes? Why hold herself so aloof?

He dragged his hand away but kept her palm planted on his chest.

'I'm not asking you to betray anyone, Ravenna. I'm not talking about some tawdry affair behind another woman's back.' Relief showed on her face and he frowned. 'How could you think that of me? After what my mother suffered from my father's infidelity?'

Ravenna blinked and he thought he read regret in her expression. 'You have your sore spots. Being treated as a mistress, as the other woman, is mine.'

'I'd never ask that of you.'

She shook her head and tried to pull away. He kept her anchored.

'But one day you'll want what you've always wanted, won't you? The dream you've had for years. The perfect wife in the perfect life.' Her eyes were huge and pleading.

'I…' Jonas flattened his mouth. He hadn't thought that

far ahead. 'I just know I can't marry Helena when I need you like this.' He'd never been so honest with a woman in his life. It made him feel raw, almost vulnerable.

'But I'm not the bride for you.' Her voice was cool, devoid of emotion.

Everything in Jonas stilled. He stared into her arresting, haunted face and felt something shift, as if the ground quaked and moved beneath their feet.

He looked at Ravenna and saw something utterly, stunningly new. Why hadn't he seen it before?

'Why not?' His fingers tightened around hers, excitement stirring.

'Oh, Jonas, don't!' Fleeting pain shadowed her eyes before she looked away to their joined hands.

'I'm serious, Ravenna.' He'd been so caught up with the list of wifely attributes he'd compiled that he'd almost ignored one of the essentials: desire for his wife. No, not just desire, he realised as Ravenna's hand trembled against him. Need. A sense of connection.

He'd come to rely on Ravenna in ways that had nothing to do with her work. Being with her completed him—emotionally as well as physically.

His mind raced. Ravenna might not have the social network and impeccable breeding he'd once wanted in a wife, but she had other things: honesty, warmth and loyalty.

With her he felt alive, whole.

'Why not, Ravenna?' The brilliance of it stunned him. 'Don't say you don't want me because I don't believe it. We're good together. We could build a wonderful future.'

She jerked her hand free and spun away, walking with quick, jerky steps to the far side of the window. She wrapped her arms round herself protectively and he frowned. What was wrong with her?

'It wouldn't work.'

'Of course it would.' He started forward but halted, perplexed, at her raised, outstretched hand.

'I'm not the sort of woman you want, remember?' He heard an echo of her old jeering tone. 'I'm not from the right family. I don't move in the right circles. The only reason I know what cutlery to use at a formal dinner is because my mother taught me to clean the silverware!' She hefted a deep breath as if waiting for him to agree.

'I don't care.' It was true. None of that mattered in the face of his need for this warm, lovely woman, who for some unfathomable reason tried to push him away.

'I'm illegitimate. Plus my mother was your father's mistress, for heaven's sake! People would talk.'

'Let them. You're not a woman to let fear of gossip rule your life.' He crossed his arms over his chest. He didn't give a damn what others thought, except for Ravenna's sake, knowing how comparisons with Silvia and Piers could hurt her. He'd just have to protect her from that.

She shook her head and he saw desperation in her face as she moved into the dawn light. He wanted to cuddle her close and make her forget her doubts, but he respected her too much to dismiss her concerns. After all, he'd been the one who wanted a wife who was aristocratic and socially assured.

'Ravenna, none of that matters any more, truly. Not now I've found you.' Why couldn't she understand?

'It will one day. You'll wake up and wonder why you settled for me. Don't you see?' She flung her arm wide in a slashing gesture. 'I've never worn jewels or haute couture in my life and wouldn't know how to start. Listen,' she added when he made to close the gap between them. 'I grew up poor. It's what I know, what I'm used to. All this—' another wide gesture '—isn't me. As a little girl my favourite dressing gown was one my mamma made from a bedspread her employer was going to throw out. I wore handmade clothes and made do with second-hand everything.'

'Which made you resourceful.' Why did she think that counted against her? 'Those silk curtains never looked so good before you wore them.' He grinned, remembering how the fabric had moulded her slim, ultra-sexy body.

'You're not listening!' She stomped her heel, making him smile. He loved her passion.

'I'm listening, sweetheart. But I don't hear anything important.' He stepped closer. 'Nothing you've said makes me stop wanting you. We can build our future together. We'll be happy, I know it. You love the Hall and so will our kids.'

Excitement sizzled in his blood as he imagined it. But a chill scudded through him as she met his eyes. She looked… defeated. In all the time he'd known her, despite everything he'd thrown at her, he'd never seen her look so bleak. She stretched out her arm to ward him off, her hand cool against his skin.

'Ravenna?' Now she worried him.

'It wouldn't work.' Ravenna swallowed hard and her fingers trembled against his chest. 'You want to make Deveson Hall into the home you never had.'

Jonas nodded, bewildered.

'You want it to be a real family home, with your children to carry the Deveson blood and traditions into another generation.' Ravenna's hand fell. Where her palm had been the dawn chill brushed his skin like a premonition of disaster.

'You'd have to give all that up if you married me. I can't be the wife you want. Ever.' She drew a sharp breath and fear drilled deep inside him. 'I can't give you those children, Jonas. Not children of your blood. The cancer treatment left me infertile.'

Her mouth twisted in a pained smile as she took in his silent shock. Then she turned and left the room, leaving him dazed and gutted.

CHAPTER FOURTEEN

RAVENNA WALKED SLOWLY along the meandering street, grateful of the shade cast by the tall houses. With her basket full of market produce she should be planning the lunch she'd cook. Mamma would need it after starting her cleaning job well before dawn and Ravenna needed sustenance before her long shift at the café.

She'd make something special, something intricate enough to stop her thoughts straying to England and Jonas.

Naturally it didn't work. It hadn't worked all week, since she'd arrived to visit her mother, now living in a tiny apartment in this large, anonymous Italian city.

She juggled the basket more securely on her arm, inhaling the scent of basil. Instantly an image sideswiped her—of Jonas tasting her home-made pesto. Of the way pleasure crinkled the corners of his eyes and his rare smile made her stomach somersault.

Ravenna blinked, hating the scratchy heat blinding her vision. She'd done the right thing, leaving that morning. What else could she have done? Stayed on as Jonas' mistress till he was ready to move on to a woman who could give him all he wanted? She'd already broken her heart, falling for a man who she couldn't have. Having an affair with him would have shattered it to irreparable smithereens.

The stark horror on his face when she'd admitted she was barren was something she carried with her every moment.

Her mouth flattened. Had she really hoped she'd reveal the truth and he wouldn't care? Not Jonas. Not the man who'd made it his mission to fill the void in his life with what he'd always dreamed of: a family of his own.

Ravenna knew about his past and guessed at his parents' neglect. She'd heard the tension in his voice as he made light of loneliness and isolation. She'd felt the tremor of guilt rack his body for tragedy he'd been unable to prevent. She'd seen his passion for the estate that was more family to him than his parents had ever been. She *understood* his need to belong there and create what he'd never had.

Ravenna tried to take solace from the fact that he'd *cared* about her. Enough to want marriage.

But that made it all worse. Better if they'd never grown close, never shared—

She shook her head. She couldn't bring herself to wish that. Even now she couldn't regret loving him.

Every limb was heavy as she turned into the old apartment building and dragged herself up the stairs. Crossing the tiny landing at the top, she took a deep breath and worked to twist her mouth into a semblance of a smile.

'I'm back.' She pushed open the door and stepped inside. 'I stopped at your favourite *pasticciera* for a treat.' Money was tight but—

'Ravenna.' The deep voice curled around her, spiralling deep to fill the aching emptiness inside. She froze as the wound in her heart that she'd tried unsuccessfully to cauterise reopened.

He was here, filling the tiny hall.

Searing grey eyes fractured her shell of composure. His dark hair had a rumpled look as if he'd tugged his hands through it. In jeans and a casual, open-necked shirt he looked devastatingly attractive and potently male.

'Jonas!' Was that her voice, that yearning gasp?

'Here, let me.' He dived to rescue the wicker basket that dangled from her nerveless fingers.

The brush of his hand on hers sent her blood racing and brought her numbed brain back to life.

Ravenna snapped her mouth shut, her brain fumbling to take in the fact he was here, not a figment of her needy imagination. 'Where's my mother?'

'She's gone out for a while. Don't worry, she's fine. She just thought to give us time alone.'

Why? What had he said to convince her mother to leave? Questions burned in Ravenna's brain but she couldn't wrap her tongue around the words. Everything was an effort. Her chest ached and she realised belatedly she'd forgotten to breathe.

'Why are you here, Jonas?'

'Shall we?' He gestured to the cramped living room.

Instinctively Ravenna shook her head. 'I can't do this, Jonas. I don't want to talk.'

Something flared in his eyes, turning them the colour of a summer storm. 'Neither do I.' Tingling spread out from her feminine core at the look on his face. 'But we need to. Please, Ravenna.'

How could she walk away? She'd done it once. She didn't have the fortitude to do it again. But did she have the self-control to face him?

'In the kitchen.' If she kept herself occupied maybe she'd be able to hear him out without revealing her feelings.

Her legs trembled as she led the way into the tiny alcove that passed for a kitchen. It shrank to minuscule as his wide shoulders filled the doorway and her heart faltered. This close she smelled his citrus and warm male scent and a pang of longing shafted through her.

'Ravenna?'

She avoided his searching look and lifted the basket from him before scooting back to the corner bench. She busied herself unloading fresh food.

'Why are you here, Jonas?'

'Won't you even look at me?' Her pulse pattered faster and she turned to wash her hands.

'Just say what you have to say, Jonas.'

'I'm sorry.'

She faltered as she flattened garlic with a knife.

'You have nothing to apologise for,' she said finally, her voice scratchy. 'You were honest. That's all I could ask.'

Her hands moved with the ease of long practice as she assembled the rest of the ingredients, peeling and chopping an onion with barely a fumble. Thank goodness for routine! She could pretend to focus on that rather than the man just a few paces away.

She wanted to cup his strained face in her palms and nuzzle that strong neck, feel again the heat of his embrace.

Ravenna blinked. Better if she could thrust him out of the door. But nothing would shift him until he was ready. She remembered his formidable power, how he'd held her weight easily that last night as he took them both to ecstasy. Heat razed her last crumbling defences and she dropped the knife on the bench with a clatter.

'I can't do this.' Her voice wobbled. 'Can you go now?' She couldn't look up, instead bracing herself on the bench so she wouldn't slump to the floor.

'No.' The word came from so close it furred the nape of her neck. 'I won't leave.'

'What?' Her head swung up. His face was so close she could count the tiny lines raying out from his eyes.

'I love you, Ravenna. I'm not leaving.'

She pressed the heel of her hand to her chest, trying to draw in enough air to stop the spots wheeling in her vision.

'You…?'

'I love you.' His eyes shimmered and she felt the warm caress of his breath on her upturned face. '*Ti amo,* Ravenna.'

'That's not possible. You didn't—'

He brushed a curl back behind her ear and her heart contracted at the tender gesture. Heat traced down her throat then dived, arrowing straight to her heart.

'I didn't say it earlier because I didn't realise.'

Ravenna shook her head, unable to summon the words to contradict him. It wasn't love he felt.

'I know that makes me a stupid, slow-witted fool.' His wry half-smile made her unwilling heart flip. 'But you see, sweetheart, I've never been in love before. I don't have any experience to draw on.' His voice hit a deep register, trawling along her bones and insinuating its way into her soul.

Trying not to hear the tension in his voice, she shook her head. 'It's not love. It's lust.'

'Is that all it was for you?'

'No, I—' She swallowed hard, watching lightning sheet across those fathomless eyes. 'You're feeling regret, that's all. You feel sorry for me.'

'Sorry? I'd like to wring your neck for walking out on me like that.' But there was no fire in his words, just pain. 'Do you know how worried I've been? Anything could have happened to you.'

Dumbfounded she stared into his hard-chiselled face. 'I can look after myself.'

His eyes bored into hers and the world quaked.

'I know,' he said at last. 'That's what I'm afraid of. That you don't need me the way I need you.'

'Jonas?' Finally she let herself register what she'd been trying to avoid—the pain drawing his features tight. Without planning it she fitted her palm against his jaw. He clamped it to the roughened silk of his skin, and she shivered as a blast of pleasure hit her at the contact.

'Do you know how I've tortured myself thinking I'd never persuade you to come back? I'm a wreck.'

He didn't look a wreck. He looked more decadently delicious than any pastry she'd ever concocted.

'I love you.' Touching his face, she felt his mouth shape the words, making them real. 'I lust after you, Ravenna, that's a given. But I love you too. I've loved you for weeks, months, I think, but I didn't realise till the ball.'

Her heart pounded on her ribs and she swayed, mesmerised by what she saw in Jonas' eyes. Could it be true?

'And I think you love me too.' His voice was raw with tension.

'Of course I do.' That was the worst of it.

Jonas gathered her close in possessive arms and Ravenna wanted to cry out at the poignant pleasure of it. 'But that doesn't change anything.' She braced herself against his hard chest as he leant in. 'Jonas! Please!'

He nuzzled her neck and Ravenna's world slid out of focus.

'Jonas, you need to listen.'

'I'm listening,' he murmured against her ear, then bit her lobe, sending pleasure streaking through her. 'And it changes everything. The way you invented objections back in England, I couldn't be sure you really cared.'

'I care.' The words slipped out unbidden. She cradled his head as he trailed fiery kisses down her throat and she arched back against his arm, letting herself steal one more desperate moment in his embrace. 'I tried not to but I couldn't help myself.'

'Even after I'd been such a bastard.' It wasn't a question. He held her so tight their heartbeats melded.

The wonder of it, having him here, having him say he loved her, was too much. Her emotions were all over the place. Hot tears leaked down her cheeks. Through the months of tests and treatment she hadn't cried but now—

'Don't cry, my love.' Jonas brushed them away with unsteady hands. 'I'll make it up to you, I swear it.'

'You can't.' She tried to tug out of his embrace but he wouldn't let her. 'Please, I can't think when you hold me.'

Jonas traced his thumb over her bottom lip. 'I'll remember that next time I want to win an argument.'

'There won't be any arguments. We—'

'Of course there will be. You're a passionate, headstrong woman.' His tone turned the words into a compliment. 'And I'm used to getting my own way. So forget right now about telling me we won't stay together. I died a thousand deaths not knowing where you were.' He threaded his fingers through her hair, holding her so she had no choice but to meet his eyes. 'It took far too long to locate you. I'm not letting you go.'

'You're forgetting one thing.' It was the hardest thing she'd ever faced, looking into Jonas' fiercely tender expression and knowing she had to pull back.

'If you're talking about children, stop right there. If it's a choice between children and you, there's no contest. It's you I want.'

For one perfect moment Ravenna stared into his face and knew he genuinely believed that. Wonder filled her, a joy that turned the dingy little kitchen into a grand, sunlit chamber, its pock-marked ceiling into a Tiepolo masterpiece.

She hugged that incandescent moment to herself a little longer then swallowed hard.

'I know you believe that, Jonas. And I love you for it.'

His embrace tightened and she'd never felt safer or more treasured. Finally she moved to pry his hands loose.

'But I can't do that to you. I know how important family is to you.' It was the dream that had sustained him since childhood. 'One day you'll regret tying yourself to me and I can't bear to watch that happen.'

'*You* are my family, Ravenna. You're all I need. How could I give you up?'

She shook her head. 'I won't strip you of your dreams, Jonas.'

His darkening gaze meshed with hers and she felt she looked right into his heart.

'They were dreams, Ravenna, concocted by a needy kid. I'm a man now and I know what I want, what I need. I need *you.* Always. For ever.' He swallowed hard and her heart went out to him. She felt the same way.

'As for kids, we can adopt, or grow old together without them, you, me and a gaggle of dogs and horses.' He shook his head. 'How many people have the chance to be with the one they love, Ravenna? Don't throw what we have away. Don't ask me to. I can't do it.'

For the first time Ravenna dared admit a sliver of hope.

'It's a gaggle of geese, not dogs,' she whispered when she found her voice.

His smile snatched her breath. 'We can have those too. Anything you want.' His smile faltered. 'Just don't send me away.'

'I can't, Jonas. I can't let you do this.' She felt stretched thin by the effort to keep strong.

'You want to see me as a lonely recluse, is that it?'

'You wouldn't be lonely long.' A knife pierced her at the thought of Helena offering Jonas comfort.

'I suppose you're right.' He gave an exaggerated sigh. 'Not with Silvia living in Deveson Hall's Dower House.'

'The Dower House? That's impossible. You hate her!'

'But if I offer her a home you'll visit her, won't you?' He nodded. 'Yes, I'm that desperate, Ravenna. Besides, she brought you up to be the woman you are, so presumably there's more to her than I thought.' He drew a deep breath. 'It may take me a while but I thought I should try to start again with her, if I can do it without the past tripping me up.'

Ravenna shook her head, pride in him stirring. Jonas truly was remarkable. He'd do that for her?

'I can't believe she agreed.'

'She'd do anything to see you happy, love. That made us unexpected allies.'

The idea boggled Ravenna's mind. 'She thought this would mend things between us?'

'It's a start, isn't it?' His eyes searched hers, his expression serious. 'None of us can know the future, Ravenna, but

I know this—I wouldn't be complete without you. I want you as my wife.' He stopped her protest with a finger to her lips. 'You can work as a chef instead of being chatelaine of the Hall. You can shock the county by wearing soft furnishings instead of buying clothes. You can do whatever you like so long as you promise to stay with me.' He hefted in a huge breath. 'I love you, Ravenna Ruggiero. My life could never be complete without you.'

Her heart was bursting. Ravenna swiped her cheek with the heel of her hand. 'That's not fair,' she gulped through a knot of emotion. 'How can I say no to that?'

His blinding smile cracked the last of her defences.

'Say yes. Say you'll marry me.'

'I'll agree to live with you.' Despite the flood of happiness, caution weighed. One day he'd realise what he gave up in taking a barren wife.

'Agreed. Live with me now and in a month we'll marry.'

Despite her battered feelings, Ravenna choked back a smile. 'Don't be impossible.' Jonas leaned in and kissed her throat, her jaw, working his way to her mouth until she gave in. 'Make it five years.' Had she really said that?

'Two months,' he shot back, his eyes gleaming.

'Four years.' Surely by then he'd realise his mistake and she would have a store of memories to sustain her.

'Three months.' Jonas slid his hand down her side, brushing the side of her breast, then letting it rest on the swell of her hip.

Ravenna's breathing hitched and her brain spun dizzily. 'Three years.'

'Oh, love, you drive a hard bargain.' He leaned in, eyes glittering, and kissed her softly on the lips.

Ravenna couldn't resist Jonas at the best of times. When he told her he loved her with every second breath she didn't have the will power to withstand him. Happiness had crept up on her and now it filled her with a blaze of optimism that finally overcame gnawing doubt.

She took his proud, patrician face in her trembling hands and kissed him back with all the urgent passion and deep, abiding love she could no longer deny.

'Don't look so worried, love,' Jonas said later as she sat, cuddled close on his lap. 'We have each other. That's all that matters. And as for the rest—' he shrugged '—we'll take each day as it comes.'

He paused, his lips twitching. 'Now about those three years. I have a counter offer…'

EPILOGUE

RAVENNA SAT IN the shade of a chestnut tree and watched Jonas, blindfolded, tumble to the ground, pulled by eager young hands. Chiara and Josh giggled as their dad groaned theatrically then reached to tickle them. There were screams as they and Vivien's son, Ben, tried to elude him but the five-year-olds were no match for Jonas' long reach.

Gleeful squeals of 'Mamma! Help!' filled the glade and with a grin Ravenna moved to get up.

'No, don't move.' Her mother was already on her feet. 'You look so comfortable. Stay.'

Ravenna subsided, content to bask in the pleasure of watching her family. She'd held out against Jonas as long as she could, eventually agreeing to marry him a year to the day after he'd arrived at the apartment in Italy. He'd used every wile to persuade her and she'd loved every minute of his loving persuasion.

He'd even followed through with his offer of a home for her mother. To their credit Mamma and Jonas were doing their best to put the past behind them and just recently her mother had moved into the Dower House permanently instead of using it as a base for short-term visits.

Jonas had mellowed too, as if the love they shared gave him the strength to accept the complexities of his parents' failed relationship and admit the possibility Piers and Mamma had, whatever their faults, genuinely cared for each other.

Every day with Jonas was a blessing. And the blessings had continued when they adopted the twins three years ago. Jonas had insisted they needn't adopt, that she was all he needed. But the love they shared was so deep and strong it seemed natural to share it further. Each day they learned together, finding parenting a challenge and a reward.

'No, Toby!' Jonas collapsed with a huff of laughter as their Basset Hound, a recent rescue dog, launched himself at them, massive ears flopping and tongue licking.

The children squealed with delight, waking a cross-breed pup that had been asleep at Ravenna's feet. With a yelp of excitement it bounded over to join the melee.

'You might have come to save me.'

Jonas stood, smiling down at her. As ever, her heart gave a skip of pleasure as she met his warm gaze. She'd been a fool ever to doubt his love.

'Sit with me?' She patted the blanket beside her.

'I thought you'd never ask.' He looked over his shoulder. 'If you think Silvia can cope?'

'Of course she can. She revels in it.'

Jonas settled himself and warmth seeped through her as he wrapped his arm around her. 'Happy, love?'

'Always.' Ravenna sank into his embrace. She glowed with excitement. She'd been cautious so long, scared to hope, but the doctor had assured her everything was normal. The miracle she'd never looked for had happened.

'Jonas, I've got something to tell you.'

'Something good?'

'Absolutely.' She lost herself in his smile. 'There's a date we need to mark on the calendar.' Her hand slipped protectively to her abdomen and his gaze followed the movement.

A muffled shout drew the twins' attention but when they looked it was to see Mamma and Daddy cuddling. They did that all the time, so Josh and Chiara turned back to the pups.

It was Silvia who watched Jonas stand and gather his wife

up in his arms as if she was the most precious thing in the world. He hugged Ravenna close and her trill of laughter floated on the warm air.

Silvia smiled. Jonas Deveson was the best thing ever to happen to her darling Ravenna.

Life was very, very good.

* * * * *

LET'S TALK
Romance

For exclusive extracts, competitions
and special offers, find us online:

f facebook.com/millsandboon

🐦 @MillsandBoon

📷 @MillsandBoonUK

Get in touch on 01413 063232

For all the latest titles coming soon, visit
millsandboon.co.uk/nextmonth

Want even more

ROMANCE?

Join our bookclub today!

'Mills & Boon books, the perfect way to escape for an hour or so.'

Miss W. Dyer

'Excellent service, promptly delivered and very good subscription choices.'

Miss A. Pearson

'You get fantastic special offers and the chance to get books before they hit the shops'

Mrs V. Hall

Visit millsandbook.co.uk/Bookclub

and save on brand new books.

MILLS & BOON

MILLS & BOON

THE HEART OF ROMANCE

A ROMANCE FOR EVERY KIND OF READER

MODERN

Prepare to be swept off your feet by sophisticated, sexy and seductive heroes, in some of the world's most glamourous and romantic locations, where power and passion collide.
8 stories per month.

HISTORICAL

Escape with historical heroes from time gone by. Whether your passion is for wicked Regency Rakes, muscled Vikings or rugged Highlanders, awaken the romance of the past.
6 stories per month.

MEDICAL

Set your pulse racing with dedicated, delectable doctors in the high-pressure world of medicine, where emotions run high and passion, comfort and love are the best medicine.
6 stories per month.

True Love

Celebrate true love with tender stories of heartfelt romance, from the rush of falling in love to the joy a new baby can bring, and a focus on the emotional heart of a relationship.
8 stories per month.

Desire

Indulge in secrets and scandal, intense drama and plenty of sizzling hot action with powerful and passionate heroes who have it all: wealth, status, good looks…everything but the right woman.
6 stories per month.

HEROES

Experience all the excitement of a gripping thriller, with an intense romance at its heart. Resourceful, true-to-life women and strong, fearless men face danger and desire - a killer combination!
8 stories per month.

DARE

Sensual love stories featuring smart, sassy heroines you'd want as a best friend, and compelling intense heroes who are worthy of them.
4 stories per month.

To see which titles are coming soon, please visit

millsandboon.co.uk/nextmonth